THE LAST VOYAGE OF THE
ODYSSEY II . . .

Fighting the swell with his left hand, spitting water, Vance reached out with his right, trying to catch any piece of wreckage floating by. Finally, he succeeded in wrapping a line around his wrist. He gasped, choking, and caught his breath. Then, still grasping the line, he draped his left arm across *Odyssey II*'s shattered side and used the line to pull himself over, into what was left of the hold. If he could stay with her, he figured, he might still have a chance.

Just as he tried to rise to his feet, however, he looked to see the mast slowly heeling over, coming straight down. He toppled backward, hoping to dodge it, but it slammed him just across the chest. The world swirled into blackness, as even the light from the blazing ship behind him seemed to flicker.

Stay conscious, he told himself. Stay alive.

Holding onto the toppled mast, using it as a brace, he managed to rise. And now the Hind had completed its gruesome handiwork and was banking. Again it was going to pass directly overhead.

By God, he thought, this thing isn't over. Those bastards are not going to get off scot-free. . . .

Books by Thomas Hoover

Fiction

PROJECT CYCLOPS *
PROJECT DAEDALUS *
THE SAMURAI STRATEGY *
CARIBBEE
THE MOGHUL

Non-Fiction

THE ZEN EXPERIENCE
ZEN CULTURE

* PUBLISHED BY BANTAM BOOKS

PROJECT CYCLOPS

Thomas
Hoover

BANTAM BOOKS

NEW YORK · TORONTO · LONDON · SYDNEY · AUCKLAND

PROJECT CYCLOPS

A Bantam Falcon Book/September 1992

Grateful acknowledgment is made to reprint from the following: "On forelands high in heaven" from More Poems from The Collected Poems of A.E. Housman. Copyright © 1936 by Barclays Bank Ltd., Copyright © 1964 by Robert E. Symons, Copyright © 1965 by Holt, Rinehart and Winston. Reprinted by permission of Henry Holt and Company, Inc.

ISBN 0-553-29520-9

Published simultaneously in the United States and Canada

PRINTED IN THE UNITED STATES OF AMERICA

OPM   0 9 8 7 6 5 4 3 2 1

PROJECT CYCLOPS

PREFACE

"Keep her above three hundred meters on the approach." Ramirez's hard voice cut through the roar of the 2,200-hp Isotov turboshafts. Down below, the cold, dusk-shrouded Aegean churned with a late autumn storm. "Any lower and there'll be surface effect."

"I'm well aware of that," the Iranian pilot muttered, a sullen response barely audible above the helicopter's noise and vibration. It stopped just short of open disrespect.

Sabri Ramirez did not mind. The two Iranians had been an unfortunate necessity, but in three days they would be dead. The others, the professionals, were the ones who counted. When he hand-picked the European terrorists now resting on the four litters in the main cabin, he had gone for the best. Each man had a track record and a purpose. Ramirez, however, was the leader, fully in control. He had planned, financed, and now commanded the operation.

In the ghostly light of late evening, his sleek cheeks, iron-shaded temples, and trim mustache gave no hint of the extensive plastic surgery that had created this, his latest face. He wore a black jumpsuit, like the others, but under his was a $2,000 Brioni charcoal double-breasted—perhaps more suited for a three-star dinner in Paris, at L'Ambroisie or La Tour d'Argent, than the operation at hand. All the same, he felt comfortably at home in this Hind-D helicopter gunship, the most lethal assault machine ever. Their operation had two objectives, and the first had just appeared on the bright green cockpit radar.

It was the 2,600-ton U.S. frigate *Glover*, Garcia class, which the National Security Agency had converted into a Mideast spy platform. Loaded with missile-tracking and communications-monitoring antennas, it had to go.

Ramirez expected no difficulties. Like the USS *Stark*, the frigate disabled by Iraqi Exocet missiles in the Persian Gulf in 1988, it was a perfect target. With only one gun, it would be child's play for a fully-armed Hind.

"Activate IFF," he ordered, glancing back at the instrument panels. "They should acquire us on radar within two minutes now."

"IFF on." Salim Khan, the still-brooding Iranian, nodded and reached for the interrogator/responsor in the panel on his right. They were using the NATO Identification System, a low-band interrogator, into which they had programmed the false Israeli Identification Friend or Foe code. The gray box would receive the electronic query, "Are you a friend?" and it would automatically reply, "Yes, this aircraft is friendly."

Ramirez watched with satisfaction as the green numbers flashed. Deception, he thought. The key to everything.

In the intelligence dossiers of Mossad, and the U.S. CIA, he was known as the Hyena, killer of hundreds in Europe and the Middle East. But his most cherished recent fact in those dossiers was the item declaring the disbanding of his private organization. He thankfully had been written off. Of course, the self-important analysts reasoned over their pipes and printouts, of course the chimera named Sabri Ramirez must be dead. His unmistakable touch had not been on a bombing in years. The playboy terrorist who flaunted silk suits, had cellars of rare vintage wines in Tripoli, Damascus,

Baghdad, and Beirut . . . that man wouldn't just retire. He had to be *gone*.

They were half right. He had wearied of the squabbles and disputes of a far-flung organization; however, he had not lost his taste for money. Or his hatred of the United States.

Now that NATO was falling apart, America was trying to take over the Middle East—aided by its European lackeys. But he had put together a plan that would end America's global military intimidation once and for all. Not coincidentally, he was going to acquire eight hundred million dollars in the process.

"We'll be exposed," he continued, "but just for about three minutes. They only have one gun, a .38 caliber DP Mark 30, mounted on the forward deck. It is in plain view. Remember I need a clear ten-second window for the Swatter. After we neutralize their main ordnance, we come about and strafe the communications gear."

He hoped this dense Iranian understood the approach profile. He had briefed the man over and over, but still he was not sure it had sunk in. He examined Salim Khan one last time—the bulky face with sunken, almost depressed eyes—and stifled a sigh of exasperation. Iranians.

Still, he had better not offend the man's much-vaunted honor. After all, Salim had single-handedly stolen the Hind gunship they were now flying from the Iranian Air Force, providing a crucial component in the overall operation. A rare prize, the Hind had been secretly purchased by the IAF from an Afghan rebel unit—which had captured it in 1987. Iran had wanted to see one up close, against the day the Soviets might turn their anti-Islamic paranoia against them and try to invade. That day had never come. And now this disaffected air force lieutenant had simply stolen it. At last, Ramirez thought with satisfaction, their valued prize would be put to use.

Salim Khan had mastered the Hind's controls years before, had flown it often, and just four days ago he had taken it up, shot his weapons operator, and used a fake identity to file a new flight plan, setting down to refuel in Rawalpindi. The theft had caused a tempest. When they discovered it, the mullahs had blamed America and engineered a demonstration in the streets of Tehran so they could bray in the press.

But by that time he had already taken it out over the gulf and landed it on the camouflaged Greek cargo ship they had waiting. After navigating the Suez Canal, that ship was now anchored safely off Crete's main port of Iráklion. For Salim Khan, who had twice been passed over for promotion to captain, the taste of revenge in that theft was sweet indeed.

"The most important part of the approach," Ramirez went on, "is to make sure we're ID'd by their VIS, their Visual Identification System. It's crucial they make our Israeli markings."

The Hind-D looked like nothing else in the world, one of a kind. Its visual profile, dark green against the sunset hues of the sky, should be unmistakable. Or so he hoped. Almost sixty feet long and over twenty feet high, it had a main rotor fifty-five feet in diameter and a heavy, retractable landing gear. The tandem stations in the nose for the weapons operator, and the pilot above him, had individual canopies, with the rear seat raised to give the pilot an unobstructed forward view. Any schoolboy should be able to identify one a mile away, as well as its Israeli markings—the blue Star of David in a white circle.

"I still think it's unnecessary," Salim Khan mumbled into his beard. "It only adds to our risk. It would be better—"

"A visual ID is essential." Ramirez cut him off. "When they make it, they'll go through the Sixth Fleet HQ in Gournes for verification, then—"

"They just acquired us on radar," the Iranian interjected, as a high-pitched alert sounded from the instrument panel and a line of green warning diodes turned red.

"Right on schedule." Ramirez nodded. "The U.S. Navy never sleeps." He turned and motioned to one of the men crouched on a litter in the main cabin, shouting above the noise. "Peretz, it's time to start earning your share."

Dore Peretz, a veteran of the Weizman Institute, was a specialist in strategic weapons and their delivery. But that was another life. Now he was free-lance. Ramirez had picked him for his technical skills, and his greed.

He rose and made his way forward, working carefully through the jumble of legs and automatic weapons. He was younger than he appeared; his prematurely salt-and-pepper hair made him look late forties, though he actually was only thirty-nine. He settled into the weapons station below Salim, pulling down his black turtleneck, the better to accommodate a flight helmet, and went to work.

"Are you ready?" he asked Salim, in perfect Farsi.

"I am ready if God is ready," the Iranian replied grimly, his eyes beginning to gleam from the strain.

Peretz reached down and switched the radio to 121.50 megahertz, the military emergency channel.

"Mayday. Mayday. Israeli Hawk One requesting permission for emergency approach." He then repeated the announcement in Hebrew. It was, of course, a pointless gesture for the illiterate Americans, but for now verisimilitude counted.

"We copy you, Hawk One. This is USS *Glover*. We've acquired you on radar," came back the response, a Southern drawl, young and slightly nervous. "What seems to be the problem?"

"One of our turboshafts has started losing oil pressure. We could use a visual check. What's your position?" He glanced down at the green radar screen and grinned. It showed the frigate's coordinates to within meters.

The radioman complied with his request, then continued. "There could be a problem, Hawk One. The storm's just pushed the sea over four feet. It's a helluva—"

"Permission to approach. We have a situation here," he continued in English.

"Have to check that with the TAO. We've got a perimeter," came back the uneasy answer.

"Fuck your perimeter, sailor." Peretz's voice was harder now. "This is Lieutenant Colonel Leon Daniel, Israeli Air Force. We've got an emergency and we're coming in. Tell *that* to your TAO, and get us perimeter clearance. We're coming by." He switched off his mike.

"Well done." Ramirez nodded his approval. "Just the right combination of entreaty and bravado. I think the Americans will be stymied. The good-neighbor policy they like to talk about."

He leaned back and wished he had a cigar. The other men waiting, crouched in the dark, had understood only some of the English. They were four Germans, a Frenchman, and a Greek.

"Conditional clearance granted," crackled the radio. "But we have to visual ID you first. Approach from vector three-two-zero. Emergency rescue op being readied, just in case."

"Roger, USS *Glover*," Peretz spoke back sharply, in his best military style. "Keep the coffee hot."

"It's always hot, sir. This is the U.S. Navy."

"Appreciated."

"Glad to be of help, Hawk One."

Peretz clicked off the radio and turned around. "I think they bought it."

"So far so good," Ramirez nodded.

He descended the three steps down into the lower cockpit, the weapons station, and stood behind Peretz, looking it over again. The Hind's offensive capability included a four-barrel Gatling-type 12.7mm machine gun in a turret under the nose, as well as 32-round packs of 57mm rockets secured on hardpoints on each stubby auxiliary wing. Finally, the wingtips carried four Swatter homing antitank missiles, two on each side. Plenty of firepower for what he intended.

"Remember," he said to Salim as he moved back up, "no hint of hostile action until after they make the ID." Would the stubborn Iranian hold steady? Stick to the procedure?

He checked his watch. Four and a half minutes should take them inside the VIS range. The altimeter showed that they were now at eleven hundred meters, and so far the Iranian was bringing her in perfectly. Of course, after the frigate confirmed they were flying a Hind . . . but by then it would be too late.

CHAPTER ONE

"I was doubling Cape Maleas when the swell, the current, and the North Wind combined to drive me sidelong off my course and send me drifting past Kythera. The force of the gusts tore my sails to tatters, and for nine days I was chased by those accursed winds across the fish-infested seas. But on the tenth I made the country of the Lotus-Eaters."

From *The Odyssey*: Book Nine

7:25 P.M.

"Do you read me, *Odyssey II?* Come in." The radio crackled on channel sixteen, the ocean mariner's open line. "Goddammit Mike, do you copy? Over."

Michael Vance was exhilarated, and scared. The salty taste of the Aegean was in his mouth as he reached for the black mike of his radio, still gripping the starboard tiller. His waterproof Ross DSC 800 was topside, since there was no other place for it.

He was lean, with leathery skin and taut tanned cheeks all the more so for his having spent the last three days fighting the sea. He had dark brown hair and a high forehead above eyebrows that set off inquiring blue eyes. His face had mileage, yet was curiously warm, with a slim nose that barely showed where it had been broken year before last—during an ARM special op in Iran.

"Is that you, Bill? Good to hear your voice, but this is a hell of a time—"

"Who else would it be, you loony gringo? Hey, I'm getting a damned lot of static. How about switching channels? Over to seventy."

"Seventy, confirmed." He pushed in the code, his fingers slippery and wet. The wind was already gusting up to thirty knots, while his boat was crabbing across the growing swell. "Okay, Lotus-Eater, you're on."

"Listen, old buddy," the voice continued, clearer now that it was digital, "our weather radar shows a squall building in the north, up in the Sporades, and it looks like it could be a real bear. It's going to be all over your butt in no time. Thought I'd better let you know. You ought to try and hole up down on the south side of Kythera."

Kythera was an island just off the southeast tip of Greece's Peloponnesos. It was now looming off Vance's starboard bow, barren mountains and sheer cliffs.

"I've been watching it," he yelled back into the mike, holding it close to shield it from the howl of wind. The gale was coming in at an angle to the waves, creating two swells running at ninety degrees, and the sea was getting short and confused. "But I think I can ride it out. I'm making probably seven or eight knots." He paused, then decided to add a little bravado. No point in admitting how worried he was. "Just a little rock and roll."

"That's horseshit, friend. This thing's for real. You'd better head for cover." It was the profane, oversmoked voice of Bill Bates, CEO of SatCom, who'd been monitoring his trip using the awesome electronics he'd installed on the little island of Andikythera, fifteen kilometers south of Kythera. "Even old Ulysses himself had that much sense, and it's common knowledge that guy didn't know fuck-all about sailing. Took him ten years to get home. Remember that inlet on the south side of the island, that little harbor at Kapsali? We put in once for a drink last year. I respectfully suggest you get your ass over there and drop anchor as soon as possible."

"And let you win? No way, José." He was jamming his weight against the starboard tiller, and the radio was distracting. As far as he was concerned, the wager with Bates was ironclad: retrace Ulysses's route in a fortnight and do it without ever touching land. "I just think you're getting worried. You suddenly remembered we've got ten large riding on this. Somebody's got to lose, and it's going to be you, pal."

"You're a headstrong idiot, Michael," Bates sputtered. "Fuck the ten grand. I don't want it and you don't need it. I'm hereby going on record as taking no responsibility for this idiotic stunt, from this point on. You're really pushing your luck."

"We both know this ain't about money. I've got a reputation to live up to." Like finding out how many ways I can kill myself, he thought. Jesus! How did I get into this?

He reached to secure the linen sail line to a wooden cleat. The heightening swell was churning over the gunwales, soaking him as it drove the bow to leeward.

"Well, for once in your life use some sense. The risk isn't worth it. Our weather radar here at the facility tells no lies, and you should see it. This is going to be a granddaddy. I've triangulated your position and you're only about four klicks off the east side of Kythera. You could still run for that little harbor down south before it hits."

"I know where I am. I can just make out the island off my starboard bow. About two o'clock." It's tempting, he told himself. Damned tempting. But not just yet.

"Then go for it." Bates coughed. "Listen, you crazy nutcake, I have to get back out to Control. We've got a major run-up of the Cyclops laser system scheduled tonight for 2100 hours. So use your head for once, goddammit, and make for that anchorage."

"Your views are taken under advisement. But a great American philosopher once said it ain't over till it's over." He pushed the thumb switch on the microphone, clicking it off. Then he switched it on again. "By the way, amigo, good luck with the test." The Cyclops was going to power the world's first laser-driven space vehicle. Who knew if it would work?

"Thanks, we may need it. Catch you again at 2300."

"See you then." If I'm still around, he thought. He clicked off his mike, then switched back to channel sixteen. The radio was the only electronic equipment he had permitted himself. He enjoyed monitoring the Greek chatter coming from the island fishing boats and trawlers, which worked nights. Lots of bragging.

Now, though, the bursts of talk on the open channel were all about the building storm. The fishing boats this night had abandoned the Aegean to the massive interisland ferries. In fact, those white multideck monsters were his real concern, more than the storm. *Odyssey II* had no radar, and his tiny mast lantern would just melt into the rain when the storm hit. Sailing in the dark and in a squall was a game of pure defense; he had to keep every sense alert—sight, hearing, even smell. He prayed the ferry lanes would be empty tonight. A Nomicos Line triple-decker could slice his little homemade toy in half without ever knowing he was there.

Odyssey II was a thirty-eight-foot wooden bark, planked construction of cypress on oak, that no sane man would have taken out of a marina. But Michael Vance was hoping to prove to the world that the fabled voyage of Ulysses from Troy back to Greece *could* have happened. Unlike anything seen afloat for almost three thousand years, his "yacht" was, in fact, an authentic replica of a single-masted Mycenaean warship. Painted lavender and gold—the ancient Greeks loved bold colors—she could have been a theme-park ride. But every time he looked her over, he felt proud.

His browned, cracked fingers gripped the wet wood as the sea churned ever higher, now blotting out the dim line of the horizon. The storm was arriving just as daylight faded— the worst moment.

Enough thinking, he ordered himself, audibly above the gale. It's bad for the reflexes. Just keep the tiller to leeward and don't shorten sail. Go for it. Just get around Kythera, then heave to and lie in the lee till the worst is over. Another five, maybe six kilometers should do it.

Vance wasn't Greek; he was American and looked it. As for Greece and things Greek, he preferred tequila over ouzo, a medium-rare sirloin to chewy grilled octopus. All the same, years ago he had gotten a Ph.D. in Greek archaeology from Yale, taught there for two years, then published a celebrated and radical theory about the Palace of Knossos on Crete. The book had caused an uproar in the scholarly community, and in the aftermath he had drifted away from the world of the ancient Greeks for several years. With this project, he liked to think, he was coming back home. He had just turned forty-four, and it was about time.

Age. More and more lately he realized he preferred old,

well-crafted things: stick-shift transmissions, tube amplifiers, vinyl recordings. Anything without numbers that glowed. *Odyssey II* was as close to that feeling as he could get.

Coming in now was his first real weather, and he had his numb, pained fingers crossed. His creation had certain historically precise features yet to be fully tested in high seas. He had built her in the style of ships in Homer's time, which meant she was hardly more than a raft with washboard sides. Four meters across the beam, with a shallow draft of a meter and a half, she was undecked except for a longitudinal gangway over the cargo and platforms at the bow and stern, protected with latticework to deflect enemy spears. It did not help much, however, against the swell. The keel extended forward at the bow, supposedly for additional lateral plane, and that was a plus when reaching with the wind abeam or tacking to windward, but now, running downwind, it increased her tendency to sheer about. All his strength was needed on the tillers just to keep her aright.

There were other problems. Maybe, he thought, Ulysses had them, too. He'd reproduced the ancient Aegean practice of tying the ends of the longitudinal wales together at the stern, then letting them extend on behind the ship and splay outward like the tail feathers of some magnificent phoenix. Although he loved the beauty of it, now that "tail" was catching the wind and making steering even tougher.

Probably should have left the damn thing off, he'd often lectured himself. But no; *Odyssey II* had to be exactly authentic . . . or what was the point? No guts, no glory. The ancient Greeks were the astronauts of their age, the Aegean their universe, and he wanted to recapture the triumphs and the fears of Homer's time, if only for a fortnight.

7:28 P.M.

"Sir, we got an RQ from the *Glover*." Alfred Konwitz, a twenty-year-old Oklahoman with a thirty-eight-inch waist and known to the evening radio shift affectionately as Big Al, lifted off his headphones and reached for his coffee, extra cream and sugar, which he kept in a special Thermos cup.

The United States has two bases on the southern Mediterranean island of Crete, strategically close to Libya and the Middle East in general. They are the naval and air base at Souda Bay, which is large enough to accommodate the entire Mediterranean Sixth Fleet, and the communications base at Gournes, in the southern outskirts of Iráklion, Crete's capital city.

He and Staff Sergeant Jack Mulhoney were at Gournes, on the fourth floor of the faceless gray building that housed operations for the massive battery of antennas. They both knew the *Glover* was a Garcia-class frigate, technically part of the Sixth Fleet, on a routine but classified intelligence-gathering assignment a hundred kilometers northwest of Souda Bay.

"They've got an Israeli chopper Mayday," Konwitz continued. "They need a verify. See if it's a scheduled op or what."

Jack Mulhoney was busy with paperwork—more damned forms every day—and did not really want to be bothered. He got off at midnight, and the staff officer had ordered it completed and on his desk, by God, by 0800 tomorrow. Or else.

"Then run it by Traffic," he said without looking up. Forms. "Maybe it's some exercise. You could call down to the Mole and see if it's on his schedule."

The Mole was Charlie Molinsky, who ran the Traffic Section on the second floor. If the Israeli chopper was on a regular op, he would have it in the computer.

"Roger." Konwitz punched in the number and asked Molinsky to check it out. As he waited, he found himself wishing he were back in Oklahoma, hunting white-tail deer on his uncle's ranch. They were as thick as jackrabbits.

He only had six months more to go, and he could not wait to get out. He had joined at age seventeen to get a crack at electronics, and—true to its word—the Navy came through. When he got out, he was going to open his own shop and get rich fixing VCRs. Hell, everybody who had one was always saying how they broke down all the time and how much they cost to fix. Who said the Japs didn't create jobs in America. . . .

Suddenly he came alive. "He's got a negative, sir. He's asking if we could get *Glover* to reconfirm."

"Christ, switch me on." Mulhoney shoved aside the pile of paper and reached for his headset. "*Glover*, this is Gournes. Do you copy? Over."

He listened a second, then continued. "Roger. We have no ID on that bogey. Repeat, negative ID. Can you reconfirm?"

While he was waiting, he punched up a computer screen and studied it. The *Glover* had reported a position at latitude 36°20′ and longitude 25°10′ at 1800 hours. And their bearing was last reported to be two-five-zero. Nothing else was in the vicinity.

Damn. He didn't like the feel of this one. His instincts were telling him something was wrong.

Then his headphones crackled. "Verified IFF. Definitely Israeli code. Do you copy?"

"I copy but I don't buy it. Proceed with caution. Configure for a bogey unless you can get a good visual."

"Roger. But can you get through to Israeli Control? There's a hell of a storm coming down out here right now, and visuals don't really cut it."

"I copy you, *Glover*. Hang on and we'll try to get something for you." He flipped off the headset and revolved in his chair, concern seeping into his ruddy features. "Al, see if the people downstairs can get through on their hot line to Israeli Air Control. Military. Ask them if they know anything about a chopper in the vicinity of the *Glover*. Tell them we need a response *now*. Priority. Could be we've got a bogey closing on one of ours, maybe using a phony IFF. I want them to clear it."

"Aye, aye, sir," he said crisply, then reached for the phone again. He spoke quickly, then waited, drumming his fingers on the vinyl desk. . . .

7:31 P.M.

As another gust hit, Vance glanced up at the rigging, praying it would hang together. Instead of canvas, the wide, shallow square sail was made of small linen cloths sewn together, like those made on the tiny looms of ancient times. It was a single-masted reefing sail, invented just in time for the Trojan War, with an upper yard fitted with a system of lines whereby it could be furled up and then secured aloft. When he got south of the island and hove to, he would drop the sea anchor and reef her, but for now he wanted every square inch.

He was tired and thirsty, but he had no time for even a sip of water. With the sea rising, waves were pounding over the primitive sideboards and soaking him to the skin. Next the squalls would come—though maybe a little rain would feel good, improve the personal hygiene. . . .

He was used to problems. For the past five years he had operated a three-yacht charter sail business out of Nassau, the Bahamas, living aboard one of the vessels, a forty-four-foot Bristol two-master christened *The Ulysses*. In fact, this whole enterprise had begun there when, after a day of sailing, he and Bill Bates were unwinding over drinks one hot and humid afternoon at a club near the Hurricane Hole Marina. Vance, attired in shorts and a T-shirt, his standard sailing outfit, was sipping his Sauza Tres Generaciones tequila and feeling great.

"You know, Bill, I've been thinking," he had said. "I want to try something that's never been done before."

"What? You mean try paying your bills on time?" Bates had laughed, knowing Vance seemed to have a perennial cash-flow problem.

"Very funny." He had ignored the crack and swirled the ice in his glass, then pulled out a piece to chew. "No, this is serious. Ever check out the paintings of the early ships on Greek vases?"

"Can't say as I have." Bates had reached down and was brushing a fleck of dirt off his perfectly white leather Sperry Top-Siders. As always, his pale blue Polo blazer remained crisp, his West Marine "Weatherbeater" cap immaculate.

"Well, hear this out. I think there's enough detail in some of the pictures I've seen to actually re-create one. And I checked it out: there's also a pretty good description of one in *The Odyssey*."

Bates had looked up from his Bacardi and Perrier. "So you want to try and build—"

"Not just build one; anybody could do that." He had leaned back, hoping to add a touch of drama to what was next. "I want to sail one through the Aegean. Do a rerun of the Odyssey, the classic quest."

"Get serious." Bates laughed.

"Couldn't be more. I want to build one—single mast, square sail—and go for it. Recreate Ulysses's Odyssey. And no nav gear. Just the stars."

"But what route would you take?" Bill was digging into the pocket of his blazer for a weathered briar pipe. "Does anybody really know?"

"I've looked into it, and just about everything Homer talked about has been located, in some place or another. We know exactly where the site of Troy was, so that'd be the spot to push off. Starting at the Dardanelles Strait, Ulysses first went north and sacked a city on the coast of Thrace. Then he took a heading almost due south, passing through the Cyclades islands and by the north side of Crete, then put in at the north shore of Africa, where—"

"So, you intend to do it by the book," Bates had interjected.

"Only way." He had sipped his tequila, feeling his excitement growing, then continued. "From there it's up to the western tip of Sicily, Polyphemus land, then northwest to Sardinia. Then over to Italy and down the west coast, where Ulysses ran afoul of Circe. Next it's south, past the Galli Islands, where the Sirens sang, after which I make the Straits of Messina and down to Malta, the island of Calypso. Finally it's northeast to Corfu, and from there it'd be a straight shot on down to Ithaca. Home plate."

"You'll never make it." Bill was thoughtfully filling his pipe.

"Bet you ten grand I can do it in a fortnight."

"I'll probably never see the money, but you're on." Bates had grabbed the bet, with a big, winner's grin. . . .

So far, it had gone virtually without a hitch. Using old paintings, he had worked up precise engineering drawings for the vessel, then engaged with a small shipyard in Istanbul to build it. The Turkish workers could scarcely believe their eyes. The ship was a Greek vase come to life, and already the world press had given him plenty of coverage. Everybody liked the idea of a long shot.

He had taken plenty of long shots sailing the Caribbean over the last eight years, but he had no experience with an early October storm in the Aegean. Tonight was building into a serious problem. All signs pointed to a typical autumn blow-out. He glanced at the low-lying clouds moving in from the north, darkening the sky and building rapidly. He knew that in these waters, light autumn breezes could easily whip into thrashing gales. Yeah, Bill's radar was right. The weather was real. And it scared him, a lot.

Well, he figured, it was time. He had been lucky so far. The Ross DSC radio still worked, and the patchwork sail hadn't ripped—yet. . . .

Then it happened. The nightmare. Without warning the winds suddenly changed around to the north, going from thirty knots to sixty in what seemed only a second. As the linen sail strained, he threw his weight against the tiller, hoping to hold his course. Now more than ever, with the storm on him, he wanted to keep on all his canvas and try to get into the lee of the island as soon as possible. It was definitely time to cut the bravado and start thinking about the sea anchor.

"*Odyssey II,* come in," the radio crackled, and he recognized Bates's voice once more. "Do you read?"

He reached down and picked up the small black mike, then yelled against the howl of wind. "I copy you, but make this quick. No time to chat."

"I had another look-see at the radar, Mike, and I just noticed something else you should know about. We show you at almost the same position as a U.S. Navy ship of some kind. Part of the Sixth Fleet probably. Take care you miss her."

He clicked the mike to transmit. This time he didn't want

to bother switching channels. "Some kind of exercise, probably. What's her class?"

"Can't tell. But she's still a hell of a lot bigger than you are, pal. They may pick you up on their radar, but again maybe not. Just take care."

"I'll keep an eye out for lights. Thanks." He clicked off the mike again, then looked around. But the Aegean, what he could see of it, remained dark and empty. Somehow, though, the black made it just that much scarier.

He leaned back into the tiller, still trying to hold as much of the wind in the sail as possible. The waves were lashing him now, cold and relentless. And *Odyssey II* was beginning to heel precariously, forcing him to apply helm, throwing his full hundred and eighty pounds against the heavy wooden portside tiller. It was one of a pair, port and starboard—the old Greek idea being that whenever a ship leaned away from the wind, lifting the windward rudder out of the water, the helmsman still had a lee rudder for control. But when he took her to starboard and tried to round the island, the wind and tides would be full abeam. With a shallow-draft, low-ballast vessel like this, that was going to be dicey. . . .

He reached for the life jacket he had secured to the mast, a new Switlik Fastnet Crew Vest MKII. Normally he did not bother, but this was not the time to go macho. It had a 35-pound buoyancy and a 4,000-pound breaking strength, enough for any seas.

Now the wind was gusting even harder, kicking up yet more swell. The Aegean sunset was concluding, its red clouds turned purple and darkening fast, a presage that visibility would shortly be a thing of the past.

The past, *à la recherche du temps perdu*. This trip, regardless of his bet with Bill, was also about recent times gone by. His father had died, the revered Michael Vance, Sr., the undisputed Grand Old Man of archaeology at Penn. It turned out to be a far greater loss than he had anticipated, like a chunk of himself torn away. He still missed their late-hours "discussions"—heated arguments, really. He had been trying to wrench away the future, the old man trying to hang on to what he knew best: the past. It had been a dynamic tension filled with mutual love. And now he felt guilty. But why? There was no reason.

He also had gone through another of life's milestones, a divorce. Eva Borodin, a dark-haired daughter of Russian aristocracy, a college sweetheart, had come back into his life after a digression of ten years. The second time around was supposed to be a charm, right?

The soap operas were wrong on that one, the same way they were about most other things in real life. Although the divorce, now a year ago, had been businesslike and amicable, it still had hurt. For the past year he had been sitting around and brooding—about life, love, middle age, death.

He still found himself wearing his wedding ring. Why? It just made him think of her even more. No, the truth was, everything reminded him of her and how much he needed her. What he had not realized—until she was gone—was that needing somebody was the richest experience of life.

He sighed into the wind. The challenge of his Odyssey enterprise was supposed to take his mind off all that. Was it working?

Maybe. But so far the jury was still out. . . .

He gripped the tiller harder and glanced up at the sail. Running downwind, the cutwater on the bow was going to be a real problem. But just another half hour, probably, and—

Christ! Bill's warning was on the mark. A massive hulk loomed dead ahead, running with no lights. It was as long as a football field, the bow towering up like a battering ram. She was moving in off his portside stern—he guessed she was making at least fifteen knots. High above the bridge, antennas and communications gear showed faintly against the twilight gloom, gray and huge. Not recommended for close encounters . . . but he still had time to tack and give her a wide berth.

He threw his weight against the tiller, veering to leeward. Once clear, he would bring the bow about and let the cutwater top her wake like a surfboard, keeping him from taking water. Then he would be on his way, into the storm and the night.

Maybe he did not even have a problem. They probably

had picked him up on their radar by now. It did not mean they would veer off course, but they might throttle her down a few notches, just to be neighborly. . . .

He was still leaning on the tiller, watching the monolithic hulk skim silently past, when he noticed a throaty roar beginning to drown out the slap of the ship's wake against the side of *Odyssey II*'s hull. After a few moments, as it grew in ominous intensity, he realized it was coming in from the south. What in hell!

He whirled to look, and spotted a chopper, altitude about eight hundred meters. What was it doing here? Had Bill been *that* worried, enough to risk sending his hot new Agusta Mark II out in this weather to . . .

No, it was way too big. When he finally saw it clearly, the stubby wings and rocket pods, he realized it was a Soviet Mi-24D, a Hind. Over the mottled camouflage paint he discerned the blue star and white background of the Israeli Air Force. Odd.

He knew they had captured one once, an export model from the Syrian Air Force, but they would never fly it this far into international airspace. It was a prize. What's more, this bird was fully armed—with dual heat-seeking missiles secured at the tips of each stubby wing, just beyond the twin rocket pods. Then it assumed an attack mode. . . .

7:43 P.M.

Sabri Ramirez stepped down to the weapons station again, gazed out through the huge bubble, and smiled. "Shut down the radar. Their IWR must not have any reason for alarm. They're probably running our IFF through Gournes right now."

The Israeli nodded, then reached over to switch off all systems that the Americans might interpret as weapons guidance. Next he clicked on the low-light TV. Unlike radar, it was a passive system that would not alert the ship that she was being ranged.

Ramirez pictured the control room of the USS *Glover*

crowded with curious young seamen glued to their monitoring screens, probably happy to have a little excitement. Their IFF would be reporting an Israeli chopper. But the minute the visual ID came through, all hell would break loose.

So far, he told himself, it had been a textbook approach. Airspeed was down to ninety-five knots, altitude eight hundred meters. Carefully, carefully. First rule. Don't spook the quarry. We don't need radar. We'll be passive, heat-seeking. No ECM they can throw at us will make any difference.

"Under two minutes now," he said. "It's time."

"No pain, no gain." Peretz flipped on the radio. "USS *Glover*, we're going to have to ditch. We have a crew of three —pilot, copilot, and navigation trainee."

"We have emergency crews on starboard side, ready to pick you up. Do you have Mae Wests?"

"Life jackets on. Standard-issue yellow. With dye markers and saltwater-activated beacons. We'll—"

"Hawk One, our Traffic guys at Gournes just reported they can't get a positive verify on you."

"Tell them to check again," Peretz suggested matter-of-factly. "Maybe they screwed up in—"

"We'll have them run it through one more time. Routine security. But you've got to keep a three-thousand-meter perimeter till—"

"Dammit, sailor, oil pressure's in the red. We're taking her by your starboard bow. Ready your crews."

Suddenly another voice came on the radio. It was older.

"Israeli Hawk One, this is Tactical Action Officer Vince Bradley. Who the hell are you? We VID you as a Mi-24 gunship."

Peretz had switched off his mike and was loosening his helmet strap. "You got it right, asshole."

7:44 P.M.

Vance watched as the Hind approached on the starboard side of the destroyer, heading straight for it and dropping altitude. What in hell was going on?

He lunged for the radio, and switched it to the military emergency frequency, hoping to pick up some clue that would explain it all. Probably not much of a chance. If this was a Sixth Fleet operation, they would be scrambling everything.

Nothing. So he flipped over and started scanning the U.S. Navy tracking frequencies—216.8 through 217.1 megahertz —in the meantime trying to keep the tiller in hand.

The radio was alive, agitated voices yelling back and forth. It was an argument, the helo claiming it was making a flyby for an emergency ditch, the frigate not exactly buying the story.

No kidding. He'd checked out the chopper in close-up as she came over, and he'd seen nothing wrong. Everything looked to be in perfect working order. The only obvious thing out of the ordinary was that she was fully armed. Whoever was flying her was using some kind of bogus Mayday to get in close. But by now it was too late to try and give the frigate a warning.

7:45 P.M.

"Perfect timing," Ramirez said, moving down to the weapons station and taking Peretz's place. "We're inside forty-five seconds. Now just keep her on the deck. First we neutralize the forward gun turret."

"Taking airspeed to fifty knots." Salim was praying now. *"Allau Akbar!"*

"USS *Glover*." Ramirez had switched on the helmet mike again. "We have a confirmed ditch. Oil pressure just went entirely. We'll be taking her by the bow."

"I repeat, who the hell are you?" the TAO's voice came back on the radio. "We still have no confirm on your IFF. If you make a pass, I'll assume hostile intent."

"Sorry. No time to play this by the book," he replied. "We're ditching."

He immediately clicked on the radar. In less than ten seconds he'd be in position to lay a Swatter directly into the forward gun turret. Command on the *Glover* knew it, and at that moment the gun was swiveling, coming around.

Suddenly a blaze streaked past them in the sky as the forward gun fired and a telltale tracer ripped by. It was intended as a warning.

But now the gun glowed on the IR interrogation screen.

Thank you very much, Ramirez thought, and flipped a switch, activating the starboard Swatter's heat-seeking guidance system.

7:46 P.M.

"Right." Alfred Konwitz snapped to attention. "Yes, *sir.*"

He slammed down the phone and whirled around to Jack Mulhoney. "Full denial, sir. Israeli Control says they have no military aircraft operating anywhere in that sector of the Aegean. They double-confirm. That's Class A. Hard."

"We're in the shit. Some son of a bitch is closing on one of ours, and we don't even know who he is." He picked up the headphones, then switched on the scrambler. "*Glover,* do you read me? I think it's a bogey. I can't tell you that officially, but you'd better alert your TAO in the next five seconds or it'll be your ass, sailor."

"This is Bradley," came back a new voice. "We just— *Jesus!*"

"*Glover,* what—?"

"Hostile action . . . do you copy? We've got a hostile."

"How many—?"

"It's visual ID'd as a Russian Mi 24-D. With Israeli markings. We're taking fire forward—"

"What are—?"

Sounds behind the radio voice had erupted in turmoil. Something catastrophic was going on.

"Al," he turned quickly, "get Command. I think we've got an Israeli-ID'd Hind taking hostile action on the *Glover.*"

He didn't realize it, but with those words he had played directly into Sabri Ramirez's hands. The scenario was now a lock.

When Jack Mulhoney turned back to his radio, he only heard static.

Vance watched as the frigate got off a warning tracer, but to no effect. The Hind ignored it, as a stream of 57mm rockets from under the chopper's stubby starboard wing flared down, while the radar-slaved machine gun beneath the nose opened fire. Then the weapons operator on the Hind loosed a starboard-mounted heat-seeking Swatter, and an instant later flames erupted on the frigate's bow, an orange and black ball where the forward gun turret had been. As it spiraled upward into the night, the turret and its magazine exploded like a giant, slow-motion cherry bomb.

He could see sailors running down the decks, could hear the sound of a shipboard fire alarm going off, the dull horn used for emergencies. They were calling all hands to station, but their response had come too late. The false-flag approach had caught the U.S. Navy off guard, its defenses down.

The radio crackled alive with a Mayday. Were there any other ships in the area? he wondered. Anybody to take out the bastards in the chopper?

Now it was banking, coming around, bringing the frigate's stern into its deadly view. Then a blaze of 57mm rockets poured in, engulfing the communications gear and antennas. Next the weapons operator loosed a second Swatter directly into the bridge.

Christ!

Seconds later it had transformed the midsection of the frigate into a ball of fire. He watched aghast as the blast flung the men on the bridge outward through the glass partition.

He plunged for cover just as the first airborne shock wave ripped *Odyssey II*'s linen sail loose from its lines. When he rose to try and grab the starboard tiller, a second shock wave caught him and flung him savagely against the mast.

The next thing he knew, he was clinging to the portside gunwale, one hand still tangled in the lines that had been ripped from the sail. The night sky had turned a blood red, reflecting down off the low-lying clouds.

Then he felt a tremor in the hull as a massive wave caught him and the pegs that held the stern together—so lovingly installed—sheared. The aft section of *Odyssey II* instantaneously began to come apart. The light woods would float— she was, after all, hardly more than a raft with sides—but she would be helpless. His handmade marvel had been reduced to a bundle of planks, barely holding together, sail in shreds, twin rudders demolished.

For a moment he counted himself lucky. His body unscathed, he probably could weather the storm by just hanging on.

Then it happened. Whether through luck or skill, the chopper's weapons operator laid another one of the Swatter missiles into the frigate's stern section, causing a massive secondary explosion, a billowing ball of fire that punched out near the waterline. This time, he knew, a wall of water would come bearing down on him, sending a terminal shock wave through what was left of *Odyssey II*.

You've got to try and keep her aright, he told himself. Try and lash yourself down with one of the lines. . . .

The wall of water hit, hurtling him over the side. He grasped for a section of gunwale, but it was too late. The wave obliterated everything. Now the swell was churning against his face as he tried to stroke back, his lungs filling with water. His arms were flailing, hands trying desperately to grasp the slippery cypress planking. The Switlik vest was holding, so he was in no danger of drowning. Yet.

Fighting the swell with his left hand, spitting water, he reached out with his right, trying to catch any piece of wreckage floating by. Finally, he succeeded in wrapping a line around his wrist. He gasped, choking, and caught his breath. Then, still grasping the line, he draped his left arm across *Odyssey II*'s shattered side and used the line to pull himself over, into what was left of the hold. If he could stay with her, he figured, he might still have a chance.

Just as he tried to rise to his feet, however, he looked up to see the mast slowly heeling over, coming straight down.

He toppled backward, hoping to dodge it, but it slammed him just across the chest. The world swirled into blackness, as even the light from the blazing ship behind him seemed to flicker.

Stay conscious, he told himself. Stay alive.

Holding onto the toppled mast, using it as a brace, he managed to rise. And now the Hind had completed its gruesome handiwork and was banking. Again it was going to pass directly overhead.

By God, he thought, this thing isn't over. Those bastards are not going to get off scot-free.

7:50 P.M.

"You used the Swatters!" Salim was shoving the throttle levers forward as he banked. His voice was incredulous. "You said we were just going to disable the TRSSCOMM system and the radars with rockets."

TRSSCOMM was short for Technical Research Ship Special Communications. The frigate was equipped with batteries of listening antennas, an elaborate system of sensors and sophisticated computers, and various hydraulic systems on the stern needed to twist and turn the various dishes. But it also was manned.

What was the point of mass murder? Ramirez had explained that the *Glover* was a spy ship that worked for the U.S. National Security Agency, the NSA. Normally it operated within a small region, in a special "hearability" area just off Crete where a fluke in the weather allowed it to eavesdrop on all the Middle East; the crew could even watch Cairo television.

Salim was stunned. Ramirez, he had suddenly realized, was a madman. It was one thing to require an occasional killing in an operation this complex—after all, he had had to shoot his weapons operator in order to steal the Hind—but an all-out attack on a U.S. frigate was pointless. The stakes had just gone through the roof.

However, Salim's younger brother, Jamal, had exactly the

opposite reaction. With a surge of pride he exclaimed, "Praise
be to God," and fell to his knees on the rear litter. This was a
leader he would follow anywhere.

The others did not share Jamal's joy. They considered
themselves professionals, and overkill was not businesslike.
However, they merely glanced at each other and kept silent.
Squabbling with Ramirez served no purpose.

"We were only going to take out their tracking capability," Salim said again, his anger growing.

"It's time you understood something." Ramirez handed
his headset to the Israeli, Dore Peretz, and stepped up from
the weapons station, his voice sounding above the roar of the
engines. "I am in charge of this operation. If I think an action
is necessary, I will take it. Does anyone here want to disagree?"

The question was answered with silence. He had just
killed dozens of men. They all knew one more would hardly
matter.

7:52 P.M.

Vance pulled himself across the planking and stretched
for a box of gear stowed beneath the stern platform. In it was
a constant traveling companion: his chrome-handled 9mm
Walther. Although the concept of downing a Hind gunship
with small-arms fire had been tested in Afghanistan and
found wanting, he was so angry his better judgment was not
fully in play.

The pistol remained in its waterproof case. Quickly he
took it out, unwrapped it, and clicked a round into the chamber. Then he tried to steady himself against the fallen mast.

The Hind was about a hundred meters away now, coming
in low. Were they going to strafe? No, they probably didn't
realize he was there.

They were about to be in for a surprise.

He could see the weapons-system operator inside the
lower bulletproof bubble. Forget it. And the pilot, seated just
above him, was similarly invulnerable. No way. Furthermore,

the dual rocket pods beneath each short wing were probably armored. Again no vulnerability.

Aside from the poorly protected gas tanks there was only one point worth the trouble. If . . .

It was about to pass directly overhead, and he saw that he was going to be lucky. One Swatter missile remained, secured on the hardpoint tip of the stubby starboard wing. It was the only shot he had.

But if he didn't get it, they would get him. One touch of the red firing button by the weapons operator and *Odyssey II* would be evaporated.

He took careful aim at the small white tube on the wing, still nestled on its launcher, and squeezed off a round. But at that instant *Odyssey II* dipped in the swell and he saw sparks fly off the fuselage instead. The chopper passed blissfully overhead, its engine a dull roar above the howl of the sea.

7:54 P.M.

"We're taking fire!" Peretz shouted from the weapons station down below.

"What? That's impossible." Ramirez whirled, then stepped in behind him to look. Lights from the control panel winked over his shoulders, while below them the Aegean was dark and gray. "Check the look-down radar."

Peretz flipped a switch on his left and scanned the screen. "There's something down there. Maybe a fishing—"

"Idiot, nobody's fishing here now. Not with this weather." He looked up and shouted to the cockpit. "Salim, take her about, one-eighty, and we'll strafe the son of a bitch."

The 12.7mm nose cannon was slaved to the radar, another of the Hind's many well-designed, and lethal, features. While Ramirez watched—he would have moved back into the gunnery seat himself, but there was no time—Dore Peretz switched on the nose cannon. When the target locked on the radar, he pushed the fire control under his right hand.

7:55 P.M.

A flare of machine-gun fire, hopping across the churning sea, caught the side of *Odyssey II* and sprayed flecks of wood around him. But the swell was making him an elusive target. The line of fire had not really done any damage, not this time.

They knew he was there, though. Now the chopper was banking and returning for another pass.

Maybe, he thought, they're going to stick with the nose cannon. They won't bother wasting rockets or a multi-thousand-dollar Swatter missile on the wreckage of a raft. The bastards are just having some target practice, a little fun and games.

He saw the flames from the nose cannon begin as the massive Hind started its second pass. This was it. *Odyssey II* was about to be history.

But not before he gave her one last blaze of glory.

Holding to the gunwale and readying himself, he took careful aim at the starboard Swatter, still perched like a thin white bird on the stubby wingtip. He steadied the Walther, on semiautomatic, and began firing—oblivious to the line of strafing coming his way.

He saw the rounds glancing off the armored wing, and the sparks guided his aim. The clip was going fast, but then . . .

Bingo.

A flare erupted, then an orange fireball, neatly severing the starboard wingtip. The missile had detonated, but just as it did, the Hind's strafing caught *Odyssey II* right down the middle, shearing her in half.

7:56 P.M.

"Stabilize her!" Peretz felt himself flung against the bulletproof bubble that shielded the weapons station. A blinding explosion jolted the Hind, and the accompanying shock wave from the detonating Swatter spun it around thirty degrees. Several gauges in the instrument panel had veered off scale.

Salim reached up and cut the power to the main rotor,

then eased the column and grabbed the collective pitch lever with his left hand. In less than a second the Hind had righted herself. Slowly the instruments began coming back as the electrical system recovered from the impact.

"Tail rotor's okay," he reported, checking the panel. "Altimeter reads five hundred meters." He looked up. "What in the name of God happened?"

"Our last Swatter detonated. The question is, why?" Ramirez answered. He was staring angrily out the high-impact plastic of his bubble at the wreckage of the starboard wing.

Dore Peretz, now in the weapons station in the nose, was talking to himself. "I got the bastard."

7:57 P.M.

He shoved the Walther into his belt and dove into the swell, the cold waters crashing against his face. The *Odyssey II* was reduced to debris. His labor of love, half a year's work, all evaporated in an instant. The Zen masters were right: never get attached to physical things.

He avoided the deadly shards of wood, then seized onto a section of the mast that had blown in his direction. The Hind was banking and turning now, assuming a heading due south. That, he realized, was the direction of Andikythera, site of SatCom's new complex. Was it their next target?

That didn't make any sense. Bill's project was commercial; it had no military value. Or at least none he could imagine.

But now he had only one thing on his mind. He secured his life vest tighter and held on to the mast, the salty Aegean in his face. The current was taking him due south, the same direction the chopper had headed.

CHAPTER TWO

"Damn it!" Ramirez looked down at the weapons' read-outs. "Did you have the Swatter armed? The system should have been off. If it was on, he could have detonated it by impact."

Peretz stared a second longer at the wreckage of the vessel below, then glanced back at his instruments and paled. "I thought it was . . . it must have malfunctioned. No fucking way—"

"Carelessness. Stupid carelessness." Ramirez bent his head and examined the wing, then checked the status read-outs on the weapons system. "We lost the starboard rocket pod, too."

Peretz took one look and realized it was true. The rocket pod had been shorn away, leaving the tangled metal of the wing completely bare. But the Hind did not need its wings for stability; they were merely for armaments.

"Well, so what? I wasted the fucker, whoever he was." He tried a smile, sending a web of lines through his tan as the lights of the weapons panel played across his face. It was the way he always disguised nervousness.

Damn you, Ramirez was thinking. An Israeli cowboy. I would kill you on the spot except that I need you. It was an arrogant mistake, and I can't let it happen again. It *won't* happen again.

He turned and moved back up to the cockpit. "What's our status?"

"Sideslip is nominal," Salim reported grimly, his dark eyes glancing down at the churning sea only a couple of hundred meters below them. "I think we're going to be all right."

"We have just had an example of how an oversight can destroy an operation," Ramirez declared, turning back to the main cabin. "We will not succeed if we get careless, lose discipline. I have planned this operation down to the last small detail. You have all been briefed, over and over." He paused and examined the men. Sometimes he felt as if he were lecturing children, but these were no children. "Each of you knows what his job is. I expect you to do it with exactness and precision. The next oversight anyone here makes will be his last. Am I understood?"

There was silence, then finally a voice came from the litters in the darkened cabin aft, barely audible above the roar of the twin engines. It was Jean-Paul Moreau, the Frenchman. He hated flying, and he particularly hated flying with an Iranian at the controls.

"What the hell happened?"

"Someone on . . . presumably a raft of some kind. We took a couple of rounds of small-arms fire." He glanced back, making sure his voice reached Peretz in the weapons station. "The last Swatter was left turned on, armed, and it must have been hit. Probably the detonator. A stupid oversight."

"Looks like the mistake was mine," came the voice of Peretz, trying, unsuccessfully, to sound contrite. "Can't win them all, baby."

Back to his smart-ass self, Ramirez thought, still gritting his teeth in anger. But he pushed it aside. "Forget it. In this business you only look back if you can profit from your mistakes. We just learned what happens when we forget our mission. The matter is closed."

"Now"—he returned his attention to the main cabin—"when we set down at the facility, I expect total discipline. Nothing less will be tolerated. Is that understood?" He motioned Peretz out of the weapons station and took his place there.

Would these men hold together the way he required? As he looked them over, he felt confident. He had had enough experience to smell success.

Sabri Ramirez had definitely been around the track. Born in Venezuela almost half a century earlier, the son of a prominent Marxist lawyer, he had become an ardent revolutionary by age twenty. At twenty-five he went off to Cuba, but it was only later, while attending Patrice Lumumba University in the Soviet Union, that he discovered his true ideological core —it turned out he actually despised "the oppressed of the earth," along with curfews, books, and lectures. No, what he really wanted to join was not the Party, but *the party*—good living, women, fame. And he wanted the last most of all. After nine months his lack of ideological fervor got him summarily expelled. He actually felt relief.

With an eye to where the action was, he emigrated to Beirut . . . and prudently became a Muslim by conversion. Then he started making contacts—Beirut had always been a good place to make contacts. The payoff was quick. He was young, obviously brilliant, and he would do anything. In the early 1970s he was recruited by the terrorist group known as the Popular Front for the Liberation of Palestine and assigned leadership of its European unit. Off he went to Paris, the posting of his dreams.

He had long fantasized about making himself a legend as one of the world's leading terrorists, and he was soon succeeding beyond his fondest imaginings. In 1974 he graduated from the PFLP and formed his own group. A Middle Eastern gun-for-hire, it was known as the Organization of the Armed Arab Struggle. The designation, he thought, had a nice revolutionary ring, which he had long since learned mattered. His new enterprise—terrorism-to-go—soon attracted such major clients as Libya and Iraq. Among his more celebrated achievements were the bombing of a French Cultural Center in West Berlin, exploding a suitcase bomb at a Marseilles railroad station, and placing an incendary device aboard the French "bullet train."

Although he never had cared about ideology, he appreciated the importance of a correct political stance in the Islamic world, and therefore he frequently posed as the leader of an "armed struggle" against the "Zionist Enemy." But always, however, at a profit. He had, in fact, perfected the fine art of extortion, pressing the "reactionary" regimes of Egypt, Jordan, Kuwait, Saudi Arabia, and the Gulf sheikdoms into paying protection money disguised as "revolutionary donations." After he engineered the 1975 OPEC incident in Vienna in which eleven oil ministers were taken hostage, and then blew up a seaside resort, killing a Kuwaiti official, he began receiving regular payoffs from all the Gulf states.

Finally, in 1984, he closed out operations under the OAAS name, moved to Damascus, and began training Syrian intelligence agents. By that time, he had become a chimera, a legend whose nickname, the Hyena, was linked to every car bomb in Europe. And by that time also, the Hyena (a name he despised) had become the stuff of popular fiction, as well as of dossiers on three continents.

Having reduced terrorism to a science—a boring science —he then temporarily retired. But now, after the American invasion of the Middle East, he had decided to come back for one last score, to do what he had been dreaming about for years. The Americans had unwittingly provided the perfect opportunity. Why not seize it? This time, however, he wanted to do it himself, not with an army of half-crazed radical Muslims. . . .

He stepped up to the cockpit and examined the rows of gauges. "Hold the airspeed under a hundred knots. And make sure you keep her on the deck."

Then he checked down below. "Peretz, this time make sure all the weapons stations are switched off. That's off."

The Israeli nodded, this time without his usual grin.

Now the Hind had begun its final approach. The low-light

TV showed a small landing pad approximately thirty meters on each side with a private helicopter parked in the middle of a black and white bull's-eye in the center. He knew that ARM—a group he had long hated—had ringed the island with a first-class industrial security system. Five years ago, he recalled, they had killed three of his operatives in Beirut, in a futile attempt to kill *him*. What's more, it never made the papers. Typical. The security system they had developed for the island was good, but it made no provision for this kind of penetration. It pleased him to at last make fools of them.

"We're coming in," Salim announced. He touched the rudder pedal with his left foot to hold their heading and grasped the collective pitch lever as he eased the engines toward idle. "There's already a helo on the pad. Looks like a new Agusta."

"I know about it. Just set down next to it, inside the landing perimeter. I want this to be simple."

Tonight, he knew, they had scheduled the first full power-up of the Cyclops. Everything depended on how that test went, but he couldn't postpone the takeover any longer. This was it. . . .

Abruptly he wondered if the damaged wing would affect stability on touchdown? They would soon find out.

8:10 P.M.

The current swept him inexorably southward, while behind him the bundle of planks that remained of *Odyssey II* was dispersing rapidly. He cursed himself for having lost the Ross DSC radio. On the other hand, he considered himself lucky just to be in one piece. Luckier than the crewmen of the USS *Glover*. It was heartrending. Seeing a tragedy coming and not being able to stop it: that was the worst possible nightmare. He wanted to go back to try and help, but the sea made it impossible.

He pulled himself over the bobbing, drifting mast, feeling it slam against his face as the sea tossed it like a matchstick. All around him lethal splinters of *Odyssey II* sliced through the water, jagged spears driven by the swell. The dark engulfed him, lightened only by the billowing remains of the Navy frigate now some thousand yards away.

Somewhere, dear God, it's got to be somewhere. Let it still be strapped to the mast. The idea seemed stupid at the time, but now . . .

He felt his way down until his fingers touched a slippery nylon cord. Was it . . . *yes.*

Maybe there is a God.

The straps were tangled, which was not supposed to happen, and fragments of cypress planking from the sides of the ship had punctured the nylon cover, but his Switlik search-and-rescue raft was still dangling from the remains of the mast. Now for one more minor miracle: Could he manage to pull it free before everything disappeared into the dark and the swell?

He flailed with one hand to keep his head afloat, while his fingers grappled with the bowline knot. Finally the knot loosened, and he wrenched it loose.

Jesus, is there going to be anything left? Would it still inflate?

He grappled with the fiberglass canister that contained the raft, then popped it open. With his last remaining strength he pulled on the tether, discharging the bottled carbon dioxide that caused the Switlik to hiss to life. Part of it. He realized the lower buoyancy tube had been ripped to shreds by the 12.7mm machine gun of the Hind that had destroyed the mast, but the upper one had somehow escaped intact. So he was half-lucky.

It was yellow, hexagonal, and it looked like heaven. He had never used one before, and he had never realized how it felt. Like an oversized inner tube.

With a surge of relief, he pulled himself aboard, inching in as he felt the swell pound over him, and then he drew out the folding oars and extended them. With his new course he knew he would miss the harbor at Kythera recommended by Bates—no way could he battle the current and make it. The vagaries of wind and sea were driving him almost due south.

It was the direction the chopper had taken—straight for the little island of Andikythera.

Could they breach SatCom's security and get in? Probably. The setup installed by ARM was industrial-level only. He had cautioned Bill about that.

He grimaced and plied his strength to the two small aluminum oars. The way the wind and seas were taking him, he would find out soon enough. Again he lamented the loss of the radio—with it he could get out a Mayday alerting any ships around that might mount a rescue of the frigate's survivors. He also could try warning the SatCom facility that trouble was headed their way. The problem was, the Hind had a top speed of over a hundred and fifty knots. If Andikythera was its destination, it probably was already there.

The cold sea stung his face and the tossing waves were making him slightly seasick, but he felt alive again. Almost by instinct he looked up to try to find the stars, loving how crisp and striking they could be over the Aegean. Nothing yet, but there were glimmers in the north. A good sign. The storm was blowing over now, the clouds starting to open up again.

If Bill tries the radio, he'll probably figure I've just vanished from the earth.

He half felt like it. As the cold autumn waters of the Aegean surged around him, its six-foot waves washing over his partially inflated Switlik, he thought about Bill Bates. He was a friend, a very good friend. Was he about to be in trouble?

Although Bates was a world-class executive, he also was a dedicated family man. He had a model wife back in Arlington and two model sons, both deposited in model private academies. His wife, a blond WASP old-fashioned enough to have the same family name as a prominent Philadelphia bank, never seemed to tire of her charity obligations, so it was his sons he took with him sailing in the summers. That was how Vance had met him, sailing with the boys in the Bahamas.

Bill was highly regarded in industry circles as the CEO's CEO, and not without reason. For one thing, less inconsequential than most would think, he *looked* the part. His steel-gray hair was always trimmed to the precise millimeter, his tanned cheeks were forever sleek from a workout at his club, or whatever club was handy on his perpetual travels. He had once claimed he knew the location of more health clubs than any man in America.

Best of all, though, he knew how to raise money. When he described a pending enterprise, he did it with the gleaming eye of the true believer. Even in a dicey investment environment, he always generated the enthusiasm sufficient to ensure that a new stock issue sold out and closed higher than the offering price on the day it was floated. The man could sell sunlamps in the Sahara.

He competed hard in everything he did. When he decided, some years after he and Vance had become acquainted, that he wanted to spend summers racing, he did not bother buying his own yacht; instead he flew to Nassau and leased the fastest boat he knew. At that moment, the vessel filling that description was the *Argonaut*, owned by Windstalker, Ltd. It was a forty-four-foot sloop, highly regarded throughout the racing fraternity. Its owner, however, never let any of his three yachts out of the harbor without first undertaking a personal checkout of the new skipper—even if it was an old friend.

Vance remembered it well. Bill manned the helm, a mahogany wheel always kept well polished, and they were making a solid eight knots on the speedo. It was one of those mornings in the islands when everything seemed as clear as a desert sky. No cruise ships were scheduled into the harbor, and the stinkpot powerboats were mercifully in limited supply. The wind was perfect and the water as smooth as a glittering mirror. Best of all, Bates was handling the helm as though he had been there all his life.

"Think we can get her up to ten knots?" he'd asked, shielding his eyes as he studied the genoa, a gleaming triangle of white above the bow.

Vance had leaned back and tested the wind. "Give her a little touch on the helm, to starboard, and I think she might come through for you." He was proud of his recent refurbishing of the boat—the latest Northstar digital satnav gear, brand-new sails that cost a fortune, a complete renovation of the instrument station down below.

Bates tapped the wheel and the genoa bellied even more. "I like this fucking boat a lot, Mike," he declared. "So here's the deal. I want to lease her for three months, take her to Norfolk, get a crew together, and get everybody comfortable with her."

"I think we can talk." Vance had to smile. The yacht would be in good hands, and a three-month charter was a dream come true for a guy in his business.

"Matter of fact, I wanted to ask you to help me out with something else, too. Some security work."

"Hey, I'm just a simple charter-boat operator. Not my line."

"Don't bullshit me, pal." He laughed. "You know SatCom is building a new industrial facility in the Aegean."

"A private space facility."

"I think American technology is getting a bum rap, Michael," he said with sudden seriousness. "I plan to change that."

"The *Journal* says you want to try and give the Europeans a run for the roses."

He looked over, the wind whipping his glistening hair. "You keep in touch pretty damned good for a simple sailor. But I tell you, if we succeed, we'll literally change the way space is used. I'll be able to put a satellite into orbit for a song. Just between us, I'm building the biggest private spaceport anywhere. The French operation in Guiana won't hold a candle to it. I've already got ten geostationary orbital slots locked up with the World Administrative Radio Conference. Even NASA better keep a grip on their jockstrap."

"Where's the money coming from? The usual suspects?"

"Who else." He laughed, then tapped the helm slightly more to starboard. "The stock was over-the-counter and it was hell and gone in three fucking hours. Bang. Out the door. Matter of fact, it's now trading almost fifteen percent above the original offering price." He shrugged. "I should have issued more. But like a stupid son of a bitch, I had a failure of nerve. Didn't go with my instincts."

"Next time, how about letting me in on the action?"

"You're a goddamn piece of work, Michael. And so's this boat. Tell you what. I'll make you a deal. I figure you're expecting about four thou a week for this baby, correct?"

"Anything for a friend."

"Right." He laughed. "I want her for twelve weeks. So . . . what if I paid you with some of my personal SatCom stock? Fifty thou worth at the current price? How's that sound?"

"Deal," Vance said, without hesitation. He'd heard a lot of big-time bull in the charter business, but Bates was a straight shooter. The temporary gap in cash flow was going to make meeting the three mortgages—one for each boat—tough, but he liked the sound of the project."

"This isn't going to leave you strapped, is it?" Bates looked a trifle worried.

"I'll manage. As I always say, two in the bush is worth one in the hand."

"Michael, half the time you don't have a pot to piss in. I know that. You're the lousiest personal-finance manager I know." He laughed out loud and tapped the helm, bringing her to port a notch. "Which is one of the world's great ironies, considering what you do for ARM."

"You hear things, too." He had never really discussed his ARM work with Bates.

"You're good. I know that. Word gets around." He paused. "Matter of fact, I wanted to ask you a favor. I was hoping you could work up a contract for me with your people. As I said, I need some security for that facility in Greece."

"What kind?"

"That's for your guys to say. It just has to be good. We're going to be installing some proprietary technology that's light-years beyond anything that's ever been seen before. And we're going to rock a lot of boats in the business. There're a hell of a lot of Europeans who'd love to know what we're up to. There's a real chance of industrial espionage."

"So what's the program? Perimeter surveillance? Security guards? We could probably arrange the subcontracting."

"I'd appreciate it. Your guys know Europe, the local scene. I've got a feeling that's going to be important."

"No problem." The truth was, this was exactly the kind of no-risk work the boys at ARM liked. Nobody shooting at you. "I'll put in a call to Paris if you like. Something probably can be arranged."

"Good." Bates nodded, as though a handshake were already involved. One more thing off his checklist. "Mainly I want some physical-security stuff. You know—fences, alarms, that kind of crap."

"We've got a guy in Athens who specializes in that. He won't give estimates over the phone, but if you'll let him look over the site, he'll price the job for you right down to the drachma. With various options. But you'd be smart to go with his top-of-the-line recommendation. Try to nickel and dime him and he'll walk. I've seen him do it."

"So what's this so-called 'top of the line' likely to run me?" Bates had asked.

"Well, there are the systems you can see and the ones you can't." He'd laughed. "The ones you can't see cost more."

"I already told you I need the best."

"Then you probably want to go MAD," Vance said, his eyes hiding a twinkle.

"What the hell are you talking about?" He looked over, annoyed and puzzled.

"Magnetic anomaly detectors. You bury special transmitting cables beneath the ground, outside the perimeter, so that they build an invisible electromagnetic field around and above their location. Anything—doesn't even have to be metal—that enters the field will distort it. If you go with the Sentrax system, made by an outfit in Switzerland called Cerberus, you can have the whole thing linked to a central console that displays the layout of the perimeter on computer screens."

"Sounds good. We're practically going to have computers in the bathrooms."

"Won't come cheap."

Bates shrugged into the wind. "As long as you guys don't

ask for the store, I see no problem. I've budgeted for security, and there's always contingency money."

"I'll see what I can do." He had glanced up and ascertained that the sun had passed the yardarm. But even if it had not, what the hell. He saw the prospects for a fat commission looming. "How about a Heineken?" He was reaching into the cooler in the well.

"You read my mind."

"By the way, want to tell me the location of the site? You've managed to keep that out of the papers so far. I'd guess it's probably an uninhabited island, right?"

"Good guess. It's north of Crete, about twenty square kilometers. It's privately owned, but I've just signed a long-term lease."

Vance tried to envision the place. Most of the Greek islands tended to be granite, with nothing growing on them but scrub cedar. "What's the terrain like?"

"That's actually what makes it so attractive. Cliffs all around the shoreline—you couldn't put in with so much as a dinghy—and then one really marvelous deepwater inlet. But the best part is, the interior is mostly level and perfect for what we need. And there's a granite mountain at one end that's ideal for our telemetry."

"A protected docking location and a natural telemetry base."

"Right. All the electronics will be set up high above the launch facility, and we can use the inlet for bringing in materials. We should only have to dredge it a bit and sink some pilings. It's well along. I've already signed off on a lot of the prime contracts." He stared at the blue horizon and adjusted the wheel again. "And I'll let you in on another secret, Michael. I've bet the ranch on this one. The stock offering wasn't nearly enough to capitalize the enterprise. I've had to raise money from everybody in town—junk bonds, the fucking banks, you name it. Just the hardware ran close to three hundred million. I've even put up my stock in all my other companies. If this project doesn't fly"—he laughed—"literally, I'm going to be joining America's homeless. I even put up my house in Arlington. Worth two million, and I owned the goddamn thing free and clear. I'll just have to hand over the keys. Dorothy'll kill me."

"Then we'll make sure nobody snoops." He popped open an ice-cold beer for Bates, then one for himself. "From land or sea."

"Land or sea." Bates hoisted his icy green bottle.

"Which actually raises an interesting question." He took a sip, cold and bracing. "How about security from the air? Fly-overs, that kind of action?"

"Let them come. There'll be nothing to see. Except for the launch pad and telemetry, everything's going to be underground. There're a lot of caves on the island—like that famous one on Antiparos. We're going to use those for the computers and assembly areas. And what we can't find in place, we'll just excavate."

It's beginning to sound a little too pat, Vance found himself thinking. But that's what security experts were for. They were the guys who got paid to find holes in a project like this. . . .

The thing that kept gnawing at his mind, however, was the phrase "by land or sea." All along he'd worried about penetration from the air. Had he been right after all?

CHAPTER THREE

Sitting at Main Control, the central desk facing the large display screen, Cally Andros had just reached a conclusion. She was getting old. Two more weeks to her thirty-fifth birthday, then a measly five years till the big four-oh. After that she could only look forward to a holding action, fighting sags and crow's-feet. Building dikes to hold back the deluge of time.

It was depressing.

She sipped at a cup of black coffee emblazoned with the SatCom logo, the laser eye of the Cyclops, and impatiently drummed her fingers on the workstation keyboard, trying not to be distracted by meditations on mortality. Tonight for the first time they would run up the superconducting coil all the way, in their most important test yet. The tech crews at the other end of the island predicted it would reach peak power in—she glanced at the huge digital clock on the blue wall next to the screen—twenty-seven minutes. . . .

What was wrong with her? She had thought that one over

a lot and decided the answer was *nothing*. She had dark Greek eyes, olive skin, and a figure that would stop a clock— a perfect size eight. But it got better. She had the best legs in the world. The absolute very best. If they wouldn't necessarily stop a timepiece, they'd sure as heck slowed a lot of traffic over the years.

No, her problem was opportunity. Whereas on paper this island was every single girl's dream—males trapped here by the carload—all the attractive/interesting men were either too young or too old or too dumb or too married. Moreover, those in the control room—mostly Ph.D.'s in their late twenties—saw her only as Dr. C. A. Andros, Director-in-Charge. There seemed to be an unspoken rule around Control that you didn't make a move on the boss lady. Anybody who could run this project had to be treated with the distance befitting authority. Especially since they believed all she really cared about was work.

Thanks a lot, whoever dreamed that one up.

The sickest part of all, though, was they were half right. She did not wish herself anywhere else in the world right now, men or no men. She occupied the center of the universe, was poised for the winner-take-all shot she could only have dreamed about five years ago, back when she was still fighting the mindless bureaucrats at NASA. With Project Cyclops she was running a half-billion-dollar gamble for the last big prize of the twentieth century. If she lived to be a hundred, she would never be handed anything this terrific ever again.

Born Calypso Andropolous thirty-four years ago, daughter of strong-minded Greek farmers, she had learned to believe in herself with a fierce, unshakable conviction. Until now, though, she had never really had the opportunity to test that faith. Until now.

It had not been an easy journey. After getting her doctorate in aerospace engineering from Cal Tech, she had struggled up through NASA's Kennedy Center bureaucracy to the position of chief analyst. But she had never achieved more than a desk job. She had wanted more, a lot more. Now, thanks to SatCom, in three days she would have it. Using a fifteen-gigawatt microwave laser nicknamed Cyclops, she was about to put SatCom in the forefront of the private race for space.

Ironically, the company had built its spaceport barely three hundred kilometers from her birthplace on the island of Naxos. She often thought about life's ironies: sometimes you had to return home to change the future. She barely remembered that rugged little island now; the images were faint and overly romantic. Those times dated back to when the junta of right-wing colonels had seized power in Greece. Soon thereafter her parents had emigrated; they and their nine-year-old daughter joining a large exodus of freedom-minded Greeks to New York. They had been there only three months when her father died—the hospital said it was pneumonia; she knew it was mourning for Greece and all he had lost. He had loved it more than life. She was afraid, down inside in a place where she didn't visit much anymore, that he loved it more than he had loved her. So along the way she tried to forget all of it, to bury her memories of Greece. And now here she was back again. In New York, Cally Andropolous had, in spite of herself, thought incessantly of Greece; back here now, all she could think about was New York.

The strongest recollection was the third floor of a walk-up tenement on Tenth Avenue and Forty-ninth Street, a section of town widely known as Hell's Kitchen—and for good reason. The schools were designed to make sociopaths of all those trapped inside; only New York's famous Bronx High School of Science, one of the finest and most competitive public institutions in the nation, offered an escape from their horror.

Accepted when she was thirteen, Calypso Andropolous graduated third in her class. For her senior science project, she created a solid-fuel rocket, using, as the phrase goes, ordinary household chemicals. And she did it all by herself, with a little help from a skinny French Canadian boy named Georges LeFarge, who lived with his mother in Soho.

By that time, she knew exactly what she wanted. Her ambition was to be the first woman in space.

Nobody said it would be easy. But after the rocket—she

and Georges had launched it from the Morton Street Pier in Greenwich Village—she felt she was on her way. She had blossomed—in every way, much to her frustration—a lot quicker than Georges did. At age seventeen his idea of sex was still to swap chemical formulas. So she finally gave up on him as a lover and decided to wait till college.

She chose Cal Tech, selected after turning down acceptances from half a dozen prestigious universities in the East. By then, Calypso Andropolous had decided she wanted to get as far away from West Forty-ninth Street as possible. And she never wanted to see another eggplant moussaka as long as she lived.

She also wanted a shorter name, and thus it was that her long Greek surname became merely Andros. That simple change had a liberating effect on her far beyond what she had expected. At last she felt truly American . . . and able to admit to loving nothing better than living off Whoppers and fries. Junk food was, in fact, the thing she missed most here. No, what she missed most was Alan. Still.

Georges had picked MIT, and she did not see him again until he came to Cal Tech for grad school. By that time she was deeply in love with Alan Harris, who was twenty years her senior. She was discovering things about herself she didn't want to know. Harris was a biochemistry professor, tall and darkly handsome, and she wanted desperately to live with him. She knew he was a notorious womanizer, but that didn't matter. She was looking for a missing father and she didn't care. It was what she *wanted*.

When he broke it off, she thought she wanted to die. The only one she had left to turn to was Georges. And they restarted a friendship as platonic as it had been back at Bronx Science, though it was deeper this time. Georges told her to forget about Harris and just concentrate on a first-rate dissertation.

It was not easy, but she did. Her project involved compressing a big computer program that calculated spacecraft trajectories into a small one that could be operated on a Hewlett-Packard hand calculator. She then devised a way to create voice commands that could free up an astronaut's hands while he—soon, she told herself, it would be *she*—handled other controls.

After reading every NASA report that NTIS had released on microfiche, she knew no one there had created anything like it. She also figured out that NASA was a hotbed of careerists, all protecting their own turf. The only obstacle to their accepting her new computer program would be the NIH syndrome—Not Invented Here. It turned out she was right, and wrong.

By happy chance, her dissertation came to the attention of Dr. Edward Olberg, a deputy director of trajectory control at the Kennedy Space Center, who hired her a week later, with a GS rating a full two grades higher than customary. He knew a good thing when he saw it. And now Dr. Cally Andros's computer work was the creation of a NASA employee. End of problem. She still wanted to be in the astronaut program, but she figured she had made a good start.

She was wrong. It turned out that she was far too valuable in the guidance section to let go. She published a lot of papers, grew very disillusioned, and was on the verge of telling them to stuff it, when . . .

An executive unknown to her, named William Bates, called one May morning three years ago, said he had read all her papers, and then offered her a job that caused her to postpone her dreams of space flight. He wanted her to head up a private space program. She was, he told her, too good to work for the government. She should be out in the real world, where things happened.

When she recovered from the shock, she felt an emotion she had not known since her first day at Bronx Science—she was scared. In the business world, the responsibilities were clear-cut and fatal. You were not blowing some anonymous taxpayer's money: it was real cash. Furthermore, your responsibilities doubled. Not only did you have to make it work, you had to make a profit. She loved the challenge, but she quaked at the enormous risk.

Finally she made a deal. Yes, she would give up a sure career for a risky long shot, but on two conditions. First, she got to pick her staff, and second, someday she would get to go into space herself.

Although he clearly thought the second demand rather farfetched for SatCom, he assented to both.

"How's it looking, Cally?" Bates was striding into Command, having just emerged from his office at the far end of the cavernous room. Fifties, gray-templed but trim, he wore a trademark open-necked white shirt and blue trousers—a touch of the yachtsman, even ashore. A former Vietnam fighter pilot, he had flown over from the company's head office in Arlington, Virginia two days ago—setting down the company's Gulfstream IV at Athens—to be on hand when the first vehicle, VX-1, went up. As he stalked up, he was his usual crabby self, seemingly never satisfied with anything that was going on.

She looked him over and stifled the horrible impulse she had sometimes to call him Alan. He was short-tempered, the way Alan Harris was, and he had the same curt voice. Otherwise, though, they were nothing alike. The mind works in strange ways.

"Cyclops countdown is right on the money, Bill. To the second. Big Benny is humming, and coil temps are nominal. Georges says it's a go for sure this time. We're going to achieve the power levels needed to lase." (They had tried two preliminary power-ups previously, but the supercomputer had shut them down in the last hour of the countdown both times.) "Looks like tonight is the night we get lucky."

Georges LeFarge had served as her personal assistant throughout the project, even though he formally headed up the computer section. These days he was still slim, almost emaciated, with a scraggly beard he seemed to leave deliberately unkempt, just as he had at Cal Tech. Bates had bestowed on him the title of Director of Computer Systems, which did not sit well with his leftist politics. His conscience wanted him to be a slave to the exploiting capitalists, not one of them. However, he always managed to cash his bonus checks. He had carried on a flirtation with Cally, sending messages back and forth on the Fujitsu's workstations, for the last two years. She had finally taken him up on it; and it was a bust all around. *C'est la vie.*

At this moment he was blended into a sea of shirt-sleeved technicians glued to the computer screens in Command Central, the nerve center of the entire operation. The young Americans all worked in a room slightly smaller than three tennis courts, with rows of light-beige workstations for the staff and three giant master screens that faced out from the far wall. The soft fluorescents, cheerful pale-blue walls spotted with posters and the large SatCom laser-eye logo, muted strains of Pink Floyd emanating from speakers somewhere in the corner, and circulated air carrying a hint of the sea—all made the perfect environment for the nineteen young workers spaced comfortably apart at the lines of desks this evening shift.

As they watched, the superconducting coil racheted increasingly larger bursts of energy into the accelerator, pumping it up. At twelve gigawatts the Cyclops should—if all went well—begin to lase.

The coil, a revolutionary new concept for storing electrical energy, was situated deep in the island's core. It was a near-perfect storage system, permitting a huge current of electricity to circulate indefinitely without resistance, ready to produce the massive, microsecond pulses of power. The heart of the system was an electromagnetic induction coil 350 feet in diameter and 50 feet high embedded in a natural cave in the island's bedrock. The coil itself was a new niobium-titanium alloy that became superconducting, storing electricity without resistance losses, at the temperature of liquid nitrogen. A vacuum vessel almost like a giant Thermos bottle surrounded the coil and its cryogenic bath.

The coil fed power into a particle accelerator that drove the complex's centerpiece, the Cyclops—a free-electron laser designed to convert the energy stored in the coil into powerful pulses of coherent microwaves. The supercomputer would then focus these with the phased-array antennas into the propulsion unit of the space vehicle. That unit contained simple dry ice—the only thing simple about the entire system—

which would be converted to plasma by the energy and expand, providing thrust for the vehicle.

"Cally, we have ten point three gigs," LeFarge announced confidently. He was absently stroking his wisp of beard. "Power is still stable."

"Good." She watched the readout on the computer screen in front of her as the numbers continued to scroll. If the Cyclops performed the way the engineers were all predicting, the world's most powerful laser was about to go critical. A thrill coursed through her.

The idea was brilliant. By directing the energy *to* a space vehicle, you kept the power plant for its rockets on the ground. Unlike conventional rockets, the vehicle's weight would be virtually all payload, instead of almost all fuel. It would cut the cost of launching anything by a factor of at least a hundred. . . .

Now a green oscilloscope next to the computer screens was reading out the buildup, a sine curve slowly increasing in frequency.

"Eleven point one," Georges announced, barely containing a boyish grin. "We're still nominal."

Cally glanced at the screen. "Let's keep our fingers crossed. Almost there."

"By the way," Bates interjected, "assuming everything goes well here tonight and the storm lets up, I've scheduled myself on the Agusta over to Kythera in the morning. A friend of mine was sailing near there, and I'm a little worried. I just tried to reach him on the radio and got no answer. Maybe his radio got swamped, but I want to find out." He was turning to head back to his office. "Now, though, I've got some calls in to Tokyo. So keep me informed on the countdown, and your feelings on the weather."

More investors, she caught herself thinking. Begging. Which must mean the money's getting tight again. But hang in there just a couple more days, Bill, and we're gonna show the world a thing or two. They'll be begging *you* to let them invest.

"I just came in to give you some moral support," Bates

continued, pausing, "and to tell you I think you're doing a terrific job."

"Bullshitting the help again?" She laughed, not quite sure she believed his tone.

"Why not? It's free." A scowl. "But just keep up the good work." He had extracted a leather tobacco pouch from his blue blazer and begun to fiddle with his heavy briar pipe. She started to ask him to please not smoke here with all the sensitive Fujitsu workstations, but then decided they were his workstations. "If this thing flies, literally, I'm going to give you a vulgar stock option. Another one. For putting up with me."

"How about a bottle of aspirin?" She made a mock face. "I don't have any time to spend the money."

"I'm going to take care of that, too. After this is over, I'm going to have you kidnapped by a Greek beachboy and taken to some deserted island where there's only one way to pass the time." He frowned back, a wry crinkle passing through the tan at the corner of his eyes. "Twenty years ago I might have tried to do it myself."

"Still hoping to get me laid?" She gave him her best look of shock, and they both had to laugh. The sexual electricity was there, whether either of them wanted to admit it or not.

"There's a time and place for everything," he went on, showing he could hint and not hint at the same time. "You're definitely working too hard."

"I can't take all the credit." She knew when to be self-effacing and when to change the subject, fast. "We owe all this to the Red Sox's oldest living fan."

By which she meant Isaac Mannheim, the retired MIT professor whose revolutionary propulsion idea had made the whole project possible. In 1969 he had demonstrated his ground-based laser concept to NASA, but they had backed away, claiming they had too much invested in conventional chemical rockets. But he knew it would work, knew it would change the way space was used, so he had taken the idea to entrepreneur William Bates and offered to sign over the patents for a piece of the profits. Bates was impressed. He took him up on the offer, raised the money, and then hired the best aerospace engineer he could find to head up the project. Together they were a perfect team.

Mannheim, with flowing white hair and tweedy suits, was now in his seventies and lived in retirement in Cambridge, Massachusetts. He was due in tomorrow, just in time to watch the first lift-off of a full-scale vehicle. When he arrived in Athens, Cally always dispatched the company Agusta to pick him up. A first-class corporation, she figured, ought to behave like one.

"If the Cyclops power-up goes off without a hitch tonight, then we should have plenty of good news for him this trip," Bates said. "I'll let you be the one to brief him."

"Oh, he'll know it all before he gets here. He calls me every day at 1700 hours, our time, to check things out. I could use him to set my watch."

"Isaac's like the voice of our conscience, always telling us to work harder and better. Well, good for him." He smiled and flicked a gold lighter. The young technicians around the room gave him a disapproving glance, but kept their silence. The boss was the boss.

Besides, everybody in Command, poised in front of their screens, had other things to worry about.

8:22 P.M.

Eric Hamblin, formerly of Sweetwater, Texas, had worked as a guard for SatCom for the past two and a half years and he loved the job. He was twenty-four, a college-dropout casualty of the go-go eighties who got to spend his afternoons hanging out on one of Greece's most beautiful islands. He was tall, thin, and bronzed to perfection. During his weekends on Crete he could almost pass for French as he cruised the German *Fräuleins* who lined the sands in their string bikinis.

Tonight he had come on duty at seven o'clock—actually a couple of minutes later than that, since he'd been on the phone to a girl from Dresden to whom he had made some pretty overreaching promises. She wanted to come back to

Crete this weekend and do it all over again. He grinned with satisfaction, kiddingly asking himself if he had the stamina.

He sighed, then strolled on down the east perimeter. The security here at this end of the island was good, as it was everywhere: the tall hurricane fence was topped with razor wire and rigged with electronic alarms. Of course you couldn't see all the security, which meant the place did not feel confining or scary. Which suited him fine. He was wearing a .38, but it was mainly for show. He wasn't sure he could hit anything if—God forbid—he should ever have to draw it.

Besides, the island was surrounded by miles and miles of water, the deep blue Aegean. The whole scene was a fucking hoot, and he gloried in it. Sea, sand, and—on weekends— hot-and-cold running German snatch. Who could ask for more?

Andikythera was, indeed, a travel poster come to life. Though it still was owned by the Greek shipbuilder Telemachus Viannos, as part of his major investment in the company, Bates had negotiated a long-term lease for SatCom, and by the time the technical staff started arriving, the few Greek shepherds on the island had been comfortably relocated to Paros. Construction began almost immediately after Bates took over, and soon it was almost like one giant Cal Tech laboratory. Everything from Big Benny, SatCom's Fujitsu supercomputer, to the phased-array microwave installation was state of the art. Here SatCom had created a launch facility that was within ten degrees latitude of Cape Canaveral, totally secure from industrial espionage, and perfectly situated to send up a major network of communication satellites.

Even now, though, the island remained unbelievably picturesque—its sharp white cliffs abutting the deep blue sea, then rising up in craggy granite to a single peak at one end, where the phased-array transmission antennas were now. Its flawless air sparkled in the mornings, then ripened to a rosy hue at sunset. For security and safety, as much as for aesthetics, the major high-technology installations had been secured deep in the island's core. Command was at one end, situated behind sealed security doors, and a tunnel from there led down to the power plant, installed a hundred and fifty meters below sea level. Guarding this small piece of paradise had been a snap. . . .

Hamblin scratched at his neck and moved on through the sand. He despised the shoes they made him wear and wished he could be barefoot, untie his ponytail and let his sandy hair flow free around . . .

What was that? The east perimeter was totally dark, but he caught a sound that almost could be . . . what? a chopper approaching? But there were no lights anywhere on the eastern horizon, and the pad was dark. Nobody flew Mr. Bates's fancy new Agusta 109 Mark II at night. *Especially* with no lights.

No mistaking it now, though. A whirlybird was coming in. He could clearly make out the heavy drumbeat of the main rotor.

8:24 P.M.

Salim altered the throttles when they were about ten meters above the pad, and they started drifting sideways. For a second it looked as though they might ram the Agusta, but then he applied the clutch, stopcocked the engines, and hit the rotor brake. The Hind safely touched down, tires skidding. They were in.

Best of all, there'd been no radar warning alert from the instrument panel. Around them the facility was dark and, as he shut down the engines, deathly quiet. The wheels of the retractable landing gear had barely settled onto the asphalt before the main hatch was open and the men were piling out, black Uzis ready, the first rounds already chambered.

8:25 P.M.

Hamblin thought briefly about raising Guard Command at the front desk on his walkie-talkie and inquiring what in hell was going on. But then he knew how they hated false alarms. Particularly when the top brass was busy, like tonight.

He turned and studied the blinding white glow surrounding the two launch vehicles, *VX-1* and *VX-2*, down by the superstructure on the western end of the island. They were basking in glory, as though anticipating tonight's power-up of the Cyclops. He automatically glanced at his watch: the big test was scheduled for about twenty minutes from now.

No, instead of running the risk of looking like a jerk by reporting the expected arrival of SatCom execs he should have known about, he'd check this out himself. Jesus, why didn't anybody tell him anything?

He mused that security precautions here had been intended to guard against infiltration through the fences, not to prevent a chopper from coming in. Guess they figured nobody would be crazy enough to try and sneak in using a helicopter.

As he moved toward the landing pad, just over a hundred yards farther on down the fenceline, he searched his memory for something he might have forgotten. No, he'd glanced over the schedule for the pad this afternoon and nothing was listed. Dr. Andros—what a fox she was, made those plump German broads look like leftover hamburger—always had been good about keeping the schedule up to date. He liked that and counted on it. But then maybe this was some kind of unscheduled situation, connected with the test. Who the hell knew?

He was about to find out. Fifty yards to go. He could see the chopper now and it was huge, much bigger than anything he'd ever known the company to use. Maybe it was a last-minute delivery. An emergency.

They had touched down, but still no landing lights. That didn't make any sense. Suddenly nothing made any sense. Another ten seconds, though, and he'd zap them with his big flashlight.

He flipped the securing strap on his .38 and tested the feel of the grip. Just to be ready.

He was thirty yards away and he could hear them talking now, though he still did not recognize all the languages. He realized right away, however, that these clowns weren't connected with SatCom. He'd had an uneasy feeling all along, and now he was sure.

Were they industrial spies trying to pull a fast one? Maybe sneak in and take some photos?

He had no time now to radio for help. He was on his own.

He drew out the .38 and cocked it. Suddenly it felt very heavy. Then in his left hand he rotated the long flashlight till his thumb felt the switch.

Now.

He flicked on the light, beaming it through the wire security fence and catching the side of the chopper—God, it was huge—just in time to see several men stepping down. They were wearing black commando outfits and they most definitely were not anybody from the company.

"You!" he yelled, his courage growing. "Stop right where you are and identi—"

One of the intruders whirled in his direction, and before he could finish, he felt a deep burning sensation in his chest that slammed him backward. Next a piercing pain erupted in his neck and his head dropped sideways. The asphalt of the pavement came up, crashing against his nose. He heard the dull thunk of silencers just as the world went forever black.

8:26 P.M.

"Pad perimeter secure," Jamal Khan, Salim's intense younger brother said in Farsi, his voice matter-of-fact. He'd just wasted some stranger; no big deal. Then he slipped the Uzi's strap over his shoulder and turned back. Come to think of it, this was the thirteenth man he'd killed with an Uzi. Maybe the number would be lucky. . . .

Ramirez looked out over the facility, confident. Posing as an electronics supplier, he had fully reconnoitered the site two months earlier, meticulously memorizing the location of everything they needed. Once again he reflected on how fortuitous its geometry was. The facility was made to be penetrated from the air.

Stelios Tritsis, their Greek, was busy scanning the walkie-

talkie channels, but he heard no alerts from any of the guards
—which meant no more surprises in this remote corner. For
reasons of safety, SatCom deliberately had located the helicopter pad as far as possible from the Cyclops and the launch
installation. All staff were engaged down at the other end.
This guard had been a loner, and he had paid for his stupidity.

"Phase two complete," Ramirez announced quietly as he
looked back at the Hind. "Now, remember. No heroics. Everybody on semiauto."

The only obvious security out here was at the entry gate
to the chopper pad. After Peretz quickly aborted its alarm by
short-circuiting the copper contacts, they moved through sin-
gle-file. Ramirez stood at the opening, studying each man one
last time and hoping he could keep them together as a team.

So far almost everything had gone according to plan. He
had hand-picked, assembled, and trained them four months
in Libya, rehearsing them for all the standard antiterrorist
techniques that might be used against them—from stun grenades to "Thunder Strips"—then afterward had rendez-
voused with them in Yemen to pick up the Hind, the other
helicopter, and the two packages. He had made cash arrangements with enough officials in both countries to ensure that
no questions would be asked.

The most unreliable team member was Salim Khan, tonight's pilot. Ramirez watched him pat a twenty-two-round
clip into his Uzi and draw back the gnarled walnut cocking
knob on the top as he stepped through the gate. He looked
trustworthy, but he really wasn't. Ramirez suspected Salim
was too bitter, was too strongly of the opinion life had given
him a screwing—which meant he was now devoted to settling the score. He liked to live on the edge, push the rules.
On the other hand, this mission was all about that, and thus
far Ramirez had exploited the Iranian to the hilt.

It also meant, however, that he had to be watched: he was
a cynical realist who held nothing but contempt for the mili-
tant cadres of young firebrands who marched through the
streets of Tehran with photos of some ayatollah attached defiantly to their chest, chanting slogans against the Great Satan

. . . while wearing jeans whose back pockets read "Made in U.S.A." Because Salim didn't believe in anything anymore, he was difficult to control. Always dicey.

Following close behind him, also carrying a black Uzi, was Jamal, his younger brother. Jamal, with crazy eyes and a coal-black beard, was the exact opposite—he only fought for a cause.

Jamal had come to Lebanon years ago to join Hizballah, a radical organization headquartered in West Beirut and the Bekáa Valley. Since he joined, as many as five hundred Hizballah had been directly involved in terrorist acts in the Middle East and Europe. He believed God wanted him to carry out a jihad, a holy crusade, against the Americans and Zionists who had surrounded and were choking the Muslim peoples. To prove his faith, he had been part of the team that commandeered a Libyan Arab Airlines 727 in flight between Zurich and Tripoli, leading to the longest hijacking in history. The plane had traveled six thousand miles, bouncing from Beirut to Athens, then Rome, again Beirut, and even Tehran before ending on its third stop in Lebanon three days later.

Miraculously Jamal had walked free. He was a hothead, but he also was a survivor. Jamal prayed five times a day, neither drank nor smoked, and had been one of the explosives experts on the U.S. Embassy job in Beirut that killed 218 Marines. He was truly a living contradiction.

That was fine with Ramirez. He could care less about Hizballah's radical politics. On the other hand, he'd always made good use of them. After Jamal's famous hijacking, Ramirez had gone to the Bekáa Valley and found him, and through him Salim—who, by stealing the Hind, had turned out to be much more valuable than his rabid younger brother. All the same, he had problems with them. Iranians sometimes had difficulty discerning the difference between fact and fantasy: as with most Muslims, they thought that saying something was so made it happen.

The tall man striding through after Jamal, nursing a slight limp, was Stelios Tritsis, their only Greek. In 1975, as a young firebrand, he had been a founding member of the famous terrorist organization Epanastaiki Organosi 17 Noemvri. In his heart he was still a radical, dedicated to forcing Greece out of NATO and ending the U.S. military domination of his country. The new American imperialism in the Persian Gulf had only proved he was right all along.

Because of an incident long ago in his youth—a torture episode at the hands of the infamous Colonels—Stelios's eyes never seemed entirely focused. He had become addicted to the morphine given to relieve the pain and never kicked it. Even so, he was their most lethal marksman, and he considered this operation his final revenge against America and her lackeys. The man didn't care, honestly didn't care, about his share of the money. Even Ramirez had to admire that.

Following him was Jean-Paul Moreau, head of the famous Action Directe, whose international wing was headquartered in Paris. Jean-Paul was tall, had long flowing blond hair and determined eyes. He also had a famous bullet scar across his cheek from an attempt in the early eighties to assassinate former Justice Minister Alain Peyrefitte with a bomb attached to his car. He merely killed the chauffeur and was wounded by the security guards. But in November 1986 he got his revenge, masterminding the murder of Georges Besse, the chairman of Renault. He wanted nothing more than for Europe to rid herself of Americans and Zionists—toward which end Action Directe had cooperated with the Lebanese Armed Revolutionary Faction on several attacks carried out in France, which was how Ramirez had first met him. In the past Action Directe had financed its operations primarily through bank robberies. After this, Moreau was told, their money problems would be over.

The next man was Wolf Helling, the lanky, balding leader of Germany's Revolutionare Zellen. Ramirez suspected his real goal in life was to look as Aryan as possible. Politically he was an anarchist—who had, in 1984, bombed a NATO fuel pipeline near Lorch in Baden-Württemberg. RZ's official aim was to pressure the U.S. out of Germany through terrorist attacks and to destroy the West German "system" by conducting guerrilla terrorism against Zionists and militarists. RZ had long-standing ties to Palestinian terrorist organizations, which was again how Ramirez had met him. How ironic for

Helling: just when he had lived to see the Zionist American military begin to depart Europe, it had become the de facto ruler of the Middle East. He wanted to teach America one final lesson: the propertied classes of the world could never be secure.

Following behind him were three beefy former members of East Germany's Stasi—now being sought by authorities in the new unified Germany for torture and other crimes of the past. With few friends left, they had thrown in their lot with RZ. They had always reminded Ramirez of the three monkeys of folklore: Rudolph Schindler, with his dark sunglasses, could see no evil; Peter Maier remained such a rabid ideologue he still could hear no evil (of Communism); and Henes Sommer spoke nothing but evil, against everyone. They were sullen and bitter, but they were perfect goons for auxiliary firepower, or should be. They were men without a country, guns for hire who already had lost everything.

Dore Peretz, their renegade Israeli, walked through last, closing the wire gate behind him. He had fixed his steady dark eyes on only one outcome: he had come for the money, the money *only*. No politics or mock heroics for him. He already had selected a seaside villa in Hadera. Despite his annoying tendency to shoot off his mouth, to make jokes at the wrong time, his contribution would be crucial. Ramirez did not wholly trust him, but he needed his computer and weapons expertise. He asked himself what Peretz would do if the chips were really down. With luck, however, that question would never have to be answered. Ramirez almost liked him—he was not sure why—and would hate to have to kill the smart-ass fucker. . . .

They were in. Command lay at one end of SatCom's setup, the two vehicles at the other, and in between was the living quarters—known as the "Bates Motel"—as well as rows of small warehouses that contained supplies for personnel and equipment maintenance, used for storage but now darkened and locked. As they moved along the walkway, carefully staying out of the circles of light that illuminated the doorways of the warehouses, their black slipovers blended into the Aegean night. The minimal lighting in this area caused him no hesitation: he had thoroughly memorized the site. He knew they would find the control center with the computers just below their present location.

Now they were approaching the entry-point to Command, the high-security "lobby." Just inside the glass-doored space a uniformed Greek guard occupied a teakwood desk, attentively studying the sports section of an Athens newspaper.

They paused in the last shadows before the open space fronting the entryway, giving Stelios Tritsis time to shuck his black pullover. Underneath he was wearing the brown uniform of a SatCom guard, complete with epaulets and the regulation .38. He also had what, upon casual inspection, looked like a SatCom photo ID.

While the others waited, holding their breath, he stepped through the glass entry doors, feigning a jaunty pace and flipping the pass impatiently against the leg of his uniform.

When the SatCom guard looked up, puzzled, and started to challenge him, Tritsis was only five feet away. He sang out a hello in Greek, then reached to scratch an itch in the small of his back. When his hand came away, it was holding a small Glock-17 automatic. The shot was directly in the forehead, a dull thunk, and the guard tumbled backward in his chair, his eyes disbelieving, his .38 still holstered. It took only seconds.

Without a word the rest of them moved in.

"What's next?" Ramirez said quietly to Peretz.

"The code for the doors has to be punched in there—" he pointed. Behind the desk was a computer terminal that reported the security status of all the sectors. Its green screen remained blank, flashing no alerts.

"Disable them," Ramirez ordered, the first test of the Israeli's technical skills. In the hours to come, he would prove indispensable. Or so he claimed. "Then deactivate the access code and we ought to be able to just walk in."

While Jamal was rearranging the guard's body, leaving him slumped over the desk as though asleep, Ramirez locked the entry doors behind them, then stepped behind the desk and dimmed the lobby lights. Finally he slipped off his flight suit and tossed it behind the desk.

Right on schedule.

They headed toward Command. He knew that if you control the brain, you are master of the body, and now they had to seize that brain. So far their smooth progress surpassed his hopes. But the next phase was crucial, allowed for no foul-ups. He still feared his *ad hoc* troops might get trigger-happy and destroy some of the critical equipment; he had even considered making them use blanks, but that was taking too big a risk.

"The gates of Paradise are about to be opened," Jamal declared through his black beard, his crazed eyes reflecting back the lights on the security door as they changed from red to green and a muted buzzer sounded. "Allah has given this to us."

Ramirez said nothing, merely straightened the hand-tailored cuffs of his charcoal Brioni. Then he stepped back to watch as the door to Command Central slowly began sliding to the left.

8:39 P.M.

Cally was thinking about how much she would love a pizza, heavy on the cheese and Italian sausage. No, just heavy on the cholesterol. Why was it that the only things that tasted good were all supposed to be bad for you? She had long ago determined never to let it bother her. Like Scarlett, she'd think about it tomorrow. The heck with it. Everybody needed a secret sin. And that was the worst part of being here on Andikythera. You couldn't just pick up a phone. . . .

She stared across the cavernous room, her stomach grumbling, and looked at the large overhead screen intended to track the space vehicle after lift-off. Then she glanced around at the rows of desks with computer workstations that lined the floor. It was almost as though she had a small army under her command. All this power, and she still couldn't order up a pizza. What was wrong with this picture? She was so preoccupied with her thoughts that she completely failed to notice the new arrivals. . . .

8:40 P.M.

As Ramirez took position, he quickly noticed everything. At the far end, beneath the huge master screens, a wide desk commanded the room. And behind it sat a dark-haired woman whose history he had committed to memory. She was the one that counted.

Odd that a woman should be in charge . . . but then a woman had even been elected president of a major Muslim country. Once. All things were possible, now and then.

It did not matter to him, not the way he knew it mattered to these two Iranians. He lived in the real world; they lived in a world that did not exist. They, he knew, would say it did not exist *yet*. Well, that was their problem, not his. . . .

Gradually, as one technician after another became aware of them standing in the doorway, all activity ceased. Ten men, dressed in black, all armed with Uzis. Their image triggered a reflexive response of fear throughout the room, nurtured by decades of terrorism in the news.

Ramirez surveyed the room. None of the American technicians had any weapons. As anticipated, he had caught the prey unprepared. Indeed, he had hoped to avoid gunfire. Keep the staff calm. They would be needed.

"You will continue, please, as you were." His voice sounded over the room, English with only a trace of accent. But that trace of accent was bloodless. The authority with which he spoke let everybody know that the command chain had just changed.

Cally turned to stare at the intruders, puzzled. They were strangers . . . now the sight of their automatic weapons registered . . . and they were armed. They sure didn't work for SatCom. How the hell did they get through facility security?

Their leader—she noted that he was wearing a sharp Italian suit, not commando mufti, and he was doing the talking— was scanning the room as though he already owned it. And, in truth, he did. Like the American embassy in Tehran, SatCom had been caught sleeping. But there was no gesturing of weapons. He seemed to want to maintain normality.

They're *terrorists*, her intuition was screaming. But no,

her rational mind answered back. It couldn't be true. Terrorism operated a universe away from Andikythera; it wasn't supposed to touch the lives of anybody outside the hot spots.

Now their spokesman was strolling down the aisle between the computer terminals, headed her way. She figured him for late forties, educated, subject to reason. He seemed rational, or at least businesslike. He could have been a SatCom VP from Arlington dropping by for a surprise inspection. The rest, except for a couple of Arabs with beards, looked like Eurotrash hoods.

"Miss Andros, I presume," the man said, then laughed. "It is a pleasure to meet you. At last."

"What are you doing here?" Her disorientation was being rapidly replaced by anger. "This is a restricted area."

The man smiled . . . almost politely . . . and seemed to ignore the question. "You are absolutely correct. Very reasonable, and proper. But please, you and your staff must just continue on and pay no attention to us. Your head-office check-in is scheduled for 2200 hours. You will, of course, report nothing amiss. Which will be true." He bowed lightly. "I'm sure they will want to know how the Cyclops power-up went. In fact, we are all anxious for the answer to that."

His words echoed off the hard, neon-lit surfaces. Command Central, its pale blue walls notwithstanding, had never seemed more stark.

"I'd appreciate it very much if you would leave," she said, holding her voice quiet. "This is private property. You are trespassing."

The man just smiled again and walked over to examine the big screens. "These things have always intrigued me. Like something in the movies. Buck Rogers." He turned back. "Please, don't let my layman's curiosity interfere with your work."

Bill, Bill. She thought of SatCom's CEO in his office, just beyond the doors at the far end of the room. You've got a radio. And you can see this room on a security monitor. Can't you—

The door at the far end opened, and there stood William Bates.

"Who the hell are you?" his voice boomed over the room.

"My name need not concern you," the terrorist in the suit answered. "Just call me Number One. But I will favor you returning your question."

"And I'll give you the same answer, Number One, or whoever the hell you are," Bates replied, not moving. "Whatever you're thinking, there's nothing here to steal. You're wasting your time. What's more, you're trespassing on American property. So take those goons with you and get the hell out the same way you came in."

"American property? Americans seem to think the whole world is their property." He smiled once more. "But let me put your mind at ease. We are not here to steal. And if you cooperate, no one in this room will be harmed."

Cally looked him over, asking herself whether she believed him. Not for a minute. She suddenly realized this man would kill anyone who got in his way; it was etched into his eyes.

"Now, Miss Andros . . . you should order your people to proceed with the countdown. My understanding is that the first vehicle is scheduled to be launched in less than sixty-five hours. We certainly want nothing to disrupt your timetable."

She stared at him more closely, puzzled. If he and these creeps weren't here for blackmail, threatening to destroy the facility, against a payoff, then what could they possibly want?

"You don't give the orders here." Bates moved toward the man. "I do." He dropped his voice as he passed Cally. "Don't do a goddamn thing." Then he looked up. "You will leave right now, or I'll call my security staff."

"That would be most unwise. At least two of them would be unable to respond." He nodded toward the door. "You are welcome to check outside. But come, we're all wasting precious time."

"You son of a bitch. I won't—"

"Well, well," the man interrupted, "could it be I am luckier than I dreamed possible? Could it be that I have the honor to be speaking to none other than William Bates? Have we snared the CEO? No, that would be too much good luck."

We're screwed, Cally thought. He knows. Now they'll hold Bill for ransom. He's pure gold. Rich and famous.

"You will kindly take a seat, Mr. Bates," the man went on.

"The hell I—"

One of the bearded men carrying an automatic weapon stepped forward and slammed the metal butt into Bates's stomach, sending him staggering backward. He tried to catch his balance, but failed and collapsed ignominiously onto the gray linoleum.

"Again, we're squandering time," the spokesman, the one in charge, continued calmly. "Where were we? Oh yes, the power-up." He turned around. "Now, Miss Andros, none of us wants that report to be late, do we? It would look bad for everybody."

CHAPTER FOUR

7:02 A.M.

When Vance caught his first clear sight of Andikythera's sheltered inlet, the storm had passed over in the night and Homer's "rosy-fingered dawn" was displaying all her splendored glory. With only a slight effort he had altered his course and reached the island. Now, as he rowed in through the still, turquoise waters, only light surface ripples lapped against his Switlik. As quickly as it had come, the turmoil in the seas had vanished. He hoped it was a good omen.

He looked down and realized the water was so crystalline he could see the bottom, now at least ten meters below. Although he had visited many islands, he had never seen anything more perfect than Andikythera. Despite being bone-tired and soaked to the skin, conditions that exacerbated his anger, the sight of the island momentarily buoyed his spirits. It reminded him of a thousand Caribbean mornings, the feeling of rebirth and renewal.

Andikythera had always been private, and never more so than now. It was an industrial site these days, pure and simple. No ferries deposited tourists here, no fishing boats docked in the mornings. Nothing but granite cliffs surrounded the secrets held inside.

The heavy construction equipment, the prefabricated buildings, the facility's high-tech components, all had come through this harbor. Now, however, the dock was deserted; the off-loading cranes and giant mechanical arms highlighted against the morning sky stood idle. Everything had been delivered, was in place, and was humming. The only vessel now tied up was a sailing yacht, Bill's twenty-eight-foot Morgan, leased specially so he could keep his hand in while here. Great boat. . . .

Abruptly he stopped rowing.

Think a minute, he told himself. You can't risk using the inlet. No way.

On the right and left sides of the harbor, steep crags of white granite speckled with scrub cypress guarded the shore, while the towering cliffs of the north mirrored the coastline of a thousand Greek islands. Unlike the postcard photos for sale everywhere on the tourist islands—featuring topless Swedish blondes and trim Italian playboys, gold chains glinting—this was the real Greece, harsh and severe. Only a few seabirds swirling over the near shore, adding their plaintive calls to the silence-breaking churn of surf pounding over the rocks, broke the silence.

He studied the island, trying to get his bearings. Just as Bill had said, it appeared to be about three miles long, maybe a couple of miles wide. As though balancing the radar-controlled mountain at one end, at the opposite terminus stood the launch vehicles, now just visible as the tip of two giant spires, gleaming in the early sunshine like huge silver bullets. And somewhere beneath this granite island, he knew, was the heart of the Cyclops, SatCom's computer-guided twenty-gigawatt laser. . . .

There was no sign of anybody monitoring his approach. The early light showed only pristine cliffs, cold and empty.

Careful now. First things first.

He rowed under a near cliff, then slipped off the yellow raft and into the knee-deep waters of the near shore, still dazzlingly clear. It reminded him again of the Caribbean. Maybe Bill unconsciously had an island there in mind when he decided to move everything here.

The water was cold, refreshing as he moved in. He collected what he needed from the raft and stood a minute wondering what to do with it. Then inspiration struck. It only weighed sixty-five pounds, so why not use it?

It was a standard Switlik, which meant inflation had been automatic. The deflation would take a while, so he started it going as he hefted the heavy yellow hulk and headed up the hill. He wanted it empty, but not entirely.

The security Dimitri Spiros had installed was high-tech and good. He had not gone to the trouble of burying cables all around the place with magnetic anomaly detectors. That would have required blasting through a lot of granite and did not really seem worth the tab. Instead he had surrounded the place with a chain-link fence and topped that with free-spinning wheels of razor wire known as Rota-Barb, which prevented an intruder from smothering the cutting edges with cloth. Then, just to make sure, across the top and at several levels below, he had added lines of Sabretape with an enclosed fiber-optic strand. A pulse of light was transmitted through the length of the tape, and if it was disturbed, detectors at a central guard location would know immediately when and where.

Now Vance had to try to penetrate a system he had actually been involved, indirectly, in setting up. The ultimate irony.

The jagged granite tore at his hands as he struggled up, picking his way through the clusters of scrub cedar that clung to the steep ascent and dragging the Switlik by its nylon straps. The cliff rose a good two hundred feet and was almost sheer, but he located enough niches to haul himself forward. Finally, exhausted and hands bleeding, he pulled himself over the top. Then he dragged up the remains of the raft.

Ahead, just in front of the towering communications mountain, he discerned ARM's industrial security installation, a ten-foot-high chain-link fence interwoven with fiber optics. Beyond it on a helicopter pad sat Bill's new Agusta, a hot 109 Mark II with all the latest modifications, including two 450-hp Allison engines. It sat there, its blue trim like ice, a ghostly apparition against the lightening sky.

Poised alongside was a brooding hulk that dwarfed the Agusta—a Soviet Mi-24D, one of its stubby wings a tangled mass of metal.

So the bastards were here. He'd guessed right.

He saw no guards around it, but who knew.

He would find out soon enough, but one thing was sure: it must have a radio on board. The U.S. Navy would be very interested in identifying the location of its hostile. Maybe he should just switch on the Hind's cockpit IFF, let it start broadcasting. If the ship that was attacked had been interrogating the Hind, there'd probably be knowledge somewhere of the codes it was transmitting.

Easy. Just take it easy. Go in behind the chopper, handle the fence, and then rush the thing from the back. If anybody's guarding it, you'll be taking them from their blind side.

Grasping the Switlik, with the Walther tucked firmly into the waist of his soaked trousers, he dashed for the corner of the fence behind the Hind. He was barefoot, the way he always sailed, and the granite felt sharp and cutting under his feet. But being barefoot was going to help him take the fence.

Okay, he thought, the fiber-optic alarm system is going to blow, no matter what. Just get in and get on the radio quick, then worry about what comes next.

He knew the only way to defeat a Rota-Barb system was at the corners, where the spinning rolls of wire intersected at a right angle. As he approached the corner, he looked up and checked out his chances. Yep, with the Switlik to smother the barbs it might just be possible.

He looped one of the nylon straps, then leaned back and heaved the raft up onto the top of the fence. It caught and was hanging there but—just as he had hoped—the strap passed over and down the other side. Next he reached through, seized it, and tied it securely to the heavy chain links of the fence. Now it would hold the raft in place as he climbed from the outside.

Holding the hand straps of the raft, he clambered up and

made it to the top. Then he rolled himself into the rubber and pushed over. A second later he dropped shoulder-first onto the asphalt of the landing pad. Home.

The razor wire had shredded the raft, and the fiber-optic security system would have detected the entry, but he was in. If any guards were left alive, they probably had other things to worry about.

Or so he hoped.

At that instant he thought he heard a sound, and whirled back. No, he had only caught the chirp of a morning bird, somewhere in the cluster of trees down toward the shore. The island again seemed as serene as a paradise.

He crouched a moment, grasping the Walther, then shoved a round into the chamber. The early morning light showed the Hind in all its glory. It was dark green, with a heavy, retractable landing gear—a magnificent machine. And a lethal one. Originally intended as an antitank weapon, the Mi-24 had quickly become a high-speed tool for air-to-ground combat. To reduce vulnerability to ground fire, its makers substituted steel and titanium for aluminum in critical components and replaced the original blade-pocket design with glassfiber-skinned rotors. . . .

The only defect of this particular example was the absence of the starboard auxiliary wing, including the rocket pod. Its arrival and accurate landing here spoke volumes for the flying skills of whoever had been at the controls. If the weapons operator had possessed comparable talent, Vance reflected, he might not be standing here now.

But, he noted again, it had Israeli markings. Had the Israelis really attacked a U.S. frigate? That made no sense. For one thing, they couldn't have flown a Hind this far without refueling. Its combat radius was only about a hundred miles.

Then he looked more closely and realized that the Israeli Star of David in a circle of white had merely been papered on. So it was a false-flag job. Which more than ever left open the question—who the hell were they?

Gripping the Walther, he slid open the door to the cargo bay and examined the darkened interior. It was empty save for a few remnants of packing crates. He climbed in and checked them over. They had been for weapons. He saw some U.S. markings on one: a crate of M79 grenade launchers. Another had contained Czech ZB-26 light machine guns, with spare boxes for C-Mag modifications, giving them 100-round capability.

Jesus! If these were just the discarded crates, what else did these guys have?

He turned and moved up the gray metal steps to the cockpit, a raised bubble above the weapons station. Nice. He settled himself, looking out the bulletproof windscreen at the first tinge of dawn breaking over the island. His first impulse was to crank her up and fly her out. He resisted it.

Switching on the IFF would be a chore; he was not even sure he knew how. He could, however, get on the airwaves.

The pilot's flight helmet was stashed on the right-hand panel where it had been tossed. He picked it up and slipped it on, then clicked on the electronics. The helicopter's main panel and screens glowed to life, a patchwork of green and red lights and LEDs. He flicked more switches overhead and the infrared and radar systems came on-line, their displays like Christmas-tree lights briskly illuminating one by one in rows.

Now for the radio.

It was Soviet-made, of course, with heavy metal knobs and a case that looked as though it could withstand World War III. He clicked it on and began scanning through the aviation channels, checking to see if anybody was out there. Maybe . . .

Nothing, except a few routine exchanges of civilian pilots. Well, he thought, could be it takes a while for the news of major world events to get down to the trenches. Word would circulate soon enough. The military channels, however, would be another matter.

The Hind had them all. He clicked over to the frequencies and began scanning. There were a lot of scrambled communications; the radio traffic was sizzling. He figured the Sixth Fleet was on full alert.

Except they didn't know where to look for their hostile. He remembered that the military emergency channel was

121.50 megahertz. He punched it in, then unhooked the black mike and switched to transmit. The green diodes blinked to red.

7:09 A.M.

Jean-Paul Moreau, who had perfect command of English, was catching the BBC on a small Sony ICF-PRO80 in Command Central, keeping abreast of the news. The World Service was just winding up its morning broadcast, circumspect as always.

". . . A reminder of the main story: there are unconfirmed rumors emanating from the southern Aegean that an American naval vessel, the USS *Glover,* was attacked by a helicopter gunship late last evening, with considerable damage and loss of life. It is said the gunship was Israeli. No confirmation or denial of this report has yet been issued by the government in Tel Aviv. And that's the end of the news from London. . . ."

"Guess we had a hit." He laughed, then switched frequencies and started monitoring the military channels.

Ramirez had also heard the broadcast, with satisfaction. The attack would soon blossom into a world event, with accusations flying. After that had played its course, he would drop his bombshell.

Now it was daylight. Time to begin phase three of the operation.

It had been a productive night. The first order of business had been to off-load their hardware. In addition to the Uzis they had carried in, they had broken out a compliment of AK-47s. The Germans had also brought out and limbered up a crate of MK760 submachine guns, fully automatic with folding stocks, as well as some Czech mortars and grenade launchers.

That was finished by 0300 hours, after which the men caught catnaps, rotating to keep at least three on guard at all times. Now that the test had gone off successfully, most of the facility staff was lounging at the blank terminals, dazed.

Ramirez, however, had no intention of letting the SatCom staff become rested. He looked over the room at the young engineers, all of whom were showing the first signs of hostage behavior. They were frightened, stressed, tired—already in the early stages of "hostile dependency." Soon they would melt, become totally pliable. But to achieve that, they could not be allowed to get enough sleep. Food also had to be kept to a minimum.

Most importantly, all telephone and computer linkages with the outside world had been cut—with the exception of one. The single telephone remaining was on the main desk down at the other end of Command. Otherwise, Peretz had methodically shut down everything, including the telemetry equipment located up on the mountain. While they would need to reactivate it later on, for the moment they could keep it on standby.

Peretz had proved reliable so far, Ramirez told himself. The man was seasoned and competent, unlike the young Muslims who acted first and thought later. An operation like this required precision, not unbridled impetuosity, which was why he valued the Israeli so highly. . . .

As he surveyed Command, he decided it was time for champagne. He had brought a small bottle, a split of Dom. . . . But what was champagne without the company of a beautiful woman. He turned toward Miss Andros—

"*Merde!*"

His meditations were interrupted by the startled voice of Moreau.

"There's a Mayday on one-twenty-one point five megahertz. It's so close, I think someone is transmitting from here on the island."

Ramirez cursed, while the buzz in Command subsided. Then Moreau continued.

"In English. He's talking about the *Glover*, and he's giving our location."

"Probably one of the guards." Ramirez paused, thinking. "But how could he know about the *Glover?*"

"Maybe he's in the Hind, monitoring the radio," Helling said, rubbing at his balding skull. "We—"

"You brought backup. Time to use it." Ramirez turned and beckoned for the three ex-Stasi: Schindler, Maier, and Sommer. It was time for the three monkeys to start earning their keep. "Go out to the chopper," he barked to them in German, "and handle it. You know what to do."

They nodded seriously and checked their Uzis. They knew exactly.

7:23 A.M.

The transmit seemed to be working, and he was getting out everything he knew—the location of the Hind, the fake nationality, the attack on the frigate. But was anybody picking it up? The heavy Soviet radio was rapidly drawing down its batteries, but he figured it was now or never. Get it out quick and hope, he thought. Pray some Navy ship in this part of the Aegean will scan it and raise the alarm.

He was still trying to piece it all together when he spied the figures, approaching from far down the central walkway. Three men dressed in black, looking just like a hit squad. He had not expected so fast a response, and for a second he was caught off guard. They must have been monitoring the radio.

If you had any sense, he told himself, you'd have expected that. You're about to have some really lousy odds.

The Hind was armored like a tank, he knew, and even the bubbles over the cockpit and the weapons station were supposedly bulletproof. *How* bulletproof, he guessed, he was about to learn.

With the three men still a distance away, he realized he had only one choice. Although he had never actually flown a Hind, this seemed an ideal time to try and find out how difficult it was.

Probably harder than he knew. He reached up and flicked on the fuel feeds, then pushed the starter. To his surprise, there came the sound of a long, dull whine that began increasing rapidly in intensity and frequency. The main rotor had kicked on—he could tell from the vibration—and the tail stabilizer, too, if the rpm dials were reporting accurately.

All right, he told himself, the dial on the right side of the panel is rotor speed. Keep it in the green. And over to the left is engine speed. Come on, baby. Go for the green. Red line means you crash and burn. Pedals, okay. But this isn't like a regular airplane; the stick is cyclic, controls the angle of your blades.

The instruments were now on-line—temperature, fuel gauges, pressure, power output. The two Isotov turboshafts were rapidly bringing up rpm now, already past three thousand. He grabbed hold of the collective, eased back on the clutch, and felt the massive machine shudder, then begin to lift off.

As the three men breached the gate leading into the asphalt-paved landing area, a fusillade of automatic-weapons fire began spattering off the bubble windscreen, leaving deep dents in the clear, globelike plastic.

So far, so good, he thought. It's holding up to manufacturer's specs.

Now for the power. It's controlled by the collective, but when you increase power you increase torque, so give her some left pedal to compensate.

The Hind had started to hover, and now he moved the columns to starboard, bringing it around. He could not reach the weapons station, but the 12.7mm machine gun in the nose had an auxiliary fire control under the command of the pilot.

With his hand on the stick, he activated the fire button. He might not be able to hit anything, but he'd definitely get somebody's attention. . . .

The machine gun just below him erupted, a deadly spray that knocked sparks off the hurricane fence surrounding the pad as the chopper slowly revolved around. Somewhere now off to his left came a new burst of automatic fire. He found himself in a full-scale firefight, trapped like a tormented bull in a pen.

But the Hind was up and hovering . . . and also beginning to slip sideways because of the damaged wing. He grappled with the collective pitch lever in his left hand, trying to regain control, but he didn't have the experience. The chopper was now poised about ten feet above the ground, its engines bellowing, nosing around and drifting dangerously.

He'd lost control. As it tilted sideways, the fence began coming up at him, aiming directly for the nose bubble. Even more unnerving, though, was the heavyset terrorist in a black pullover who was standing directly in front of the bubble and firing his Uzi point-blank. Worse still, he was handling it like second nature.

The plastic splintered with a high-pitched shriek as the rounds caught it head-on. The curvature had helped before, but now the gunman was able to fire straight into it. The game was about to be up.

He ducked for the floor of the cockpit just as the bubble windscreen detonated, spewing shards of plastic both outward and inward. Now the helicopter was coming about and lifting off again, pulling up strands of the wire fence that had gotten tangled in the landing gear.

No time to worry about it. He rose up, grasped the collective, and urged more power, trying to compensate for the torque. But the mottled gray behemoth was increasingly unstable, shunting sideways, drifting over the security fence and spiraling upward toward the mountain that bristled with SatCom's communications gear. The gunner holding the Uzi slipped in another clip and raised up to finish him off, but at that instant Vance squeezed the fire button one last time and the man danced a pirouette, disappearing from view.

As he started to spiral in earnest, more automatic fire ricocheted off the fuselage. Then came a sickening whine.

The stabilizer, he thought. They must have hit the damned stabilizer. This is going to be a very short trip.

Panic caught him as the Hind started into autorotation, round and round like a bumper-car ride at an amusement park.

He cut the power—hoping he could bring her down using the energy stored in the blades—then quickly put the right pedal to the floor, held the collective down, and tried to keep rotor speed in the green. He was drifting to the east now, headed for a copse of trees halfway up the mountain. Not a bad place to set down, he thought, and started to flare the blades with the stick, hoping he could bring her in with the collective. The Hind was still spinning in autorotation, but not yet dangerously. Slowly, slowly . . .

He was about thirty feet above the trees when a splatter of automatic fire erupted from the open doorway. He whirled around to see the terrorist he'd bulldozed into the fence now hanging onto the metal step and trying to pull himself in.

What now . . . !

The man—Vance guessed he was pushing forty, with a face of timeless brutality—was covered with blood and his aim was hampered by trying to hold the Uzi as he fired one-handed, the other hand grasping the step. He was cursing in German. . . .

At that instant the Hind took a sickening dip, and the Uzi clattered onto the doorway pallet as the terrorist relinquished it to try to hold on with both hands.

But he was losing it, his hands slippery with his own blood, and all that held him now was the torn section of his own shirt that had somehow sleeved over the step. Then his grasp gave way entirely, and he dangled for a moment by the shirt before it ripped through and he fell, a trailing scream. He landed somewhere in the trees twenty feet below, leaving only the shirt.

In the meantime the Hind continued spiraling and drifting down, and Vance looked out to see the gray granite of the side of the mountain moving toward him, with only a bramble of trees in between. But at least the chopper's autorotation was bringing him in for a soft crash.

He braced himself as a clump of trees slapped against the side of the fuselage. Then the twelve-ton helicopter plunged into them, its landing gear collapsing as it crunched to a stop. He felt himself flung forward, accompanied by the metallic splatter of the rotor collapsing against the granite, shearing and knocking the fuselage sideways in a series of jolts. As the two turboshaft engines automatically shut down, he held onto the seat straps and reflected that this was his first and probably last turn at the stick of a Hind. And all he'd managed to do was total it.

Heck of a way to start a morning.

The Uzi was still lying on the floor of the cabin, while the shirt of the man he had shot was wrapped around the metal step and lodged beneath the crushed landing gear.

When he reached back and checked to see that the Walther 9mm was still secured in his belt, he noticed that his arm had been lacerated by the jagged plastic of the shattered canopy. He noticed it, but he didn't feel it. He was feeling nothing, only a surge of adrenaline and the certain knowledge he had to get out fast, with the Uzi.

He scooped it up and stumbled through the doorway, to the sound of muted gunfire down the hill, as the other two hoods continued to advance.

He had the German's automatic now, but the last thing he wanted was a shootout. Nonetheless, rounds of fire sang around him as he ripped the black shirt loose from the chopper's step and felt the pockets. One contained what seemed like a small leather packet.

He yanked it out, then plunged in a direction that would bring the Hind between him and the other two assailants. But when he tried to catch his footing in the green bramble of brush, he fell on his shoulder and rolled, feeling a spasm of pain. Christ, this was no longer any fun!

About twenty feet away was an even denser copse of cypress scrub than the one he had crashed in. If he could make that, he told himself, he'd have some cover. He just had to get there in one piece.

Half scrambling, half rolling, he headed for the thicket of trees, occasionally loosing a round of covering fire down the hill. Then he felt the scratchy hardness of the low brush and threw himself into the bramble. Dirt spattered as rounds of fire—or was it flecks of granite?—ricocheted around him, and then he felt a nick across one shoulder—he was not sure from what. A couple more rounds cut past, but now they were going wide.

He collapsed into the dense bramble and tried to catch his breath. What next? The Uzi still had a half-full clip. Maybe he could hold them off.

He stilled his breathing and listened, but heard nothing. The mountainside was deathly quiet, so much so he could almost hear the crash of waves on the shore below. It was probably only wishful imagination, but the quiet gave hope he might temporarily be out of danger.

He turned and looked up the mountain, finally able to see it clearly. The near hillside was covered with brush, the only objects visible above the green being the tip of a high-tech jungle. SatCom had a hell of a communications installation. Outlined against the blue sky were huge parabolic antennas used for microwave uplinks, a phased-array transmission system for powering the space vehicles, a myriad of dishes for satellite uplinks and downlinks, and various other antennas used for conventional radio. It was all set inside a high-security hurricane fence with a gray cinderblock control hut at the near corner.

Well, he thought, with that battery of antennas, there's surely a way to do what has to be done next . . .

This time he wouldn't waste radio access with Maydays.

9:35 A.M.

As the landing announcement sounded through British Air flight 1101 from London to Athens, Isaac Mannheim took off his thick spectacles, wiped them futilely with a greasy handkerchief, settled them back, and stared down. The plane was now on final approach, and he had already taken down his flight bag and stuffed it under the seat in preparation, ready to march off.

Mannheim was professor emeritus at MIT, Department of Engineering, and he retained the intellectual curiosity of a mischievous schoolboy. He had the flowing white hair of a nineteenth-century European philosopher, the burning eyes of a Jules Verne visionary, the single-minded enthusiasm of a born inventor, the discursive knowledge of a Renaissance man, and the self-assurance of a true genius—which he was.

Wearing a tweedy checked suit, a frayed brown overcoat, smudgy horn-rims, and a Boston Red Sox baseball cap, he also looked every bit as eccentric as his reputation said. The baseball cap was tribute to another of his eclectic concerns—

the statistics of that particular team. Those he kept on a computer file and subjected to daily updates.

As Issac Mannheim saw it, he was the undisputed father of Project Cyclops; Bill Bates was merely in charge of its delivery room down on Andikythera. It was a half-truth, perhaps, but not entirely untrue either. He had dreamed up the idea and proved in his MIT lab that it could work. The rest, he figured, was merely scaling it up—which any dimwit with half a billion dollars could do with ease. He had already seen to the hard part.

Mannheim liked to check in on his baby every other week, just to make sure that Bates—who was going to make a fortune off *his* idea—was doing it right. Although the long flight to Athens and then the helicopter ride down to Andikythera were starting to make him feel his seventy-five years, he did not really mind. When you're my age, he'd claim, you don't have time to sit around on your butt all day.

He always flew British Air from London rather than taking a direct Olympic flight from Boston, mainly because he was an Anglophile but also because he wasn't quite sure he trusted Greek maintenance. Isaac Mannheim was old school in all things.

As the tires screeched onto the asphalt, he glanced out the window again, marveling how small the Athens airport was. But then his mind quickly traveled on to other pressing matters: namely, the day's agenda. He was anxious to go over the power-up data number by number with Georges LeFarge. The young French Canadian had been his best student in Cambridge, ten years ago, and Isaac Mannheim was secretly pleased, very pleased, that Georges had been given a leading role in the project. Together, years ago, they had ironed out many of the technical problems in the system. The work back then had been done on a lab bench, and a shoestring, but LeFarge knew everything that could go wrong. With Georges as Director of Computer Systems here, Mannheim knew the project was in good hands, at least the crucial computer part of it.

When the doors opened, he was one of the first to step out of the BA 757 and down the steel stairway onto the runway. He reflected that he'd had a good flight this time, with only an hour layover in Heathrow's infamously crowded Terminal Four. Now, as the airport bus arrived to carry the bleary-eyed London passengers into the Athens terminal, he anticipated getting an early start on the day.

He glanced down toward the far end of the airport, the civilian aviation terminal, expecting to catch sight of Bates's blue-and-white-striped Agusta helicopter. Funny, he couldn't see it today; usually you could.

It was odd; they were always here, waiting. Customary promptness was just one more example of how well that young Dr. Andros was handling the project. He chafed to admit it, but she was pretty damned good. Although he had long scoffed at the idea that women could compete successfully with male engineers, he had to admit she was as professional as any male project manager he'd ever worked with.

Carrying his overstuffed black briefcase in his left hand and his tattered nylon flight bag in his right, he waited till the airport bus was almost full before stepping on. Airport buses, he noted as an engineer, operated on the old-time LIFO computer storage principle: last in, first out. No random access.

And he was indeed first out as they pulled into the sheltered awning of the terminal. The Athens morning sun was already burning through the growing layer of brown haze. He thought ruefully how it would look from the south, down around Piraeus, as they flew out. From there Athens seemed to be encased in an ugly brown tomb.

World air quality was yet another of the topics weighing on his mind these days. It was, in fact, a frequent subject of the long letters he addressed to another former student, an average-IQ Danish boy majoring in physics whom he had seen fit to flunk in junior-year thermodynamics. Afterward Mannheim had taken the lad aside and bluntly suggested he might wish to consider a less intellectually demanding career path.

The advice had been heeded, and these days he was doing reasonably well at his cushy new job, down in Washington. Still, Isaac Mannheim felt it necessary to post the boy long typewritten letters from time to time concerning various avenues for self-improvement.

Yes, he had turned out reasonably well after all, considering, but he still needed to work harder. Don't be a slacker, John; nobody ever got ahead that way. The forty-second President of the United States, Johan Hansen, read his old professor's missives, usually written on the back of semilog graph paper or whatever was handy, and dutifully answered every one of them. Maybe he was afraid he'd get another "F" and a humiliating lecture.

Isaac Mannheim stared around the half-filled terminal, wondering. The SatCom pilot usually met him right at the gate, but today nobody was there. Incompetent Greeks. This one, in fact, was particularly feckless: just out of the Greek Air Force with no real grasp of the value of time.

Or had Dr. Andros forgotten he was arriving? That was hard to imagine, since he had talked with her just before he left Cambridge. One thing you had to say for her, she never forgot appointments. Strange.

No helicopter. No pilot. Damned peculiar. He had no alternative but to phone Dr. Andros on her private line.

He walked over to the booth near the entrance to the terminal lobby and got some drachmas. Then he located a pay phone and placed the call.

She answered on the first ring. Good.

"Cally, what in blazes is going on down there?" He tried to open the conversation as diplomatically as he knew how. "I'm here, sitting on my butt in the Athens airport, as though I had nothing else to do. I don't see Alex anywhere. Or the Agusta. You're going to have to get rid of that boy if this happens again. Where in hell are they?"

A long uncomfortable pause ensued, and it sounded as though she was listening to someone else. Finally she answered in a shaky voice.

"Dr. Mannheim, it's been a *very* long night here. Maybe you—"

"Well, how did the power-up go? I need to go over the data with Georges right away."

"Dr. Mannheim, maybe—" The phone seemed to go

dead. Then she came back on. "The Mark II is temporarily out of service. Can you take the ferry?"

"What! You know perfectly well that damned thing only runs once a week. And that was yesterday. Now what about the Agusta?"

"It's . . . it's just not possible. So—"

"Tell you what, then, I'll just rent one here. It'll cost a few dollars, but I can't wait around all day."

"Isaac, I—" She never used his first name, at least not to him, but he took no notice.

"Don't worry about it. It'll just go into project overhead. Be a tax write-off for Bates." He laughed, without noticeable humor. "He understands all about such things."

"That's awfully expensive," she said, her voice still sounding strange. "Maybe it'd be better to wait—"

"Damn it. I'll be there in a couple of hours."

"Dr. Mannheim . . ." Her voice would have sounded an alarm to most people. But then most people listened. Isaac Mannheim rarely bothered. Especially where women were concerned. You simply did what had to be done. It was that simple, but most women seemed unable to fathom matters of such obvious transparency.

He slammed down the phone and strode out into the morning sunshine. The private aviation terminal was about a half mile down an ill-paved road, but he decided the walk would do him good. The breeze would feel refreshing after the smoky, stuffy terminal. The problem was, Athens was already getting hot. That's why he liked the islands. They were always cooler this time of year.

CHAPTER FIVE

Vance stared up the mountain, puzzled. The silence baffled him, and then he realized why. He was not hearing the usual high-tension hum of transformers; nothing was operating. They had shut down the power.

He heaved a sigh, then dropped down beside a tree trunk and clicked out the magazine of the black Uzi. It had about fifteen rounds left, so the time had come to start making them count. Here, amid the brush, he had a chance to lie low for a while and figure out what to do next. Besides feeling thirst and fatigue, he had a throbbing sprain in his shoulder, incurred somehow during the crash of the chopper. But the pain was helping to clear his mind.

Maybe, he thought, he could find some provisions stowed in the Hind, left or overlooked. A stray canteen or some MREs. But did he want to risk going back down?

The answer was yes because—even more important—the radio might still be operating. It was definitely time to activate the warranty on this job.

But first things first. Who are these creeps?

Hoping to find out something, he pulled out the leather packet he had retrieved from the terrorist's torn shirt and cracked it open. Crumpled inside was a wad of Yemeni dinars, and a crinkled ID card in German. On the back was a phrase scrawled in English . . . it looked like *The Resistance Front for a Free*—it was smudged, but yes—*Europe.*

Back when he and Bates had first talked about the security question, Bill had insisted ARM focus on industrial security. Truthfully, there hadn't been any real thought given to antiterrorist measures. It had just seemed unimaginable. Looked at another way, though, Bates had been trying to be cost-effective, had gambled on an assumption. Now it was beginning to look as though that had been a bad bet.

Although for a ground-based setup Dimitri's handiwork— contracted out of Athens—was top-notch, it had made no provisions against aerial penetration. From land or sea. That haunting phrase kept coming back. But Bill had laughed it off, and the client was always supposed to be right.

Besides, the SatCom facility already had a nest of radars up on the hill, there as part of the Cyclops and also to monitor the local weather. Why clutter up the place any more? The fact was, these guys had probably come in under the facility's electronic eyes anyway, using the Hind's ability to detect an interrogation and keep low enough to avoid a significant radar signature. The background noise from the choppy sea must have been enough to mask their approach.

Maybe Spiros should have considered that, but at this point such meditations amounted to Monday-morning quarterbacking. So now the parameters of the job had changed, from industrial security to counterterrorism. SatCom was fortunate in its choice of security services, because an ARM job always came with a guarantee: if a problem came up, the boys would be there immediately to solve it. Which meant that alerting Paris was now his first priority. Until reinforcements arrived, though, he was ARM's on-site rep.

Lots of problems came to mind. First off, he was operating on the perimeter: he had no map of the facility, no idea where to find the hostages. However, the communications station up the hill represented a redoubt he probably could defend reasonably well, unless they brought up some really heavy artillery. Maybe there would be some way to disrupt the proceedings, provide a diversion.

Sooner or later, he figured, there's bound to be some action out of the U.S. air and naval base down at Souda Bay, on Crete. Hopefully somebody down at Gournes had picked up his Mayday.

But even if they had, could they send in a team? This was Greek soil, and Greeks tended to be fussy about their sovereignty. Now that NATO had no idea what its new mission was, America's heavy presence in Europe more and more looked like Yankee imperialism. They might convince the Greeks to let them bring in the Navy SEALs or even the antiterrorist Delta Force from Fort Bragg in Fayetteville, North Carolina, but that would require a lot of negotiation, might take days. Time could run out by then. And the Greeks had no capability themselves to do anything but make matters worse.

He looked down the hill, toward the half-visible wreckage of the Hind. Okay, he thought, time to see about that radio. Slowly he rose, chambered a round in the Uzi with a hard click, and started through the brush. The Greek scrub tore through his thin shirt and rasped at his skin, while the morning sun, glimmering off the proud silver spires of the vehicles at the other end of the island, beat down. The island remained eerily calm, the sleep of the dead. The takeover was complete, no question about that.

Through the brush the wreckage of the Hind showed its mottled coloring, a mix of grays and tans among the green of the branches. As he approached, he could discern no sign of his attackers, which either meant they were pros and lying in wait for him or they were amateurs and had fled.

He looked around the copse of scrub cypress, then gingerly stepped through the open doorway. By some miracle the electronics were still lined up in rows of readiness, lights and LEDs glowing. A tough bird. And the radio was still operating, and on. Dawn had long since ripened the clear blue of the sky, and he could feel the beat of warm sunshine on the shattered bubble of the canopy. Now, he knew, the terrorists would be scanning the military frequencies, so it was time to be circumspect and use some caution for a change.

He checked it over. Good, it had sideband. That was perfect, because he figured they probably wouldn't monitor those offbeat marine frequencies. If he could raise Spiros in Athens, he could then contact Paris. They could put together a team overnight and fly it down.

He fiddled with the sideband channels, hoping. He heard some amateur action and a ship-to-shore—funny, he thought, that the minute yachtsmen put to sea they're anxious to get in contact with someone on dry land. What would Ulysses have done with a shortwave radio? Talked back to the Sirens? . . .

The broadcasts, however, were mainly about the weather. Sailors did not waste their time on world events. When that news finally trickled down, however, these sideband channels would probably no longer be safe to use—maybe they weren't now, but he had to take the risk. . . .

He tried a few frequencies and then he got lucky. It was a Greek ham operator, probably having a second cup of strong native coffee and waiting for the traffic in Athens to subside. As are all amateurs, he was delighted to talk. He sounded youthful and enthusiastic, eager to help.

"I read you, Ulysses. You're coming in loud and clear on SSB 432.124 megahertz. This is SV5VMS, Athens. What is your callsign?"

"Don't have a handle," Vance replied into the mike, in Greek. "This is a Mayday."

"I copy." The voice suddenly grew serious. "What is your location?"

He paused a second, wondering what to say. No, he couldn't take a chance. Who knew who else was listening in?

"Don't have that either. What I need is a phone patch to a number in Athens. Can you set it up?"

"No problem," came the confident response, using the international English phrase. Vance tried to imagine what he looked like. Probably mid-twenties, with the swagger acquired by all young Greek men along with their first motorscooter. They wanted to impress you with how wonderful their country was, and they also wanted you to know that they were the biggest stud in all the land. "But whoever you want may be gone to work by now."

"This guy probably won't even be out of bed yet. He's a night owl," Vance replied into the mike. He didn't add that the best thing Dimitri did at night was handle an infrared-mounted H&K MP5. "It's Athens city code and the number is 21776." He knew that Spiros kept a lovely whitewashed house on the western side of town, just out of the major smog centers.

Moments later the patch was through and he had Spiros on the radio. The patch was scratchy and full of static, but not so much he couldn't hear.

"Michael, you woke me up. I hope the world just ended." It was Spiros's gruff voice. A thirty-year veteran of an antiterrorist unit in Brussels, he was as tough as he sounded. "By the way, everybody's heard about that Odyssey stunt of yours. Are you in trouble already? We've got a pool going on you. I have ten thousand drachmas saying you'll never make it."

"I appreciate the confidence. Anyway, you can start spending the money. You'll be relieved to know I blew it. She sank on me."

"Too bad." He laughed. "So what was the problem?"

"Mostly it was some twelve-mil machine-gun fire. Took the wind right out of her sails. I took a swim and then I think a 57mm Euclid finished her off.

"That's Russian." The voice quickly grew serious. "Sounds like you made the wrong people mad. Who in hell did it?"

"Don't know, but they're very meticulous about their work. They used a false-flag approach and shelled an American frigate down here north of Crete. Should be making the news any time now."

"Sounds like somebody's getting hot about inviting the Sixth Fleet out of the Med." Then Spiros's pensive tone turned businesslike. "Are you okay? Where are you now?"

"I'm fine, I think. But you've got to get some of the boys down here."

"What do you mean?"

"Remember that job you did for Bill Bates?" Maybe, he thought, we can talk around the problem. "Looks like the security didn't stick."

"That was a good job," Spiros said with a growl. "Need some updating?"

"It's going to be a little more than that. I think maybe a dozen hostiles, give or take, came in by chopper. A Hind-D. Had all the factory extras."

"Had?"

"It just met with an accident."

"And I'll bet you had nothing to do with it." He laughed. "So what kind of hardware do they have?"

"Uzis for sure. Probably also some grenade launchers. Also light machine guns, ZB-26. The odds are good they're going to be here for a while. They've dug in and it's a long swim to anywhere."

"Should we be having this conversation on the phone?" Caution was entering his voice. "Can we secure up these communications?"

"Right now we've got no choice," Vance answered. "Nothing where I am is secure." Including my skin, he thought.

"All right, then, give it to me fast." He was all business. "What do you have on nationality?"

"It has a Beirut feel about it. But I managed to get some material off one of them, and I think he was a former East German Stasi type. Whoever they are, they're operating under some phony front name."

"I read you. Usual terrorist MO?"

"Best I can tell."

"Then we have to worry about civilians. That's going to make it tougher."

"Bill may be among them. And all his staff."

"Bad news."

"He's a prize."

"What do you think their game is?" Spiros asked after a pause. "Ransom?"

"That'd be my first guess. Though it doesn't synch with the attack on the U.S. ship—unless it was intended as a deliberate diversion. Maybe they're planning something else. But my hunch is money's involved. Anyway, we'll find out soon enough."

"You're damned right we will." The line was silent for a moment as static intervened. "Well, this will teach us to guarantee our work. It's going to be an expensive insurance policy."

"Nothing in life is supposed to be easy."

"So we keep finding out." He seemed to be thinking. "You know, I sent the layout to Paris when the job was finished. For the files." He didn't want to mention Pierre Armont, the head of ARM, on an unsecured line. "I'll see what the office there can get together for us."

"Do we have any people left on site?" Vance asked.

"Just contract," Spiros responded. "Locals and probably not worth much."

"Well, whoever they are, chances are good they've been neutralized by now. As a matter of fact, I fear the worst."

"That's our motto. Assume everything will go to hell and then work around it."

"Time to get off the air. I'll try to raise you at 1700 hours. On 2150 megahertz. By that time you'd better have the team lined up and ready to move in. I owe Bates this one. A nice clean job."

"Right. Who do you think we ought to use?"

"Anybody who worked on the security here would be good."

"That's got to be me," Spiros said ruefully.

"Okay. Beyond that, we'll need a first-class SWAT team. This one is going to be rough. We need somebody who can handle explosives like a brain surgeon, maybe Marcel, out of Antwerp. Get him if you can find him sober. Also, we probably could use a negotiator. Somebody who can keep them busy while we get the real insertion in place. And a good sniper will be essential. Lots of friendlies."

"Okay. That sounds like Reggie. I'll run some names past Paris. But what are you going to do in the meantime?"

"Well, they know I'm here, but they don't know who I am. I'll concentrate on staying alive, and try to find out whatever I can about the MO. Catch you at 1700."

"Talk to you then," Dimitri said, and hung up.

Right, Vance thought. I'd definitely rather be in Philadelphia.

8:39 A.M.

"It's a go in five," Caroline Shaeffer announced in a stage whisper, leaning over his shoulder. A blond Ohio debutante, she was press secretary—a job she had fought for and loved —and she structured the President's media appearances with the bloodless efficiency of a Nazi drill sergeant. This hastily arranged breakfast speech at New York's Plaza was no different. She had put it together in less than ten days, and anybody who mattered in New York politics was in attendance, smiling their way through stale *prosciutto con melone* and soggy eggs Benedict, for an awe-inspiring hour of "quality time" with Johan Hansen.

The head table had the usual crowd: Mayor Jarvis, senators, representatives, state senators, state officials of every stripe, even the borough presidents. Hansen was almost as popular as Ronald Reagan had been in his heyday. The election was coming up in less than six weeks, and Johan Hansen held a commanding lead—twenty-eight points if you believed the latest *Newsweek*/Gallup poll. A "nonpolitical" event in the middle of the campaign allowed everybody to show up for a photo, regardless of party. President Hansen's speech was scheduled to begin at 8:44 A.M. sharp, perfectly timed to let *Today* and *Good Morning America* carry the opening remarks live eastern and central and not have to look like the networks were trailing CNN, indeed wiping its ass, yet again. In any case, it would definitely make the evening news on all three. Precisely as Hansen intended.

Johan Hansen, whose perfect white hair and granite chin

made him look every inch a chief of state, had mixed feelings about his trips to the Big Apple. He relished the automatic media attention they received (Caroline claimed that whereas $2-million-a-year network anchors usually considered themselves above travel, in New York one or two might deign to show up), but chafed at the mechanics—the helicopters, traffic jams, awesome security. He also despised political food, which was why Caroline had packed his own private breakfast of shredded wheat and skimmed milk, to be downed discreetly while everybody else was busy clogging their arteries.

He was speaking on worldwide nuclear disarmament, and he intended his address to be a warm-up for one at the United Nations General Assembly three weeks hence (which meant another damned trip to New York). After opening with his standard stump remarks, all partisan digs excised, he would then go on to assure his audience that the New World truly was here—which always got everybody in a receptive mood. He would then remind them that three years earlier (i.e., "When I assumed this office"), America was still spending $7 billion a year on new nuclear warheads. He had put an end to that, but now it was time to take the next step. Total nuclear disarmament worldwide. It was a stance that normally received polite applause at best, and stony silence at worst. But it never failed to make the news.

This morning the broadcast networks and CNN had combined their resources—after all, the space was limited—to provide pool coverage. Although the usual ganglia of lights and wires were reduced to an absolute minimum, the back of the room still looked like a makeshift convention bureau. The broadcast correspondents all had their own "instant analysis" cameras set up, and the print people were all next to their own newly installed, dedicated phones.

Johan Hansen's acquisition of the Oval Office had come at the end of a hard-fought election battle that saw several firsts in American politics. For one thing, it proved, finally, that America truly was the land of opportunity. He was a first-generation Danish American, and he was Jewish—the latter being a part of his heritage that seldom, if ever, got press play.

He scarcely noticed either. In truth, it was only on his father's side—which in Judaism did not really count. Hansen's father, Joost, had been a young Copenhagen college student in 1943 when the people of Denmark one night heroically evacuated all the country's Jews to Sweden, out of the looming grasp of the Nazis. Shortly thereafter he had married Hansen's mother, a Swede named Erica who had helped in the evacuation, and then, after the war, they had emigrated to America. Joost Hansen had finished his doctorate in physics at Princeton—being a promising physicist was one of the reasons he could so readily get into the United States—and then had gone to work at Los Alamos.

On the liner that brought them, the birth of Johan Hansen was due any minute, and one hour after it docked on the pier on the west side of New York, he came bawling into the world —a brand-new citizen and native-born, thereby eligible by a matter of minutes to be President someday. Who could have known?

Young Johan remembered little of Princeton, New Jersey, but in Los Alamos he had gloried in the clear air of the mountains, had loved the old White Sands rocket test area where they vacationed, had loved everything about America. He'd gone on to try engineering at MIT, but he had soon realized he didn't have the makings to follow in his father's technical footsteps. He cared too much about human affairs to stay in the bloodless world of formulas and machines.

As a result, he shifted to political science, and after graduating he became an aide to one of Massachusetts's liberal congressmen. Eventually he ran for the House on his own. The Democratic primary was a model of rough-and-tumble Boston politics, but he won a squeaker and became a full-fledged member at thirty-one.

Thus began a career that continued through the Senate and, after two terms, to the Presidency. He had achieved his ambitions, and his soaring popularity was all the more amazing for accruing to a man who had restructured the military during the painful transition of the United States to a post-

Cold-War economy. Turning swords into plowshares was never as easy as it sounded, but America's excess armaments capacity had gone back to reinvigorate her high-tech sectors. If you could make an F-15, he had declared, you could by-God make anything. Now retool and get on with it. America had.

In his most important contribution to history, however, John Hansen had presided over the dismantling of more than half the world's nuclear arsenal. It's easy, he'd declared to the Russians, we just do nothing. And in so doing, the tritium in all those warheads will simply decay. End of bombs. You monitor our plants at Oak Ridge and Savannah River; we monitor you; and together we watch the nuclear threat to humanity simply tick away.

It was working, he often noted with pride. Maybe we're not going to melt the planet after all. Not only would future generations thank him; there would *be* future generations. But would they know enough history to appreciate what he'd done? he wondered ruefully. Only if the dismal state of American education could be improved . . .

It was now 8:40 A.M. and the television lights had been switched on, turning the fake gold leaf on the ceiling into an intense white. The TelePrompTer had been readied, and the Secret Service detail was making last-minute checks around the room as unobtrusively as conditions would permit. Correspondents, for their own part, were poring over an advance copy of the text that Caroline's aide had just passed out, making notes for the brief question period scheduled to follow.

The time was 8:41 when she walked up behind him and laid down a large gray envelope marked Top Secret. It was, she whispered, a couple of pages fresh off the secure fax that had been installed in the room just down the hall.

What was it? he wondered. Some eleventh-hour revisions by Jordan McCormick, a young new speechwriter from Harvard who liked to tinker till the very last minute? Puzzled, he ripped open the envelope. The first page was a covering memo from his personal secretary, Alicia Winston. Miss Winston, as she insisted on being called, was a spinster, fifty-eight, who guarded access to Johan Hansen with the ferocity of a pit bull. Get past her, junior members of Congress often declared, and you're home free. It was, however, more often a dream than a realization. Seduction was frequently discussed.

Alicia's note was brief and pointed. The second page, it said, was a copy of a fax that had just arrived on her desk from Ed Briggs, head of the Joint Chiefs. Hansen's chief of staff, Morton Davies, had asked her to fax it on to New York immediately. They both knew Morton was not a man to squander time.

Hansen glanced over to see a white phone, complete with scrambler, being nestled next to the official text of his speech. When he scanned the second sheet, he knew why.

"He's on the line," Caroline said.

He nodded and checked his watch. Eight forty-three. Shit. "Caroline, tell them there's been a five-minute hold. And see if you can have them kill those damned lights."

"You've got it." She signaled to the pool producer, pointed to the lights, and made a slashing motion across her throat. With a puzzled nod, he immediately complied, barking an order to his lighting director.

Hansen picked up the phone. "Ed, what the hell is this about? I'm looking at the fax. You say this happened over six hours ago?"

"Mr. President, that came in about ten minutes ago from naval intel. They've been trying to get the story straight. The BBC was carrying a rumor, but it was soft. We wanted to get all the facts before—"

"It was in the Med?" Hansen impatiently cut him off. "Why so long—?"

"They claim they took all this time trying to nail down who's responsible, and they still don't know for sure. All they've got that's hard is what I sent you. A frigate under contract to NSA got hit. About fifty known casualties. It could be our friends the Israelis, up to their old tricks, or it could be somebody who wants us to think it's them."

"Ed, I'm staring down half the press in the country right now, as we speak. I can't do anything till I get back. But check with Alicia. I think I'm scheduled in around noon, and I'd like to try and have a statement out by three today."

"All right, Mr. President, we'll do what we can. Let me secure-fax Morton everything I've got so far, and he can forward anything he thinks might help. But we've got to talk. This could be a tough call."

"What are the Israelis saying?"

"Their military intel told Morton they don't know a damned thing about it. But their embassy here's already on red alert, getting ready to start pushing out smoke."

"Typical." Hansen had no love for Israel. In his view, their intransigence had caused the lion's share of America's problems in the Middle East. They never told the truth about anything until three days later, when it was too late to matter. In the meantime, they just did whatever they wanted.

"Well, this time I almost think they may be straight," Briggs said. "It doesn't have any of their trademarks. For one thing, it had their name all over it—not their style."

Hansen scanned the fax again, noting the large-print Top Secret across the top, and tried to make it sink in. Concentration was difficult, considering the expectant stirrings in the room, the clank of silverware. But this was nothing short of a major episode. What did it mean?

"Okay, Ed, I want to see you first thing. And bring Bob with you"—Robert Barnes was his assistant, Navy—"in case we need to scramble out of Crete."

"Roger, sir. I'll have Alicia get everything we need set up in the Sit Room."

"Good." Hansen hung up the phone and looked around the room. Damn. Who was trying to screw up the Med? Already he had a bad feeling it might involve terrorists, but where did they get the Soviet helicopter?

Okay, he told himself, time to call in all the heavy guns, all the advisers who get paid so much to do your thinking.

He would face his first problem when the press got hold of the story. He could already see the cartoons, that bastard in the Moonie-owned *Washington Times* who was always accusing him of being a pansy on defense. They'd want blood, an eye for an eye, while he was trying his best to change that way of thinking.

This latest stupidity damned sure wasn't going to make it any easier.

With that grim thought, he smiled his widest smile and signaled Caroline to alert the pool producer to switch on the television lights.

8:14 A.M.

"What happened?" Ramirez asked. Helling had alerted him by walkie-talkie and summoned him to the lobby. There the Germans were returning, Henes Sommer covered with blood and being carried by Rudolph Schindler and Peter Maier.

"Henes got caught in a firefight. Then he tried to take the chopper . . . and fell." Schindler was struggling to find the words, thinking that he would have to be the one to tell Henes's wife, in what used to be East Berlin. Henes Sommer, forty-five, had joined Ramirez's operation out of idealism, as a step toward driving the Zionist scourge from Europe. Ramirez had made the operation sound so easy.

"It's even worse," Helling said slowly, addressing his words to Ramirez. "He must have been a guard who escaped our notice, but he managed to start the Hind. Then he crashed it against the hillside."

"Why didn't you go after him and kill him?" Ramirez asked quietly, his anger smoldering.

"There was no need. He's trapped up there. For now he can rot." An uncomfortable pause ensued before he continued. "Besides, he's armed. We probably should wait till nightfall. What can he do?"

He can do a lot, Ramirez was thinking. This could be trouble.

The three Germans had been brought along as a favor to Wolf Helling, and now they had demonstrated just how worthless they actually were. Under ordinary circumstances, he would have shot them all on the spot, as an example to the rest of the team.

"You say the Hind has been crashed?" he went on, his eyes hidden behind his shades.

"We don't need it any more. What does that matter?" Helling shrugged, not sure he believed his own words. "In any case, this is what comes of having amateurs involved."

Schindler's eyes darkened in resentment. It had never really occurred to him until this moment that his and his friends' lives were at risk.

Ramirez was trying hard to mask his own chagrin, telling himself he should never have sent these untried goons out to do a man's work. A good attorney never asked a question in court that he didn't already know the answer to; and you never turned your back on an operation if you weren't already fully certain how it would turn out. That was one mistake he didn't plan to make again.

"Life is never simple," he said, turning back to the German threesome. The wounded man was wheezing from a hole in his chest. "There's only one thing to do with him."

He withdrew a Walther from inside his coat and, with great precision, shot Henes Sommer directly between the eyes, as calmly as though dispatching a racehorse with a broken leg. The body slumped into the arms of Rudolph Schindler, who looked on in horror.

"It was merely a minor miscalculation, but now it's been handled." He turned to Helling. "Now go back and watch the hill. And try to act like a professional."

The German nodded. He dared not tell Ramirez the true extent of their trouble. Not only had the mysterious stranger escaped with Henes's Uzi, he also still might have a radio, if the Hind had not been totally wrecked. Helling, their boss, didn't seem yet aware of this problem. If it was still working, what would he do?

"Now," Ramirez continued, "rather than waste our time on fruitless recriminations, we must proceed."

He turned and walked back through the doors leading into Command. Across the room, past the rows of computer terminals, Bates sat at the Main Command desk, talking to Dr. Andros.

"Problem?" Bates asked, looking up. Although he had not slept all night, his blue blazer remained immaculate. "Having some trouble, you son of a bitch?"

"You will be relieved to know nothing is amiss," Ramirez replied as smoothly as he could manage. "One of your guards, it would seem, decided to make a nuisance of himself. But he has been neutralized."

Bates did not believe it. He had overheard the broadcast on the BBC, and now he was starting to put it all together. These thugs had come in by chopper, after attacking a U.S. ship. They must have left the attack helicopter out on the pad. But somebody got to it . . .

"Now, Miss Andros . . ." Ramirez lifted a clipboard from her desk and examined it. "My, my, today we all have a busy schedule. Review the test data from the power-up, final calibrations of the Cyclops, flight prep of the vehicle. . . ." He put it down. "Yes, it does look like a busy day. For us all. All you have to do is cooperate, and no one here will be harmed."

The second chopper is on its way now, he was thinking, if everything was on schedule. The next item was the launch vehicle.

He estimated they would need a day and a half to make the retrofit. The scheduled first test launch had been programmed for three days away—now it was two—so there was ample time . . . exactly as he had planned.

9:27 A.M.

Vance leaned back against the scrub cypress and listened to the whistle of the light wind through the granite outcroppings. He had perched himself on one of the rugged cliffs, from which he could see virtually everything that went on aboveground. Around him ants crawled, oblivious to the heat of the sun, which now seared the bone-colored rocks on all sides, while down below the languorous surf beckoned. How ironic, and tragic: all the violence and killing, right here in the middle of paradise.

He had managed to remove the battery-powered radio from the Hind; it would serve as his lifeline to the rest of the world. The military channels were all scrambled now, which told him that plenty was going on out there over the blue horizon. Trouble was, all communications had been secured. He had no idea what was happening.

What the hell to do next? He was barefoot—with nothing but an Uzi, a 9mm, and a radio.

He felt waves of grogginess ripple over him as the sun continued to climb. He was dead tired, and in spite of himself he sensed his mind drifting in the heat, his body losing its edge. Pulling himself together, he snapped alert. This was no time to ease up. He noticed that some of the men had left the command section and gone down to Launch Control, the flight-prep sector. They were carrying AK-47s now. Much better for sniper work.

They know I've only got an Uzi, he reminded himself, which is why they realize they're in no danger. From up here it'd be next to useless. But with a scope, those Kalashnikovs are bad news. . . .

At that moment he heard a dull roar, coming in from the south. Was it somebody who'd picked up his radio Mayday? He squinted against the sun and tried to see. As he watched, a dark, mottled shape appeared over the blue horizon. It was another helicopter—not a Hind this time.

As it came in for a landing at the pad down by Launch Control, Vance checked it over. It was a Sikorsky S-61R, military, with a main rotor almost sixty feet across, a retractable tricycle landing gear, and a rear cargo ramp. It went back to the sixties—the U.S. had used them to lift astronauts from the sea—but it was a warhorse and reliable as hell. It had an amphibious hull, twin General Electric turboshaft engines located up close to the drive gearbox, and an advanced flight-control system. Whether or not this one had the latest bells and whistles, he did know its speed was over a hundred and sixty miles per hour and its range was over six hundred miles.

What's that all about? he wondered. Is this the getaway car?

Whatever it was, they were not landing on the regular pad; they were putting her down as close as they could to the vehicles.

No, he decided, what they're doing is setting up something, getting ready for the big show.

He already had a feeling he knew what it was going to be. The *modus* was standard operating procedure. But this was going to be a waiting game, at least for a while, and he thought about trying to catch a couple of winks. There was nothing to be done now. He'd have to wait till dark.

To pass the time, he clicked on the radio again, to see if they were using walkie-talkies. After scanning the civilian channels he finally got a burst of traffic. They were chatting, all right—a lot of coded talk in a mixture of German, English, and French.

He paused a minute, even picked up the mike, attached by a coiled black cord to the radio, and pushed the red button. But then he thought better of it and clicked it off. The time would come soon enough to get in on the fun, but not yet.

9:32 A.M.

Jamal Khan, the younger brother of Salim, watched as the Sikorsky set down, then pushed the starter button on the white electric cart, urging it to life. This was the moment he had been waiting for. Nothing he had ever done in years past matched up to this, not even the airline hijackings. The only drawback was his comrades. Like, for example, this wise-ass Israeli, Peretz.

Dore Peretz, for his own part, waited until the cart—a three-wheel, on-site mover—had started, and then he swung onto the back. Neither spoke as they silently motored through the sunshine, the breeze in their hair, headed for the just-landed helo.

The sparkling morning did not improve the atmosphere

between the two men: only the sunshine contributed warmth to the moment. Peretz had contempt for the Iranian's arrogance and intensity; the bearded Iranian resented the Israeli's technical skills, his attitude, and the fact that he was Israeli. None of it could easily be forgiven. Jamal further could not forgive the Israeli for having no commitment to driving the Americans from the Middle East, for being here only for the money.

When they reached the Sikorsky, now settled on the tarmac, Jamal pulled the cart to a halt, then switched off the motor and stepped down. It would take all hands to manage the off-loading.

Helling and the two other Germans were already waiting in the sunshine, and as Jamal looked them over, he found himself liking them even less than he did Peretz. The truth was, they were little more than bureaucrats, regardless of whatever they called themselves. They ranted about America being the prisoner of the Zionists, but it was just rhetoric . . .

The door of the Sikorsky was opening now and "Abdoullah," the first of the three Pakistani engineers, was emerging, followed by "Rais" and "Shujat." All three had their dark hair swathed in a traditional Palestinian black and white *kufflyeh*, part of their "disguise."

Jamal tried not to smile as he watched them— grim-faced college boys—awkwardly slam clips into their Uzis and look around, as though they were about to lead an assault. It was a wonderful joke.

"Abdoullah" actually had a Ph.D. in nuclear engineering from Berkeley. While in America he had developed a taste for the good life—cars, designer clothes, and gold jewelry—and then when he came back and went to work at Kahuta, Pakistan's top-secret uranium enrichment plant, he had discovered sex.

The instrument of this discovery was a hard-eyed Palestinian girl, Ramala, whose fiery politics were matched only by her skills in bed. He became a convert to her and then to her cause—which played directly into the hands of Ramirez. Ramirez had, Jamal knew, been working on this setup for five years. Money here, information there, it all had finally paid off.

Of all Ramirez's recruits, "Abdoullah's" contribution had been the most crucial, since he had been the one who had arranged the theft of the two items now crated and ready in the cargo bay of the Sikorsky. He and his two engineer-colleagues spoke English by choice, and to Jamal they looked almost identical, all with new coal-black beards and designer "commando" sweatbands under their *kaffiyeh*. They were trying to get with the look of revolutionary chic, he thought with disdain. They'd just made the big time, but they still thought they were in a Chuck Norris movie. Fortunately, they'd already served their main purpose. In two more days, they would be totally expendable.

The Sikorsky had landed approximately fifty yards from the entrance to the blockhouse of the launch facility, placing them a mere two hundred yards away from the SatCom space vehicles, *VX-1* and *VX-2*. Those spires seemed to preside over everything, casting long shadows, and the three Pakistani engineers paused, still gripping their Uzis, to gaze up and admire them.

"Don't stand there gawking." Peretz curtly brought them to attention. "We've got to get moving. If anybody has started any satellite recon of this place, we could be on TV by now. A U.S. KH-12 can read the address on a fucking postcard." He signaled for the pilot to release the rear entry ramp. "Let's get going. We're taking them in immediately."

The Pakistanis saluted in paramilitary style, secured their Uzis into their black leg-holsters, and moved expectantly to the rear of the helo. As the ramp slowly came down, there strapped and waiting in the aft bay were two wooden crates cushioned in a bed of clear plastic bubble-wrap, each approximately a meter square and weighing just under a hundred kilos.

Phase four had begun.

CHAPTER SIX

12:03 P.M.

Cally Andros felt disgusted, physically nauseated. And partly it was with herself. Blame the victim. She wondered if all hostages felt this way: powerless, angry, and scared. What would she feel next? She had heard that strange things happened to your mind when you lost all control. You started forgetting recent events and remembering oddities from long ago, childhood memories you'd totally repressed, stashed away somewhere down in the lower cortex. It had already started, dwelling on her father's death and blaming herself, when the real reason was his overwork and grief.

And other memories were creeping in, little things that only the child inside would regard as anything but trivial. That first bumbling sexual disaster, in the Cal Tech dorm that weekend, when she got drunk, then threw up on his pillow. She'd repressed that one completely, never told *anybody* about that, hoping the memory would just go away. God! It was horrible. And now it was back, right at the top of the remembrance file.

More memories, the first year at Bronx Science, when her very first real date stood her up, and she ended up sitting home all night crying and praying everybody was going to believe her when she told them she'd had the cramps and couldn't go out after all. (They didn't. Everybody found out exactly what had happened.)

Humiliations? Stupid things that meant so much at the time that they stuck. You felt your life had been a string of mistakes and you wanted to go back and get it right before you checked out. And try as you might, you didn't care at all about the triumphs—degrees, ceremonies, honors. No, all you could remember were the little, trivial things, joys and sadnesses that were yours alone. Remembrances of trivialities past. That's what being a hostage was all about.

On the other hand—and she hated herself for this feeling —there was something almost erotic about men with so much sudden, ill-gotten power. Evil had its own allure, just as surely as good. Were they just two opposite sides of the same emotion? Wasn't Satan the real hero of *Paradise Lost*? Was Ramirez that same figure? The sexiness of power. Bill Bates had the same aura. . . .

Georges and his young staff engineers were sitting listlessly and staring at their computer screens, looking exhausted and defeated. Bill had been confined to his office, where he could do nothing but fume since his radio had been shut down and there was now only one phone remaining connected to the outside world—the one on her desk, which they monitored.

It got worse. Isaac was coming in, which meant they'd have a real prize for a hostage. As if Bill weren't enough, to have a famous American Jewish professor in hand would be the topping on their whole grab.

She tried to catch Georges's eye, across the room. He seemed to be drowsing at his terminal, almost as though nothing had happened. Since he had always held a political stance slightly to the left of Che Guevara, maybe he secretly enjoyed being taken hostage by these self-appointed enemies of American Capitalism.

No . . . she saw an eyelid flutter . . . he was just faking his calm. He was scared to death. And he was thinking. About what?

She had done some thinking of her own, about the guy who called himself Number One, the terrorist now sitting at the other end of Command, calmly smoking a thin cigar. As she examined him, the gray temples and perfect tan, the beige sunglasses, she began to find his appearance a little incongruous. What was it?

Well, for one thing, he looked too perfect. Something about him . . . He had to be at least in his late forties, but nobody's face looked like that at his age. It was too smooth, too tight.

Plastic surgery. The bastard had changed his appearance. So who was he, really? He hadn't given his name, but his face must have mattered once. Who?

Try and put it together, she told herself. He's not Middle Eastern. Maybe he's trying to pass as an Arab, but he's not fooling me. No, he's *Latin*. It's in the way he moves, the way he brushes at his sleeve, the way he holds his cigar. He's just like Domingo, the guy in junior year, who thought he was God's gift to the feminine gender.

Yes, Domingo was a Latin caricature, but this guy has all the same moves. They can't escape it. They're just so proud of being male. The ironic part was, half the time Domingo couldn't get it up unless some act of violence was involved. He liked to dominate, or be dominated. Power was what he was all about. Power.

Think. Can you use that some way to get to this guy?

No, she told herself, this killer has all the power he needs. He's about image. And money.

She moved through the rows of workstations, now merely flashing updates of the status of the various components of the Cyclops system. The power plant was idling now, the superconducting coil in standby mode. The crew of technicians, armed with a punch list of post–power-up items, was checking out the Cyclops itself. The test had been a total success.

"Miss Andros, you are a beautiful woman." Ramirez glanced up as she approached. He had seemed to be meditating on his cigar, inspecting the ash as he slowly allowed it to accumulate. "I was wondering why a creature of such beauty would want to submit herself to this kind of manly trade?"

"Not as 'manly' a trade as yours. Killing for profit." She felt her anger coming back, and her courage. "As far as I'm concerned, there's no difference between a so-called 'terrorist' and a common murderer. You disgust me."

His face flushed for a millisecond as he impassively drew on his cigar. "It would be better if you would consider me, and the rest of these men, as economic freedom fighters. Perhaps I'm a modern-day Robin Hood."

"Right." She felt like spitting on him, a definitely unladylike response. "You steal from the rich and give to yourself. But you've made a big mistake this time. All you're going to do is ruin SatCom."

"Ruin you?" He seemed amused at the notion, taking another puff on his cigar. "I have no desire to *ruin* your precious American corporation. As a matter of fact, I'm going to make you the beneficiary of a billion dollars' worth of free publicity. Truly, no money in the world could purchase what I am about to do for you. And all I want in return is to borrow your Cyclops laser for a few days. If anything, you should pay *me* . . . though there will be others to do that."

"I don't know who you expect to come up with any money. It sure as hell isn't going to be SatCom. We're totally tapped out. If this launch doesn't meet our schedule, day after tomorrow, a bunch of banks in Geneva and Tokyo are going to take us over. And I doubt very much they're going to pay off you and your goons. They'll tell you to go screw yourself."

"They can do whatever they wish. They're not the ones who're going to pay." There was no trace of sarcasm in his voice. "We are going to make the Americans pay. For their crimes against the Muslim peoples of the world."

"That's a lot of crap." She hated the man, really hated him. "You don't care a damn about the 'Muslim peoples,' do you, *señor?*"

He pulled up sharply and stared at her, startled. For the

first time since he had barged in, he seemed momentarily at a loss for words. But he covered it quickly by reaching out to tap his cigar ash into a half-filled trash can.

"What are you suggesting?"

"You're a fake, through and through." Keep him on the defensive, she thought. "As phony as they come. Who are you, really?"

His composure was returning, an instinct for chivalry that could operate on autopilot if need be. "I'm flattered by your interest in me, but who I am need not concern you. All you need to worry about is following my instructions. Then you and I will get along nicely."

"Listen, you creep, there's no way we are going to get along, nicely or otherwise." She felt her resolve growing. "You don't know me. I'm going to fight you with everything I have. You're going to have to kill me to stop me."

"Do yourself a favor, Miss Andros." He pulled again on his cigar, inhaling the harsh smoke. "Don't make that necessary."

1:17 P.M.

Isaac Mannheim gazed down through the glass partition of the old Bell Jetranger and wondered again what he was seeing. The pilot couldn't raise Command on the radio, and now he was grumbling that the pad looked unsafe.

The boy had a point. The surrounding hurricane fence had been half ripped away, and there was oil everywhere on the asphalt. The place looked as though a raging bull elephant had powered its way through, knocking aside everything in its wake. What in blazes had happened? A tornado?

He surveyed the area, and something even more ominous caught his eye. What was it, that thing half-buried in the trees, about two-thirds the way up the mountain? Now he strained to see through the smudgy windows, just making out the wreckage of some sort of military helicopter.

Next he turned and looked in the other direction, down toward the launch vehicles. That's odd. Another helicopter was parked down there. It was big, a military gray, but no one was around it.

"It looks like there was a crash on the pad or something," the young Greek pilot shouted over the roar of the engines, his dark, serious eyes fixed gravely on the scene. His name, sewn in Greek on his tan shirt, was Mikis; his father owned the 1981 Jetranger, and the business. Flying this far from Athens meant he would have to refuel to make it back, and nobody was around to take care of that. Moreover, the situation definitely looked unsafe.

"I can see that," Mannheim responded dryly, his voice faint above the noise. "Which is why you need to be careful. We don't want to add another casualty."

"Something funny is definitely going on," Mikis continued, to no one in particular. He had already discovered the eccentric American professor with a baseball cap didn't care all that much for small talk. And he had no patience whatsoever for small talk that pointed out the obvious. "I don't like this, but I'll have to put her down. I'm already on my auxiliary tank."

For once Mannheim allowed his thoughts to stray to the concerns of someone else. "There's an airfield at Kythera. You could make it there, if you just touched down here and dropped me off."

"Are you sure you want to do that?" Mikis was gripping the stick, frowning behind his aviator shades. "We can't raise anybody here on the radio, and now there's this mess. Let me take you to Kythera with me. The whole deal looks weird."

"No," Mannheim shouted back. "I have to find out what's happened."

This project is like Sarah, he thought, his estranged daughter coming to mind. I had to do everything I knew how to try to keep her from making the wrong decisions. Then he remembered ruefully that she had gone ahead and made them anyway. But he had been there always, ready to give her advice.

Mikis shrugged, clearly worried, and gave the Jetranger some pedal, circling to search for signs of life. There was nothing. The bleak granite cliffs were barren, and the cool blue of the light surf washed against an empty shoreline. He had not seen this space facility before, but everybody had heard about it. The most impressive sight was, of course, those silver spires down at the other end of the island. Those had to be their vehicles, but nobody was around them now. Puzzled, he examined the huge dormitory-type residence in the middle of the island and the supply buildings, lined along a paved segment connecting the landing pad with the main building, and still saw no one.

"Look, I'm going to just drop you off and then get the hell out of here," he yelled over. He was easing up on the collective, taking her in. "I'll buy petrol on Kythera. I don't see anybody around, and this place gives me the creeps."

"You've done all you need to," Mannheim shouted back. "Something . . ."

His voice trailed off as he finally saw some movement. A figure was coming down the mountain, carrying what looked like an automatic weapon.

"We'd better make this quick."

1:21 P.M.

Vance was moving as fast as he could and watching as the helicopter—now about a thousand yards from the pad—began its final approach.

Friend or foe? With the second arrival in as many hours, the place resembled an airport. He assumed by now they surely had seen the wreckage of the Hind, but they seemed determined to come in anyway.

He watched as the old Bell gingerly began to hover above the landing pad, the pilot dispensing with preliminaries. While it was settling in, he chambered a round in the Uzi, pulled back the gnarled cocking lever on the top, and continued on down the hill at a brisk pace. With any luck he would beat the guys in black. Or maybe they were deliberately keeping a low profile, hoping to lure in the prey. They were also luring him out, he knew, but he had to take the chance.

He was moving quickly, the sharp rocks cutting into his

feet, and now only a hundred yards or so remained between him and the approaching helo.

Only then did he first notice he had bumped Bill's new Agusta when he tried to fly the Hind, leaving a bad dent. Now he owed Bates for repairs. Great. He wondered fleetingly if SatCom had terrorist insurance.

There was now an opening in the pad's protective fence, where the Hind had ripped it away, and as the din of the approaching helicopter rang in his ears, he raced across the last clearing, headed for it. But his instincts caused him to look around, and just in time . . .

Approaching on the run down the asphalt road leading from the launch facility were three of the terrorists. He recognized two of them as his earlier assailants, together with a third who looked like he might actually know what he was doing. They must have seen the arriving Jetranger, and now they were coming out to give it a welcome.

The way they were moving, and the AK-47s they were carrying, told him a lot. The chopper's occupants were the good guys.

As the Bell settled in and its door opened, he dropped onto the granite and nestled the metal stock of the Uzi against his cheek. It felt warm from the morning sun, like the touch of a comfortable friend. He flipped the fire control to semiautomatic and caught the approaching goons in the metal sight. Then he gently squeezed the trigger.

The Uzi kicked back, sending a round upward into the morning air. He realized he was out of practice. Next time he would handle it better, but for now he had blown the operation.

The three in black who had been running toward the landing pad dropped onto the asphalt and opened fire, spattering flecks of granite around him as he took cover. Then he looked up to see an elderly man fairly tumble out of the chopper and make a dash for the safety of the SatCom Agusta. He need not have hurried; no one was shooting at *him*.

As the Jetranger started to lift off, however, the gunmen's focus switched away from Vance, and he realized they had no intention of letting it escape. As it left the pad and banked to gain altitude, the lead terrorist dropped to a prone position on the asphalt and took aim directly at the cockpit, where the pilot was just visible behind the glare of the windscreen. With a range of only fifty yards, Vance realized, taking him out would be easy.

It was. The AK-47 was on full auto, and one burst splintered away the windscreen, exploding it and leaving what remained spattered with blood. The pilot was thrown against the shattered glass, then left hanging halfway through. He never knew what hit him.

The fuselage began to pirouette into a sickening spiral, but the firing continued, as though to kill what was already dead. The gunman's obsessed, Vance thought. He's also emptying his magazine.

Now's the time. Make a move while he's still distracted. These thugs want the old man alive, whoever he is. So why not try and ruin their day, get him before they do.

The Bell continued to autorotate in a series of circles. Then it abruptly nosed straight downward, and a second later it veered toward the side of the cliff abutting the sea. A splintering crash replaced the sound of the engine as the rotors slammed against the granite, shearing away—whereupon the fuselage bounced down the steep wall of the cliff and into the water. In moments the seabed swallowed it up.

In the meantime Vance had reached the landing pad, a few meters away from the old man, who was stumbling distractedly across the asphalt, staring in the direction the chopper had disappeared and so shocked by the sight he seemed not to realize he was walking directly into the hands of the men who had killed the pilot.

Vance wanted to shout, but then he thought better of it. What was the point? The old man clearly was unable to think. He had to be pulled out quickly and with a minimum of risk. No, the best thing to do was lay down a line of covering fire and go for him.

He opened up the Uzi on semiauto and dashed for the Agusta.

1:25 P.M.

Wolf Helling hit the ground rolling, bringing up his Kalashnikov, set on automatic. The renegade guard was back to shoot it out, firing from somewhere in the area of the pad.

Good. He was going to trap the fucker. This time he would handle the situation personally; he would not have to depend on a bunch of incompetent East German Stasi burnouts.

He glanced back and saw the two trailing behind him. When the guard had opened fire, they'd dived and stumbled pell-mell for the cover of the storage sheds. They wouldn't be any help, but he'd known that already.

It didn't matter. This was going to be one-on-one. And easy.

The chopper had been lost, which was a shame. Although Ramirez's orders were to seize it when it arrived, that had not been possible. You win some, you lose some.

Amid the gunfire the old man had reached the SatCom helicopter, while the guard was now making a dash for its protection, too, even as he covered himself with another spray from the automatic that the damn fools had let him get.

Fortunately his aim was wild again, probably because he was running, and the rounds sailed by harmlessly. And he was in the open.

Now.

Helling trained his AK-47, long barrel and heavy clip, on him and pulled the trigger. . . .

His clip was empty.

Scheisse! He cursed himself for having used the gun on automatic. At ten pops a second, you could wipe out a 35-round clip before you could sneeze.

Still cursing, he pushed the button releasing the clip and slammed in another. But he was too late; by that time the guard had disappeared behind the SatCom helicopter. The two East Germans were firing randomly and ineffectually from the safety of the storage sheds, holding their weapons around the corners and spraying blindly. Idiots. They were providing cover, but since they had no idea where they were aiming, they were endangering him at least as much as their target.

And now the bastard had reached the cover of the helicopter. He was safe for the moment. But only for the moment.

1:27 P.M.

"Don't shoot," Isaac Mannheim shouted as he saw the unshaven, barefoot man roll next to him, an Uzi giving off bursts of rounds.

"Get down," Vance yelled back, then shoved him onto the asphalt beside the blue-and-white Agusta. "You picked a hell of a time to come visiting. There're some new natives, and they're not overly friendly."

"Who are you?" The old man's ancient eyes were brimming with alarm and confusion. "What are you doing here?"

"At the moment I'm trying to keep you alive." Vance checked the clip of the Uzi. There were about seven rounds left. With three hoods out there, all with Kalashnikovs, seven rounds would not go very far.

Was anything usable in the Agusta? he asked himself. He peered through the glass of the cockpit, searching. It looked empty. Except for—

A blast of fire careened by the canopy, and he again yanked Mannheim down onto the asphalt. Then he cautiously raised up enough to recon the situation.

The hoods were all advancing now, scurrying forward from building to building as they gave covering blasts from their automatics. However, the two farthest back did not seem to be overly enthusiastic.

"They're going to kill us, too," Mannheim stammered. "Can you—?"

"Just stay down," Vance interrupted him. "I'm probably the one they want to get rid of. If they'd wanted you dead, believe me, you would be by now."

He opened the door and hurriedly surveyed the cockpit more closely. Yes, he had seen it right . . .

Attached to the back firewall, ready for emergency use, was a rack of smoke grenades, factory fresh, the kind used for signaling in case the helo went down.

He remembered that grenade smoke was designed to cling to the ground rather than rise, and with a burn time between one and two minutes, a good grenade could produce a quarter million cubic feet of HC smoke.

Maybe, he thought, I just got lucky.

He peeled one off the rack and checked it over. Yep, American M-18, which everybody knew was the best. The can was about the size of a Diet Coke, and it was military gray. It even gave the flavor on the side—this one was red, but they also came in yellow and white. Nice to have around if you went down in wooded terrain.

He looked toward the gunmen approaching and made the decision on the spot. With a quick motion he clenched the handle with his right hand and yanked the steel pin with his left. When he looked up again, they had closed the distance, now only about thirty yards. Time for a touchdown.

He drew back and lobbed the can directly at the lead terrorist.

The time delay was one and a half seconds. It landed just in front of the first man, bounced once, and blew—an eruption of red that engulfed him.

Beautiful.

With a quick twist he yanked the rack from the side of the cockpit and began hurling the cans as fast as he could. Finally, he grabbed the startled old professor by the arm, then dropped the last grenade at their feet.

"Time to move the party. There's cover in the rocks up there."

Mannheim stumbled backward as the smoke bomb exploded, and Vance realized he would never make it. He would have to be dragged, or carried. And since dragging was out of the question, there really was only one option.

He bent down and grabbed the old man around the waist, then lifted him over his shoulder. It turned out he was hardly more than skin and bones, maybe a hundred and fifty pounds, tops. After spending the last four days heaving the tillers of the late, lamented *Odyssey II*, the load seemed like a feather.

Some more random gunfire exploded behind them as he struggled and stumbled up the rocky slope, but now a dense cloud of red completely obliterated the scene below. The M-18 grenades were still billowing, totally obscuring the landing pad and the roadway.

When they reached the first clump of brush leading up the mountain, he settled Mannheim onto the ground. The old professor was choking from the smoke, totally disoriented, and babbling. Vance clapped a hand over his mouth, then urged him onward.

"No talking. If they find us, we're going to have some really lousy odds."

He removed his hand, and immediately Mannheim started again.

"Whoever you are, I guess I have to thank you for saving my life." He puffed over the stones. "Who are you?"

"I'm a friend of Bill Bates, the man supposedly in charge around here."

"I'm Isaac Mannheim. This project—"

"The godfather." Vance looked him over. "Bill's talked about you. MIT, right?"

"The Cyclops is my—"

"Nice to meet you. Now who in the hell are these thugs?"

"I have no idea."

"Well, we can assume they're not part of Bill's technical support team." He glanced down the hill, toward the drifting cloud of red smoke, then back at the old man. "But if you've been involved in this project, then you must know the layout here."

"I know it very well. But—"

"Good. We're going to have to keep moving, at least till it gets dark, but while we're doing that, I want you to get me up to speed on where things are. Give me the setup. And tell me how many personnel are here and where they are."

Mannheim pointed down the hill, at a point just past the storage sheds. "The people are housed in the Bates Motel, which is over there, beyond that row of buildings."

Vance looked it over. At the moment it seemed deserted. "Where's the entrance?"

"You can go in directly from the connecting corridor underground, or you can use the front entrance, there."

"What if the entrance topside were locked? Then it would be secure, right?"

"I suppose so." He still seemed disoriented, though he was recovering. "Of course there are fire exits at various places in the underground network, as well as the security lobby over there. And then, the storage sheds can be accessed from below."

"But all of those entry-points can be sealed, right?"

"Yes. In fact, they can be sealed electronically, from Command. The staff controls everything from there."

Vance looked down at the white surf rippled across the blue. "So if somebody wanted to take over this place, that's where they would start, right? Hit that and you're in like a bandit. It's the head office."

"That's correct." Mannheim nodded.

"Good. We know where to focus. Now you're going to tell me how I can get there."

CHAPTER SEVEN

2:18 P.M.

Pierre Armont was forty-six, with gray temples and a body appropriate to an Olympic wrestler. He had full cheeks, a heavy mustache, and suspicious dark eyes that constantly searched his surroundings. It was an innate survival instinct.

He never went out without a tie and a perfect shoeshine, not to mention a crisp military bearing that sat as comfortably on him as a birthright. He prided himself on his ability to instill discipline while at the same time leading his men. Although he liked to command, he wanted to do it from the front, where the action was.

Here in Paris he ran a worldwide business from a gray stone townhouse situated on the Left Bank in an obscure cul-de-sac at the intersection of Saint-Andre des Arts and rue de l'Ancienne Comédie. Fifty meters away from his ivy-covered doorway, the rue de Seine wound down to the river, playing host to one of Paris's finer open-air produce markets, while farther down, rows of small galleries displayed the latest in Neo-Deconstructionist painting and sculpture. An avid amateur chef and art collector, he found the location ideal. From his house, where the French aviator Saint-Exupéry once wrote, he could march a few paces, along cobblestones as old as Chartres, and acquire a freshly plucked pheasant, a plump grouse, aromatic black truffles just hours away from the countryside, or an abstract landscape whose paint was scarcely dry. It was the best of all worlds: everything he loved was just meters away, and yet his secretive courtyard provided perfect urban privacy and security, with only the occasional blue-jeaned student from the Académie de Beaux-Arts wandering into his courtyard to sketch. He was rich and he knew how to live well; he also risked his life on a regular basis.

He claimed it made his *foie gras* taste even better.

He worked behind a wide oak desk flanked by a line of state-of-the-art communications equipment, and along one walnut-paneled wall stood rows of files secured inside teak-wood-camouflaged safes. His wide oak desk could have belonged in the office of a travel agent with a very select clientele. However, it served another purpose entirely: it was where he planned operations for ARM.

Pierre Armont headed up the Association of Retired Mercenaries, and he had been busy all day. But he was used to emergencies. What other people called problems, ARM thought of as business.

The Association of Retired Mercenaries was a secretive but loose group of former members of various antiterrorist organizations. The name was an inside joke, because they were far from retired. Although they were not listed in the Paris phone book, governments who needed their services somehow always knew how to find Pierre. ARM took on nasty counterterrorism actions that could not occur officially. They rescued hostages unreported in newspapers, and they had terminated more than a few unpleasant individuals in covert actions that never made the evening news.

At the moment, as he was thinking over the insertion strategy for Andikythera, he was gazing down on his private courtyard and noticing that the honking from the boulevard Saint-Germain indicated that Paris's mid-afternoon traffic had ground to a halt. Again. He had just hung up the scrambled phone, after a thirty-minute conversation with Reggie Hall, the second today. London was on board, so everything was a go. He was looking forward to this one. Some *bâtards* had mucked with an ARM job. They had to be taken down.

Armont was retired from France's antiterrorist Groupement d'Intervention de la Gendarmerie Nationale, known as GIGN, ideal experience for his present occupation. Over the years "Gigene" had carried out, among other things, VIP protection in high-threat situations and general antiterrorist ops. Mostly commandos in their twenties and early thirties, Gigene operatives had to pass a grueling series of tests, including firing an H&K MP5 one-handed while swinging through a window in a quick entry called the pendulum technique. Known for their skills in inserting by helicopter, either by rappelling or by parachuting, they could also swim half a mile under water and come out blasting, using their specially loaded Norma ammo.

Armont's particular claim to fame was the invention of a sophisticated slingshot that fired deadly steel balls for a silent kill. He had trained antiterrorist units in a number of France's former colonies, and had secretly provided tactical guidance for the Saudi National Guard when they ejected radical Muslims from the Great Mosque at Mecca.

These days, however, he was a private citizen and ran a simple business. And as with all well-run businesses, the customer was king. If problems arose, they had to be resolved; if a job did not stick, you sent in a repair team. An American member of ARM named Michael Vance, who normally did not participate in the operations end of the business, had turned up at the wrong place at the right time. A Reuters confirmation of the loss of the U.S. communications ship definitely meant some bad action had gone down in the eastern Med. Vance's analysis that it was a preliminary to seizure of the SatCom facility on Andikythera probably was correct. Armont's secretary had spent the day on the phone trying to reach the island, but all commercial communications with the site were down. There was no way that should have happened, even with last night's rough storm.

He had liked Michael Vance the minute he met him,

three years earlier. He considered Mike reliable in completing his assignments—be they quick access to a "secure" bank computer file or a paper trail of wire transfers stretching from Miami to Nassau to Geneva to Bogotá. Vance's regular missions for ARM, however, were those kinds of transactions, not the street action, and Armont could only hope he could also manage the rougher end of the business.

The organization had checked out the man extensively, as they did all new members, and ARM's computer probably knew as much about him as he did himself. It was an oddball story: son of a famous Penn archaeologist, he had been by turns an archaeologist himself, a yachtsman, and a low-level spook. After he finished his doctorate at Yale and had taught there for two semesters, he had published his dissertation—claiming the famous Palace of Minos in Crete was actually a hallowed necropolis—as a book. It had caused a lot of flap, and to get away for a while, he had taken a vacation in Nassau to do some big-game fishing. Before the trip ended, he had bought an old forty-four-foot Bristol sailboat in need of massive restoration. It was a classic wooden vessel, which meant that no sooner had he finished varnishing the thing from one end to the other than he had to start over again.

But he apparently liked the life. Or maybe he just enjoyed giving the academic snakepit a rest. The computer could not get into his mind. Whatever the reason, however, the sailboat, which had begun as a diversion, soon became something else. By the time he had finished refurbishing her, she was the most beautiful yacht in the Caribbean, and everybody around Nassau wanted a shot at the helm. He had a charter business on his hands.

Then his saga took yet another turn. The Nassau Yacht Club, and the new Hurricane Hole Marina across the bridge on Paradise Island, comprised a yachting fraternity that included a lot of bankers. Nassau, after all, had over three hundred foreign commercial banks, and its "see no evil" approach to regulation and reporting made it a natural haven for drug receipts. With a lot of bankers as clients, before long Vance knew more than any man should about offshore money laundering. He did not like that part of the scene, but the bankers loved his yacht, and they paid cash.

As he once told it, he eventually found out why. At least for one of them. One sunny afternoon the vice president of the European Consolidated Commercial Bank, an attractive blond-haired young Swiss mover known to Vance only as "Werner," was docking The Ulysses at Hurricane Hole, bringing her back from a three-day sail, when the DEA swooped down, flanked by the local Bahamian police. Armed with warrants, they searched the boat and soon uncovered fifty kilos of Colombian export produce. Seems "Werner" had sailed The Ulysses to some prearranged point and taken it on, planning to have divers stash the packages in the rudder-trunk air pocket of one of the giant cruise ships that tied up at Nassau's four-berth dock. Vance heard about it when he got a call from the harbormaster advising him that his prized Bristol had just been seized as evidence in a coke bust. He was out of business.

That afternoon Bill Bates had coincidentally flown in on Merv Griffin's Paradise Island commuter airline and come over to Hurricane Hole, wanting to charter The Ulysses for a week of sailing and fishing. Vance had to inform him his favorite Bahamian yacht had just acquired a new owner.

Bates could not believe he had flown into such a screwup. Vance was having his own problems with disbelief, too, but paying the mortgage was his more immediate concern. The DEA had the boat, but before long he wouldn't have to worry about that any more. That problem, and the boat, would soon belong to the mortgage-holding bank over on Bay Street.

He immediately slapped the DEA with a two-million-dollar lawsuit, just to put on some heat. His lawyer claimed he didn't have a hope in hell.

But two weeks later a Bahamian judge, after lunch with the mortgage-holding banker, summarily ordered the DEA to release the yacht. To Vance's surprise, the U.S. Drug Enforcement Administration cheerfully complied and turned it over the same afternoon. He immediately dropped the lawsuit, writing off the whole affair as a triumph for truth, justice, and the Bahamian way of banking. Or so it seemed.

Only later did he unearth the Byzantine complexities of what really had happened. The affair had somehow come to the attention of The Company, and there had been a flurry of phone calls to the DEA in New Orleans from Langley, Virginia. A month later, while he was in the States attending a Yale alumni function, he'd found himself talking to two earnest Washington bureaucrats, who congratulated him on beating the system. Huh?

They then described their need for a "financial consultant" in Nassau, somebody who knew the right people. Maybe he would consider taking the job; it could merely be a favor for—they hinted broadly—a favor.

Here was the problem: the CIA desperately needed help in trying to keep track of the cocaine millions being laundered through Nassau's go-go banks. The Company wanted some local assistance getting certain off-the-record audits, from clean bankers who were tired of Nassau being a haven for dirty cash.

He hated drugs and drug money, so he had seen nothing wrong with the idea. He even ended up training some greenhorns out of Langley in the subtle art of tracing wire transfers. Two years later he got his payoff. They formed their own in-house desk to do what he had been doing and retired him. He was, it turned out, too successful.

But the word on such skills got around, and two months later Pierre Armont had approached him about joining ARM. They needed somebody good at tracing hot money, frequently the most reliable trail of a terrorist operation, and everybody close to the business had identified him as the best around.

By that time he had formally incorporated a charter operation in Nassau as Windstalker, Ltd., with three boats, three mortgages, and a big monthly nut. So he had signed on, only later discovering that along with ARM's extra cash came a lot of travel, many responsibilities, and occasional death threats. He took them seriously enough to start carrying his own protection, a chrome-plated 9mm Walther. Armont approved.

Vance had always been well paid. It was expected. Anybody who hired ARM—usually because there was nowhere else left to turn—knew the best did not come cheap. A good two-week op could pull down fifty thousand pounds sterling for every man on the team, which was why the boys drove BMWs and drank twelve-year-old Scotch. But no client ever complained about the price. Or if they did, they didn't complain to Pierre. Payment was always cash, half up front and the rest on delivery. Any client who welshed on the follow-through would be making a very ill-considered career decision.

He pulled the blinds and turned to his desk. Faxes sent via ARM's secure, encrypted system covered the surface. The team was coming together. His secretary Emile, a young Frenchman who came in mornings and worked in the next room, had already booked the necessary flights. By 1800 hours tomorrow everybody would be assembled in Athens and ready to insert.

Armont intended to lead the operation himself . . . unless Vance, as the man on the ground, proved the logical choice. Since he was already in place, always the best location, he would in any case have to be point man.

He had talked the job over with "Hans" in Frankfurt at 1030 hours, just after he had gotten the call from Athens, and together they had picked six operatives. Vance would make seven. He calculated that would be plenty.

"Hans" was the nom de guerre of a former GSG-9, Germany's green-beret-sporting Grenzschutzgruppen 9. GSG-9, headquartered at St. Augustin just outside Bonn, had a nine-million-dollar underground training range that included a communications and intel unit, aircraft mockups, an engineer unit, a weapons unit, an equipment unit, a training unit, and a strike unit. In his fifteen years with GSG-9, Hans had been known to achieve 95 percent accuracy with an H&K MP9 when firing from a moving vehicle or even rappelling down a rope from a hovering chopper. Now retired, he brought to ARM many talents: as well as participating in the on-site op, he usually acted as liaison officer because of his flawless English.

He also knew which old-timers from GSG-9—that was anybody over thirty-five—were looking for an op, and if the job required some younger talent he used his connections to get current members temporarily released from their units. When needed, he could arrange for special-purpose weapons otherwise "unavailable" or restricted. Once, when a sniper-assault situation called for a hot new IR scope, he borrowed one from the St. Augustin armory overnight, made a drawing, then had it copied in Brussels by noon the next day. He knew where to find ARM field operatives and what shape they were in—which ones had been shot up, broken legs in parachute drops, or gone over the edge with a case of nerves and too much booze.

Best of all, though, he could usually locate a wanted terrorist. GSG-9 was hooked directly into a massive computer in Wiesbaden informally known as the Kommissar. Hans could still tap into the Kommissar, which tracked various world terrorist groups, constantly updating everything known about their methods, their membership, and—most importantly—their movements.

These days he operated a rundown biergarten in Frankfurt, at least as his cover, and there were suspicions he managed to drink up a lot of its profits. In any case, he was in ARM for the money, and he never pretended otherwise. So when Armont rang him, he was immediately all ears. Never failed.

"Pierre, *allo! Comment allez vous?*" Even at ten-thirty in the morning Hans could be cheerful. Armont, definitely a night person, never understood how he did it.

"*Bien*, considering." Armont knew Hans was more comfortable in English than in French, and he hated speaking German. "What're you doing for the next couple of days?"

"Got something?" The German's interest immediately perked up.

"There's a little cleanup . . ."

After he gave him a quick briefing on the situation via their secure phone, Hans was extremely unhappy.

"Dimitri screwed up. It's not our problem."

"*I* say it's our problem," Pierre replied. "We guarantee our work and you're either in, or you're out. Permanently. Those are the rules."

"All right." Hans sighed. "Can't blame me for not liking it, though."

"So who do you think we need?" Armont asked. Hans knew the people better than he did.

"Well, we definitely should have Reggie," he replied straightaway. "He's the best negotiator we've got, and also he can get us some of the hardware we'll be needing."

The man in question was Reginald Hall. Just under fifty, he was a stocky ex–small-arms instructor, regimental sergeant major, retired, of the SAS, Britain's Special Air Service. In the old days he headed up a unit known in the press as the CRW, Counter Revolutionary Warfare section, called "the special projects blokes" by those on the inside.

He finally quit after successfully leading an assault on the Iranian embassy in London on 5 May 1980—which, to his astonished dismay, was televised live. He'd gotten famous overnight, and after thinking it over for a weekend, he decided the time had come to cash it in. These days he ran a small company that purportedly bought and sold used sports firearms. That was a polite way of saying he dabbled in the international arms trade, though not in a big way. But whenever ARM needed a special piece of equipment, as often as not Reggie found a way to take care of it.

He did not do it for love. Even though he was happily retired down in Dorset, Thomas Hardy country, with a plump Welsh common-law wife, he occasionally slipped away —much to her chagrin—to take on special ops for ARM. Maybe his neighbors thought he had bought their matching Jaguars with his army pension or the sale of used Mausers.

"I'll call him as soon as we hang up. He spent some time in the Emirates or some damn place and claims to speak a little Arabic." He was thinking. "Okay, who else could we use?"

"How about the Flying Dutchmen?" Hans said.

He was referring to the Voorst brothers, Willem and Hugo, both former members of the Royal Dutch Marines' "Whiskey Company." That was the nickname of a special group officially known as the Marine Close Combat Unit. Both bachelors, though never short of women, they lived in

Amsterdam and took on any security job that looked like it would pay. They also ran a part-time aircraft charter operation.

"We might need a chopper for the insert. Think they can handle it on such short notice?"

The Voorst brothers would occasionally arrange, through their old connections, for a Dutch military helicopter to get lost in paperwork for a weekend. Whiskey Company was a club, and everybody was going to retire someday. What went around came around. Besides, there was plenty of spare change in it for those who made the arrangements.

"With nobody paying? It'll take some fast talking."

"So far, this thing's being done on spec. We're just making good on a job."

"Don't remind me," Hans groaned. "Don't want to hear it. I think we'd better just rent something in Athens." He paused. "But I also think we ought to take along the Hunter. He'd be the man to handle grenades. He loves those damned things better than his wife."

They were both thinking of Marcel, formerly of the Belgian ESI, Escadron Special d'Intervention. While with ESI, he had fathered their famous four-man units, pairs of two-man teams, and had come up with the idea of carrying a spare magazine on the strong-side wrist to facilitate rapid mag change. ESI was known informally as Diana Unit, and since Diana was the huntress of mythology, Marcel had become known as the Hunter. But not till after he had earned the sobriquet. A former Belgian paratrooper, ex-Angola, he got the nickname after a special op there, when he had saved an entire ARM team by taking out a room of terrorists with three stun grenades, tear gas, and an Uzi—while wearing an antiflash hood called a balaclava plus a gas mask, a little like working under water. Marcel liked the nickname.

"I'll see if I can reach him. The Antwerp number."

"Well, we'll probably need him." Hans paused. "And Vance is already on site. That'll make all the difference."

"He's good. If you can get all the others, I think we'll have what we need."

"Then, let's get started. I'll try to reach everybody and

have them in Athens by late tomorrow. Fax me an equipment list and I'll talk that over with Spiros. See what he can get together for us down there and save having to ship it."

"You know, *mon cher*," Hans had said, "this is no way to start a day."

1:29 P.M.

"It was there for the National Security Agency, the NSA," admitted Theodore Brock, his special assistant for national security affairs. The atmosphere in the Oval Office was heating up.

"I'm now well aware of that," the President snapped, not bothering to hide his annoyance. "What I'm not well aware of is who the hell authorized it?"

The Oval Office, in the southeast corner of the White House West Wing, was, in the eyes of many, a small, unimposing prize for all the effort required to take up residence. John Hanson, however, seemed not to notice. He commandeered whatever space he happened to occupy and made it seem an extension of his own spirit. In fact, he rather liked the minimalist quarters, heritage of a time when U.S. presidents had much less weight on their shoulders. From here the wide world opened out. For one thing, the communications here and in the Situation Room in the basement put the planet at his fingertips. Next to a gigantic push-button multiline telephone was another, highly secure and modernistic, digital voice transmission system that could take him anywhere.

As the old-fashioned Danish grandfather clock—his only personal item in the office—began to chime the half hour, he glanced once more over the crisis summary that Alicia Winston had hastily assembled and had waiting on his desk when he returned from New York. Her office was conveniently just behind one of the three doors that led into the Oval Office. Another led to his personal study, passing through a small kitchen, from which now came the aroma of fresh-brewed Jamaican Blue Mountain coffee. The third opened onto a corridor, with the standard six Secret Service people, through which he expected to see his national security adviser appear at 1:45 P.M. Then, according to his schedule, he had to try to put all this out of his mind at 2:30, when he was due to host a delegation of troglodytes from the Hill. Nuclear disarmament did not have a lot of friends in Tennessee and Washington State. He was going to have to make some concessions, he knew, but politics was about compromise, always had been.

"Apparently the ship was put into place without authorization," Brock went on. "There was some back-channel request from NASA. They wanted to keep tabs on a space project on an island in the Aegean."

"SatCom. Now we're spying on Americans, is that it?" Hansen leaned back in his high, Kevlar-protected chair and tossed a telling glance toward Morton Davies, his chief of staff, who monitored most of his incoming calls. They both had received an earful on the Cyclops project from his old professor, Isaac Mannheim—who claimed it would demonstrate to the world that America's private sector still had plenty of life left, could stand up to the Europeans and the Japanese when it came to innovation. SatCom's independence from government, at least to Mannheim's way of thinking, was precisely its greatest virtue.

"Well, damn NSA," he continued. "This is an outrage."

He recalled that he'd sent the new director, Al Giramonti, a pointedly worded memo on that very subject. When John Hansen took office, the National Security Agency was still liberally exercising its capacity to monitor every phone call in America from its vast array of listening antennas at Fort Meade. He had resolved to terminate the practice. He thought he had.

"It was just routine surveillance," Brock insisted, squirming. He was in his late fifties, bright, with horn-rimmed glasses and a high forehead. He also was black, and he felt he had more than the usual obligation to make his President look good. "There was a satellite test launching in the works. The whole project has been kept under wraps, and NASA wanted to know what was going on. The National Security Agency had a platform in the area, so it all more or less meshed. There was nothing—"

"And what do the Israelis have to say for themselves?" the President pushed on. "The Hind had their markings."

"They deny they had anything to do with it." He squinted toward Hansen, trying to seem knowledgeable yet uncommitted. Which way was the wind going to blow next? "Even though the helo was plainly ID'd by—"

"That's what they claimed in '67," Hansen fumed, cutting him off, "when they strafed, torpedoed, and napalmed NSA's *Liberty*, which was clearly in international waters. They were hoping to prolong the Six-Day War long enough to roll into Syria, and they didn't want us to monitor their plans. So they took careful pains to knock out all our SIGINT capability in the region, just happening to kill a dozen seamen in the process. Afterwards the lying fuckers told our embassy in Tel Aviv it was all a mistake and sent flowers. If anybody else in the world had done that, we'd have nuked them."

"Well, at the time the *Glover* was hit, it wasn't monitoring Israeli SIGINT," Brock noted, adjusting his glasses. "We think they're clean on this one. At least what we have from Fort Meade so far seems to bear that out. They're still running a computer analysis, though, pulling out all the voice and code used by the Israeli Air Force during that time. We didn't have that capability back in 1967. In a few more hours we'll be able to put that question to rest, one way or another."

"Okay, maybe we should go slow till then. So in the meantime, let's take them at their word for a moment and examine the other possibilities." Hansen revolved in his chair and stared out the bulletproof window behind him. The Washington sky was growing overcast. And the clock was running. This whole screwup would be in tomorrow's *Washington Post*, garbled, just as sure as the sun was going to come up. CNN had already picked up the BBC's "rumor" and was running it on their "Headline" service, hinting the U.S. intelligence community had been caught with its pants around its ankles, again.

"There's more," Brock said, interrupting his thoughts. "The Iranians have been screaming about a stolen Hind for four days, blaming us, of course. But they've quietly let Mossad know they think it may have strayed into Pakistan, maybe as a diversion, and then ended up heading out for one of the Gulf states, probably Yemen. The Israelis have reason to believe it was delivered to a Yemeni-flagged freighter in the Persian Gulf, then taken through the Suez Canal and into the eastern Med. After that, all contact was lost."

Iran, the President thought. Pakistan. None of it sorted into a picture. Unless . . .

"Incidentally," Morton Davies, Chief of Staff, interjected, "the Israelis also have one other bit of intel that seems to have somehow gotten lost in all of NSA's Cray supercomputers. An Israeli 'fishing trawler' picked up a Mayday they triangulated as coming from somewhere north of Crete. It supposedly claimed—the transmission was a bit garbled—to emanate from the very Hind that had attacked the ship. The broadcast said that terrorists had taken over the SatCom facility on the island of Andikythera. If that's true, it would be the one that the *Glover* was monitoring."

Hansen stared at him. "Are we supposed to believe any of this? That unknown terrorists are behind this whole thing? That's exactly the kind of disinformation the Israelis have used on us in the past. Besides, it doesn't click. If terrorists did do it, they'd damned sure want the credit. Nobody throws a rock this size through your window unless there's a note attached. So where is it?"

That's when the import of what Davies had said hit him. SatCom. It was going to be the pride of America, a symbol . . . My God, it was a rocket launch facility.

He reached down and touched the blue button on the desk intercom on the right side of his desk.

"Alicia."

"Sir," came back the crisp reply.

"Have NSA send over any recent PHOTOINT they have on the Greek island of Andikythera. By hand. I want it yesterday."

"Yes, sir."

"Ted," he said, turning back to Brock, "somehow this time

I've got an uncomfortable feeling the medium may be the message."

1:49 P.M.

"To understand the operation of this facility," Isaac Mannheim was saying, "you need to appreciate the technology we've installed here." He was resting against the trunk of a tree, gazing wearily down the mountain at the sunbaked asphalt of the facility stretching below.

"I've already got a rough idea how it works," Vance replied. He was pondering the quiet down below. "It's the people I want to know more about."

"Well, of course, that's my primary concern as well." The old man shrugged. "But we are on the verge of an experiment that will change the world for all time. That's just as important."

"Not in my book."

"Perhaps. But all the same, I think I should tell you a few technical details about the facility. Since you say you're familiar with its general workings, you probably know that its heart is a twenty-gigawatt laser we call the Cyclops. Using it, we can send a high-energy beam hundreds of miles into space without losing appreciable energy. Our plan is to use that beam of energy, which we can direct very accurately, to power a satellite launch vehicle."

"I understand that."

"Excellent," he said, as though encouraging a student. Then he pushed on. "In any case, the Cyclops itself is a repetitive-pulsed, free-electron laser, which means the computer can tune it continuously to the most energy-efficient wavelength, a crucial feature. It starts with an intense beam of electrons which it accelerates to high velocity, then passes through an array of magnets we call the 'wiggler.' Those magnets are arranged in a line but they alternate in polarity, which causes the electrons passing through to experience rapid variations in magnetic-field strength and direction. What happens is, the alternating magnetic field 'wiggles' the beam of electrons into a wave, causing them to emit a microwave pulse—which is itself then passed back and forth, gaining strength at every pass. Eventually it saturates at a level roughly equal to the power of Grand Coulee Dam, and then—"

"Maybe you ought to get to the point," Vance said, feeling he was receiving a college lecture. He used to *give* college lectures, for chrissake, in archaeology. Were they just as tedious? he suddenly wondered.

"Of course." He pushed on, oblivious. "The whole operation is controlled by our Fujitsu supercomputer. The hardest part is getting the microwave pulses and the electron pulses to overlap perfectly in the wiggler. That part of the Cyclops, called the coaxial phase shifter, requires delicate fine-tuning. The alignment has to be critically adjusted, the focusing perfect, the cavity length—"

"Get back to the vehicle. I think I've heard all I need to know about the wonders of the Cyclops."

"Very well. The energy is focused, in bursts, from up there." He turned and pointed up the mountain. "That installation is a phased-array microwave transmission system, which delivers it to the spacecraft. To a port located on the sides of the vehicles down there. The port is a special heat-resistant crystal of synthetic diamond. Once inside, the beam is directed downward into the nozzle, where it strikes dry ice and creates plasma, producing thrust. The vehicle is single-stage-to-orbit."

"Nothing is burned." Vance had to admit it was a nifty idea. If you could do it.

"That's correct. The laser beam creates a shock wave, a burst of superheated gas moving at supersonic velocity out of the nozzle. By pulsing the beam, we form a detonation wave that hits the nozzle chamber and—"

"So it's really Star Wars in reverse," Vance interjected. "Bates is using all that fancy research in high-powered lasers to put up a satellite instead of shooting one down."

"The power is comparable. The superconducting coil we use to store power can pulse as high as twenty-five billion watts. The dry ice that is the 'propellant' is only about three hundred kilograms, a tiny percentage of the vehicle's weight, and since the vehicle is virtually all payload, we should be able to put it into a hundred-nautical-mile orbit in a matter of minutes. The beam energy will be roughly five hundred gigawatts per second and—"

"I get the picture," Vance interjected, tired of numbers. "But what you're really saying is that this transmission system up here on the mountain is the key to everything. If it goes down, end of show."

He was thinking. The terrorists had not destroyed anything, at least not up here. Which probably meant they intended to use it. The prospect chilled him.

"Okay, let's work backward to where the people are," he continued. "What's down below us here? The power has to get up here somehow."

"We're at one end of the island, down a bit from Command, which is underground. That's where the computer is, which handles the output frequencies of the Cyclops and also the trajectory analysis. It gets data from a radar up here on the mountain and uses that to provide guidance for the laser beam as the vehicle gains altitude. There are giant servo-mechanisms that keep the parabolic antennas trained on the vehicle as it lifts off the pad and heads into orbit. They also retrieve all the telemetry from the spacecraft, and—"

"What's belowground down there?" He was pointing toward the vehicles.

"That area has an excavated space below it for the multi-cavity amplifier bay. It's—"

"The what?"

"That's where the free-electron laser, the Cyclops, begins pumping up. Then the energy is sent up here"—he pointed back up the mountain—"to the phased-array transmission system."

"Right. So underground it's shaped something like a dumbbell, with the technical management staff at this end and then the operating people down there. What's in between? Just a big connecting tunnel?"

"Correct. And, of course, the communications conduits. For all the wiring."

Okay, Vance thought. Now we're getting somewhere. The terrorists will be split up. That's going to make things easier, and harder. They could be taken out one group at a time, but there also could be hostages at peril all over the place. These situations are always a lot cleaner when all the hostages are in one location.

"Any other connections?"

"Well, there's really only one." He shrugged, and ran his hand through his mane of white hair. Vance thought it made him look like an aging lion. "As you can imagine, these levels of power mean there are enormous quantities of waste heat. So Bates tunneled water conduits between a submerged pumping station on the other side of the island and a number of locations."

Vance's pulse quickened. "What do they lead to?"

"They run from the computer in Command, and the power plant down at the other end of the island, right beneath where we are now and . . . actually, one leads up to those heat exchangers there—" He was pointing up the mountain, past a large cinderblock building at the edge of the phased-array radar installation.

A tunnel filled with water, Vance thought. There's been enough swimming for a while. But if the system is off, then maybe . . .

"Then there must be an entry-point up there somewhere."

He smiled and nodded wistfully. "I assume there must be. But I don't know where it is."

"Think it's big enough for somebody to get into?"

"It should be. Everything was overengineered, since we weren't sure how much waste heat there would be."

"So all I have to do is get into the heat exchanger, then hope there's some air left in Bill's granite water pipe."

The old man looked worried. "Do you realize the kind of energy that goes through that conduit? If they should turn on the pumps, you'd be drowned in an instant and then dumped out to sea."

"I've already been drowned once on this trip. Another time won't matter." He shrugged. "But I've got to get inside and find out how many terrorists there are and where they're keeping the people." Once I figure out their deployment, he was thinking, we can plan the assault.

"It's dangerous," Mannheim mumbled. "That conduit was never intended to have anybody—"

"I'm forewarned." He was apprehensively rising to his feet and wincing at his aches. "All you have to do is get me inside."

2:36 P.M.

Georges LeFarge felt like he was getting a fever. Or maybe the room was just growing hot. All he knew was, he was miserable. He swabbed at his face with a moist paper towel and tried to breathe normally, telling himself he had to keep going, had to stick by Cally. This was no time to give in to these creeps and get sick.

Ardent and intense, Georges looked every inch the computer hacker he was; but he also was one of the finest aerospace engineers ever to come out of Cal Tech. Although his long hair and so-so beard were intended to deliver a fierce political statement, his benign blue eyes negated the message. He was an idealist, but one filled with love, not hate. His politics were as simplistic as his technical skills were state-of-the-art: he never managed to understand why everyone in the world did not act *rationally*.

He had grown up in New York's Soho district, living in a mammoth, sparsely furnished loft with his mother, a widely praised painter of massive, abstract oils—usually in black and ocher. Her depressing paintings were huge, but her income only occasionally was, and Georges's memory of his childhood was years of alternating caviar and spaghetti. His French Canadian father had long since returned to a log-and-clay cabin in northern Quebec, never to be heard from again.

He also remembered his mother's string of lovers, an emotional intrusion he never quite came to accept. The day he went off to MIT, on a National Merit Scholarship, was the happiest of his life. Or at least he had thought so until he got a call from Cally Andros asking him to come to work for SatCom.

He was now thirty-four, single, and he loved girls, or the idea of girls. No, the truth was that he loved one girl, and had forever. She was now his boss. After years of separation, they had finally dabbled at an affair here on Andikythera, but he had to admit it hadn't worked. At first it had seemed a good idea, his boyhood dream come true, but now he had realized maybe they were better off just being friends. She became a different person in bed, and one he found slightly terrifying.

But given what had just happened, all that seemed part of another, forgotten place and time.

In addition to having a fever, he was bone-tired and his neck ached. But he wanted desperately to stay alert. He stroked the wispy beard he had been trying to grow for the last four months, gazed at the terminal, and warned himself to stop thinking like an engineer and try to think like a terrorist. These European criminals had shown up just in time for the first space shot, which meant they had something planned that needed a vehicle. They weren't going to hold the facility for ransom: there was nothing here they could steal. Also, they had been very careful not to damage any of the systems.

Which meant their real program, whatever it was, needed the Cyclops to work and a vehicle to lift off. If that didn't happen, they were screwed. So, he thought, you sabotage Thursday's shot and you nix their plot, whatever it is.

But Cally would have a fit. Mr. Bates needed a success, and soon, or the whole SatCom gamble would go down the tubes. It was a lose-lose scenario. What to do?

Simple. Just keep working for now and hope. What else was there?

On the screen in front of him now was the output of a program in progress, this one called HI-VOLT, which was a daily low-power warm-up of the coils of the phased-array radar system on the mountain. The computer methodically checked all the power systems for any hint of malfunction, and the program had to be run, rain or shine. It was now time to kick on the pumps and heat exchangers and get going. Something to do. . . .

The cursor was flashing, ready for the "power on" command. He hit the Enter key, activating the pumps for the heat exchangers, then turned to see Cally approaching, winding her way through the workstations, led by the head terrorist, the fucker who called himself Number One. LeFarge could not get over the fact the bastard looked like an executive from the Arlington office, only better dressed.

"Georges, you've got to kill HI-VOLT," Cally said. Although she looked normal, there was extreme anxiety in her voice. The strain was coming through. "We have to do a different run." She was passing her fingers nervously through her hair. He loved her dark, Mediterranean tresses. "A trajectory analysis using SORT."

The Fujitsu supercomputer they were using was programmed with a special NASA program developed by Mc-Donnell-Douglas Astronautics Co. Called SORT, an abbreviation for Simulation and Optimization of Rocket Trajectories, it minimized the laser energy required for an insertion trajectory into low earth orbit. It also calculated the on-board nozzle vectors to adjust altitude while the vehicle was in flight. Midcourse corrections. All you had to do was program everything in.

"Now? But I just started—"

"Here's a list of what he wants." She glanced at Number One again, then handed over a sheet of blue paper.

He took it and looked down. Maybe they were about to tip their hand. But what could they know about computers?

He finally focused on the sheet. What? These weren't satellite trajectories, these were longitude and latitude coordinates. Then he studied it more carefully. They were abort targets.

CHAPTER EIGHT

2:37 P.M.

The conduit was roughly a meter and a half in diameter and pitch dark. He had expected that and had extracted a waterproof flashlight from an emergency kit in the wreckage of the Hind. It was helping, but not all that much. With the heat exchangers off, no water was flowing. The stone walls were merely moist, the curved sides covered with slime.

The tunnel sloped downward from the installation on the mountain as a gentle incline, and although the gray algae that swathed its sides now covered him, he had found niches in the granite to hang onto as he worked his way down.

Then it had leveled out, matching the terrain, and that was when he encountered the first water, now up around his waist. The radars up the hill, he realized, were only one of the producers of waste heat. Ahead, the tunnel he was in seemed to join a larger one from another site, as part of a general confluence.

Thank God all the systems are in standby, he thought. If

those massive pumps down by the shore start up, they'll produce a raging torrent that'll leave no place to hide. . . .

As he splashed through the dark, he found himself pondering if this was what he had been placed on the planet to do. Maybe he should never have left Yale. The pay was decent, the hours leisurely, the company congenial. Poking around in the hidden secrets of the past always gave solace to the spirit. What did humanity think about three thousand years ago? Five thousand? Five hundred? What were their loves, their hates, their fears, their dreams? Were they the same as ours? And why did humanity always need to worship something? Where did the drive come from to create—poetry, music, painting? These were all marvelous mysteries that we might never unravel, but they were among the most noble questions anyone could ask. What makes us human? It was the immortal quandary.

But when you asked that, you also had to ask the flip-side question. How could humanity create so much that was bad at the same time? So much tyranny, greed, hurt? How did all that beauty and ugliness get mixed up together down in our genes? Maybe he was about to find out more about the evil in the heart of man, coming up. . . .

He splashed and paddled his way onward, his flashlight sending a puny beam ahead, and tried to relate his location to the rest of the facility. Before entering through the heat exchanger atop the mountain, he had grilled Mannheim on the specifics of site layout. The old man, however, hadn't really known much about the nuts and bolts of the facility; his head was out in space somewhere. All the same, Vance found himself liking him, in spite of his encroaching senility. Even Homer was said to nod. Just hope you live long enough to get senile yourself.

Back to business. Ahead, settled into the top of the conduit, was a metal door just large enough for a man to work through. What was that for? he wondered. Maintenance access? If so, it must lead into the main facility somewhere.

He felt his way around the curved sides of the conduit, searching for flaws in the granite where he could get a handhold. Then he reached up and tested the door.

The metal was beginning to rust from the seawater, but it still looked workable. A large black wheel in the center, inset with gears, operated sliding bolts that fit into the frame.

This has to be fast, he told himself. Do a quick reconnoiter of the place and make mental notes. Look for entry-points and escape routes. Then get back in time for the radio chat with Pierre. About three hours, two to be on the safe side.

He braced himself against the stone sides of the conduit and—holding the flashlight with one hand—tried to budge the metal wheel.

Nothing. The contact with seawater had frozen it with rust. He tried again, shoving the flashlight into his belt and, grappling in the dark, twisting the wheel with both hands. Was it moving?

He felt a faint vibration make its way down the stone walls of the conduit, then there was a hum of huge electric motors starting somewhere. Somebody was turning on the systems.

He listened as the vibration continued to grow, and now the water level was beginning to rise, as the pumps down by the shore began priming. Were they about to turn them on full blast? The involuntary rush of his pulse and his breathing made him abruptly aware of how close the confining tunnel felt, the tight hermetic sense of claustrophobia. For the first time since landing on Andikythera he felt real fear. He hated the dark, the enclosed space, and now he was trapped.

Idiot, how did you get yourself into this? You're going to be drowned in about thirty seconds.

Now the roar of water began to overwhelm the hum of the pumps. The conduit was filling rapidly, and flow had begun. He realized that only about a foot of airspace remained at the top. Praying for a miracle, he heaved against the metal wheel one last time, and finally felt it break loose, begin to turn.

2:38 P.M.

"Abdoullah" had finished unpacking the second crate, and now he examined what he had: two fifteen-kiloton nuclear devices, made using enriched uranium-235 from the Kahuta Nuclear Research Center. He smiled again to think they had been smuggled out right from under the noses of the officials at Kahuta, directly up the security elevators leading down to the U^{235} centrifuge at Level Five.

The research center was situated more or less in between the sister cities of Rawalpindi and Islamabad, in northeast Pakistan, where it was surrounded by barren, scrub-brush rolling hills that looked toward the looming border of Afghanistan. Kahuta was the heart of Pakistan's nuclear-weapons program, and its many levels of high-security infrastructure were buried deep belowground. The only structure visible to a satellite was the telltale concrete cupola and an adjacent environmental-control plant for air filtration. Security was tight, with high fences, watchtowers, and an army barracks near at hand.

The security was for a reason. In 1975 Pakistan began acquiring hardware and technology for a plant capable of producing weapons-grade uranium. Bombs require 90 percent enrichment, and when the U.S. discovered the project, it had threatened to cut off aid if any uranium was enriched beyond 5 percent. Pakistan agreed, then went right ahead. Between 1977 and 1980, using dummy corporations and transshipments through third countries, the government smuggled from West Germany an entire plant for converting uranium powder into uranium hexafluoride, a compound easily gasified and then enriched. Two years later the Nuclear Research Center purchased a ton of specially hardened "maraging" steel, from West Germany, which was delivered already fabricated into round bars whose diameter exactly matched that of the (also) German gas centrifuges under construction at Kahuta. Shortly thereafter, the plant at Dera Ghazi Khan was on-line, producing uranium hexafluoride feedstock for the Kahuta enrichment facility, and the Kahuta facility was using it to turn out U^{235} enriched uranium in abundance.

At the same time, Pakistani operatives were hastening to acquire high-speed American electronic switches called krytrons, the triggering devices for a bomb. Their efforts to obtain nuclear detonators required several tries, but eventually they got what they needed. They dispensed with aboveground testing of the nuclear devices they had assembled, having procured the necessary data from China, and instead just went ahead and made their bombs. They then secured them on Level Five of the Kahuta reprocessing facility—against the day they would be needed.

Until now. Liberating two of those well-guarded A-bombs had required a lot of unofficial cooperation from the plant's security forces. Batteries of surface-to-air missiles protected Kahuta from air penetration, and elite paratroopers and army tanks reinforced the many checkpoints, making sure that no vehicle, official or private, could enter or leave the complex without a stamped authorization by the security chief. Only a *lot* of money in the right hands could make two of the devices disappear. Sabri Ramirez had seen to that small technicality. . . .

Abdoullah patted one of the nuclear weapons casually and admired it. The bomb itself was a half meter in diameter, its outer casing of Octol carefully packed inside a polished steel sheath embedded with wires. Expensive but available commercially, Octol was a 70–30 mixture of cyclotetramethylenetetranitramine and trinitrotoluene, known colloquially as HMX and TNT. It was stable, powerful, and the triggering agent of choice for nuclear devices. Inside the Octol encasing each device were twenty-five kilograms of 93 percent enriched U^{235}. When the external Octol sphere was evenly detonated, it would compress the uranium core sufficiently to create a "critical mass," causing the naturally occurring radioactive decay of the uranium to focus in upon itself. Once the radiation intensified, it started an avalanche, an instantaneous chain reaction of atom-splitting that converted the uranium's mass into enormous quantities of energy.

The trick to making it work was an even, synchronous implosion of the outer sphere, which was the job of the high-tech krytron detonator switches. . . .

Which, Abdoullah realized, were still in the Sikorsky. The krytrons were packed separately and handled as though they were finest crystal.

"Rais," he said, looking up and addressing his Berkeley classmate now standing by the door, "I need the detonators."

"Well, they're in the cockpit, where we stowed them." He was tightening his commando sweatband, itching to try out his Uzi, still unfamiliar. Would the others notice? In any case, he wasn't here to run errands.

"Then go get them, for chrissake." He had considered Rais to be an asshole from the day they first met in the Advanced Quantum Mechanics class at college. Nothing that had happened since had in any way undermined that conviction. The guy thought he was hot stuff, God's gift to the world. It was not a view that anybody who knew him shared.

"Why don't *you* go get them?" Rais said, not moving.

"Because I want to check these babies over and make sure everything is a go." What a jerk. "Come on, man, don't start giving me a lot of shit, okay? This is serious. Everybody's got to pull his weight around here."

Rais hesitated, his manhood on the line, and then decided to capitulate. At least for now. Abdoullah was starting to throw his weight around, get on the nerves. The guy was real close to stepping out of line.

"All right, fuck it." He clicked the safety on his Uzi on and off and on, then holstered it.

"As long as you're at it, why don't you just take them directly down to the clean room. We'll be assembling everything there anyway, since that's where the elevator is they use to go up and prep the vehicles."

"That's cool. See you down there." Rais closed the door and walked out into the Greek sunshine. He was starting to like this fucking place.

2:39 P.M.

Vance shoved the metal door open just as the roar of the onrushing water reached the confluence at the intersection of the tunnel, a mere hundred yards ahead. The tunnel was almost full now, the water flow increasing.

They're about to turn on the Cyclops, he thought. You've got about fifteen seconds left.

He pulled himself through the metal door, soaked but alive, and rolled onto a cement floor. With his last remaining strength he reached over and tipped the metal door shut, then grabbed the wheel and gave it a twist. Down below he could feel the wall of water surge by.

He thought he was going to faint, but instead he took a deep breath and pulled out the flashlight. . . .

. . . And found himself in a communications conduit, consisting of a concrete floor with styrofoam insulation over-head. All around him stretched what seemed miles of coaxial cables, wrapped in huge circular strands. The conduit also contained fiber-optics bundles for carrying computer data to guide the parabolic antennas up on the mountain as they tracked the space vehicle.

The major contents of the conduit, however, were mas-sive copper power-transmission cables. What had Mannheim warned? How many gigawatts per second? The numbers were too mind-boggling to comprehend, or bother remem-bering. All they meant was that if the Cyclops were suddenly turned on, the Gaussian fields of electromagnetic flux would probably rearrange his brain cells permanently.

He rose and moved down the conduit, feeling along its curved sides, his back braced against the large bundle of power wires in the center while ahead of him the darkness gaped. A few yards farther, though, and the probing beam of his flashlight revealed a terminus where some of the shielded fiber optics had been shunted off into the wall, passing through a heavy metal sleeve.

Although it was welded into a steel plate bolted to the side of the wall, large handles allowed the bolts to be turned without the aid of special wrenches. Whoever designed the fiber optics for this tunnel, he thought, didn't want a lot of Greek workmen down here waving tools around after a long lunch of guzzling retsina. The fibers were too vulnerable to stand up to any banging.

He grasped the handles and began to twist one, finding the bolts well lubricated. After four turns, it opened. The second yielded just as easily. Then the third and the fourth.

He took a deep breath, thinking this might be his first encounter with the hostages, and the terrorists. Then he slid the metal plate back away from the wall and tried to peer through. The opening was approximately a meter wide, with the bundle of fiber-optics cables directly through the middle. Still, he found just enough clearance to slip past and into the freezing cold of the room used to prep the payloads for the vehicles.

2:40 P.M.

"What's this all about?" LeFarge looked again at the sheet, then up at Number One. "SORT is intended to calculate orbital parameters. Optimize them."

"And if there is an abort? It has to go down somewhere."

"You're talking about a prespecified abort?" LeFarge was trying to sound dumb. "The Cyclops can't power an ICBM." It probably could, but he didn't want to mention that.

The terrorist who called himself Number One was not impressed. "That's a question we will let the computer decide. I happen to believe it can. You just send it up, then you abort. When you fail to achieve orbital velocity, it comes down. The nose has a reentry shield, since you are planning to reuse the vehicle. It should work very nicely."

Georges looked at Cally. He did not want to admit it, but this guy was right. He had thought about that a lot. Any private spaceport could be seized by terrorists and turned into a missile launch site. Was that their plan?

"I won't do it," he heard himself saying. "I refuse."

"That is a mistake," Number One replied calmly. "I will simply shoot one of your technicians here every five minutes until you begin." He smiled. "Would you like to pick the first? Preferably someone you can manage without."

"You're bluffing." He felt a chill. Something told him what he had just said wasn't true. This man, with his expensive suit and haircut, meant every word. He was a killer. Georges knew he had never met anyone remotely like him.

"Young man, you are an amateur." His eyes had grown narrow, almost disappearing behind his gray aviator shades. "Amateurs do not know the first thing about bluffing. Now don't try my patience."

He turned and gestured one of the technicians toward them. He was a young man in his mid-twenties. He came forward and Number One asked his name.

"I'm Chris Schneider," he said. His blond hair and blue eyes attested to the fact. His father was a German farmer in Ohio, his mother a primary-school teacher. He had taken a degree in Engineering from Ohio State, then stumbled upon the dream job of his life. He was now thinking about moving to Greece.

"I'm sorry to have to make an example of you, Chris," Number One said, drawing out his Walther. . . .

2:41 P.M.

Vance realized he was in a satellite "clean room," painted a septic white with bright fluorescents overhead. Along one wall were steel tables, several of which held giant "glove boxes" that enabled a worker to handle satellite components without human contamination. Alongside those were instruments to measure ambient ionization and dust. Other systems in the room included banks of electronic equipment about whose function he could only speculate.

And what was that? . . . there, just above the door . . . it looked like a closed-circuit TV monitor, black-and-white. It seemed to be displaying the vague movements of a large control room, one with banks of computer screens in long rows and marshalled lines of technicians monitoring them. He studied the picture for a second, wondering why it seemed so familiar, and then he realized it looked just like TV shots of the Kennedy Space Center.

Shivering from the cold, he moved closer to the screen, which was just clear enough to allow him to make out some of the figures in what had to be the command center. However, he saw only staffers; no sign of Bill Bates. One individual stood out, his suit and tie a marked contrast to the general open-shirt atmosphere, and he looked like he was giving the orders. He was now chatting with a woman and another, younger man, seated at a keyboard.

Then the well-dressed guy turned and beckoned one of the staffers forward. He said something to him and then— Jesus!—he pulled a pistol. . . .

2:42 P.M.

"No!" Cally screamed, but it was already too late. Before Chris Schneider even saw it coming, Ramirez shot him precisely between the eyes, neatly and without fanfare. The precision was almost clinical, and he was dead by the time he collapsed onto the gray linoleum tiles of the floor. His body lay motionless, his head nestled in a growing pool of dark blood.

Georges LeFarge looked on unbelieving. Had he really seen it? No, it was too grotesque. Chris, murdered in cold blood right before his eyes. They had been talking only yesterday about going to Crete for the weekend, maybe renting a car. . . . Death had always been an abstraction, never anything to view up close. He had never seen a body. He had never even imagined such things could really happen; it was only in the movies, right? Until this moment he had never confronted actual murder ever in his life.

Calypso Andros felt a shock, then a surge of emotional Novocain as her adrenaline pumped. Right then and there she decided that she was going to kill this bastard herself, personally, with her own hands. Number One, whoever he was, was a monster. No revenge . . .

Then the superego intervened. *He's* still got the gun. Wait, and get the son of a bitch when he's not expecting it.

"Georges," she said quietly, finally collecting herself, "you'd better do what he says."

LeFarge was still too astonished to think, let alone talk.

This horror was outside every realm of reason. He had no way to file it within any known category contained in his mind.

"She is giving you excellent advice," Number One was saying. "You would be wise to listen. In any case, I merely want you to demonstrate the technical capabilities of this system." He smiled as though nothing had happened. "An intellectual exercise."

Georges looked at Cally and watched her nod. Her eyes seemed almost empty. Was it shock? How could she manage to carry on?

Well, he thought, if she can do it, then so can I.

Slowly he revolved and examined the computer terminal in front of him. The cool green of the screen was all that remained recognizable, the only thing to which he could still relate.

"All right." He barely heard his own words as he glanced down at the sheet. "I'll see if I can put in a run."

The room around them was paralyzed in time, the single thunk of the pistol having reverberated louder than a cannon shot. Like Georges, none of the other young technicians had ever witnessed an overt act of violence. It produced a new reality, a jolt that made the senses suddenly grow sharper, the hearing more acute, the periphery of vision wider.

Still in shock, he typed an instruction into his Fujitsu workstation, telling it to start back-calculating the trajectory of an abort splashdown for various locations. Then he began typing in the numbers on the sheet. The first coordinates, he realized at once, were somewhere close. But where?

2:43 P.M.

Vance watched the control room freeze as the body slumped to the floor, and he felt his fingers involuntarily bunch into a fist. The bastards were killing hostages already. They definitely were terrorists, right out of the textbook. Kill one, and frighten a thousand. Except they might not stop with one. He foresaw a long day. And night.

The victim had been hardly more than a college kid. Murdered at random, and for no other apparent reason than to frighten the rest into submission. A technique that was as old as brutality. But that terrorist trick, management by intimidation, worked both ways. Take away their Uzis and these smug bastards could just as easily be turned into quivering Jell-O. All human beings had psychological pressure points that could be accessed. What separated the wheat from the chaff was what happened when somebody got to those points. He often wondered what *he* would do. He prayed he would never have to find out. . . .

Then he watched as the young man at the terminal began typing in something off a sheet of paper. Whatever the terrorist had intended to accomplish by his wanton murder, apparently it had worked. The other technicians were all staring down at their screens, scared to move. Whatever had gone on, everybody was back to business. But what did these thugs want?

Sadly he turned away from the screen to reexamine his surroundings . . . and noticed a workstation, situated off to the left side of the door. What had Bill once said? They practically had computer terminals in the bathrooms. This one obviously was intended for quick communications with the command crews from here in this freezing white room.

Keeping an eye on the TV monitor, he moved over to take a look. Instructions began appearing on the bright green screen, indicating it was tied into a computer network at the facility. Yes, somebody—probably the young analyst out there —was typing in a complex series of commands. Above that, on the screen, another sequence had been aborted. It had been some sort of run called HI-VOLT. That must have been what had jolted him when he was out in the conduit.

He studied the screen, trying to figure out what was going on. Only the hum of air conditioning broke the silence, and the quiet helped him to think. . . .

Of course! These bastards were planning to use the Cyclops—or worse, its spacecraft—to . . . what?

He recalled seeing the second chopper arrive and the boys unload two crates. Its cargo wasn't going to be a Christmas present to the world. Whatever it was, they were poised to deliver it just about anywhere on the globe.

So what was their target? He studied the computer screen, hoping to get an inkling. But he saw only numbers. In pairs. They looked like . . . latitude and longitude. Coordinates. What did that mean? The first ones were nearby, maybe somewhere near Crete. So what were they doing? Reprogramming the vehicle into a missile? Terrific.

That was the first half of the bad news. The second half was that whatever they were up to, there also seemed a good chance they might try to blow up the SatCom facility after they were finished, just to cover their tracks. Dead men make no IDs in some faraway courtroom years from now.

He could probably terminate that plan by just sabotaging some of the fiber optics in the conduit, thereby putting the whole facility out of commission. But that would screw Bill too, and probably end up costing SatCom millions. Bates was close enough to being suicidal already. This was probably going to put him over the edge in any case.

Keep that as a last-ditch option, he told himself. And besides, everything at the moment was only guesswork. The thing to do first was to get a better handle on the situation without the terrorists knowing. The question was how.

He looked around the room again, wondering. And then his eye fell on the terminal and a thought dawned. Why not see if you can interrupt the computer run in progress and have a chat with the analyst at the keyboard, the one with the beard now typing in the numbers appearing on the green screen?

He reached down and tested one of the keys, but nothing happened. The data being typed in just kept on coming. What now? How to cut into the system and send him a little personal E-mail? Get his attention. Something. Then he realized the keyboard had an on/off switch, which was currently shunting it out of the system.

Guess that's to keep somebody from screwing up a run by leaning against it, he thought. How much time is there? Any minute now somebody could come wandering in. Probably this window of opportunity only had a few minutes to go.

He switched on the keyboard and again gave a letter a tap. This time it instantly appeared on the screen, highlighted. A glance at the TV monitor told him that the startled analyst at the keyboard had frozen his fingers in mid-tap, bringing everything to a halt.

Quickly he started typing, hoping that none of the terrorists had the brains to be monitoring the computers.

DON'T STOP. JUST ANSWER.

The young analyst, he could tell from the monitor, had a funny look on his face, obvious even through his scraggly beard. But he was cool.

WHO ARE YOU? came back the answer.

A FRIEND. NEED INFORMATION. FAST. HOW MANY TERRORISTS?

TEN. The reply appeared. BUT I THINK ONE WAS KILLED.

Plus those who came in on the Sikorsky this morning, Vance thought. Looked like another three. Then he typed in another question.

WHAT DO THEY WANT?

DON'T KNOW. MAYBE USE VEHICLES. The typing was quick and experienced. THEY SAY FACILITY TO KEEP OPERATING NORMALLY.

WHERE IS BATES? Vance typed back. IS HE OKAY?

IN HIS OFFICE. THINK HE'S OKAY.

That's a relief, he thought. Guess Bill's still got some hostage value to them.

TELL HIM ULYSSES HAS LANDED. BE OF GOOD CHEER.

The answer came back. WHO ARE YOU? I'M SCARED. THEY KILLED CHRIS.

I SAW IT. BUT THAT'S PROBABLY ALL FOR A WHILE. STANDARD TERROR TACTICS. NOW ERASE THIS CONVERSATION.

Something was typed on the screen and their words immediately all disappeared. And just in time. . . .

2:48 P.M.

Rais had finished retrieving the box of krytrons from the cockpit of the Huey and was headed down the elevator for the area directly below and south of the launch facility, the clean room where SatCom's expensive communications satellites were going to be prepped for launch. Abdoullah was a jerk, but he had been right about that: it was the obvious location to install the detonators and set the timing mechanisms.

As the elevator door opened, his Uzi was still holstered just below his right hip and in his hands was the box of detonators, all carefully secured in their beds of bubble-wrap. He stepped into the hallway, then headed down for the closed door of the clean room.

2:58 P.M.

"William Bates, I must say, made a wise choice when he hired you to run this project, Miss Andros," Ramirez was saying. He had just lit a new cigar. "I have to commend his judgment."

"Well, if you think I'm doing such a great job, you'd better let me go on doing it," Cally managed to answer, trying to get a grip on herself. She had her arms crossed, mainly to try to keep her hands from shaking. When Chris was shot, she was so stunned she'd repressed the horror. Now the numbness was wearing off and she wanted to scream. Just one long wail to purge everything. She was biting her lip to try to repress the impulse. "I need to go down to the launch facility and check with the tech crews."

Toughen up and think, she told herself. These terrorists are up to something, and the sooner you figure out what it is, the better for everybody.

"As a matter of fact"—he nodded—"I need to go down myself and see how things are proceeding. So why don't we both go, Miss Andros."

"Around here I'm called Dr. Andros." She was feeling her control coming back. Two could play the power game.

"But of course." He nodded. "In a professional environment we all like to be treated accordingly. I respect that, and expect no less myself." He surveyed the room, its SatCom technicians still stunned. Then his eye caught the tall, bearded Iranian, Salim, now lounging by the door with his Uzi, and motioned him over.

"Get this body out of here."

The Iranian nodded and strolled over. Cally studied him, wondering. She had been trying to size up the team for some time, and she still had not figured them all out. But this one, heavy-set and defiantly bearded, seemed somewhat at odds with the others. He clearly had no taste to clean up Number One's murder; you could see it in his eyes.

"Where—?"

"In the lobby. It's disrupting the professional environment."

He nodded again and without a word grabbed Chris Schneider by the shoulders and began dragging him past.

"Dr. Andros"—Number One turned back to her—"already I feel closer to you than I do to half of my men. I think you and I will make a good team."

"You have got to be fucking kidding."

He merely laughed, then spoke to another of the terrorists, a young Arab. After apparently ordering him to stay behind in Command to keep an eye on things, he motioned Cally to lead the way through the security doors.

They edged around Salim, still moving the body, and out into the lobby. The first thing she noticed was that the guard was missing from the front security station. Instead a wide dark stain covered the desk. Blood.

She whirled on Number One. "What happened to Milos, you bastard?"

"Regrettably he is no longer with us." He shrugged, not pausing as he took her arm and shoved her on.

"You mean you murdered him, too?" She felt herself about to explode. She had loved that Greek, who spent more time worrying about soccer scores than he did about security.

Thinking about his death, she felt a wave of nausea sweep over her. "You bloodthirsty—"

"Please, we're going to try to be professionals, remember," he interrupted her calmly. "We will be working together in the days ahead, and animosity will serve no purpose."

She thought of several responses, but squelched them all. Talking wasn't going to make things any better. In that respect, he was right. Talk would have no effect.

They were facing the tunnel leading to the mechanical-systems sector at the other end of the island. The large metal doors, operated from the security system at the desk, had been opened, slid back, and permanently secured. The short-circuiting of the security system had disabled all the electronic locks in the facility.

Scrutinizing them, she felt sadness. All the months of fine-tuning and technical calibration throughout the facility, had all that effort been wasted? Probably not, she suspected. These goons, true to their word, had taken great pains not to disturb anything in Command. So far everything had apparently conformed to their plan, except for something to do with a helicopter. Whatever that was, it had taken them by surprise. What was it?

Ramirez said nothing as they started down the asphalt pavement of the underground passageway. Over a thousand meters long and illuminated by fluorescent lighting, its cinderblock walls were wide and high enough to accommodate a standard Greek truck or two small lorries. Cally noted the deserted guard desk at the far end. Had he been killed as well? she wondered.

"Let me put your mind at ease," Number One announced, as though reading her thoughts. "The other guards have merely been disarmed and locked in their quarters. As I said, we have no desire for any unnecessary bloodshed."

"More lies?" She tossed her hair.

"You should try to believe me. Again, trust will make things easier for us both."

She pushed past the doors at the end of the passageway and together they entered the first sector, Launch Control.

Beyond, another set of doors led to the giant underground installation for the superconducting coil, which fed into a massive glass tube holding the wiggler, heart of the Cyclops. Above that, now unseen, stood the launch vehicles, "rockets" that carried no fuel.

Neither was yet primed; they planned to ready the vehicle designated VX-1 just before launch. In fact, nothing had happened since the test the night before. Tech crews were checking the instruments, knowing only that a communications breakdown with Command had occurred and some strange visitors had shown up in a helicopter. *Something* was going on, but nobody knew what.

"A very impressive installation," Number One said, watching as the technicians all nodded their greetings. "Incidentally, there is no point in alarming any of them now. For the moment, you should just proceed normally."

"That's why you're here, right?" she shot back. "To make sure there's all this normality. Things were pretty normal before you and your band of thugs barged in."

"We are colleagues now, Dr. Andros. I'm here to observe the lift-off we all are so anxious for. Please, for starters I would like to tag along and have you show me around. You're a congenial guide."

You bet, she thought. You'll discover how "congenial" I am soon enough.

Of course, she had not yet formulated a strategy. One bright spot was the voice on the radio this morning? Was somebody on the island still free? She had peeked out into the lobby long enough to learn that the mysterious "guard" had shot one of the Germans and then escaped. So who was it? That was what she wanted to find out next. . . .

But first, business. She approached Jordan Jaegar, a young Cal Tech graduate and friend of Georges who had been with the project from the start.

"J.J., how long did the coil temperature stay nominal?"

Although he had a master's in mechanical engineering, Jordan sported shoulder-length hair and had just gotten a tattoo on his right bicep—an elaborate rendering of his initials, J.J., which he much preferred to be called. He liked the fact Dr. Andros remembered that.

"For just over twenty-one minutes," he announced with pride, his eyes discreetly taking in her hourglass figure. "Long enough. Then it started creeping up, but we'd have almost inserted into orbit by that time. And after twenty-nine minutes it was only five degrees Celsius higher. No sweat, Dr. Andros."

Who, J.J. was wondering, was this hotshot standing next to Dr. Andros? He had seen a lot of SatCom brass come and go, but this dude was definitely new. What was his scene? No question, though, the boss lady was really pissed about something. She also did not seem interested in introducing this new creep to anyone. Fine. There was enough to worry about without more head-office brass.

Cally nodded. "The on–line readout in Command showed that the Cyclops reached saturation at twelve point three-five gigawatts."

"Right," J.J. agreed. "The wiggler went critical and we used the phased array to dissipate the energy." He beamed. "Hell, we could have sent her up last night. The whole thing was textbook."

He knew she already knew all that. But he figured there was no harm in impressing this front-office creep that all the money they'd spent hadn't been wasted. SatCom was definitely on-budget from *his* section. Management *had* to be happy. Payoff time was just around the corner. This time next week, SatCom's stock was going to be pure gold. After VX-1 went up, there wouldn't be any more shit from Arlington. They'd be passing out stock bonuses like fucking peppermints. He figured a hot new Nissan was definitely in his future.

"Good," Dr. Andros said, but she seemed distracted, having trouble staying focused. Something was definitely wrong, but she was hiding it. "How about sending a data summary to my terminal in Command."

Cally walked on past J.J., thinking as fast as she could. None of the technicians here knew what had happened. When they found out, were they going to fall apart, endangering everybody and everything? Maybe, she thought, it would be better now to just continue normally as long as possible.

Number One, whoever he was, wasn't carrying an Uzi now; instead he had a 9mm skillfully concealed beneath his double-breasted. It was all very stylish. He was keeping the takeover on low profile, at least down here where the vehicles were. Maybe, she told herself, he doesn't feel as sure of himself here, or maybe he needs to keep their plans a secret. So they're definitely up to something.

As they walked past the massive steel housings enclosing the wiggler's controls, Ramirez suddenly paused and cleared his throat.

"Dr. Andros, what is the payload for the test launching? You certainly wouldn't put a multimillion-dollar communications satellite at peril during your maiden run."

He isn't stupid, she thought. He understands the economics of the satellite business.

"It's just a test. With a dummy payload."

"Good. We will have a real payload for you. It won't be low-cost, but it will definitely get you some attention. We—"

At that moment his walkie-talkie crackled.

3:00 P.M.

Abdoullah had completed his inspection and, together with Shujat, was loading the crates back onto the small trucks intended to move them down to the clean room.

"We'll have to adjust the timers very carefully," he was saying to Shujat, now bent over with him, "make sure they're synched critically with the trajectory."

The second Pakistani engineer nodded. "Right. So we'll do it when the trajectory computer runs are completed. That's scheduled for 2200 hours tonight."

"Sounds good." Abdoullah clicked on his black walkie-talkie, a small Kenwood, and tried to sound professional. "Firebird Two to Firebird One. Do you read?"

There was a burst of static, and then Ramirez's voice sounded. "I copy you, Firebird Two. Any problems?"

"Negative. The items look in perfect condition. We are taking them down to the clean room now to install the detonators."

"Fine," Ramirez replied. "I'll meet you there." The radio voice paused. "Incidentally, be aware there is somebody loose on the island who seems a trifle out of synch with the situation."

"Where is he?" He was signaling for Shujat to come over and listen. Having a problem or two always made things more fun.

"Probably up at the communications complex on the mountain. So far he's only been a nuisance, but the matter will have to be resolved. In the meantime, don't let anything slow down your work. We need to be prepared for the next phase, including whatever time flexibility we might need."

Abdoullah did not exactly like the sound of that. He had a troubling feeling that Number One wasn't exactly telling everybody the whole plan. He was not a man you instinctively trusted. Who the hell *was* he, really. Of course, in this business you didn't necessarily trust anybody, but still, when you were working together it was nice to think that everybody was on the same wavelength.

In his view, a lot of questions still needed answering. Like where had the money come from to mount this operation? The preparations, the bribes, the equipment and the second chopper, the Sikorsky—the Hind, he knew, had been stolen —the payments to all the third parties involved. Everything had required money, tons of it, but the man known as Number One clearly had all he needed. So how had this character come up with all those millions of bucks?

His intuition told him that not everybody was going to make it to the safe house in Malta when the time came. At the moment he had confidence only in Rais and Shujat. And Rais was a jerk. In fact, he hadn't seen him since he went out to get the krytrons from the cockpit of the Sikorsky, but he should be down in the clean room by now. . . .

3:01 P.M.

Vance heard a sound outside the clean room, footsteps. Somebody was approaching, but not with a walk that suggested familiarity with the place.

This might turn out to be his hoped-for break. Maybe he was about to have a nice face-to-face with one of the terrorists. At last, an opportunity for some answers.

He slipped back against the wall next to the door, his wet clothes chilling him in the low temperature. But he sensed that things were about to warm up. The person behind the door paused for a second, then shoved it open. A box appeared, then a face. It was young and cocky.

"Don't even *think* about making a sound, asshole." He slapped his Walther against the guy's cheek, then yanked the Uzi from his leg holster and pulled him into the room. Next he kicked the door shut and shoved his new guest to the floor. The box he was carrying thumped down beside him.

In the glare of the fluorescents the "terrorist" looked like an aging graduate student, except he was wearing a Palestinian *kaffiyeh*. Vance ripped it away, rolled him over, and inserted the Uzi into his mouth. A metal barrel loosening the teeth, he knew, did marvels for a wiseguy's powers of concentration. That was one of the first lessons he'd picked up from the boys at ARM. And this one was no exception. He stared up, genuine terror in his eyes, and moaned.

"Speak English? Just nod."

He dipped his forehead forward, eyes still in shock.

"Good. Now we're going to play Twenty Questions. That's about the number of teeth you've got, so each time I get an answer I don't buy, one of them goes. And when we run out of teeth, you won't be able to talk any more, so I'll just blow your head off. Okay, how're we doing? We understand each other so far?"

He nodded again and gave an airless grunt.

"Great. Looks like we're on a roll. Now, how many more of your team is in there? Hold up fingers. Very slowly. I was never good at fast arithmetic."

His eyes were cloudy, but he managed to lift five fingers.

This guy is one of the new arrivals, Vance thought. I counted three of them. So that means two others are down here as well. Those first guys were the pros, but this kid barely knows which end of an Uzi to hold.

"Do they know you came back here?" He rattled the barrel of the Uzi around in his mouth, just to keep him focused.

Again he nodded, even more terrified.

Okay, he thought, we're going to have to make this a short chat.

"Are there hostages down here?"

Again the man nodded.

"How many?"

He just shrugged, clearly having no idea.

Well, Vance thought, maybe it's time to get this show on the road.

He slowly removed the barrel, then ripped off a portion of the *kaffiyeh* lying on the floor, balled it, and stuffed it into his mouth. Next he tore off a longer strip and tied it around his head, securing the gag. The eyes were still terrified.

"By the way," he said, "what's in the box?"

A new look of even-greater horror entered the eyes. He's really scared now, Vance thought. Interesting.

"Well, well, maybe we ought to take a look."

He reached over and opened the lid. There, nestled inside several layers of bubble-wrap, were what looked like large, oversized blue transistors.

Bingo, he thought, what have we here? Could it be these are the tickets to the upcoming show. This ain't chopped liver.

"Okay, pal, on your feet. We're going to get moving. Just you and me. And we're going to take along your little box of toys. You can tell me what they are later."

The young terrorist started to rise, gingerly.

"See that opening over there"—he pointed—"where the wires enter into the conduit? We're going through there, you first. You're about to have some experience in mountain climbing. The workout might do you good."

That was when the door opened.

CHAPTER NINE

3:18 Г.М.

Vance cocked the Pakistani's Uzi and trained it on the door, not sure what to do. The fear was that he might inadvertently kill a friendly. Hostage situations always presented that harrowing possibility. Quick identifications and quick decisions were what made good antiterrorist teams. He was afraid he had neither skill. He wasn't even that great a shot.

But events were to break his way for a change. As the door swung in, he saw a woman framed there. He needed only to lock eyes with her to know she was a friendly. Okay, one ID out of the way. Then a man behind her, dressed in a tailored charcoal suit, reached out to seize her and pull her in front of him.

No good. As Vance watched, mesmerized, she elbowed him in the chin, sending him reeling backward and out into the hallway. Then, before he could recover, she slammed the door, using her other elbow to hit the blue Airlock button next to the frame. With electronic efficiency, the red Sealed light above the door blinked on and bolts around the edges clicked into place.

She turned, still shaking, and looked at him. "Please tell me you're not one of them, too."

"No way. I'm just a tourist." Vance examined her and liked her on the spot. She was a stunner, with dark hair and an eye-catching sweater emblazoned with the SatCom logo— one of those take-charge women made for the modern age. Exhibit A: she'd just iced the thug in the hallway. "And who are you?"

Instead of answering, she glanced over at the Pakistani, his mouth gagged. "I see you've already met one of our new guests."

"We got acquainted informally. Not exactly a meaningful relationship." He stared at the door, wondering how long it would hold. "By the way, is that guy outside who I think he is? Didn't he just shoot somebody in your control room?"

"He did. And you were probably about to be next." She took time to examine him more closely. He couldn't tell if she liked what she saw, but her look quickly turned to puzzlement. "You're soaking wet."

"I had an afternoon dip."

"What? You swam here?" She looked about the room, then back. "How—"

"In a manner of speaking."

"Who are you?"

"Mike Vance." He extended his hand. "Friend of Bill's. It's a long story. In real life I run a sailboat charter operation back in the Bahamas. And you?"

"Cally Andros. I run *this* place, or at least I did until last night." She shook his hand, tentatively. "So what are you doing here?"

"As I said. Just an island tourist. But I've got to tell you, Greek hospitality isn't what it used to be." He reached down and picked up the box with the krytrons. "Now what do you say we get out of here before that guy outside comes blasting in?"

"Through that door?" She laughed. "That's an inch and a

half of steel. Even better, it's fail-safe, which means that if the electronics fail, it stays in the locked mode anyway."

He liked her snappy answers. "Nothing lasts forever. I strongly recommend we do ourselves a favor and move along." He turned and indicated the open panel where the wiring entered. "How does the back way sound to you?"

"You came in through *there?*" She clearly was startled. "You're either very smart, or very stupid. That's where—"

"I'll tell you what's really stupid. Standing around while those goons figure out how to take out that door. Because there's something in here I've got a feeling they're going to want back very badly."

"You mean him?" She pointed at the Pakistani, still gagged, hunching down on the floor.

"This one? Doubt that. He's just a water carrier. No, I'm talking about the gadgets inside this box."

"What . . . ?"

"Check them out." He passed it over. "What do you think?"

She lifted out one of the glass-covered units, three wires extending from one end, and her dark eyes widened. "My God, do you know what this is?"

"Tell me."

"It's a krytron." She rotated it in her hand, gently, as though it were crystal. "I've never actually seen one before, only pictures. You can trigger a nuclear device with one of these. They're worth millions on the black market."

"Guess we just made the Fortune Five Hundred." He laughed. "If we live long enough to cash them in. Should be lots of buyers around the Middle East."

"Do you realize—?"

"The nightmare's finally come true? Looks that way." He sighed. "Terrorists are building a bomb. Or, more likely, they've managed to steal one somewhere."

"One?" She shivered from the cold and pulled at her sweater. "There must be more than one, if they've got all these detonators."

"But a bomb is just another chunk of enriched uranium without these, right?"

"Well, if they're planning to do more than threaten . . . Oh, my God." She froze. "That explains why they've got Georges changing trajectories. They—"

"What! Are they tinkering with your rockets?"

"So far just the computer-guidance part. But if they put a bomb on *VX-1*, who knows what they could end up doing?"

"How does nuclear blackmail sound? But nobody goes to this much trouble just to shake down a corporation. There're lots of easier ways." He paused to ponder. "Ten to one it's not SatCom they're holding for ransom. They're aiming for a lot higher stakes. They're probably planning to shake down a country somewhere. No prizes for guessing which one."

"The U.S.," she guessed anyway. "Think they can get away with it?"

"Probably not without these." He closed the box. "Maybe we've just pulled the plug. So let's take these and get out of here."

She glanced down at the surly Pakistani. "What about him?"

"We could take him with us, as a bargaining chip, but I don't think he's worth the bother." Vance reached over and turned his face up. "How about it? Do your buddies out there care whether you live or die?"

His eyes betrayed his fear they did not.

"Didn't really think so," Vance revolved back. "I say we leave him. They'll probably execute him anyway, for being a screwup and losing these." He tucked the box under his arm, then turned back one last time. "Tell your chief we're going to take good care of them. They're the world's insurance policy." He pointed toward the opening into the wiring shaft. "Want to go first?"

"The conduit?" She frowned.

"You get used to it. It's just—"

"I really can't believe any of this is happening." She turned, walked over, and—with only minor hesitation—began climbing through.

At that moment, the Pakistani suddenly rolled to his feet and lunged for the sealed door. Vance whirled to try and catch him, but it was too late. He had already thrown his body against the release button. The seal clicked off, and in an instant their security evaporated.

"Go!" he turned back and yelled, but she was already through.

What now? he wondered fleetingly. Stay and shoot it out, or disappear.

The second option had more appeal.

He dived for the open grate of the conduit, but the door was already opening. The Paki couldn't yell, but when the door slid back, he pushed through . . . and was cut down by a fusillade of automatic-weapons fire. The impact blew him back into the room, sending his riddled body full length across the floor.

Vance swung around the Uzi and laid down a blast of covering fire through the doorway, which had the effect of clearing the opening for a second. He got off a couple of last rounds, just for good measure, then turned and hurled himself into the communications shaft.

No sooner had he pulled himself inside than rounds of fire began ricocheting through behind him. The aim, however, was wide, and he managed to flatten himself and stay out of the way.

Then the firing abruptly stopped.

They must have seen what's in here, he realized, all the wiring.

"Are you all right?" It was Cally's voice, somewhere in the dark ahead.

"I'm doing fine." He paused, hating the next part. "Only one small problem."

"What—?"

"I managed to drop our insurance policy on the floor in there. They're back in business."

3:20 P.M.

Isaac Mannheim checked his watch and then gazed down the hill, marking the time with growing impatience. Coping with inactivity, he felt, was the most extraordinarily difficult task in life. In fact, he never understood how anybody could retire, when three lifetimes would not be adequate for all one's dreams. The tall man who had saved his life earlier in the day had departed almost an hour and a half ago. Where was he? This waiting around was not accomplishing a damned thing.

He rose off the rock where he'd been sitting, and stretched. Enough of this lollygagging about; he had to get down there and find out what was happening. Already he assumed that something had interfered with the schedule. This afternoon's agenda included a communications power-up of the servomechanisms that guided the phased-array transmitter through the trajectory. He had even warned the tall stranger about it before he descended into the conduit. Well, he seemed to carry luck around with him, because the power-up had begun, then suddenly halted. But that meant somebody was mucking with the timetable. It was necessary to stop these people, whoever they were, from causing any more interference.

In times like these, he figured, it paid to be pragmatic. So give them a piece of whatever it was they wanted and they'd go away. It always worked. Even the student sit-ins of the sixties could have been tamed with a few gestures, a handful of concessions. If he'd been in charge, the problem would have disappeared.

So this time he would take the initiative. These people had no reason to want to stop the project—which meant, logically, that they had to be after something else. So why not just let them have it and then get on with matters?

After squinting at his watch one last time, he shrugged and started down the hill, working his way through the rocks and scrub brush. The sun beat down fiercely, making him thirsty and weak, while the sharp rocks pierced the lightweight shoes he had worn for the plane. But the other, sturdier pair he had packed was lost with the helicopter. . . .

Well, so be it. The first rule of life was to make do with what you had, manage around problems, and he intended to do exactly that. Shrugging again, he gingerly continued his climb. On his left he was passing the landing pad, with the slightly beat up Agusta, the sight of which momentarily discomfited him. But surely Bates had it insured. Still, the whole business was damned irritating, start to finish.

As he walked onto the asphalt of the connecting roadway and headed for the entrance to Command, he puzzled over how these thugs could have penetrated the facility in the first place and why Security had not handled the problem. That was bloody well what SatCom was paying its layabout Greek guards to do. They should have nipped the whole mess in the bud.

He turned and scanned the mountain one last time, but still spied nobody. The chap who saved his life must have gotten lost. Or killed.

With a shrug he walked directly up to the SatCom entry lobby and shoved open the glass door. To his surprise nobody was manning the security station. And an ominous dark stain covered the desk. Why hadn't anybody cleaned that up?

Readying his lecture, he dug out his security card and headed across toward the door to Command.

3:21 P.M.

"Let them go," Ramirez said. "We have what we need." He bent down and picked up the box.

"What about the woman?" Wolf Helling asked. "Can we work without her?"

"She'll be back." Ramirez seemed to be thinking aloud. "I'll see to it."

"But—"

"There are ways." He cut him off. "It's not a problem."

"What do you want us to do here?" Helling inquired finally, skepticism in his voice. He stepped over to look at the body of Rais, staring down dispassionately. One less amateur to deal with. He had shot the Pakistani by accident, but the kid was unreliable. And this job had no room for unreliability.

"Just get on with arming the devices," he said, checking his Rolex. "I'm going back to Command." It's time, he was thinking, for an important phone call.

3:39 P.M.

"I figure it like this," Vance said, trying to sound confident. "We take out the guy in charge, behead the dragon, and we've solved a large part of the problem. He seems to like shooting people, even his own men." He paused, then looked at her. "By the way, do you know who he is? Could be a real help."

"I have no idea," Cally said, shaking her head. "Just that he's a killer." She was straightening her clothes after climbing out of the conduit and through the heat exchanger. "He murdered Chris for no reason. Why would he do that?" Her voice began to choke, and she stopped.

Vance reached over and patted her hand. She had been through a lot. "He needs to scare you and everybody working for you. But try and hang on. You'll be getting some professional reinforcements soon. A few friends of mine known as ARM."

"ARM? Isn't that the security bunch that wired this facility in the first place?" She stared at him, then made a face. "Some job."

"What can I say?" He winced. "They don't usually have these problems."

"And now these same guys are going to come back and save us? That's really comforting."

"Try thinking positive." It was the best he could do.

She clearly viewed that response as inadequate, but she was too exhausted to argue. "Well, at this point I don't have any better ideas. But I'm worried about what may happen if there's a lot of shooting."

"Part of our job is to try and make sure nobody gets hurt. Keep the friendlies out of harm's way."

"Great." Her spunk was coming back. "We're probably going to have to keep them out of the way of your incompetent rescuers as well."

"Have faith. These guys've had plenty of experience. It won't be the first time."

"And what about you?" She looked him over again. "How much experience have *you* had?"

"You want an honest answer?"

"I take it that means none."

"Pretty close. So till they get here we just ad-lib." He settled under a tree and leaned back against the trunk. "Now, how about describing their leading man. I didn't get a very good look at him."

She was quiet for a moment, as though to collect her memories, and then she produced a description so thorough it would have impressed a Mossad intelligence officer. By the time she finished, Vance was grinning.

"Well, what do you know. He's alive after all. Looks like ARM is in for some unfinished business."

"What do you mean?"

"I think you just described somebody who slipped past Pierre in Beirut about five years ago. He's been in the terrorist game a long, long time, but he hasn't been heard from since. Everybody started believing he was dead. Or hoping."

"You know who he is?"

"It could only be one guy, Sabri Ramirez." He felt mixed emotions. This would be a real prize for Pierre and the others, *if* they could get him. The problem was getting him. Nobody had ever managed to come close.

"Who's that?"

Vance wondered if he really ought to tell her. Or shade the truth down a bit.

"Let me put it like this. He's no ordinary criminal. He's probably murdered a hundred people if you added up all the bombings. Mossad has been trying to assassinate the bastard for fifteen years." Vance leaned back, his mind churning, and touched his fingertips together. "This puts things in a whole new perspective. I knew he was a pro, had to be, but we're about to go up against the world's number-one terrorist. The king." His blue eyes grew thoughtful. "I've got to warn Pierre ASAP. The tactics may have to be changed."

"What's that supposed to mean?"

"If Ramirez thinks he's trapped, he'll just lash out. Always happens. He goes crazy and gets irrational when he's cornered, which means negotiations are useless."

"Jesus." She shuddered, her eyes seeming to go momentarily blank. "I didn't sign on for this."

"Makes two of us." He settled back in the grass, then yanked up a handful, fresh and fragrant, and sniffed it. "I came for sun and sea. Not to help rekill a dead man."

"What's that supposed to mean?" She plopped down beside him under the tree.

"Seems reasonable to guess he's been quote dead unquote for five years because he wants to be. It's not a bad condition to be in. For one thing, people stop looking for you. You can start reusing your old hideaways. And then you can put together a really big score. The Hyena returns."

"The Hyena?"

"That's what Mossad calls him. The story is he hates it, but it sort of sums up his line of work. The Hyena. The world's number-one killer-for-hire."

"God. I knew there was something about him, although in a way he seemed so . . . the man in the Brooks Brothers suit. But when he gunned down Chris in cold blood . . . still, this goes way beyond anything I could ever have dreamed."

"Looks like SatCom just made the big time. Right up there with the OPEC ministers he kidnapped in 1975, then auctioned off all over the Middle East. This is even bigger. It's going to be the crown jewel of his career." He stopped to muse. "What's it like to be famous and officially dead at the same time?"

"Maybe the best thing would be if he were really dead."

"You read my mind."

2:18 P.M.

"Mr. President." It was the voice of Alicia on the intercom. "There's a call holding on line three. It's Dr. Mannheim."

He glanced up, distracted. In the interest of more space, the operation had moved from the Oval Office to the Cabinet Room, where Stuart's wooden-jawed portrait of George

Washington gazed down on the papers strewn around the eight-sided table. Seated there with him were his chief of staff, Morton Davies; the special assistant for national security affairs, Theodore Brock; head of the Joint Chiefs, Ed Briggs; as well as the head of the CIA and the secretary of defense. The Vice President was giving a speech at a California fund-raiser, but his contribution was not particularly desired, or missed. Let him make speeches and wave the flag.

He reached over and picked up the handset. "Tell him I'll get back to him. Is he at home?"

"He's calling from somewhere in Greece. The SatCom—"

"Damn. Can't I call him back? I really don't have time—"

"I think you might want to take this, sir." Her voice was crisp and neutral as always, but he knew what the edge in her intonation meant. This is priority.

"SatCom?" Suddenly it clicked. He had been too distracted for the name to register at first.

"He's almost babbling. Something about a helicopter. He's—"

"Put him on. And have the damned thing traced." He hit the speaker button.

"Isaac. What's—"

"Johan, he's got a gun at my head." The voice was unmistakable. It had made students quake for forty years. It had made *him* quake. Now it was quivering. He had never heard his old professor in such a state. Very, very unlike Isaac.

"Dr. Mannheim?"

"They made me call this number. I know I'm not supposed—"

"Who's they?" The connection was intermittent, but he still could make it out.

"The . . ." He paused, then seemed to be reading. "The Resistance Front for a Free Europe. They've taken over the SatCom facility here, everybody. They shot down my helicopter. They killed—"

"What did you say? Helicopter?" Hansen's pulse quickened. Was Isaac talking about the Israeli Hind that had attacked the *Glover?* And what was this Resistance Front—for something or other . . . "Free Europe?" Europe was already free. Maybe too damned free, given all the ethnic turmoil.

The connection chattered, then another voice sounded. Hansen noted a trace of an accent, but he couldn't identify it. "Johan Hansen, this is to inform you that all the American engineers here are safe at the moment. We have no desire to harm anyone. We merely want our demand addressed."

Hansen glanced at Brock, who nodded, then pushed a button next to the phone that allowed him to record both sides of the conversation.

"This had better not be a prank."

"It's no prank. The staff of SatCom is now hostage."

"Listen, whoever you are, the United States of America doesn't negotiate with hostage takers. We never have before and we're not about to start now."

"I'm afraid the rules of the past no longer apply. In fact, I have no desire to negotiate either. There is nothing to negotiate. We have a very simple demand. And you have no alternative."

"You've got that backwards, whoever you are. *You* have no alternatives. You can release whatever hostages you have and get the hell out of there. That's your one option."

"We would be delighted to comply. As I said to you, we merely have a small nonnegotiable demand. I assume we are being recorded, but you may wish to take notes nonetheless. In case you have any questions."

"If you're talking about ransom, I can tell you now it's absolutely unthinkable."

"That kind of intransigence will get us nowhere." He sighed, a faint hiss over the line, and then continued. "You may consider our demand as merely a small repayment to the Muslim peoples, large portions of whose homeland America has seen fit to devastate. That payment will be eight hundred million dollars, to be delivered according to conditions that will be specified by fax. I assume you will wish some time to make the arrangements. You have twenty-four hours."

"You're out of your mind," Hansen said firmly. "You've got a hell of a nerve even—"

"Don't make me repeat myself. I will fax you the bank

information. As I said, you have twenty-four hours. If you have not wire-transferred the funds by that time, an American military installation in Europe will be incinerated. And without your frigate *Glover*, sent to spy on the Islamic peoples of the region, you will have no inkling where that installation will be."

"Just what do you think you're going to do?"

"The same thing America once did to Japan. Only this time with a little help from one of your so-called 'non-nuclear' allies."

Hansen pulled up short. Was this the nightmare every U.S. President had feared—a nuclear device in the hands of terrorists. No, this took it one step further; the terrorists had just seized the means to deliver the device. It was that nightmare compounded.

He glanced at Ed Briggs, whose face had just turned ashen. They both were thinking the same thing: What kind of military action was possible? The answer was not going to be simple. Then he turned back to the phone.

"Listen, I want . . ." He paused, because the line had gone dead.

9:04 P.M.

"How does an ETA of 0200 hours sound to you?" Dimitri Spiros was using an unsecured radio, but he had no choice. "That'll give us about twenty-nine hours. Enough time to get everything together."

"I'll have the welcome mat out." Vance's radio voice was interrupted periodically with static. The man sounded stressed out, but Spiros had already interrogated him about the overall situation.

"Our plan right now is to come in by seaplane, set down two klicks to the north, and stage the actual insertion using Zodiacs. Pierre wants to get everything together here in Athens by 1600 hours tomorrow. That's firm. We'll have a briefing and then—you know the rest."

"Try not to overfly this place. It's pretty small and there are lots of islands down in this part of the world."

"Michael, I'm Greek, for godsake." He bristled. "We'll make it, seas permitting. And the weather looks like a go for now."

"All right, here's the drill. Right now there are friendlies in Command and down at Launch. You have the plans for that, right?"

"Right. And how about the Bates Motel?"

"The living quarters? At the moment I think they've got some friendlies in there, too, but it's currently cut off from the rest of the facility, no communications of any kind, and it's not heavily guarded. We can worry about it last. The heavy hitters and the hardware will be at the two other places."

"What else do you know?" Spiros pressed.

"It gets even better. These guys have got at least one nuclear device. All signs are they have plans—probably to use the Cyclops system for delivery."

"I don't like the sound of that," Spiros said. "Who's leading it?"

"This is the very best part. I think it might be Ramirez."

"Sabri? The Hyena?"

"Could be."

He snorted in disbelief. "No way. The Kommissar has had him dead for three years."

"The Hyena has many lives. I actually got a look at him. Plastic surgery, maybe, but I've got a feeling it's none other than." There was a pause as Vance seemed to be checking something. "You know, we probably should cut this short. These guys have long ears. But just a word of warning: don't underestimate what he's capable of. I saw him shoot a staffer here in cold blood, just to get everybody's attention. When the time comes, things are going to get rough."

"That's how we're used to playing. Until somebody shows us a better way."

"Well, there's a good chance they're planning to arm at least one of the vehicles. After that it's anybody's guess."

"Nuclear blackmail?"

"Could be. Anyway, the fun part is, I got hold of the triggering mechanisms. For about five minutes."

"And then you politely gave them back?"

"It's a long story."

"Aren't they all," Spiros said. Then, "Well, do us all a favor, stay alive till we can make the insertion."

"That's an idea I could get with."

"By the way, do you have anything on their schedule? When does the balloon go up?"

"I don't know. You might hear something at your end. Ramirez has got to be talking to somebody by now. Demands, the usual. We need to find out what he wants. Maybe it'll all be over by the time you get here."

"Don't count on it. These things take a while. In the meantime, I'll get Pierre to have Hans chat up the Kommissar. If Germany's intel computer files have anything, he can probably pull it out quick enough."

"I do have another information source." Vance paused. "A new partner. And she's tough."

"She? What the hell are you talking about? Michael, this is not really the time for such things."

"I should get to fraternize with the hostages. One of the perks. Otherwise what do I get out of this job? She also happens to be the one who runs this place. She gave Ramirez the slip." A laugh sounded over the line, mixed with the static. "Incidentally, she doesn't think too much of your security job."

"Very funny." Spiros's gruff voice suggested he didn't mean it. "But maybe you should send her back inside. Might actually be safer there."

"Highly doubtful."

"All right. What about Bates?"

"The word is he's still okay. But they know who he is and I expect they'll put on the pressure when the time comes. There's an old professor here, too, the guy who dreamed this whole thing up, and they've got him. Name's Mannheim. First name Isaac. Why don't you find out anything you can about him. I had him here with me, but when I went down to reconnoiter, he disappeared. My guess is he wandered off and got himself taken."

"Sounds like you're on the case. Let's synchronize and talk again tomorrow at 0800 hours, local."

"Okay. We're counting on you. Don't mind telling you I'm scared. We're outgunned and Ramirez has started killing people."

"Michael, we're working as fast as we can. Just be by a radio tomorrow." Dimitri Spiros switched off the microphone and lapsed into troubled thought.

3:29 P.M.

Events were getting serious enough that the operation had been moved down to the Situation Room, in the White House basement. Scarcely twenty feet on a side, it was dominated by a teak conference table, with leather-bound chairs lining the walls. Although it appeared cramped by corporate standards, especially when the full National Security Council met, its close quarters intensified the focus needed for international crisis management. Besides, in the new age of electronic decisions, it was state-of-the-art, making up in technology what it lacked in spaciousness. Installed behind the dark walnut panels that covered three of the walls was the latest in high-tech electronic equipment, including a variety of telecommunications terminals, video monitors, and apparatus for projecting and manipulating images on the large screen on the fourth wall—normally concealed by a drawn curtain but now open and ready.

"We'll have to work through Joint Special Operations Command," the President was saying as he looked around the room. The five people there were intensely at work—their coat jackets crumpled across the chairs, shirt sleeves pushed back, ties loosened or off. They included Chief of Staff Morton Davies, Special Assistant for National Security Affairs Ted Brock, and Head of the Joint Chiefs Ed Briggs. "So we're about to find out if this country has any counterterrorist assault capability."

Special Operations Command had been created in the eighties after the string of embarrassing communication snafus during the Grenada invasion. Headquartered at MacDill Air Force Base in Florida, it had overall control and supervision of America's major commando units.

"I guess the first decision they'll have to make," he continued, "is who we should send in."

There were two options. The Navy had a 175-frogman unit, Sea-Air-Land Team Six, operating out of the Little Creek Naval Amphibious Base near Norfolk, Virginia. SEAL Team Six specialized in underwater demolitions, clandestine coastal infiltrations, hand-to-hand operations. The other unit trained to carry out hostage-rescue missions was Delta Force, headquartered in a classified installation at Fort Bragg. The SEALs were high profile, whereas everybody denied the very existence of Delta's assault team—called "shooters" in military parlance. Delta Force was probably the worst-kept secret in America.

"Shouldn't we hold up a minute and talk first about the hostages?" Morton Davies wondered aloud. "How much risk is there?"

"There's always risk," Hansen declared. "With anything you do in this office, there's always a downside. What was it Harry Truman said about the place where the buck stops? Well, I've got an uncomfortable feeling I'm about to find out what he was talking about." He turned and hit the intercom. "Alicia, get hold of Admiral Cutter and tell him to get over here. We've got to get Special Operations in on this ASAP."

"Yes, sir," came the quick reply. Despite the migraine now increasing her tension, she continued to offer Johan Hansen total support. In fact, she rejoiced at the opportunity. His wife, off somewhere dedicating flower parks in America's inner cities, certainly provided none.

That, at least, was what Alicia Winston preferred to think.

"Another worry I've got," the President continued after he had clicked off the intercom, "is how to keep this out of the press as long as possible. If there's any truth to their bomb hints, we'll need to try and minimize the panic factor.

From here on, every aspect, even the smallest insignificant detail, is classified. Top Secret."

"The Israelis will most certainly get with that," Ted Brock observed wryly, nervously cleaning his horn-rims for what seemed the tenth time that hour. The strain was all over his face.

"Now," the President continued, "SatCom is on Andikythera. Do we have any KH-12 PHOTOINT of the island here yet?"

"It's in, Mr. President," Briggs said, then pushed two green buttons on an electronic console on the conference table. A photo came up on the screen behind them, a dull black-and-white rectangle.

"That's it?" Hansen said, annoyed. He scanned the photo, then looked around. "Ed, there's not enough detail here to use. How long before we can get some computer enhancement of this? A blowup."

"I thought you would want that," Briggs answered, "so I've already made the arrangements. We're on-line to NSA. We should be able to get it in about ten minutes."

"Then we'll wait." He switched off the screen and turned back. "Okay, we have to start planning our first move. For the moment let's talk about logistics. If we have to make an insert, what do we need?"

"Well, to begin with, ISA would have to have twenty-four hours, minimum, to get somebody in there on the ground to gather enough intel to support a move," Briggs announced, almost apologetically.

The President sighed. ISA was the Army's Intelligence Support Activity, which provided intelligence for Delta Force and SEAL Team Six. As an intelligence organization, ISA was required to secure Central Intelligence Agency approval before entering foreign countries—which meant institutional gridlock and bureaucratic tie-ups before they could even get started.

"Then forget it. We'll just have to use satellite PHOTOINT and pray. The next problem is, who can we get there and how long would it take?" He knew that the Air Force's Special Operations Wing and the Army Task Force

160 supported long-range missions by Delta Force and the SEALs. Were they ready?

"Well, let's back up a second," Briggs interjected. "We can't just send in a task force cold. They'd need to practice an assault on something resembling the same kind of terrain."

No country in Europe, the President knew, had ever given permission for American commando bases on their territory. So why would they suddenly permit an assault rehearsal?

"That's going to be a tough sell. We're talking about Greek soil. But if these terrorists really have a nuclear device, then the government of Greece might well take an interest in what happens to it. Still, we don't know for sure. It'd be—"

"They'd damned well better take an interest," Briggs declared. "If these terrorists plan a demonstration bombing, they could just be thinking about the air and naval facility at Souda Bay. Which would mean taking out the western end of Crete. Every anti-American in the world would doubtless cheer. They'd claim that our presence in a country makes it a military target. There'd be a groundswell of sentiment worldwide to send us packing. Everywhere."

The chief of staff was thinking. "Do you suppose these fuckers have really got a bomb? What did he mean about checking with our closest allies?"

The President had already been pondering that. "Well, the Israelis have a nuclear arsenal, of course, but they also have enough safeguards to take care of anything. They even shot down one of their own planes once when it accidentally strayed over the Dimona plutonium-reprocessing facility. *Nobody* is going to steal one of theirs. The same goes for South Africa."

"So who does that leave?" Stubbs asked. He had a feeling he already knew.

"Let's save the obvious for last," Hansen answered. "And let me give you a quick briefing on who's in the bomb business on this planet. It just happens to be a particular interest of mine."

He leaned back. "In the Middle East proper, only one country presently has full capability. That is, obviously,

Israel. They have, in fact, a lot more bombs than anybody realizes. Their plutonium-reprocessing plant at Dimona extracts plutonium from the spent fuel in their research reactor there, and CIA claims they've got at least two hundred strategic nuclear weapons. Normal plutonium bombs need eight kilograms of the stuff, but we think they've come up with a sophisticated way to make one with five. Then there're the tactical nukes. They've got nuclear artillery shells, nuclear landmines in the Golan Heights, and hundreds of low-yield neutron bombs. That's more or less common knowledge, but what's less well known is that they've also got fusion capability—H-bombs. Which, God help us, I assume is not our problem here today. Then there's Libya, though they're still trying to get enough enriched uranium together to become a credible threat. Having only one or two bombs means that if you start anything, somebody else is going to finish it, so you need a lot before you get going. Iraq, thankfully, has been put out of business. Of course, there's still India, which has plenty of unrestricted plutonium and they've even claimed they could make a bomb in a month. We happen to think they've already done it. Because . . ." He paused. "Because we know damned well Pakistan has."

"There's your non-Caucasian in the fuel supply," Davies noted. "The fuckers."

The special assistant for national security affairs, Theodore Brock, who happened to be black, did not find Davies's Alabama good-old-boy remark especially amusing.

"Exactly," Hansen continued, wondering when he would have a good public excuse to send Davies to greener pastures. "That's got to be the 'ally' the bastard was talking about. It's a Muslim country, and their controls are a joke. It's the obvious choice."

Brock agreed solemnly. "We can start with an inquiry through their embassy. But it's going to be sticky."

The President nodded, wishing he had a hot line to the desk of every head of state in the world. It would make this kind of crisis so much more manageable.

Part of the problem, he thought, was how do you ask somebody if they've lost something that they've never admitted having in the first place? A marvel of diplomacy was in order. Still, he would have to do it. At worst, a denial wouldn't prove the terrorists did not have a bomb, but if the answer was affirmative, then knowing the size of the device could be crucial.

"We're receiving the enhanced satellite photos now." Briggs was pulling the first sheet off the machine. "Looks like ten-meter grids." He scanned over it. "But I don't see much. There're two big rockets here, but they seem to be all right."

"Which is in line with their threat to use them," Hansen observed dryly.

"I don't suppose a surgical air strike is possible?" Briggs wondered aloud. If the Gulf War had shown anything, it was the power of air superiority.

Hansen tried unsuccessfully to smile. "You're asking me to go to the Greek government and ask them if they would mind terribly if we bombed one of the islands in their Aegean tourist paradise, their cash cow. And, by the way, we'd probably kill a few hundred Greek civilians in the process. But we'd explain that we need to do this because I got an unsettling phone call. With no proof of anything." He sighed. "Keep thinking. This has to be a commando insertion. And, frankly, I'd just as soon Athens got a phone call *after* it happened, not before. For a lot of reasons."

"You know, there's something funny right here." Briggs was bent over, squinting. "Here, next to what appears to be a radar complex." He looked up. "Gentlemen, I think I've located our Hind. Or what's left of it. Looks like it was smashed into the side of the mountain, just below where the radars are."

"Let me have a look." The President stepped over. "You mean there?" He picked up a magnifying glass. "I'm no expert, but whatever it is, it's big. It could be a Soviet assault helicopter, you're right."

"There appear to be two other choppers on the site as well." Briggs continued to study the photo. "One down here on the helipad looks to be a light commercial model. But there's another one over here, down by the launch vehicles. It's bigger."

The President looked. "You're right. I see them. That big one down by the vehicles is probably how they brought in the damned bomb, if they actually have one. Most likely the Hind wasn't up to the job, maybe took some fire from the *Glover*. So they used a second one to deliver the package. Nice logistics."

"Too damned nice. I'm beginning to believe this is in no way a hoax."

"Roger." Ted Brock had been on the phone and now was hanging up. "That was Special Operations Command, sir. Cutter's people want to use a Delta task force, but they'll need at least forty-eight hours to get them in place for an operation."

"Forty-eight hours!" Hansen exploded. "Our crack counterterrorist assault force needs two days just to get into position to do what they're trained for?"

"Well, we'll be using an Air Force C-130 to deploy the Deltas to Souda Bay. And then they'd need at least two Combat Talons for the final insertion. Those are all kept down at the Air Force's First Special Operations Wing, you know, Hurlburt Field in Florida."

"I know that, Ted," Hansen said.

Brock nodded sheepishly, then continued. "Well, after the insertion, they'd need support from our long-range HH-53 Pave-Low choppers, but only three are flying at the moment. And—"

"I get the picture." The President cut him off. "Transportation is lousy and half the equipment we need is somewhere else or in maintenance. Any other bad news?"

"One thing, an assault would have to be at night. It's the only way that makes any sense. Which means more special equipment. If they go in during daylight, it's going to be a slaughter of the hostages, particularly if these bastards are armed the way we have to assume. And from the looks of everything so far, I'd say they know how the game is played. Which means that even if we do our best, it's going to be tricky. They're going to assume we're coming. The way I figure it, even with no rehearsals, forty-eight hours would be tight."

"We invest millions training the finest counterterrorist units in the world and then they can't be deployed in less than half a week?" He exhaled angrily, remembering a classified internal Pentagon study that claimed the best time to launch a successful assault with the least number of casualties among hostages was within twenty-four hours of their capture. "It's a goddamn outrage."

"Forty-eight hours, minimum, Mr. President. And even so, that's pushing it." He squirmed. "There's a lot of paperwork that'll have to be processed, and—"

"Well, tell Cutter to get the Special Forces mobilized and moving," Hansen interjected. "In the meantime, our job is going to be to try and find out what happened. Do they really have a nuke, and if they do, how in hell did they get it and what are they planning to do with it?"

Chapter Ten

9:22 P.M.

"It's very simple," Ramirez said to Jean-Paul Moreau. After the phone call, he had sent Mannheim to the Bates Motel and returned to Launch. Let Washington stew awhile. They were probably now trying to figure out how to get their antiterrorist units into Greece. Their nightmare logistics would be fun to watch. "We have to find them. And get him. Alive if possible, but we can't be fussy. The time to do it will be just after midnight, when we're finished here."

Moreau disagreed. "I'd say the sooner the better. The longer they're free, the more problems they can cause." Crossing Ramirez was not something to be done lightly, but he felt strongly that the operation was not going as smoothly as it should have. It was time for a little damage control.

"Well, he's probably back on the mountain," Ramirez said calmly. "If you want to, then go on up and get him. Take the RPG-7; it's light. But be careful you don't damage anything."

He was right about the weight. At slightly over ten kilos, the RPG-7 was one of the best bangs-for-the-ounce around. It was a guerrilla special, a Soviet-designed 40mm launcher that loosed a rocket with an oversize hollow-charge rocket-warhead 85mm in diameter. Fired from the shoulder, it was deadly against lightly armored vehicles and structures. Used on personnel, it was lethal. They had brought along a Pakistani clone of the latest Soviet model, a two-piece version that was easy to move about, yet assembled quickly.

"But remember," Ramirez went on, "so far all we have to show for trying to take out this nuisance is a wrecked helo. Don't botch it again."

"That was because you left the work to German amateurs," Moreau remarked dryly. "This time I'll take care of it myself. Personally."

"I'm counting on that," Ramirez said, his eyes expressionless behind his gray shades.

9:43 P.M.

"We'll be working together, kid," Dore Peretz was saying. "We're a team." He swept back his mane of salt-and-pepper hair, then moved next to Georges LeFarge. The young engineer didn't like anything about the Israeli, right down to the cheap aftershave he was wearing, but he had to admit the guy seemed unfazed by all the hardware that controlled Big Benny, the Fujitsu supercomputer.

It was a correct assessment. Dore Peretz was definitely in his element. He had taken his Ph.D. from the University of Chicago in 1984, then returned to Israel to accept a high-paying research job at the Weizman Institute, Israel's top-secret nuclear facility near Tel Aviv. During the next seven years he had advanced to the level of senior institute scientist, becoming an expert in every technology connected with nuclear weapons.

From the specialty of mass destruction he graduated to another hot topic—the emerging preeminence of smart weapons. Conventional delivery technologies, the war in the Gulf had shown, were no match for the new "smart" antimissile systems. It was back to the drawing board. What Israel needed in her arsenal was the *next* generation of weaponry.

He had gone on to head up a research team that played computerized war games, studying the "what ifs" of whole new generations of technologies matched against each other. The end result of this fascination was that he became a computer and missile-guidance expert—which, when added to his knowledge of nuclear weapons, made him a double-threat man.

It also made him perfect for what Sabri Ramirez wanted to do.

When Ramirez found him, he already had departed the institute, and also for reasons that suited Ramirez perfectly. Whereas Dore Peretz had an IQ off the scale, his social development was considered—even by those who tried to like him—as scarcely progressed beyond the infantile. His was an independent . . . make that irreverent . . . temperament that was bound to clash with the bureaucracy of a straitlaced place like the institute. He had particular trouble fitting in with the deadly-serious, high-security environment that surrounded military contract research. The problem had been obvious from the first day he arrived, but his genius was such that it had been overlooked and worked around by both sides. His final rupture with the Israeli defense establishment resulted from what—to his mind—was a totally compelling event.

He had personally developed a computer-assist program that provided special procedures for the quick arming of a nuclear device in case Israel found itself facing an imminent attack. It was important, and it worked.

He had expected, reasonably enough, a rousing financial tribute for this effort, or at the very least a citation. What he got instead was screwed. When the yearly Summary of Technical Research arrived on his desk January last, he discovered the computer program had been "created" by the vice president in charge of his section, with the "assistance" of someone named Dr. D. Peretz.

A reaming by an incompetent bureaucrat whom he had hated from the beginning was the last straw. He resigned in traditional style, papering the institute with a fusillade of memos that reviewed in detail the failings of its top management and then for good measure scrambling the electronic combination on his personal safe as he was readying to walk out the door.

At that point he did not know what he wanted to do next, but he was damned sure it would not involve further interaction with a bureaucracy.

Being no dummy, he also fully anticipated the response to his outrage. And sure enough, he found he had transformed himself into a high-profile security risk that Mossad suddenly found very interesting. Israel's intelligence service remembered all too well the case of Mordecai Vanunu, the thirty-one-year-old technician who had worked at the plutonium separation facility at the Dimona complex for nine years, then left in a huff and sold pictures and a detailed description of the facility to the London *Sunday Times*. Mossad had no intention of letting it happen again.

Dore Peretz was interrogated for weeks, threatened repeatedly, then placed under close surveillance. They had no grounds to arrest him, but they were going to intimidate the hell out of him.

Their harassment, however, achieved precisely the opposite effect. They galvanized his anger. In a degree of soul searching quite foreign to his normal mental activity, he found himself wondering why he owed Israel such allegiance in the first place. *This* was their thanks for all his service.

So why not give it back to the bastards, in spades? He became a "scientific adviser" to the PLO.

That only confirmed Mossad's fears and intensified their harassment: his phone was tapped, his mail opened, his stylish Tel Aviv apartment repeatedly and blatantly searched in his absence. The overall effect was cumulative, rendering him an ever-more-vociferous critic of Israel's conservative coalition government.

It was at this time, when his name was being linked to the PLO, that Sabri Ramirez got wind of him and knew he had found a gold mine—a disaffected, activist Israeli nuclear and rocket expert looking for a cause. He sounded perfect, and he was. Ramirez approached him at a demonstration supporting a Palestinian homeland, and made him an offer he could not refuse. How would he like to get rich? He would not need to betray his country, merely lend his skills to help teach the Americans a lesson.

Fuck Israel, he had declared. Then in a lower voice he had added—come to that, fuck the Palestinians, who were basically a pain in the ass. Acquiring personal wealth was a much more inspiring cause. He could not get work in Israel, *any* kind of work, and he was fast running through his savings.

Ramirez advanced him thirty thousand American dollars on the spot, in crisp hundreds. He immediately dropped his PLO affiliation and began lowering his profile—much to Mossad's relief. Their surveillance eased up as they gratefully turned to more pressing matters, and four months later he took advantage of his new freedom to slip into Jordan one night and from there make his way, a week later, to Beirut. It was in that ravaged city that he and Sabri Ramirez worked out the technical details of the plan. . . .

Which thus far had gone perfectly.

"We'll be modifying the payload," he announced, turning to the keyboard. "Therefore the weight will be different, so we'll have to factor that into the SORT program on the Fujitsu and run it again."

Shit, LeFarge thought, he knows about SORT. Which probably means he knows everything he needs to make *VX-1* fly.

9:45 P.M.

"I have a question," Michael Vance was saying. They were still resting on the hill, and he felt himself fighting back waves of exhaustion. "Could they get that vehicle down there off the ground without you being in Command?"

"I hate to admit it"—Calypso Andros exhaled ruefully and leaned back against the tree—"but they probably could. We've already had a final test of the power-up, everything.

The Fujitsu has all the controls set. There's nothing left to do except initiate the launch routine and then let the computer take over."

"So Bill was about to be rich." He grinned, then picked up a small white stone and flung it down the hill. "He might even have been able to pay off our bet. If I'd won."

"What bet was that?"

"Long ago and in another country." He shrugged, hardly caring anymore. "It was a damned stupid stunt. We had a sailor's bet, and I lost. As it happens, your new guests here pitched in to help. But those are the breaks."

"Well, let's talk about the real world." She seemed scarcely to hear what he had said. Or maybe she wasn't interested. Vance sensed she was trying to feign normality, adopting a facade that denied the horror of watching her young technician being shot dead. "Do you think they're going to kill anybody else?"

What should I say? he wondered. Feed her a comforting lie, or tell her the truth? He looked her over and decided on the latter.

"Hate to say it, but if it's really Ramirez, he'll kill anybody he vaguely feels like. I saw him hit a U.S. frigate with a Swatter. You've got to call that mass murder. A ton of casualties, and for no good reason." He caught himself before he said more, the memory still chilling. "Then again, I'd guess he's not going to take out anybody important or technically crucial, at least for now. Which should include Bates and Mannheim. He's got to be figuring he can use the big names for headlines and leverage, if he needs it."

"I can't believe that the U.S. isn't going to send in the Marines, especially when they find out he's got a bomb."

"Don't get your hopes up. There are a couple of problems with that. The first is that they may not be allowed on Greek soil, and even if they are, it could take several days for them to mount an operation."

"That's one." She looked at him. "What's the other?"

"The other is that if the U.S. should decide to mount an assault, it could well turn into a bloodbath. I'm almost wishing they don't. Delta Force and the SEALs are well trained, but as far as anybody knows, they've never been used to carry out a straight hostage-rescue. They'd probably come in here like John Wayne and tear this place apart. I don't even want to think about the carnage." His voice trailed off. "Take it from me. The people ARM is sending in are better suited for the job at hand. They also can deploy a lot quicker than the U.S. government."

"Well, somebody better come. And soon." She had caught a strand of her tangled hair and was twisting it, distractedly making the tangle worse. "What do you think these thugs really want?"

"I'd guess money's part of the package. But since Ramirez doesn't seem to be trying to extort SatCom, at least not yet, he probably has something bigger in mind." He slowly turned to her. "Tell me something. These vehicles are intended to go into orbit, right? But what if one didn't make it." He had a sudden thought. "Or what if one of them *did* make it, and then the orbital trajectory got altered somehow? Retrofire and reentry. You could set it down pretty much where you wanted, couldn't you?"

She stared at him uncertainly. "What are you suggesting?"

"That there are two ways to play this. Somebody could use these vehicles to deliver a bomb someplace. Or they could be used to put a bomb into orbit, to be delivered later." He leaned back. "Am I right or not?"

Her eyes darkened, and she suddenly found herself sorry she had ever come back to Greece. For *this*. Then she caught herself and answered him. "I suppose either one is possible. The reentry trajectory is precisely controlled. In fact, we power it down, more or less like the space shuttle."

"And the whole thing can be done within an hour or so, right? That is, once it's in orbit."

"A low-earth insertion means a full orbit of about ninety minutes for a satellite." She was thinking. "If the vehicle itself stays in orbit, then—"

"Everything would still be controlled from down here, correct?"

"We beam power up to the vehicle using the Cyclops.

That's the whole idea." She was thinking. "What you're saying is, once they get a vehicle, and a bomb, into orbit, they've got a loaded gun pointed at any place they choose."

"Doesn't that sound like the worst-case scenario?"

"They'll never pull it off." It was more a hope than a statement of fact.

"How are you going to stop them? If Ramirez thinks you're not cooperating, then all he has to do is start killing more of your staff until you do." He looked down the hill, where the facility was now dark except for the yellow sodium lights around the storage sheds and the blaze of floods that illuminated the two vehicles. "But I definitely think they're going to try some kind of launch. You said they're being very careful not to disturb anything. So what are the possibilities?"

"The easiest thing would be not to bother putting it into orbit at all," she answered after a moment. "In fact, Number One or Sabri Ramirez or whoever he is had Georges running some trajectory aborts. It all fits."

"Also, you've got two vehicles, and that box had enough detonators for several bombs. So, say they had two nuclear devices? They use the first one as a small demo, to prove they're serious. Sort of like we did on Hiroshima. And hold the second one in reserve. For more blackmail." He reached up and touched the bark of the tree above. "But any way you look at it, they seem to be dead serious about delivering a nuke somewhere. Where?"

"You know, there's a U.S. base not far from here."

"Souda Bay?"

"It's on Crete."

"So close they probably couldn't miss." He thought about it. "Taking out that base could decimate the U.S. Sixth Fleet. It would be a very attention-getting demonstration. Think they could really do it?"

"Crete would just be a short hop for *VX-1.*"

"It's easy and it's a nightmare. Sounds pretty good for . . . uh-oh." He pointed down. Moving through the shadows at the far edge of the facility, past the bright circles cast by the sodium lights, was a group of black figures. "Guess it had to happen."

9:46 P.M.

"But I'm still finishing the trajectory-default analysis I was supposed to do," LeFarge said to Dore Peretz, hoping he could stall. "I'm only half—"

"I'm telling you to abort those runs." The truth, Peretz reflected, was that Ramirez had jumped the gun on the trajectory analysis. Maybe he just wanted to keep this computer jockey busy, or maybe he didn't understand the technical side of things well enough. In any case, it had to be redone since the crucial payload parameters were going to be new, a substantial weight differential that would impact the power input controls. "Kill what you're doing and let me see what you've got so far. If you're on the right track, then we'll do a quick rerun with revised numbers."

LeFarge grimaced, then turned back to the keyboard and gave the order to abort, directing the output to the battery of printers. The quiet hum of zipping lasers began, barely audible above the ambient noise of the room. When the first printer finished, Peretz ripped out the stack of paper and began looking it over.

"All right." He nodded with satisfaction. "This is enough. The power inputs"—he pointed—"right here, will need to be reentered to conform to the altered weight coefficients of the new payload. I'll have to get them."

He turned away and clicked on his black Kenwood walkie-talkie. Moments later he was asking somebody some technical questions. He then waited, humming to himself, while the answers were procured. Finally he nodded and jotted them down on the bottom of the printout.

"Got it. You double-verified, right? Okay. Ten-four." He clicked off the handset and looked up. "All fixed." He walked back and laid down the paper on LeFarge's desk. "Okay, start over and run it with these."

Georges looked at the numbers. The new payload was 98.3 kilograms. There it was. What now?

He knew the answer. He had no choice but to give Peretz what he wanted. He had planned to make some changes in SORT that would screw up the whole launch routine, but now, with the Israeli looking over his shoulder, that was going to be impossible. This creep knew exactly how the program worked. He probably could spot any changes a mile away.

Cally, Cally, where are you? Are you okay? Are you getting help? Let me know where you are, at least. I can't stop these guys all by myself.

He sighed, tugged at his wisp of beard, and called up the data input file for SORT. Then he began inserting the new parameters. Around Command the other staffers were perfunctorily carrying out housekeeping chores at their workstations, the routine checks and runs they did every day. LeFarge suspected the stakes had just been raised, but he had no idea what they were.

9:48 P.M.

She looked down. "Where? I don't see anything."

"Over there. By the side of the sheds. There's a saying: in the darkness, only the shadows move. See them?" He rose and looked around. "Guess we'd better start thinking up a plan here."

Although trees shielded the base of the mountain, the top had been cleared and flattened to accommodate the battery of antennas. The only possible protection was a low cinderblock structure on the side nearest the facility.

"You're right," she said finally, squinting. "I do think I see something. Yes. They look like they're headed our way. Toward the trees and then right up the hill. Oh, shit."

The sight made something click in her head, and her fear turned again to anger. Terrorists, she knew, always planned to wear down their captives, make them pliable. She wasn't going to let it happen.

"Looks like three or maybe four." Who needed this? he sighed to himself. "Uh-oh, I think I see something else. They're carrying something with them and I don't like the looks of what I think it is."

As he stared down, he was wondering: How would they

choose to try and take the mountain? A direct assault? A two-pronged pincer? Or would they use some other technique? And what were they carrying? Some of the hardware they'd brought in the Hind?

"At least we've got the high ground," he continued finally, trying to think through the odds. "Let's hope that counts for something. It's mostly open, so we can see them." Then he reflected on the downside. "But they can see us if we make a run for the top of the hill. It's too far. So there's not much we can do except just wait. The one little Uzi isn't going to do much good."

"Let's think a minute," she said, turning and looking up the hill. "They're about to pass through the trees down there, which should give us enough time to get to the block-house. . . ." She pointed. There at the dark crest was the cinderblock emplacement that housed the on-site operation controls for the radars. "Let's go up there. I've just had an idea."

"I'm game." He nodded, feeling his adrenaline starting to build again. "Standing here is not going to do anything for us."

It was a quick climb, through the slivers of granite out-cropping that cut their way out of the shallow soil. When they reached the cinderblock structure, she punched in a security code on the keypad beside its black steel door and shoved it open. "If they haven't shut down the terminal in here yet, maybe I can get Georges on the computer net. He can shunt over control of those servomechanisms up there and then . . ."

He followed her inside. As he did, fluorescent lights clicked on to reveal an array of radar screens and a main computer terminal. "Hey, can we kill the beacon?" He frowned. "Whatever you're planning better be doable in the dark."

"No problem." She activated the terminal, then pointed toward the door. "The light switch is right there. Think you can handle it?"

He clicked it off and let the wisecrack pass. Then he turned back. "Now what?"

"God, I've never had anybody coming to kill me. The stories are right. It really does concentrate the mind." She began typing on the keyboard. "I had a thought. We're networked into the Fujitsu from all over the facility with LAN, so—"

"And that's computer lingo for a local-area network, or something."

"Right." She nodded. "At one point we had to hook all the workstations together, for a special test. Part of this area was connected into the network, so we could do some of the work from up here, but we always kept the larger servomechanisms on the main system, for safety reasons. Georges set it all up so everything has to be operated from down there, where the power drain can be monitored. Right now I need to get hold of him and have him do some things."

She was still typing. And then she got what she wanted.

9:51 P.M.

. . . HELLO, SOHO. BLUEBIRD NEEDS A FAVOR. CAN YOU SWITCH ON THE SERVOS?

LeFarge stared at the screen, not believing his eyes. Cally was on the LAN. A window had appeared at the lower right-hand of his screen, and her terminal ID was . . . terrific, it was the blockhouse up the hill.

He slipped a glance at Peretz, standing over by the water cooler, then quickly typed in an acknowledgment.

SOHO NEVER LETS BLUEBIRD DOWN

Then came the specific directions. She was asking him to switch control of the servos for Radar One over to her terminal. What was she doing? The radars were always controlled by Big Benny, the Fujitsu here in Command. He grimaced. Switching the big radar over to her workstation was a tall order. And the Israeli bastard was waiting for his SORT run. So now the trick was to try to do both things at once.

He split the screen and went to work.

9:52 P.M.

"Georges is a genius," she said, turning back, "but this may not actually be possible. Nobody's ever done it before."

"Whatever you're planning had better be possible or we've got to begin thinking up a Plan B, and quick." He was staring out the open door. "Because our new friends are definitely on their way and ready for a close encounter."

"Georges has got to hook this terminal directly to the Fujitsu—which isn't how we normally use it—and then give me control of the routine that runs the servos. In effect he has to put them on manual."

"Don't think you're going to manage it in time," he said. He was thinking this was no time to get experimental, but he decided to keep the thought to himself. Instead he nervously checked the Uzi. Three rounds were left in the last remaining clip. He regretted all the random firing he had done over the last few hours. Now every round had to be hoarded as though it were the last. On the other hand, maybe he was lucky just to have the damned Uzi at all, along with the few puny rounds left. The trick now was to try not to have to use them.

Down below them the four black figures had already moved past the helicopter landing pad and were about to be swallowed up in the copse of trees that began at the base of the hill. But now a sliver of moon had appeared from behind a bank of clouds in the east, casting an eerie pale glow onto the scene. He found himself deeply wishing for an IR scope, which would be a great help, bring them right up.

"I just lost them in the trees," he said, turning back. "Which means we've got about five minutes left for whatever you've got in mind."

"Trust me." She was still typing. "This workstation just logged onto the big system, so the main servo program is now accessible from here. Georges, I love you. Now all I have to do is try and override the internal checks that go through the Fujitsu down in Command."

Vance was staring, not quite sure what he was expected to say. "Then what?"

"Hopefully it's a surprise," she laughed, a trifle grimly.

"Just be quiet and let me work." Then her voice swelled with anger. "The bastards. This is going to be a pleasure. After what they did to Chris, maybe I'll get to return the favor."

Vance started to say something, but stopped when he noticed the first signs of motion at the edge of the copse of brush. The killers were emerging, and the sight gave him a chill. They're the hunters and we're the quarry, he thought. It's going to be like a giant turkey-shoot, played with automatics.

"You know . . ." He turned back. "There's still time for you to give yourself up. They'd probably rather have you alive anyway. You could do the white-flag thing and I could use the confusion to try and make it into the brush down there, toward the shore. Those guys are carrying something that looks suspiciously like heavy weaponry. But that's a riddle we don't want to solve empirically."

"Look, trust me," she shot back. "I know what I'm doing . . . I think. Don't you have any faith?"

"We may not know each other well enough to be having this conversation."

"As a matter of fact, you're exactly right." She hurriedly finished typing. "Okay, Georges has the control set up now and we're on line. Hang on."

She reached down to flip a large red switch on the side of the console. Immediately one of the large green cathode-ray tubes began to glow. What it showed, however, was not the usual sweeping line going round and round. Instead it displayed the crisp outline of the VX-1 space vehicle at the other end of the island. Next she flipped another switch, then reached for a mouse that was connected to the keyboard. She zipped it across, and the focus of the radar picture changed, almost as though it were a zoom lens. The image of the vehicle became larger and smaller. He realized the radar could be focused.

Then she called in another routine.

"I'm going to cut the power for a second, take it down across the facility and onto the base of the mountain, and then I'll power up again."

He watched as the outline of the island, in exquisite detail, swept over the screen.

"I thought this thing was only for transmission. How can it be sending back images?"

"There's the phased-array section for powering the vehicle with microwaves—that's part of the Cyclops—but we also have to have a guidance section, for keeping the beam on track. The Cyclops is the gun, but the guidance radar here is what we use to aim it." She was concentrating on the screen. "Now, where do you think our friends are down there?"

"They're probably halfway up the hill by now."

"Let's take a look." She brought down the focus, then began scanning.

"Hold on." He stayed her hand, bringing the mouse to a halt, and then pointing to the lower left corner of the large screen. "Didn't something move just then, right there?"

"Where?"

"There." He took the mouse and guided the image to center screen. "Where is that in the real world? It's got to be close."

She zipped the mouse again, bringing up the detail. A number scrolled at the bottom of the screen. "Four hundred meters, to be exact."

9:59 P.M.

As Moreau emerged from the last copse of cypress, he scanned the mountain, towering upward in the moonlit night, and wondered where the bastard would be holed up. There was one obvious place—in the cinderblock control house.

Yeah, ten to one that's where he had to be. The guy was stupid, riding a lucky streak. It was over.

On the other hand, he thought, there's no reason not to take this slow. Just in case. The fucker wasn't *that* stupid.

He looked down as a limb of thorny bramble caught his black trousers, tearing a hole near the knee. *"Je m'en fiche!"*

Although he lived by terrorism, Jean-Paul was a confirmed denizen of Paris's *rive gauche* and he had little use for roughing it here on this godforsaken island in the bowels of the Aegean. Who needed it? On the other hand, tonight's expedition promised some diversion. It was always a pleasure to take out some jerk who was specializing in making a bloody nuisance of himself. If he could assassinate the chairman of Renault, he figured, he could handle this asshole guard.

Moreau had brought along Stelios Tritsis, reasoning that a native Greek could best guide them up this rugged mountain, but he also had Helling's two Stasi fuck-ups. *Merde!* What a lousy idea it had been to include them in the first place. Ramirez had lost sight of his better judgment.

He looked back to check them over. They were carrying the RPG-7, as ordered, but he doubted they had the slightest idea how it was fired. Though possibly they were teachable retardates.

He revolved and stared up the mountain, wondering whether the blockhouse contained any technical apparatus that he had to be wary of. Maybe, he thought, I'd better just use a stun grenade. . . .

What was that? He checked through the IR scope of his Kalashnikov just to be sure: one of the giant radar dishes was turning.

What in hell did that mean?

Then he caught a flicker of light from the blockhouse. So the bastard *was* in there. But was he trying to pull something?

Okay, time to get serious. The place is well away from the radars and antennas. So just send a stun grenade through the door and take out the fucker's eardrums. No frags: no muss, no fuss. Then clean up the place at leisure.

He motioned for Schindler and Maier to bring up the launcher. . . .

10:01 P.M.

"What are you doing?" Peretz asked. He sensed the kid at the terminal was up to something because he'd split the screen and was typing in a second batch of commands on the lower half.

CC to Ian NET.RAD

"Just some systems cleanup." LeFarge tried to lie as convincingly as he knew how.

EXPN to JRAD

"Better not try to bullshit me, pal. It could be very unhealthy."

LeFarge was already aware of that. But he kept on typing, trying to look as casual as he could. Almost, almost there.

10:02 P.M.

"The bastard is in the blockhouse. There." Moreau motioned for the first German Stasi, Schindler. "But get a move on. He may be up to something."

With Moreau directing them, they quickly slipped the two sections of the launcher together to form a single tube approximately a meter and a half in length. The rocket grenade on the forward end looked like a round arrowhead, while the back was flared to dissipate the exhaust gases. The sight and rangefinder occupied the center, and just in front of that was the handgrip and trigger.

When they had finished, he checked it over, then surveyed the mountain, where the heavy servomechanisms controlling the radars continued to rotate.

Wait a minute, he told himself with a sudden chill in his groin. Something's wrong. He's tilting the radar dishes *down*.

Mon Dieu!

"Get ready."

10:03 P.M.

"We just ran out of time," Vance said, slamming the door shut. "Looks like they've got a grenade launcher. If they can manage to blast through this door, it's going to ruin our day, once and for all."

"Georges is still on-line, and I'm turning the servos as fast as I can." Her voice betrayed the strain.

"Well, get on with it. They're setting up to fire. I'd guess you've got about thirty seconds to pull off this miracle of yours."

"I think a hundred and sixty degrees will do it," she said, her voice now deceptively mechanical, all business. Suddenly he could envision her running this facility and barking orders right and left. "We're at one-twenty now. I just don't know if I can focus it in time. Georges always handled this."

She was tapping on the keyboard, some message to LeFarge. A cryptic reply appeared on the screen, next to what appeared to Vance to be computer garbage. Then the motion of the giant servomechanisms seemed to pick up speed. The radar antennas were swiveling around, and down.

"We're almost ready. Let me get Georges to transfer the power controls to full manual."

"Christ!" He cocked his Uzi.

"Look," she exploded. "I'm doing my part. How about you doing yours? Slow them down."

"I don't want to waste any rounds until it's absolutely necessary."

But it looked like that time had come. He opened the door again and stepped through. Down below, the moon glistened on the rocks, and one of the gunmen was aiming a grenade launcher. "How long—?"

"Just a couple more seconds now. . . ."

"It's now or never." He took careful aim on the man holding the launcher. "I'm going to count to five."

That was when he heard her say, "Got it."

10:04 P.M.

"All right," Moreau barked, "fire on three."

Schindler had just finished fine-adjusting the crosshairs, the rangefinder portion of the complex optical sight. With in-flight stability for the rocket provided by tail fins that folded out after launch, the RPG-7 had a 500-meter range against static targets. Though a crosswind could affect the accuracy, tonight, thankfully, there was none. This one couldn't miss, if there wasn't a sudden gust.

He tested the trigger confidently, sights on the open doorway, and hoped Moreau was right when he claimed the concussion grenade would render anybody inside totally incapacitated.

His eyes on the target, he failed to notice a flashing green light that had just clicked on next to the main antenna up above, atop the mountain. . . .

. . . When jet fighters are launched from carriers, it is standard practice to turn off an aircraft's radars until the planes are airborne, the reason being that the energy in the intense electromagnetic radiation can literally knock a man flat with an invisible wave. Memorable things happened to the eyes and ears. In this case, however, the radar could have no such total effect, since the random clumps of trees down the hill scattered and diffused the energy. It was, however, one of the most powerful radars on earth. . . .

10:05 P.M.

Vance watched as something hit the men below, something that seemed like a giant, invisible mallet. They stumbled backward, while a grenade rocketed harmlessly into the night sky.

"Congratulations." He lowered his Uzi. "I'm impressed. I think our new friends down there are, too. Yep, you made a very definite impression. Now, how about leaving that thing on long enough for us to get out of here and back up the hill? Maybe just fry the bastards for a while."

"How does eight minutes sound to you?"

"Should be time enough for us to scurry back down the rabbit hole. Maybe take a moonlight swim in a tunnel." He was liking her more and more all the time. Not a bad piece of work.

"I'll tell Georges to cut the power in eight," she said.

Then she added, "Look, why don't we head for the hotel. You look bushed."

"You mean go down to the Bates Motel?" I'm being invited to a motel by this woman? He smiled. I must be dreaming.

"We can cut around by the shore. That's probably the last place anybody is going to look for us now."

"Sounds good." It did. He was dead tired and hungry. Tomorrow was going to be a long, long day.

"The other reason I want to go down is to try and find Isaac," she added.

"The half-cracked professor?"

"Well, he only seems that way. Behind all those eccentricities is a mind you wouldn't believe. But whatever we find, I think we both need to knock off for a while and get recharged."

"Let's give it a try. I think everybody's brain, and nerves, could use a breather. I *know* mine could."

"We're out of here." She was already typing instructions into the keyboard.

CHAPTER ELEVEN

9:15 P.M.

Fayette-Nam—as they called Fayetteville, North Carolina, in the 1960s—hosts the largest army base in the world: Fort Bragg, home of the XVIII Airborne Corps. Breaking the monotony of the harsh red Carolina clay around it, the town sports a variety of go-go bars, honkytonks, and tattoo parlors to refresh and spiritually solace the base's hundred thousand personnel. Known far and wide as a "macho post," Fort Bragg houses front-line units ready to mobilize on a moment's notice. During the Persian Gulf crisis, they were among the first to ship.

The post deserves its macho reputation for a number of reasons, not the least being a highly classified square-mile compound, referred to locally as the Ranch, that nestles in a remote and secure corner of its sprawling 135,000 acres. There, protected by a twelve-foot-high fence, with armed guards and video cameras along the perimeter, is the nerve center for Delta Force, America's primary answer to terrorism. Now part of the Joint Special Operations Command—

informally known as "jay-soc"—Delta Force is the pick of the U.S. Special Forces, a unit of some seventy men specifically organized, equipped, and trained to take down terrorist situations. Of course, Delta Force formally does not exist—"The only Delta we know about is the airline," goes the official quip.

Although they rarely have an opportunity to display their capability, Delta personnel practice free-fall parachute jumps from thirty thousand feet, assault tactics on aircraft using live ammo and "hostages," high-tech demolitions, scuba insertions, free-climbing techniques on buildings and rock faces— all the skills needed to take terrorists by surprise, neutralize them, and rescue hostages. The leadership of this nonexistent organization occupies a large windowless concrete building topped by a fifty-foot communications bubble—which recently replaced Delta's former shabby quarters in the old Fort Bragg stockade.

Since the late 1980s, Delta Force has been led by Major General Eric Nichols, a fifty-three-year-old Special Forces veteran of Vietnam who holds an advanced degree in nuclear engineering. He is short—barely five feet ten—with darting gray eyes and an old scar down his left cheek. He also moves with the deftness of a large cat. Like his hand-picked men, he is highly intelligent, physically honed to perfection, and possessed of a powerful survival instinct. His only weakness is a taste for Cuban cigars, which he satisfies with Montecristos smuggled to him by resistance forces on the island—acquaintances whose identity no conceivable amount of torture could extract.

When Nichols breached the open doorway of the new officers' lounge, those in attendance were deep in a cosmic game of five-card stud, with two—Lieutenant Manny Jackson and Captain Philip Sexton—particularly engrossed, hoping desperately that the hand they now had in play would somehow miraculously recoup their staggering losses for the evening. He paused a moment, involuntarily, and surveyed the men, feeling a surge of pride, as always, in the way they carried themselves. A bearing that in others might have seemed arrogance on them only affirmed their competent self-assurance.

And why not? Usually fewer than half a dozen volunteers finished out of a class of fifty: a lightweight like Chuck Norris wouldn't stand a chance. Mostly in their early thirties, with the powerful shoulders of bodybuilders, the "shooters" of Delta Force did not resemble run-of-the-mill service types. For one thing, since they had to be ready for a clandestine op at a moment's notice, they deliberately looked as unmilitary as possible, right down to their shaggy civilian haircuts. Although they wore olive-drab one-piece jumpsuits during daily training, here—informally "off the Ranch"—it was sports shirts, tattered jeans, and sneakers.

Naturally he noticed the poker game—bending the regs was, after all, Delta Force's modus operandi—and he just as routinely suppressed a smile. He simply wouldn't "see" it.

But with the monetary stakes he counted on the table, he realized that his news could not have come at a worse time. On the other hand, legitimate ops were few and far between, and they were always eager for action. Some real excitement, at last. He knew every man in the vinyl-trimmed gray room would feel a rush of adrenaline.

He took a deep breath and broke up the party.

"Heads up, you screw-offs." It was his everyday formal greeting. "Bad news and good news. Report to the briefing room at 2130 hours, with all personal gear. Be ready to ship."

There was a scramble to salute, followed by a frenzied bustle to collect the money still lying on the table. In seconds everybody was reaching for his jacket. They had only fifteen minutes, but they were always packed.

The briefing room was a windowless space next to the Ranch's new headquarters building. It contained a long metal table in the center, blackboards and maps around the walls, and the far end was chockablock with video screens and electronic gear. As the unit members filed in, they noticed that maps of the eastern Mediterranean now plastered the left-hand wall. Next to these they saw blowups of KH-12 photos of a small island, identified only by latitude and longitude coordinates.

"All right, listen up," Nichols began, almost the instant they had settled. He had just fired up a brand-new Cuban Montecristo and was still trying to get it stoked to his satisfaction. "I've picked twenty-three men. I'll read off the list, and if you don't hear your name, you're dismissed."

He read the list, watched much of the room clear, and then continued.

"Okay, you're God's chosen. I picked the guys I happen to think are best suited to the way I see the op shaping up. To begin with, we're going to be airborne by 2300 hours, which a check of your watches will inform you is less than an hour away. Which means no bullshit between now and when we ship out. We'll be flying Bess—everybody's favorite C-130—with two in-flight refuelings. Destination officially classified, but if you guessed Souda Bay I'd have to say 'no comment.' Wherever it is we're going, we're scheduled in at 1630 hours local tomorrow. For now I want to go over the general outlines of the op. There'll be a detailed briefing after we land. In the meantime, I've put together a packet of maps and materials for everybody to study on the plane. I suggest you hone your reading skills. Now, here's what I'm authorized to tell you."

They listened intently and without interruption as he proceeded to give a rundown. They would be making a scuba insertion onto a Greek island—operational maps with the general geography were in the packet—where an unknown number of hostiles had seized an American industrial facility and were holding hostages. He then provided a rough description of the SatCom facility using satellite maps. They would rehearse the insertion at an appropriate location in the vicinity and then chopper to a carrier some twenty klicks south of the island, where they would undergo their final prep.

It was a thorough, if circumspect, briefing—which was what they expected. Since its inception, Delta had always operated on a top-security basis. Information always came as late into an operation as possible, on the theory that it was a two-edged sword and lives were at stake. Frequently the command did not divulge the real background and strategic purpose of an op until after its conclusion, thereby avoiding sending in men with extractable information.

Questions? Right away they all had plenty. What was the layout of the facility on the island? How many hostiles were there? How were they equipped? What was the disposition of the hostages? How many? Was their objective merely to extract the friendlies, or were they also ordered to "neutralize" all the hostiles?

Answer: You'll get a further briefing at the appropriate time.

The biggest question of all, however, was why the urgency? Why was Delta being called in to take down a situation that had no military dimensions. Where were the civilian SWAT teams? If this was merely an industrial matter, why wasn't somebody negotiating?

They knew "Bess" was already being loaded with the gear the brass would think they would need. In addition, however, each man had certain nonissue items, something to take along as a talisman for luck—a backup handgun strapped onto the ankle, an extra knife. Carrying such paraphernalia was against the regs, of course, but Major General Nichols always took such niceties in stride. If the job got done, he had selective blind spots as far as such things were concerned.

Nichols actually knew a lot more than he had told his men. He had already planned the op in his head. For the insertion, backup would be provided by two Apaches that would be armed and ready to carry out a rocket attack on the facility radars and the two launch vehicles. Once they had secured the hostages, they were going to treat the terrorists to a goddamn big surprise. There would be no place to hide. If he had to, he was prepared to blow the place to hell. Let the insurance companies worry about it.

11:43 P.M.

The electric sign MEETING IN PROGRESS over the door to the Situation Room had been illuminated for hours. Inside, Hansen sat in a tall swivel chair at one end of a long table staring at a detailed map of the eastern Mediterranean now being projected on the giant screen at the end of the room. In the subdued, recessed lighting, half-drunk cups of cold coffee stood around the central teakwood table. A fourth pot was already brewing in the kitchenette, while the rotund Chairman of the Joint Chiefs, Edward Briggs, had resorted to doing knee bends to stay alert.

"All right," Hansen was saying, "we've got the Special Forces in the game. That gives us a military option. But I'm wondering . . . maybe we should just go ahead and evacuate Souda. At the minimum get the Sixth Fleet out of there. As a safety precaution. We could manufacture some exercise that would at least get most of our assets clear."

If the bastards had a nuke, he was thinking, a well-placed hit could make Pearl Harbor look like a minor skirmish. Right now the entire complement of carriers in the Mediterranean was there, not to mention destroyers, frigates, and a classified number of aircraft. The destruction would run in the untold billions; the loss of life would be incalculable.

"Where would we deploy them?" Briggs rose, bent over one last time to stretch his muscles, then straightened. "Assuming we could get them clear within twenty-four hours, which would be pushing our luck, we'd have to figure out what to do next."

"Well, assuming there's available draft, we could deploy some of them around the island. We'd give those bastards who hijacked the place a little something to occupy their minds. Might make them think long and hard about getting back to Beirut or wherever the hell they came from."

"You're talking about a tall order. I don't think we could really mobilize and evacuate the base in that kind of time frame. And even if we could, our operations in the Med would be disrupted to the point it would take us months to recover."

"Well, Ed," the President snapped, "those are the kinds of problems you're supposedly being paid to solve. If we're not mobile, then what the hell are we doing in the Med in the first place?" The question was rhetorical, but it stung—as intended.

"I'll see if I can get a scenario ready for you by 0800 hours tomorrow." He tried not to squirm. They both knew he had already cut the orders deploying Fort Bragg's Special Forces to Souda, to be ready in case an assault was needed. The last resort. "In the meantime, I certainly could arrange for the base to go on a practice alert—cancel all leave and get everybody on a ship-out basis."

"I think you should do that, at the very least." Should I inform the Greek government? Hansen wondered again. No, let's see if this can be handled without opening a can of worms about whose sovereign rights are uppermost here. The relationship with Greece had, for all its ups and downs, been generally cordial. With any luck they would never have to be involved or, with supreme good fortune, even know. . . .

"Then have Alicia get Johnson over at the Pentagon on the line," Briggs said, "and he can cut the orders. We've never moved this fast before, so we're about to find out where our glitches are. Don't be surprised if there aren't plenty."

"Just be happy if the American taxpayer never finds out what he's getting for his money," the President responded. "And speaking of money, we've been faxed a string of account numbers for a bank in Geneva. This is going to have to come out of a budget somewhere, so who do I stiff to pay off these bastards? Or make them temporarily *think* I'm paying them off. It's got to be some discretionary fund that has minimal accountability. And I don't want the CIA within a mile of this: that place is like a sieve."

Briggs pondered. "I can probably come up with the money by juggling some of the active accounts in Procurement. Cash flow is a marvelous thing if it's handled right. You can rob Peter to pay Paul, and then make Peter whole by robbing somebody else. Then the end of the fiscal year comes around and you withhold payment from some contractor while you hold an 'investigation.'" He smiled. "Believe me, there are ways."

The President wasn't smiling. "Don't tell me. I don't think I want to hear this. But if you're going to play bingo with the books, then you'd damned well better do it quick, and on the QT."

"That'll be the easiest part. I've already got some ideas."

"Just make sure I don't end up with another Iran-Contra brouhaha on my neck. I won't be able to plead senility and let a few fall guys take the rap."

Briggs had foreseen as well the glare of television lights in the Senate hearing room. Worse still, it did not take too challenging a flight of imagination to figure out who would end up being the patsy. He would have to fall on his sword to protect the Presidency. Washington had a grand tradition of that. He could kiss good-bye to a comfortable retirement in Arizona next to a golf link.

"You can be sure I will take the utmost care, Mr. President." And he was smiling even though Hansen was not.

"All right, now about the Special Forces. Once we get them to Souda Bay, I want a quick rehearsal and then I want them deployed just offshore, on the *Kennedy*, ready to move. Which means that whatever support they'll need has to be ready by the time they arrive. What have you got on that?"

"A task force shipped out for Souda tonight, Mr. President. Their C-130 is already in the air. The problems are at the other end. Once they're in-theater, we're still looking at a prep time of twelve hours, minimum. There's just no way they can mount an assault any sooner than that."

The President winced, already thinking about his other problem. If they *did* have a nuclear device, or devices, whose was it? The signs all pointed in one direction. The Israelis claimed the stolen Iranian Hind had stopped over in Pakistan. There probably was no need to look any further. But now he needed somehow to get a confirmation. Or was the threat of a bomb just a hoax?

He had a meeting at ten o'clock in the morning with the Pakistani ambassador. It would have to be handled delicately, with a lot of circumlocutions and diplomatic niceties, but he damn well intended to get some plain answers.

10:41 P.M.

"So this is the Bates Motel I've heard so much about," Vance said, casting a glance down the dull, cinderblock walls. "Hitchcock's version had a lot more character."

"You're right," Cally agreed. "But wait till you see what it's like upstairs. It sort of gives new meaning to the phrase 'no frills.' A hell of a place to cut corners, given all the money Bill poured into this facility, but he said he wasn't building a resort." She gestured around the utilities room, where a maze of insulated steam and hot-water pipes crisscrossed above their heads like a huge white forest. "Anyway, welcome back to the slightly unreal real world."

"Maybe what we need is less reality, not more. But if you can find us a beer, I think I could start getting the hang of the place. Let's just try not to bump into anybody."

"Okay, my feeling is that if we stay out of Level Three, upstairs, we'll be all right. That's got to be where they're holding everybody who's not on duty. Locked away for safe-keeping."

They had entered Level One via a trapdoor in the stone water conduit that picked up waste heat from the environmental control unit in the residential quarters. Around them now was silence, save for the clicks and hums of motors and pumps.

"All right, who do we see about something to eat?" He had just finished drinking deeply from a spigot on one of the incoming cold-water pipes. Even though he was still soaking wet from the trip through the conduit, he was feeling severely dehydrated and the water tasted delicious, as though it had come from a well deep in the island's core. It had.

"You see me," she replied. "We're going to head straight for the kitchen. There's got to be something edible there. So let's take the elevator up and see what's on the menu. I think today was supposed to be calamari."

"I'd settle for a simple American T-bone if you've got one in the freezer. The more American the better. I'm sort of down on Greece at the moment."

"You can have pretty much what you want here. As long

as it's not a pizza or a decent hamburger." She was pushing the button to summon the elevator. The lights above the door told the story of the facility: three levels, with the top being the living quarters; Level Two being services such as food preparation and laundry; Level One, utilities.

"Hit two," she said as the bell chimed, and she stepped on, taking one last glance about the basement. The elevator whisked them up quickly, then opened onto another empty hallway.

"You know," she said, her voice virtually a whisper, "this corridor is almost always full of people. I guess they really do have everybody confined to quarters. Lucky us."

"They're thorough, and they know what they're doing. They—"

That's when he noticed the line of explosives that had been placed along the wall next to the elevator, neat yellow bars of Semtex, wrapped in cellophane. The first was wired to a detonator, which was in turn connected to a digital timer.

"Hello, take a look." He nodded down. "Guess my wild hunch was right. They're not planning to leave any witnesses when this is over. When they're finished, they'll just pack everybody in here and blow up the place. Nice and tidy. Won't even interfere with the computers, just in case they need to keep them running for a while after they leave."

He bent down and examined the timer, now scrolling the minutes in red numbers. It was set to blow in just over twenty-nine hours.

"Guess we just got the inside track on their timetable."

"My God," she said, looking at the device as though it were a cobra. "Can't we just turn it off?"

"Sooner or later we'd better, but it's still got plenty of time left on it." His voice turned slightly wistful. "Tell you the truth, I'd rather some of the guys from ARM did it. I'm slightly chicken when it comes to bomb-squad operations. Cut the wrong wire and . . . eternity takes on a whole new perspective." He shrugged. "Also, there's a chance it's booby-trapped somehow. The thing's a little too obvious, sitting out here in plain view. When something looks too easy, I always get suspicious. Maybe for no reason, but . . ." He motioned her away. "I suggest we forget about that for now and focus on finding a steak. I also wouldn't fling a hot shower back in your face."

"That's only on Level Three. It may have to wait." She took his arm. "Come on. I don't like being around bombs, even if they have timers."

She led the way down the abandoned corridor, its lighting fluorescent and its floor covered with gray industrial carpet. There was a total, almost palpable silence about the place that made it feel all the more eerie and abandoned. It seemed utterly strange and alien.

"The kitchen is in here," she said, pushing open a large steel door. Vance stepped in and surveyed it: all the fixtures needed for a mess that served several hundred people three meals daily. In fact, it looked as though the evening's cleanup operation had been halted in mid-wash. Dirty pots sat cold on the big industrial stoves, and piles of half-peeled vegetables were on the wide aluminum tables. The storage lockers, refrigerators, and freezers were located across the room, opposite.

"By the way." He had a sudden thought. "This place must have TV monitors somewhere, am I right? Every other place here does."

"Well, you're right and you're wrong. It does, but they're on the blink. It always seemed like a stupid idea anyway, almost like spying, and then one day somebody just cut the wires. Probably one of the cooks. I never bothered getting them fixed. I just couldn't think of any good reason to bother."

"Well, for once laziness paid off. Maybe we're safe here for a while." He had opened the freezer. "Hello, Lady Luck has decided to get with the program." He was pulling out two thick steaks. "Care to join me?"

"Those are there for Bill," she noted, then laughed. "I'd still rather have a pizza, but I don't guess he'll mind if we dip into his private stock."

"So I repeat the question." He was already unwrapping two, both thick.

"Yes, of course. I'm famished." She shivered. "And I also wouldn't mind a set of dry clothes."

"Maybe one of these will warm you up." He was popping the steaks into a gleaming white microwave for a quick thaw.

"Right."

"And while dinner is coming along, how about drawing me a diagram of what's up there. Maybe we can go up later, take a look around."

"Let's eat first. I'm too wired to think." She switched on one of the large, black electric grills. "My vote is that we just sit tight for now."

And why not? This man with the sexy eyes and healthy laugh attracted her. Mercurial in his spirits, he appeared willing to take chances. Just the way she remembered her father. And Alan. But she wondered why he was here risking his life for a bunch of total strangers. Even Alan wouldn't have done that.

"You know, Mike Vance, I have to tell you, you don't look much like a commando."

"Guess what? I'm not."

"You know what I mean. For that matter, you don't look like the guys who came and installed our wonderful security system. I'd like to know your real story."

"How are retired archaeologists supposed to look? But I wasn't good enough at it, or maybe I was too good at it—I'm not sure which—and as a result I ended up doing what I really wanted to for a living. Running a sailboat business." He looked her over. "You seem to like what you're doing, too. And from what I've seen, I'd say Bill's getting a bargain, no matter what he's paying you."

She laughed. "I'd say you're an even better bargain. He's getting you for free."

"Freebies are only a deal if they pan out." He lifted their steaks out of the microwave and flipped them onto the grill. They immediately sizzled deliciously, a sound he had loved since he was a child growing up in Pennsylvania. It all mingled together with the scent of trees and summer.

"God, those smell great." She came over to take a look. "I

think the aroma is giving me some backbone. There's nothing like the smell of grease."

"I figured you'd come around." He patted her chastely on the back, half imagining it was farther down, then lifted one of the steaks to see how they were going. Well. Just like his spirits.

But now she was moving off again into a space of her own. She scrutinized his weathered face, feeling a little hopeful that maybe, finally, she had run across somebody like Alan. Though she still hardly knew a damned thing about him.

"With people I meet for the first time, I like to play a little game," she said finally. "It's always interesting to try and guess. What are they really like? Does character show?"

"What happens if you guess right?" He nudged a steak. "Do you own their soul? Like some primitive tribes think a photograph captures their spirit?"

"Guess you'll have to find out, won't you?" She checked him over again.

"Okay." He smiled and gave her the same look back. "But it's only fair if we both get to play. So, if one of us hits the truth, what happens then. Do we get to go for Double Jeopardy?"

"Be warned. The prince who learns the princess's secrets can end up getting more than he bargained for." She came back, full of feeling. Then she paused for a second, thinking, and began. "All right, I get to go first. Woman's prerogative. And I want to start with the sailboat—what did you call it? *Odyssey II?*—and what it says about you. I think it means you're a doer, not a talker. I like that."

"Maybe." He felt uncomfortable, not sure what to say, so he decided to let it pass. "Now it's my turn." He leaned back and examined her, hoping to get it right. Make a good first impression. Ignore the fact she's a knockout, he lectured himself, at least for now. Look for the inner woman.

"You like it here," he started. "But the isolation means everybody knows everybody. No privacy. And you're a very private person. So—to use that famous cliché—you bury yourself in your work. You could be happier."

"That goes for you, too," she quickly began, a little startled that his first insight had been so close to the mark. "And you're a loner. The good news is . . . I think you're pretty loyal. To friends. To women. The downside is you keep your friends to a close circle."

"Hey, I'd almost think you've been reading my mail." He seemed vaguely discomfited. "But I'll bet you suffer from the same malady. You made some tight friends early on, but not much in that department since. They're all engineers, and mostly you talk shop. Oh, and no women. You want them but you don't respect them enough. They're not as committed as you are. In fact, your last good friend was in college. Sometimes you have trouble getting next to anybody."

"Well, for the record I'll admit that my best friend was from *before* college, and it's a he. Georges." She decided to skip over the matter of Alan Harris. He had been a friend as well as a lover. A good friend, or so she thought. Once. "But I think the buzzer just went off. Game over."

"Whoa, don't bail out now, just when it's getting good. This was your idea, remember? And I'm not through." He leaned back. "Okay, let's really get tough. Go personal. You figure falling for some guy might just end up breaking your heart. Maybe it already happened to you once or twice. So these days you don't let things go too far." He rubbed at his chin as he studied her. "How'm I doing?"

"The rules of the game don't include having to answer questions." She took a deep breath. Mike Vance was definitely better at this than she'd reckoned. "But if you want to keep going, we'll have round two. Back to you. I'd guess you're always in control, or you want to be. So what happens is, you co-opt the things and people around you, make them work for you. And from the way things have gone so far, I'd say luck seems to be on your side; some people are like that and you're one of them."

"Don't be too sure." He checked the steaks again, then flipped them over. They were coming along nicely, the fat around the edge beginning to char the way he liked. "Luck always has a way of running out eventually."

"Tell me about it . . ." she said, letting her voice trail off.

"But I'd also guess you're a homebody in your soul. You

like a roaring fire and a glass of wine and a good book over going out to paint the town."

"And you're probably just the opposite. You want to be out in the sun and wind and rain. Sitting around bores you."

"Guilty." He nodded. "Now for round three. That glass of wine you have with the book is probably something tame. Say, Chablis."

"You drink . . . mmmm, let me see. Scotch is too mundane. I'll bet it's tequila. Straight."

"You're psychic. But you missed the lime."

"Oh, I almost forgot the most important thing." She grew somber. "You like a good battle. So taking on these thugs is going to be the most fun you've had all week."

"That's where you just went off the track." His eyes narrowed, the corners crinkling. "We're definitely on the wrong end of the odds here. These bastards are dug in, they've probably got A-bombs, and we know for sure they've got a lot of helpless people in their grasp. That's not a recipe for heroics. It's more like one for pending tragedy." He paused, deciding it was definitely time to change the subject. "Speaking of tragedies, it would be a major one if we didn't have a Greek salad to go with those steaks."

He walked over and checked the fridge. Sure enough, there was a massive bowl of ripe, red tomatoes sitting next to a pile of crisp cucumbers. Most important of all, there was a huge chunk of white feta cheese. Yep, the chef had to be Greek. And up there, on a high kitchen shelf, were rows and rows of olives, curing in brine. Throw them all together with a little oregano, lemon juice, and olive oil, and the traditional side dish of Greece was theirs.

"Just the stuff." He pulled down a jar of olive oil and one of dark Greek olives. Then he selected some tomatoes and a cucumber and went to work.

"You know, you're not a half-bad Greek chef. My mother would have loved you. You're making that salad exactly the way she used to." She made a face. "Every day. God, did I get sick of them. All I wanted to eat was french fries. So when I finally got away, off at college, I practically lived on cheeseburgers and pizza for years after that."

"Shame on you. This is very wholesome. Very good for your state of mind." He finished slicing the tomatoes, then opened the fridge and fished out a couple of brown bottles of the local beer. "Retsina would be the thing, but this will have to do." He looked over. "By the way, how're the steaks coming?"

"Looks like our feast is ready." She pulled them off the grill and onto plates. "How long has it been since you ate?"

"Think it's about two days now." He finished tossing the salad and served them each a hearty helping. "Didn't realize how famished I was till I smelled those T-bones broiling." He popped the caps on the beers and handed her one. "*Bon appétit.* Better eat hearty, because this may be the last food we're going to see for a while."

She took a bite, then looked up, chewing. "It's delicious. And I want to say one more thing about our game a while ago." She stopped to swallow. "And I mean this. It's always a little sad when I see a person who can do a lot of things but doesn't really find total satisfaction in any of them. Nothing they ever do really makes them happy. And I think that's you, really. I'll bet that whenever you're doing one thing, you're always thinking about some other things you could be doing. Which means you're never really content. You always want more."

"That's pretty deep stuff." He had launched hungrily into his steak. "Maybe you're right, but I'm not going to come out and admit it. It's too damning. So let me put it like this. Maybe I happen to think it's possible to care about a lot of things at once. That's—"

"Such as?"

"Well, okay, I'll give you a 'for instance.' I like sailing around these islands, but all the time I'm doing it, I'm thinking about what it must have been like two, three thousand years ago. The archaeology. It's intrigued me as long as I can remember. My dad was the same; he spent his life digging around in Crete. I thought that was the most marvelous thing in the world, so I did it, too. For years. Even wrote a book about that island once. I loved the place. Still do."

"That's funny. I was born practically in the shadow of

Crete, and yet I've only been there a couple of times." She sighed. "Well, what happened? I mean to your love affair with Crete. Sounds like that's what it was."

"Maybe I loved the place too much. I don't know." He paused to take a drink of the beer, cold and refreshing. "Well, when you love somebody, or something, you want to find out everything there is to know about them. But when I did that, and told what I'd concluded was the real story, or what I passionately believed was the real story, nobody wanted to hear it. I had some ideas about the island's ancient age of glory that didn't jibe with the standard theories. Made me very unpopular in the world of academia. Scholars don't like their boats to be rocked."

"And you let that get you down?" She snorted. Being a woman, she'd had an uphill battle all her life. Men could be such babies sometimes. "See, when the world's against you, that's when you're supposed to fight hardest. That's always been my rule. I'm not a quitter. Ever."

He winced and stopped eating. "Hey, I'm back, aren't I? In Greece." He looked at her, impulsively wanting to touch her again. "But it's nice to have somebody like you to pitch in and help. Maybe we'll manage something together."

"Maybe you should have had somebody around the first time." God, he was really reminding her of Alan. The same buttons. "Maybe you're not as tough as you think."

"Adversity depresses me. Like bad weather. I prefer life without too many psychodramas." And this Greek fireball, he told himself, had psychodrama written large all over her. Still . . .

"Then the question now is what I should do." She looked at him, taking a last bite. "Go back, or stay with you."

"We need to learn from Ulysses's experience with the Cyclops," Vance said, clicking back into the real world. "The one-eyed giant had trapped him and his crew and was devouring them one by one. So how did they overcome him? They got him plastered on some good Greek wine, then put out his eye with a burning post. That done, they proceeded to exploit his disability."

"What are you saying?" She frowned.

"This guy is killing off your people, right? Pierre is coming in with his crew to try and take this place down, but in the meantime it would be good if we took a shot at putting out their eyes."

"Put out their eyes?" She was still puzzled.

"It's a metaphor. It would be extremely helpful if we could blind them enough that they didn't know ARM was coming in. Couldn't 'see' the team. Maybe shut down the radars, something."

"Michael"—it was the first time she had used his name, and she liked it—"that's why we're in this mess in the first place. There are no radars that could spot an insertion. That's how these bastards got in here in the first place. Bill gets the Saddam Hussein Military Preparedness Award. There *is* no radar to monitor the shore."

He laughed. "Okay, but now that oversight has turned into a plus. What's good for the goose is good for the you-know-what. If there are no peripheral radars, then they're not going to know where Pierre and the boys make their insertion."

"Right. The bad guys are already blind. It's got to make a difference."

"Then what we need to do"—he was thinking aloud—"is to get them all together in one place."

"They're not going to let it happen." She was questing, too. "Unless . . . unless we can *make* it happen. Something . . ."

"Keep thinking," he said. "I don't have any ideas either, but somebody better come up with one."

"Well, let's go back up on the mountain before they find us here," she said finally, clearly itching to get going and do *something*. "We're going to screw these guys, wait and see."

Vance nodded, wishing he could believe it as confidently as she did.

10:49 P.M.

Sabri Ramirez stood watching as the last of the krytron detonators was secured in the ganglia of wiring that surrounded the explosive Octol sphere. Now one of the bombs was armed. He liked the looks of it. The next—

"They haven't come back yet," Wolf Helling said, interrupting his thoughts. "Do you think there was a problem?" He was warily watching the bomb and its timer being assembled, trying to calm his nerves. This was not like playing with a yellow lump of Sematach. One false move and you would be vaporized. Any man who pretended it didn't scare him was a liar, or worse, a fool. Maybe both.

The bomb did not frighten Ramirez; his mind did not dwell on risk. He assumed the Pakis knew their job—they damned well better. No, his current concern also was what had happened to Moreau. He had expected his unit to return before now. So far they had taken over an hour on what should have been a simple operation. With hostages dispersed in three locations, Ramirez feared that things were getting spread thin. Gamal had been keeping watch over the guards and the off-duty shifts on Level Three of the accommodations facility, while Peretz was holding things together in Command, but still it would be better if four of the team were not out chasing over the island trying to find some rogue guard. He had tried to reach them on his walkie-talkie, but so far he had not been able to raise anybody. That was particularly troubling. Why should all the radios suddenly go dead?

"If there was some difficulty up the hill, surely they're handling it." Ramirez tried to push aside his misgivings. He actually felt it was true, or should be true. He had checked out Moreau's credentials carefully, investigating beyond the popular myth, and what he had found did nothing to diminish the legend of the blond demon, Jean-Paul. . . .

"Now, we're ready to secure this baby into the payload container," Abdoullah was saying. "I measured it already, and it should fit with no problem. But we'll need to hook up the detonators with the telemetry interface, and for that we need

Peretz's input. He'll use the Fujitsu in Command to blow this thing, but it all has to be synchronized with the trajectory control."

"He's there now," Ramirez said, "updating the trajectory runs. That's scheduled to be completed in"—he checked his watch—"about twenty minutes. When he gets through, we can go ahead with the detonators. Everything is on schedule."

For some reason Abdoullah did not like the precise tone of Ramirez's voice. Right, he thought, everything is on schedule. So when Shujat and I have finished our part, what then? Will we be "accidentally" gunned down, the way Rais was? You claimed that was a screwup, but you're not the kind of guy who makes that kind of mistake. Okay, so maybe Rais got careless. Was that your way of making an example of him?

He motioned Shujat to help lift the first shiny sphere into the heat-resistant Teflon payload container. On a conventional launch, the container was designed to be deployed by radio command when the VX-1 vehicle had captured low earth orbit. The nose of the vehicle would open and eject it, after which the satellite payload would release. This launch, however, was—

"Hey, they're back," Helling announced, watching the door of the clean room open.

Ramirez looked up, and realized immediately that something was wrong. Jean-Paul Moreau's eyes seemed slightly unfocused, and his sense of balance was obviously impaired —a man stumbling out of a centrifuge. He also was rubbing at his ears, as though his head were buzzing.

"What in hell happened?" He had never seen anyone with quite this set of symptoms before. They looked like men who had been too close when a homemade bomb went off.

"The bastard was up on the hill, and he managed to get control of one of the radars. Let me tell you, there's nothing like it in the world. You feel your head is going to explode. I can barely hear." He then lapsed into French curses.

Stelios Tritsis still had said nothing. He merely watched as Rudolph Schindler and Peter Maier set down the RPG-7 and collapsed onto the floor.

"Then let him go for now." Ramirez wanted to kill them all, then and there. "But get that damned thing out of here." He indicated the grenade launcher. "And the rest of you with it. Take turns getting some sleep and report back to me at 0600 hours. We'll soon have our hands full. The natives here are going to start getting restless. When that happens, the next man who fucks up will have to answer to me."

They all knew what that meant.

11:16 P.M.

Dore Peretz had just finished checking over the trajectory analyses and he was satisfied that guidance would not pose a problem. With SORT controlling the trajectory at lift-off, a vehicle could be set down with pinpoint accuracy. Midcourse correction, abort—the whole setup was going to be a cake-walk.

The kid LeFarge was good, good enough to make him think he could do without the Andros bitch. Right now nothing indicated that it could not all be handled from right here in Command, with the staff at hand.

Okay, he thought, one more chore out of the way. Now it's time to start setting up the telemetry hookup with the radio-controlled detonators. . . .

CHAPTER TWELVE

10:05 P.M.

"Is there anything we need to go over again?" Pierre
Armont inquired, looking around the dusty, aging Athens
hangar with a feeling of wary confidence. The weatherbeaten
benches and tables were cluttered with maps of Andikythera
and blueprints of the SatCom facility, scattered among half-
empty bottles of ouzo and Metaxa. He had just completed his
final briefing, which meant the time had come to board the
Cessna seaplane that would be their insertion platform. The
team seemed ready. Hans had come through with the troops
they needed; Reggie sat bleary-eyed but prepared, nursing a
final brandy; the brothers Voorst of the Royal Dutch Marines
were austerely sipping coffee; Dimitri Spiros was quietly
meditating on the condition of the equipment; and Marcel of
the Belgian ESI was sketching one last paper run-through of
the insertion.

When nobody spoke, Armont glanced at his watch and
frowned. This final briefing had run longer than expected, but
he had to cover more than the usual number of complexities.

For one thing, the hostages apparently were scattered all over the place, always a problem. Unless the team could strike several locations simultaneously, the element of surprise would be forfeited. That meant the insertion had to be totally secure, giving the team time to split up, get positioned, and stage the final assault with split-second coordination. Carrying out one op was dicey enough: he was looking at three, all at once. The alternate strategy would be to focus exclusively on Ramirez. Take him out first, blow their command structure, and hope the others would fold.

The decision on *that* option would have to be made in about two hours, just before they set down the plane two kilometers west of the island and boarded the Zodiacs for insertion. That was when Vance was scheduled to radio his intel on the disposition of the hostiles and the friendlies. What a stroke of luck to have him there, a point man already in place to guide the team in.

"All right, then," Spiros said, finally coming alive, "let's do a final check of the equipment. We need to double-inventory the lists and make sure everything got delivered. I don't want to hear a lot of crap from you guys if somebody can't find something later on."

The others nodded. Dimitri had had to scramble to get all the hardware together, and Reginald Hall had had to make some expensive last-minute arrangements to obtain a set of balaclava antiflash hoods for everybody. When there were hostages everywhere, the safest way to storm the terrorists was with nonlethal flash grenades, which produced a blinding explosion and smoke but did not spew out iron fragments. But their use required the assault to function in the momentarily disruptive environment they created. The hoods, which protected the wearer's face and eyes from the smoke and flash, were crucial. And since your local hardware store did not stock them, he had borrowed a set from the Greek Dimoria Eidikon Apostolon, a SWAT unit of the Athens city police trained to provide hostage rescue, securing six on a "no questions asked" basis, even though everybody there knew they had only one use.

Word of the hostage-taking down on Andikythera had not

yet leaked out to the world, so DEA had not been consulted. But their record of security at the Athens Hellinikon Airport was so miserable he doubted they ever would be considered for a job like this. Though the DEA had trained with the German GSG-9, the British SAS, and the Royal Dutch Marines, they still were basically just cops. A real antiterrorist operation would be out of their league.

DEA had no illusions about that, and they also knew that Spiros was with ARM, arguably the best private antiterrorist organization in the world. So if they granted Dimitri a favor, they knew they could someday call on ARM to repay in kind. In the antiterrorist community, everybody was on the same team. Everybody understood the meaning of *quid pro quo*.

Most of the rest of the equipment had been retrieved from the ARM stocks the organization kept stored in Athens. Governments frowned on the transportation of heavy weaponry around Europe, so the association found it convenient to have its own private stocks at terminals in London, Paris, and Athens. It made life simpler all around.

Reggie Hall had dictated the equipment list as he drove in to London in his black Jaguar, cursing the glut of traffic on the A21. Once he reached the ARM office there, a small inconspicuous townhouse in South Kensington, he faxed the list to Athens, then caught a plane. Dimitri had checked out the list against the ARM inventory in the warehouse and quickly procured whatever was lacking. It had been packaged into crates, then taken by lorry to this small side terminal of the Hellinikon Airport, ready to be loaded on the unobtrusive Cessna seaplane he had leased for the operation.

By that time the rest of the team had already started arriving. Then, two and a half hours ago, Pierre had begun the briefing.

A counterterrorist operation always had several objectives: protecting the lives of hostages and procuring their safe release, isolating and containing the incident, recovering seized property, and preventing the escape of the offenders. But this time there was a twist to the usual rules. In a special-threat situation like this, possibly involving nuclear weapons, the recovery of those devices was the paramount priority.

The way Armont had planned the assault, ARM could manage with a seven-man team instead of the nine most special-reaction outfits normally used. He would be team leader, which meant his responsibilities included supervision as well as being in charge of planning and execution, controlling cover and entry elements, and determining special needs.

Since Vance was already on the ground, he would be point man, providing reconnaissance and recommending primary and alternate routes of approach. The point man in an assault also led the entry element during approach and assisted the defense men in the security. Finally, he was expected to pitch in and help with the pyrotechnics as needed.

The defense man would be Marcel, the Belgian, who would cover for the Voorst brothers during the assault and provide security for Vance during the approach. He would also double as point man when required and protect the entry team from ambush during approach. Another duty was to cover the entry element during withdrawal and handle the heavy equipment.

Hans would serve as the rear security man, following the entry element during movement and providing close cover during withdrawal. He would be second in command, and also would bring in whatever equipment was needed.

Since Reggie was a crack shot, the best, he would be the standoff sniper, maintaining surveillance on the subject area from a fixed position, monitoring radio frequencies, and providing intelligence on hostile movements. He also would neutralize by selective fire anybody who posed an imminent threat to the entry team.

Spiros would be the observer, keeping a record of everything for an after-action summary, providing security for Reggie, and assisting in locating hostile personnel. He would relieve Hall as necessary, and handle the CS or smoke if Pierre signaled for it.

That was it for assignments. Everybody would be doing more or less what they always did. So far so good.

The next item was intelligence. Normally you tried to gather as much as you could on-scene, and presumably Vance was taking care of that. For the rest of it, Armont had dug up blueprints for all the buildings from the files, and on the plane from Paris he had meticulously numbered the levels, sectorized the windows, and labeled all the openings, ventilation shafts, et cetera. At the briefing just completed, he had used the blueprints to designate primary and secondary entry-points. He would fine-tune his strategy with Vance by radio once they had made the insertion; and then, after he had located all the terrorists and confirmed the situation of the hostages, they would use the blueprints to plan the assault.

Next came the equipment. Since the assault would be at night, they would need vision capabilities. That included M17A1 7×50 binoculars, starlight scopes, and infrared scopes. Then the radios, which had to be multichanneled, with one channel reserved strictly for the team, and have cryptographic (secure voice) capability. The surveillance radio package—compact in size, with a short antenna—included a lapel mike, push-to-talk button, and earpiece. All members of the team would have a radio, worn in a comfortable position and out of the way. As usual they would employ strict communication discipline, using their established call signs and codes as much as possible.

Other personal equipment included chemical light wands, luminous tape, gloves, protective glasses, disposable inserts for hearing protection, black combat boots, lightweight body armor, balaclavas, flashlights, knives, first-aid pouches. Insertion gear included grapple hooks, several hundred feet of half-inch fibrous nylon rope, locking snaplinks, and rappelling harnesses.

Finally there was the weaponry. Everybody would carry a .45 caliber automatic pistol and a .38 caliber revolver with a special four-inch barrel. The assault team would use H&K MP5s except for Armont and Hall: Pierre preferred a Steyr-Mannlicher AUG and Reggie had brought along an Enfield L85A1, in addition to his usual AK-47. Then, just in case, they had the heavy stuff: M203 40mm launcher systems, M520–30 and M620A shotguns, modified 1200 pump shotguns, and 9mm PSDs. God help us, Armont thought, if we need all this.

Naturally there also were grenades. They had plenty of the standard M26 fragmentation type, but since these frequently were next to useless in a hostage situation, they planned to rely more on stun grenades and smoke grenades. The same was true of the AN-M14 incendiary hand grenade, a two-pound container of thermite that burned at over four thousand degrees Fahrenheit for half a minute. It was fine for burning up a truck, but not recommended for a room full of hostages. Better for that was the M15 smoke grenade, which spewed white phosphorus over an area of about fifteen yards. Smoke, of course, could work both ways, also slowing up the deploying team.

Last but not least were the tear-gas grenades. To temporarily neutralize an entire room, ARM had long used the M7 tear-gas grenade, which dispersed CN, chloraceteophenone. It was not a gas but a white crystalline powder similar to sugar that attacked the eyes, causing watering and partial closing, and simulated a burning sensation on the skin. If conditions seemed to require, they sometimes used a stronger chemical agent called CS—military shorthand for orthochlorobenzalmalononitrile. It, too, was a white crystalline powder similar to talc that produced immediate irritating effects that lasted from five to ten minutes. The agent (in a cloud form) caused a severe burning sensation of the chest. The eyes closed involuntarily, the nose ran, moist skin burned and stung—thereby rendering anybody in the immediate area incapable of effective action. He would choose which one to use when the time came. . . .

After Hans had helped Dimitri double-inventory the equipment list, Armont looked over the dark-brown crates one last time, then gave the go-ahead for loading. One good thing, he thought: since Andikythera is Greek, we won't be crossing any international borders; nothing will have to be smuggled through customs.

Reggie, impatient as always, was eyeing the clock at the far end of the hangar. "We've already filed the fight plan. I think it's time we made this a go op. What time is the next radio check with Vance?"

"That's scheduled for 2340 hours," Armont answered.

"After we're airborne. We'll go over the blueprints and compare them against the disposition of the friendlies and hostiles using his intel. Then we can decide the best way to take the place down."

The boys are getting itchy, he told himself. They want to get this over with and get back to their lives. Who can blame them? This screwup never should have happened in the first place. Spiros let the client set the parameters for a job—which violates the first rule. He is going to have a lot to answer for when this is over. But settling that will have to wait till later.

"All right," he said, starting up the Cessna's metal stairs and heading for the cockpit. "Let's get tower clearance and roll."

11:32 P.M.

The technicians in Command were all sprawled across their desks, demoralized and still in shock. Georges LeFarge shared their mood. Cally had disappeared hours ago, and he was beginning to think he was on his own.

The trajectories that Peretz wanted computed were finished. Now the Israeli wanted to work on the telemetry. And he wanted to do it himself. He had taken his place at the console and started programming a new set of instructions into Big Benny, the Fujitsu supercomputer. It looked as if he was coordinating some of the trajectory telemetry with the electronic signaling to the vehicle, and he was setting some sort of timer.

LeFarge pondered the significance of these actions. He wants something to happen when the *VX-1* aborts and begins descent, he told himself. And it has to be done with split-second timing. What can he be planning?

He felt helpless as he sat watching, the control room around him now silent and listless. Locked out of his own computer, he felt rudderless and lost. He was realizing computers were a friend that could easily be turned against you.

It was a moment of recognition that brought with it pure anguish.

10:01 A.M.

Dr. Abdoul Kirwani, ambassador of the Islamic Republic of Pakistan to the United States of America, sat rigidly facing the small desk in the Oval Office. When the call requesting a meeting had come from Johan Hansen's chief of staff the previous evening, he had hastily sent a secure telex to Islamabad to inquire if he needed any updating.

He did. And it was a disaster.

"It's past due time we met personally, Mr. Ambassador," President Johan Hansen was saying. "I regret that the press of affairs over the last month forced me to postpone receiving you sooner. State tells me your credentials are impeccable and you're doing a first-class job of getting up to speed."

Abdoul Kirwani nodded his thanks, modestly but with ill-concealed pride. He was a tall, elegant man with a trim mustache and deep, inquisitive eyes. Some said he could have been a double for Omar Sharif. A deeply guarded secret was that he cared more about the ragas of Indian classical music than he did about diplomacy. He had made no secret, however, of his admiration for Johan Hansen. The American President's refocus of *the* superpower's priorities was a refreshing breath of rationality and sanity in an irrational, insane world.

All of which made this particular meeting even more distressing.

"Thank you, Mr. President. My government wishes me to express its appreciation for the excellent cooperation we have received and the traditional American hospitality my family and I have enjoyed since we arrived. Shireen, I must say, loves this country as much as I do. She studied at Smith many years ago, and is especially fond of New England." He smiled. "We Pakistanis always yearn for places with a cool climate."

"Then perhaps someday you'll accord me the honor of letting Christin and me show you my new presidential hide-

away in the Berkshires." Hansen smiled back, chafing to cut
the diplomatic bullshit. "Perhaps sometime this autumn. We
think it's one of the most beautiful spots on earth."

"We would be most honored." He nodded again, reading
the President's mind-state perfectly.

"Now." Hansen could contain himself no longer. "I want
you to understand, Mr. Ambassador, that what I am about to
say is not directed toward you personally. My staff tells me
you have been a private advocate, for some years now, of
reducing and even eliminating nuclear weapons worldwide.
That, as you know, is my desire as well. So you and I see eye
to eye. Unfortunately, however, we live in a world where
realities still assume precedence over noble ambitions."

"I agree with you, Mr. President, sadly but wholeheart-
edly." The Pakistani ambassador nodded lightly, dreading
what he knew was about to come. So the U.S. already knows,
he realized. This disaster is going to turn out even worse than
I'd feared.

"The topic of nuclear proliferation brings us, I am afraid,
to the subject at hand. You will forgive me if we set aside our
views on the scenic American countryside for another day.
Time, unfortunately, is short. I think you will understand why
when you hear what I have to say." Hansen leaned back in
his heavy chair, hoping he had given the right signals. He had
been entirely sincere when he said he liked Kirwani and did
not relish the task immediately at hand. "Mr. Ambassador,
you will not be surprised to learn that this country is well
aware of the gross violations of the nuclear nonproliferation
treaty that have taken place since Pakistan refused to sign in
1968. The entire world knows about your uranium hexafluoride plant at Dera Ghazi Khan, and the Kahuta facility where
it is enriched using German centrifuges. We also know what
that enriched uranium"—he glanced down at his notes—"in
the ninety-five percent range, is being used for. However, we
have not been able to dissuade your government from the
course it has taken." He paused. "Quite frankly, there's not a
hell of a lot we could do about it without having to make
some very undiplomatic accusations against our staunchest
ally on the Asian subcontinent."

Kirwani turned slightly pale. Although he worried about India's growing nuclear capacities as much as the next Pakistani, he still did not particularly like the idea of his country having its own secret nuclear program, developed in part to counter India's. The world needed more dialogue, he believed, not more destruction.

However, he wasn't being paid to defend his personal views. "Mr. President, I'm not authorized to discuss the strategic security arrangements of my country, as I am sure you can appreciate."

"Yes," Hansen said, "I can appreciate a hell of a lot, Mr. Ambassador. For instance, I can appreciate the multi-billions in military and economic assistance we've lavished on Pakistan over the years. There are those in this administration who think that gives us the right to a hearing. You know, back when Ronald Reagan was President, his administration argued that we could slow down Pakistan's nuclear program by giving you every other possible kind of military aid. So we poured in everything you asked. However, all that aid seems not to have slowed your government's nuclear efforts for so much as a minute.

"In fact," Hansen went on, the memory still making him seethe, "what you did was turn to China for the data you needed to manufacture nuclear weapons without testing. That was the thanks we got. Then—"

"An unproven accusation, Mr. President," Kirwani interjected lamely.

"Yes, China denied it, too, but the Reagan administration took it seriously enough that they halted formal approval of a trade pact with China for almost a year in retaliation. We had hard evidence, believe me. And then—"

"Mr. President, we are not, I'm sure, here to give each other history lectures. Certainly neither of us has forgotten that during those years there were 120,000 Soviet troops in Afghanistan, just over our border. We had legitimate security concerns that could not always—I am speaking hypothetically, of course—be addressed with a strictly conventional deterrent." Kirwani tried to smile. "You do understand, of course, that this conversation is entirely hypothetical."

"Of course, so let's travel a little farther into never-never land. What we do know is that the Soviet threat in Afghanistan is now a thing of the past; world conditions have changed dramatically; and there are those in Congress who may choose to wonder why Pakistan still has any justification to stockpile—hypothetically, of course—these 'unconventional' weapons. American aid is not written in stone. Now, is that diplomatic enough for you, Mr. Ambassador?"

"We are allies, Mr. President," Kirwani replied calmly, "and allies work in concert toward mutual goals, each bringing to their alliance whatever contribution can further the ends of both. I do hope your government believes it has received as much as it has contributed over the years."

Hansen tried not to smile. We *never* "receive" as much as we "contribute," he was thinking. But then that's how the damned game is played.

"In the interest of diplomacy, Mr. Ambassador, I suggest we move this 'theoretical' discussion along. We have reason to believe that a certain number of 'unconventional' weapons may now be in hands neither of us would wish. The question is, how many weapons are involved and what is their yield?"

Ambassador Kirwani had been expecting the inquiry. It was like waiting for the other shoe to drop. The government in Islamabad was beside itself, appalled that controls had been so lax and that now the world was going to know exactly the extent of Pakistan's nuclear program. Before this ghastly situation was resolved, years of secrecy were going to be blown away. Yet in truth part of him was half-relieved that the cat was out of the bag, finally. For either India *or* Pakistan to loose nuclear weapons on the Asian subcontinent would be to unleash the wrath of Allah upon billions of innocents. It was truly unthinkable.

"You do understand, Mr. President, that before this conversation continues we must both agree that it never took place. Furthermore, even if it should take place, it would be purely hypothetical."

After Hansen nodded grimly, Kirwani continued. "We both know the Israelis have had uranium bombs, not to mention hydrogen bombs, for many years and yet they have never admitted it publicly. By maintaining a diplomatic fiction they have kept their Arab neighbors quiet on the subject. They are never called to account. The government of Pakistan merely asks to be accorded the same latitude to conduct our security arrangements as we best see fit. The Israelis know it is not in their interest to rattle nuclear sabers, and we know that as well." He edged forward in his chair. "That is, assuming we possessed such sabers, which I in no way acknowledge."

"I think we're beginning to understand each other." Hansen nodded. "So perhaps that counts as progress. Of course this conversation never took place, and lest you're wondering, I don't have the Oval Office bugged, the way that idiot Nixon did. I believe terms like 'confidentiality' and 'off the record' still have meaning."

Kirwani found himself yearning for a cigarette, though he knew smoking was forbidden here in this presidential sanctuary.

"Very well, then, speaking hypothetically and confidentially, I am authorized to inform your government that we have reason to believe that there may be two uranium bombs, in the fifteen-kiloton-yield range, that may be . . . in the wrong hands somewhere in the world. Needless to say, my government is extremely concerned about this and is currently taking steps to establish a full . . . accounting of the situation." Kirwani realized it sounded lame. But his government had authorized him to deliver those words only.

"God help us," Hansen sighed. It's true. Or maybe just a coincidence. "When were these hypothetical weapons found to be missing?"

"If such a thing were to be true," Kirwani continued, ever cautious, "it might well have been just over a week ago." A final pause. "And we have no idea where they are."

12:15 A.M.

Ramirez watched with satisfaction as Abdoullah and Shujat began loading the first device into the payload capsule. Shujat had carefully attached the wiring of the krytrons to a "black box" of computer chips, which was itself connected to a radio receiver, part of the telemetry for *VX-1*. With the bomb primed, the unsuspecting SatCom crew could now move the weapon—its fifteen kilograms of weapons-grade U^{235} waiting to be imploded upon itself—up the gantry and into the satellite bay of *VX-1*. That completed, work would begin on preparing the second device, which was going to serve as a backup.

When Peretz finished, only the computer would know the location of the first target. Total security, which meant nobody would be able to activate any antimissile defense systems. All of Europe would be at risk, though the real target would in fact be among the most obvious. With the U.S.'s entire Mediterranean Sixth Fleet now anchored at Souda Bay, a nuclear explosion there would change the equation of power throughout Europe and the Middle East.

It was high time. The so-called Eastern Bloc had turned its back on its Muslim friends in the region, leaving them to fend for themselves. The East had betrayed the Arab cause, just as it had betrayed him.

In the old days, Eastern European governments hired him in desperation, then half the time tried to kill him after he had carried out their objectives. Even a long-term purchaser of his services, Romania's Nicolae Ceausescu, had eventually turned against him. But he had seen it coming, even back when he had been the personal gun-for-hire of that late strongman, enjoying the hospitality of his plush seaside resort.

That time, his Beretta 9mm had saved the day. And now, here, now that the launch time for the first vehicle was drawing near, he was feeling more and more comfortable about the 9mm under his jacket. This *ad hoc* collection of operatives he had brought along was going to start getting edgy, more so as the hours ticked by.

The first to crack, he knew, would be the two remaining Pakistani engineers. But they were amateurs, which meant they posed no real threat. More than that, their usefulness was soon going to be at an end. . . .

No, they weren't the problem now. The problem was going to be egress when this was all over. But the old man who had been the President's professor years ago was a hostage made in heaven. And then, of course, there was the CEO, Bates. Nobody was going to shoot down a chopper with those two luminaries aboard.

Although egress was the long-term consideration, there also was a short-term concern. Salim was reporting from Command that the radio had a lot of scrambled traffic. The airwaves were beginning to have the feeling of an assault in the making. . . .

"Okay, we're ready," Shujat announced, standing back to admire his handiwork: the armed bomb nestled in its case, surrounded with bubble-wrap. The truck that would take it from the clean room to the gantry area was standing alongside the bench. The weapon itself, accompanied by its electronics, weighed over a hundred kilograms, but they used a forklift to lower it down. Very carefully.

Shujat was nervous. Although Octol was an extremely stable compound, which made it an ideal explosive to implode the enriched uranium, still . . . your instincts said to be careful. One nice thing about a nuke, though: if it went off accidentally, you'd never know. You'd be vaporized before your neurons and synapses had a chance to get their act together. You were *gone,* baby. Atoms.

"Take it up and get it on the vehicle," Ramirez ordered. "From now on we work straight through."

The two Pakistanis nodded and began slipping a large plastic covering around the crate. The clean-room procedure, which they were following, involved encasing a satellite payload in a sterile plastic wrap to protect it from contamination when it was being transferred to the gantry area. They zipped up the plastic, after which Shujat unsealed the airlock door and returned to help Abdoullah roll the white three-wheeled truck through.

Down the hallway they glided, with all the insouciance of two grocery boys delivering a case of beer. The launch facility was compact and efficient, and the gantry elevator was only some fifty meters from the clean room. The hallway itself was now deserted, as all the SatCom personnel were dutifully in their prescribed work areas. Via computer messages Peretz had advised the SatCom tech crews that the Arlington office had put the launch schedule on a crash basis and everybody had to stay at his post. There had been grumbling, but everybody was determined to get with the program. After all, SatCom was a team.

An electronic eye opened the sealed doors leading into the gantry area. It, too, was spotlessly clean, with technicians busying to ready the elevator. Everything was being prepared for a countdown.

Ramirez looked the scene over, straightening his tie. How ironic, and amusing, to have all these fresh-faced young Americans doing your bidding. The sense of power, and irony, was delicious.

"This is the new payload," he announced, with the authority that had long since become second nature. "Open the elevator and take it up."

J.J. was there and he looked Ramirez over again, still wondering who this guy was. Dr. Andros hadn't been around for a while, and all of a sudden this asshole was calling the shots. Was he Bill Bates's new second-in-command? It didn't make any sense, but then something funny was definitely going on. The communications system with Command was all screwed up; nobody could reach Dr. Andros; everybody was ordered to stay at their posts and not take a break; and there had even been what sounded like gunfire from the sector where the clean room was. None of these things boded well.

But he said nothing, just nodded in acquiescence and opened the door leading to the gantry module. The two new SatCom technicians, who had also shown up with the new AIC (asshole in charge), rolled on the cart—which was carrying some mysterious new payload.

The gantry elevator itself operated inside a mobile tower that rolled on rails, thereby allowing it to be motored next to the vehicle and—at the lower level—opened into the launch facility. From the lower level, technicians could insert the payload module, which then would be hoisted to the top of the gantry and inserted into the vehicle's nose cone. When the vehicle was fully prepped and ready for launch, they would roll the gantry, with its elevator, some fifty meters down the track.

Until thirty minutes earlier, the gantry elevator had been stationed at the midpoint of the vehicle, where technicians were loading the "propellant" and making the final adjustments to the quartz mirrors and nozzles. Now that they had finished that task, they could begin the countdown. Only the payload remained to be installed.

J.J. watched as the technicians secured the trolley, its plastic-wrapped package, and the two new dudes—a couple of camel jockeys some of the guys said they thought they'd seen at Berkeley—into the module and closed the door. In half an hour's time it would be installed and the countdown could begin.

11:24 P.M.

Willem Voorst was at the controls of the Cessna as they powered through the Aegean night, their heading 210 as they closed rapidly on Andikythera. He was holding their altitude at five hundred meters, their airspeed just under a hundred knots, barely above stall. When they were about ten klicks out, he would take the plane down to two hundred meters, then set down about two kilometers northeast of the island. The last stage of the insertion would be via two Zodiac rubber raiding craft and then, finally, scuba.

Everything still looked like a go. Reggie was leading Hans and the rest of the team through a final review of the facility blueprints, while Armont was in the cockpit, on the sideband radio to Vance. . . .

"Roger, Sirene," Vance was saying, "we're in the communications blockhouse, up on the mountain, so we're a little out of touch, but our best guess is that Terror One is still down at Launch. Everybody else is scattered all over the facility. That suggests an obvious option."

"Copy, Ulysses," Armont replied. "That means Plan B. We'll have to take down that point, and then secure the devices. Behead the dragon, then see what's left."

"My hunch," Vance concurred, "is that if you take out Ramirez the rest of them will fold. He's their main man. But I suggest extreme caution. He's a pro."

"Copy that, Ulysses. Hang on while I put you on standby. Don't go away."

"I copy."

Armont paused to search the sea below with his IR goggles while he scanned the military frequencies. Neither pleased him. A new storm was growing, building in intensity, and it would complicate matters. But even worse, the military frequencies on the radio were abuzz.

"Reggie, something's going on around here and I don't like it," he shouted back to the cabin, his voice strong above the roar of the engines as he scanned frequencies. "There's too much radio traffic in the area, all scrambled. What do you think? I'm worried the Americans are—"

Then it came. The radio crackled in crisp military English. "Unidentified aircraft, this is United States Navy warship Yankee Bravo. You are entering a controlled sector. This airspace is currently off limits to civilian aviation. Please identify yourself. Repeat, we must have your ID and destination."

"Shit," Armont blanched. He turned back to the cabin and motioned for Dimitri Spiros to come to the cockpit and take the headset.

"Give them the cover. We're a medical charter. Delivering emergency blood supplies to Apollonion General in Heraklion. Strictly civilian."

Spiros nodded, took the headset, and settled himself in the copilot's seat. "This is Icarus Aviation's Delta One. We have an approved flight plan from Athens to Iráklion, Crete. What's the problem, Yankee Bravo?"

"Icarus Delta One, we've got an exercise under way for the next seventy-two hours. No civilian aircraft are allowed within a sector from latitude 33°30' to 36°30' and longitude 20°00' to 22°30'. We're going to vector you back to Athens."

Spiros switched off his mike and yelled back at Armont. "Problem. Looks like the U.S. Navy's cordoned off

Andikythera. It's hot. Doesn't sound like they're going to take no for an answer."

"So that's what all the radio activity was about." Armont's dark eyes flashed satisfaction that at least one mystery was solved, but they quickly turned grim. "Well, we've got to go in. Give them the cover again and insist it's an emergency. They can check it out. It's all in the flight plan we filed." Which was, of course, bogus. The routing was intended to take them directly over Andikythera, where they would ditch. "See if they'll buy the 'medical emergency' story and give us an IFF and clearance," he continued. "But whatever happens, we're damned sure not to turn back."

"I'll give it a shot," Spiros yelled, "but I don't think it's going to happen. They're going to insist we exit from the area, then file another flight plan that takes us around it. Standard."

"Well, try anyway," Armont barked, knowing that the Greek was right. Things were definitely headed off the track.

Spiros clicked on the mike. "Yankee Bravo, we have a flight plan filed with Athens Control. Nobody advised us this airspace was off limits. We're making an emergency delivery of blood plasma to the Apollonion General Hospital in Iráklion. We filed a manifest with the flight plan. It's a perishable cargo and we have to have it in their hands by 0600 hours tomorrow."

"Sorry about that, Delta One, but this airspace has been quarantined to all civilian traffic as of 2100 hours. No matter what's on your manifest. You're going to have to radio Athens and amend your filing."

Spiros shrugged, clicked off his mike, and glanced back with an "I told you so" look. "Now what? They've acquired us on radar, so there's no way we can proceed. We try it and they'll scramble something and escort us out of the area at gunpoint. I'd say we're reamed."

It was a tough call, but Armont made it without hesitation. He strode toward the cockpit and shouted to Voorst, "Take her down to three hundred meters. And get ready."

The Dutchman nodded as Armont stepped back to the cabin. "Okay, gentlemen, listen up. We have to make a decision and I think we'd better vote on it. We've got three options. We can cancel the op and turn back; we can go on the deck and try our luck at evading their radar; or we can abort and take our chances. If we do that, they'll probably mount a search, but with any luck we'll be written off. I say we do it. Word of warning, though—if we screw this one up, the organization is going to take some heat."

The men looked at each other, each doing his own quick calculus. It wouldn't be the first time ARM had found itself having to work outside the system to save the system. Frequently the group or government that hired them ended up —for political expediency—formally denouncing whatever they had done. But it was a flap accompanied by a wink, and it always dissipated after any obligatory moral indignation was ventilated. This time, however, if the op went sour it might not be so easy to explain away.

Reginald Hall, the most conservative of them all, looked the most worried. He had a good civilian cover and he wanted to keep it that way. "You know, if we get picked up and detained, it's going to be bloody sticky. Half of the new chaps at Special Projects these days think I raise radishes for a living. It would be bloody awkward to end up in a Greek jail, or worse. Don't think I'd get invited to the Queen's Birthday anymore."

Hans was smiling. "Reggie, you old fossil, let me get this straight. You don't mind getting killed on an op, but you don't want to get embarrassed socially. I'd say you've got a priorities problem."

"The difference," Hall replied testily, "is that I can control what happens on a regular op. But now you're saying we might have to fight our way through the U.S. Navy just to get in. That's bloody imprudent, mates."

"Well," Armont interjected, shouting as he gazed around the cabin, "I'm waiting. We're still about thirty klicks out, which means that if we ditch her now, an insert tonight is out of the question. Plus, we'll be exposed. I'm waiting to hear a veto. If we're going to risk everybody's balls just to save Vance, it's got to be unanimous. Whatever we do, we do together." He paused. "I know what you're thinking—can

Vance handle it for another twenty-four hours? Personally, I think he can put together enough moves to gain us the time, but who knows." He looked around with an air of finality. "Okay, I take it silence is consent."

That was when Willem shouted from the cockpit. "Pierre, we've just acquired an 'escort.' About fifteen klicks out and closing fast."

"All right, lads," Armont ordered. "Time to get the show going. Break out the Zodiacs and assemble your gear."

The cabin erupted in action. They had been expecting to deplane at sea, but this was not how they had planned to do it.

"I've suspected all along we were a bunch of damned fools," Armont laughed as he strode toward the cockpit. "Now I know for sure." He glanced at his watch. "Sixty seconds."

He passed Spiros as he reclaimed the copilot's seat next to Willem Voorst. "What was our ETA for Andikythera?"

"We would have made the set-down site in twenty-three more minutes."

"Okay, I've got to alert Michael." He flicked on the sideband. "Ulysses, do you copy?"

"Loud and clear, Sirene."

"Looks like we've got a problem, old buddy. The trusty USN has shut down the airspace around the island. Closed it to commercial traffic."

"Don't like the sound of that. It's getting a little lonesome down here."

"From the look of things, it may get worse. We're going to have to slip the original insertion. We'll need another twenty-four hours. Can you hang on that long?"

"Hey, I'm making new friends all the time. No problem. The downside is that the rockets may start going up. I'm still trying to get a handle on that end of it. Now it sounds like I may have to look into trying to reschedule things a little."

"We need a breather," Armont said. "Our options don't look too good at this end. But we'll be there, so don't believe anything you hear on the radio. All things may not be what they appear."

"Copy that. Have a nice day."

"Roger." Armont clicked off the mike. "All right." He turned and motioned Spiros back to the cockpit. "Tell them we're losing radio contact. And our navigation gear is going. Say we're going to have to reduce altitude and fly with a compass and visuals. Maybe that will muddy things long enough to get us down."

Dimitri Spiros hit the radio and delivered the message. To total disbelief.

"That's a crock, Delta One. Assume a heading of three-four-zero immediately and get the hell out of this airspace. Immediately. Do you acknowledge?"

"Transmission breaking up," Spiros replied, toggling the switch back and forth as he did to add some credibility to his assertion.

"That's more bullshit, Delta One. Either you acknowledge or—"

Spiros switched off the microphone. "We've got to put her in. Now."

11:26 P.M.

Captain Jake Morton was piloting the F-14D Super Tomcat and he honestly couldn't believe this was all that serious. He and his radar-intercept officer, Frank Brady, had been scrambled on short notice and, though he relished the chance to clock a little flight time, he felt in his bones that this was a red herring.

He didn't even have a wingman, which told him that Command on the *Kennedy* probably wasn't too excited either. The blip on the VSD, vertical simulation display, was some tin can cruising just above the chop down there, pulling around a hundred knots and now losing altitude. Obviously just some civilian asshole, who wasn't going to make it unless he pulled out damned soon. He had to be close to stall.

Problem was, though, the bogey had responded to the *Kennedy*'s radio room with some "medical charter" malarky and then shut down. What was that all about? And now?

Were these guys really having radio and nav problems, like they'd said, or were they about to try something funny, some amateur attempt at evasion?

Well, he thought, if that's their game, they're pretty fucking dumb. So what the hell was the real story? He'd learned one thing in fifteen years of Navy: when you didn't know what *could* happen, you planned for the worst.

He switched on the intercom and ordered Brady to turn on the television-camera system (TCS), the F-14's powerful nose video, and use the radar to focus it, bringing up the image from down below for computer optimization.

"Yankee Bravo, this is Birdseye," he said into his helmet mike. "That bogey that ID'd itself as Icarus Delta One has still got a heading of about two-seventy, but now he's definitely losing altitude. In fact, he's practically in the drink. We're trying to get him on the TCS and take a look."

"Roger," came back the voice. "We've lost radio contact. Advise extreme caution. Whoever the hell he is, he's a bogey. I want him the hell out of this airspace. Don't waste time with the TCS. Get a visual."

"Copy, Yankee Bravo, want me to fly down for a look-see?"

"Confirmed, Birdseye. And assume you've got a hostile on your hands. Caution advised. Repeat, assume he's a hostile."

"Roger. We copy."

Morton tapped the stick and his F-14 banked into a steep dive, 74,000 pounds of steel plummeting downward.

What am I doing? he asked himself again as he watched his altimeter begin to spin. I buzz the guy and I'll probably scare hell out of him. He'll wind up in the soup for sure. And if he still doesn't respond, then what? Am I supposed to shoot down a civilian?

The very thought made his new mustache itch, a clear sign of nerves. Such things had been done before, but Captain Jake Morton had never done them and he had no interest in starting a new trend in his career. He had a wife and kids he still had to look in the face.

On the other hand, a close encounter would definitely get their attention. But then, these were international waters, and

the legality of interdicting civilian traffic was not all that obvious, and might be even less obvious in a court of law some
faraway day. Particularly if it really was a medical emergency
situation like those bozos down there claimed. Could make
for exceptionally bad press. Which didn't do a thing for pro-
motions in the U.S. Navy.

11:31 P.M.

"All right," Armont said, reaching for the microphone.
"We've got to confirm with Mike. He's got to know what's
going on."

He flicked the dial on the radio. "Ulysses, do you read?
Come in."

"I copy. What's the story?"

"Insert is a definite abort. Repeat, abort insert. We're expecting some company. Red, white, and blue."

"That's going to blow everything."

"You've got a roger, Ulysses."

"How far are you from Andikythera?"

"Looks like about twenty klicks," Armont answered.

"You were timed for 0200. Can you still make it tonight at
all?"

"Doubtful. Even with the two Zodiacs and outboards, by
the time we reached there it'd be almost daylight. We may
have to revise the insert, plus twenty-four."

"How about your gear?" Vance's voice betrayed his concern. "We'll need hardware. The hostiles are loaded for bear.
You—"

"We'll do what we can. We don't like it either. . . . Uh-
oh." He had just glanced at the radar. "Company's here,
Ulysses. Stay up on this frequency."

"Copy."

Armont turned to Voorst. "Okay, we've got to ditch *now*.
That's probably an F-14"—he pointed to the radar screen—
"and he's going to be on us in less than two minutes. We have
to give him something to talk about back in the briefing
room."

Willem Voorst was staring through the cockpit windscreen at the dark, choppy sea skimming by just below the fuselage. "Hang on."

The ARM gear was packed in waterproof containers, and the Zodiac rafts were by the doors, ready to eject.

Willem loosened his flight helmet and dropped the flaps. "I hope this baby is insured by somebody."

"It's insured," Armont said, grimacing to think of the paperwork that lay ahead. "We just had a malfunction. That's my professional opinion."

11:33 P.M.

The storm had cut visuals to a minimum, and the puddle hopper down there was still not responding. Morton figured if giving the guy a flyby didn't get his attention, then Command would want to hand him a little heat, say a tracer from the Tomcat's 20mm cannon. He prayed it wouldn't come to that, because that might well cause the guy to pee in his pants and go down for sure.

What the hell was going on, anyway? The wing had shipped out of Souda, battle-ready, with less than an hour's notice. There still hadn't been a briefing. The whole thing was some top-secret exercise nobody could figure. And now this bullshit.

He thought again about the rumor going around the flight deck of the *Kennedy* that an AWACS had been brought up from Saudi to monitor all air traffic in the area. What the hell was that about? Command had dropped a hint about terrorists, but this whole mobilization seemed like using a Phoenix missile on a mosquito.

Then, just as he had feared, the radio crackled again. "Birdseye, this is the TAO. I've just got you authorization to lay a tracer alongside that bogey if he refuses to acknowledge your flyby."

"Please repeat for verify." Morton had expected it, but he wasn't about to jeopardize his career over a misunderstood radio transmission.

"You have positive authorization to lay one tracer in the vicinity of Icarus Delta One. Monitor her response and we will advise follow-up procedure."

"Roger. But first let me try to raise them on the radio one last time." That cooks it, Morton told himself. Guess they want to play hardball with these assholes. Whatever this so-called "exercise" is all about, somebody upstairs is taking it all very seriously.

But then who knew? Maybe those guys down there were terrorists. Word had already reached the *Kennedy*'s lower decks about the *Glover* being shot all to hell in a false-flag attack, which meant caution was the byword. The rumor mill also had it that terrorists had seized one of the small Greek islands in this area. Was that it? Was the Navy's quarantine intended to keep them from bringing in reinforcements? To interdict them if they tried to get away? Had the U.S. Navy been made into a watchdog?—a pretty lowly station after the glories in the Gulf.

He spoke over the cockpit intercom, the ICS, advising Brady of the authorization. It was a formality, since Frank had monitored all the radio talk.

Brady said, "Shit," then flipped on the F-14's weapons station and armed it.

"We're hot."

11:38 P.M.

The radio crackled again, and this time Willem Voorst flicked a switch so the entire cabin could hear.

"Delta One, this is Captain Jake Morton, United States Navy. I'm giving you one last warning. You have been instructed to alter your heading to three-four-zero and exit this airspace. If you do not comply, I am authorized to employ whatever degree of force is necessary to make sure you do not proceed. What is your intention? I repeat, what is your intention?"

"All right," Armont said, "this is it."

The pontoons bounced across the chop as Voorst touched

down. He reversed the props and in seconds had brought the Cessna to an abrupt halt, its frail fuselage bobbing like a cork. With the storm coming up, the sea was rougher than it looked.

Hans immediately opened the door, then nodded back to the cabin and reached for the line attached to the first raft. He had done this dozens of times before, but it always was scary. You had to watch out for the motor, inflate the raft from the doorway, then get your gear in, all the while keeping hold of the line. Do it wrong and you could lose the whole thing.

"Okay, Reggie," Armont yelled, "time to earn your share."

"What bloody share? It's fifteen percent of nothing." Hall sighed and stared out the Cessna's open doorway. Even in the dim moonlight he could see the whitecaps thrown up by the chop, and he felt his testicles tighten. "This is going to be a hell of an insertion." He recinched the straps of the backpack containing his gear.

Armont watched him swing out and down, knowing he hated the moment, then motioned for Hugo Voorst to step up to the doorway. "Hurry. We may be eating some cannon fire any time now."

Voorst moved up quickly. He glanced toward the cockpit one last time, then seized his gear and dropped down. His brother, who was still setting the charge, would be the last out.

"Our new escort is going to have us dead to rights in about sixty seconds," Willem announced from up front. "Everybody out, now."

Armont was securing the last of the gear needed for the insertion and the assault, readying it to be passed through the hatch, while Willem Voorst was just finishing with the charge of C-4.

Armont looked around the cabin one last time, hoping they had gotten everything they absolutely needed. Several crates of backup gear would have to be left, but unexpected contingencies went with the territory. With that sober last thought, he signaled to Voorst, who was ready with the detonator. "Set it for forty-five seconds. That should be enough."

As the Dutchman nodded, he reached for the rope and dropped.

Willem spun the dials on the timer, then wrapped it against the dull orange stick of C-4 and tossed it into the copilot's seat. In seconds he was at the open doorway, swinging down the line and into the dark below.

11:40 P.M.

Now Morton was really puzzled. The pilot had just gone into the drink. What had happened? Maybe, he was thinking, he should call in a Huey for a rescue op?

No, this setup was starting to smell to high heaven. They had refused to change their heading, so the bastards had to be up to no good. No legitimate civilian aircraft would ignore a U.S. Navy wave-off. . . .

Now . . . finally he could make a visual, rough through the downpour, but it looked like . . . it was a fucking seaplane. So instead of responding to orders to vector out of the airspace, they had settled in. Wiseguys.

Well, even with the stormy sea down there, they still could take off, leave the same way they came in, and nothing would be made of it. First, though, they needed a short lesson in aviation protocol.

"Frank, let me handle this. I'm going to get their fucking attention." Using his right thumb, he toggled the weapons selector on the side of the throttle quadrant down from SP/PH, past SW, and into the setting marked GUNS. The 20mm cannon was primed with two tracers, which should give the bastards something to think about.

Now the red radar lock on his HUD was flashing. That asshole down there, whoever it was, was in for a big fucking surprise . . .

His thumb was about to depress the red "fire" button when the first explosion came: down below a giant fireball illuminated the night sky, followed by secondaries! Jesus!

Medical supplies, right! That innocent-looking little

Cessna was a flying munitions bin. They really *were* terrorists.

A pillar of black smoke now covered the entire area. He ordered Brady to switch off the weapons station, and then, his hand trembling, he toggled his oxygen regulator up a notch, trying to catch his breath as he pulled back on the stick.

11:45 P.M.

"Ulysses," Armont's voice was coming over the radio, mixed with static. "Do you copy?"

At least they're okay, Vance thought. "Transmission is lousy, Sirene. What happened?"

"We had to take a swim. About twenty klicks too soon."

"Which means we definitely scratch the original ETA, right? Does the twenty-four still look firm?"

"Assuming we don't get any more surprises. This one is turning into a bitch."

"Don't they all?" Vance said.

"Everybody is in good shape. So nothing else has changed."

Vance looked around the mountain and wished he could believe that. The whole thing could have been over in another three or four hours. Now the terrorists had time to arm the vehicles and maybe even get one up. Life was about to get a lot more complicated.

He finally spoke into the mike. "Let's keep in radio contact. The deployment here keeps changing. Who knows what it'll be like by then."

"We roger that." Armont spoke quickly to somebody else, then came back. "There should be plenty of time to chat."

"For you, maybe, but I'm not so sure how much spare time there's going to be on this end. I'll try to hold everything down till 0200 tomorrow, but it's going to be tough. If you can't raise me, then just proceed as planned. I'll be expendable."

"That's a touching sentiment, Ulysses, but you know that's not the way we work. Our people always come first."

"Keep thinking that way. It's an inspiring concept."

"Okay, we'll review procedures and wait to hear from you. That's all for now."

"Roger. Have fun." He sighed.

12:23 A.M.

Up ahead through the dark rain loomed the rugged atoll of an island. It was not large enough to have any vegetation; it really was only a giant granite outcropping that nearly disappeared every time a breaker washed over it. This, Pierre reflected with chagrin, is going to be our staging area, as well as our new home for a full day. A little camouflage would handle the problem of detection by any snooping USN flyovers, but the boys weren't going to get much sleep.

"This is a hell of a deployment base," Reggie was saying, his voice barely audible over the sputter of the two outboards. The two black Zodiac rafts were now side by side, keeping together. His normally florid complexion had turned even more deeply ruddy from the cold and frustration. "How in bloody hell did it come to this?"

Armont was so frustrated he could barely manage a civil answer. "It came to this because we let a client spec a job. We left a piece of security to the client, always a bad idea." He climbed over the side of the Zodiac, splashing through the surf, and began securing the first line to a jagged outcropping. Around them the cold waves of the Aegean lapped through the rain. Dawn was hours away, and there was nothing to do now—except recriminate.

Dimitri Spiros, who had installed the security system for the SatCom facility, waded ashore looking as sheepish as he felt. He had only himself to blame for the penetration, he knew, and he had no intention of trying to defend it now.

"What can I say?" He grimaced and caught the line Hans was tossing to him. "I should have put my foot down. Sometimes pleasing the client up front means not pleasing him at the end. If something goes wrong, it's always your fault, not his. Human nature. I didn't listen to my own better judgment. Bates claimed they had enough security, and I let him get away with it."

"It's in the past now," Armont said, biting his tongue. "We all keep learning from our mistakes. Just as long as the education doesn't get too expensive."

Hans was setting up the camouflage that would cover them during the daylight hours to come. They had prepared for most contingencies and had brought enough camouflage netting to cover them and the rafts, which they now had dragged onto the atoll to serve as beds. They would take turns sleeping, letting whoever felt like it grab a few winks.

Now Armont was staring into the dark sky, thinking . . . thinking there must be a better way to pay for your caviar.

CHAPTER THIRTEEN

11:47 P.M.

"We're on our own," Vance said, clicking off the mike and looking around the darkened blockhouse. "Marooned."

Cally, who had been listening to the radio exchange, already had other things to think about. She was engaged by the computer terminal, checking out the status of the facility.

"Hate to tell you this, but it's worse than you know." She was staring at the screen. "They've taken over the Fujitsu. They've locked out all the other workstations and there's a countdown in process. Look! Somebody's on Big Benny who knows all about SORT."

"About what? Sort?"

"SORT's the program that sets up the automatic lift-off sequence. Once it's started, it proceeds like clockwork. The Cyclops comes up to power; the radars are all switched on; and the vehicle's electronics go to full alert status. The main console in Command controls everything and nothing can prevent the launch from proceeding unless it's stopped from there."

"How long have we got?"

"It's in the abbreviated mode. That's a six-hour count-down."

He looked at her. "So you're saying we've got roughly six hours to get down there and stop it?"

"Six hours on the nose."

"How about your friend, Georges?"

"He's logged off the computer. Like I said, it's somebody else. They must have brought along their own specialist. Guess they came prepared."

"One more problem," Vance observed with a sigh. "First Ramirez, and then this one. Guess we'll have to neutralize him, too. If that's the only way to stop the launch. This is getting dirtier all the time."

"There's no way to do it except get into Command," Cally went on. "But even then shutting it down's not that simple. Once it goes into auto mode, you can't just flip a switch. But still, that's the only place—"

"You're talking about a frontal assault that could get bloody," Vance said. "They might kill more of your technicians. No, the assault will have to wait for ARM. We're going to need to work a different way." He paused. "Maybe it's time we blew up something."

"You mean—?"

"What's the definition of a terrorist? It's somebody who uses well-placed acts of violence to disrupt society's normal functions, right? Murder one and frighten a thousand. A terrorist is somebody who takes on a more powerful organization by hit-and-run tactics. Scaring them."

"So?" She looked at him quizzically, her dark eyes puzzled.

"Well, they've taken over the facility now, which means they're the establishment, and *we're* the outsiders. The tables are turned, which means we have to become terrorists against *them.*"

"But—"

"We don't have much to work with, so we're going to have to do some improvising." He turned thoughtful, scratching at his chin. "How about some 'mollys'—throw together some gasoline, sulfuric acid, sugar . . . and maybe a little potassium chlorate for ignition?"

"Mollys? You mean—"

"Molotov cocktails. And if you design them for acid ignition, then you can blow them with a bullet. Not a bad little standoff bomb."

"I'm not so keen on blowing up equipment. It's hard enough to get things to work around here when we try."

"Ditto the fiber-optics cables, I suppose?"

"That would be even worse. We'd be down for months."

"Okay, nothing crucial." He strolled to the open doorway and looked down the hill, pondering. "We just need to put something out of commission that could be fixed easily later on. And you know what: I think I see the perfect target."

"What are you talking about?" She rose, stepped over, and followed his gaze.

"Right down there. That gantry. It's the only way to prep the satellite payload, right? Maybe we could take that out. It would keep them from installing a bomb, put them out of business without damaging the vehicle. Nothing serious. They won't be able to use it, but you can put it back into operating condition in a couple of days, with the right parts. Think that's possible?"

She seemed disposed to the concept, though still none too keen. "Okay, but I've got a better idea. How about just blowing up a portion of the rails it moves on? Then they couldn't roll it away from the vehicle to launch."

"Sounds intelligent to me, but I've got a hunch we'd better not wait too long." He was feeling energized after the steak. "Matter of fact, I'd say there's no time like the present. Where can we find some chemicals? Even the kitchen would be a place to start."

"I've got a better idea," she interjected. "There's a construction shed. It might have something left from back when."

"Then why don't we go down and have a look?" he mused. "Figure out if there's anything we can liberate."

"That's fine with me." She sighed, not sounding as though

she meant it. "All we have to do is manage to get down there without being spotted and killed."

"I don't know how much more excitement I can take." He definitely felt out of control, human prey, and he hated every minute of it.

"That goes for me, too." But she was already switching off the workstation.

By now the trek down the hill was getting to be all too familiar—the bristly Greek scrub, the rough outcroppings. Some nightbirds twittered nervously, but otherwise only their labored breathing broke the silence. The harshness of the terrain made him think again about the Greek character, ancient and modern. To stand up to a land like this, you had to be tough.

Which brought his thoughts again to the dark-haired woman by his side. Once in a while you ran across somebody with whom you absolutely clicked. He believed in love at first sight—he had been an incorrigible romantic all his life—and this was definitely the feeling he had now. And he thought—well, hoped—she felt the same. Could it be true? Maybe it was just the fact they were working together. They were both strong-willed, and he sensed real potential for friction.

"What are you going to do when this is all over?" she was asking, a wistful tone entering her voice. "Just go back to sailing?"

"You sound as though you already assume it's *going* to be over." He laughed, in spite of himself. Was she thinking the same thing? "I admire your optimism. But to tell you the truth, if we live through this, I'm hoping to try my Odyssey trek all over again." He took her hand as they navigated the stones. "Want to come along? Make it a twosome?"

"Maybe." Her tone said she was intrigued, and she didn't drop his hand. "It sounded pretty heroic."

"Well, it was mainly just . . . a challenge." He shrugged, continuing on down the dark trail. "Calling it heroic is maybe a bit much."

"No way." Her voice had a wonderful finality. "I think your attempt to recreate the voyage of Ulysses was a heroic undertaking. Period." She paused. "You know, maybe I shouldn't tell you this, but you remind me an awful lot of somebody I used to know."

"Who's that?"

"His name doesn't matter, but it was Alan Harris. He was a biochemistry professor. Tall like you, older than me. I guess I made a fool of myself over him, looking back."

Vance didn't know quite what to say. "What happened?"

"What do you think happened? Older guy, smart, lovesick student looking for . . . never mind. When I think about it, I don't know whether to laugh or cry." Then her mood abruptly changed. "Okay, the construction shed is right over there." She was pointing through the dark and the light spatters of rain that had suddenly appeared. Was it beginning to storm again? "It's always locked, but it's got its own separate computer control, so it won't be shut down like everything else. All anybody has to do to get in is just to code in a requisition. That's how we keep inventory."

He led the way, keeping to the shadows. "Well, can you tell it to 'open sesame' and let us in?"

She nodded, then entered a small portico next to the entryway. There, on a terminal, she typed in the code that would disconnect the heavy electronic locks on the shed's door. Moments later he heard a click and watched the green diodes on the locks start to glow. Next it swung open and the fluorescent lights came on to reveal a perfect high-tech fabrication shop, with rows of precision machine tools lined up in neat rows, the floors spotless. Looking around, he wondered what kind of chemicals he could scrounge. There had to be something. . . .

12:10 A.M.

"Everything checks here," Wolf Helling said, looking at the wide board of lights in Launch Control. "The Pakis went up on the elevator and wired in the device. Nobody here had any inkling what it is." He was speaking on his walkie-talkie to Dore Peretz, who was still operating the Fujitsu out of Command. "I think we're ready."

"Then you'd better roll the gantry the hell back, away from the vehicle," Peretz's voice barked. "My next item in the countdown is to test the alignment on the Cyclops, make sure the vehicle is receiving power."

"Okay," Helling replied. "The electronics are all in a positive state of mind here, but I guess you can't be too safe. By the way, how's everybody doing there? Having any trouble?"

"Our guests are getting with the program," came the answer. "I've even got an engineer friend here named Georges who's going to be a great help when the time comes. Small attitude problem, but nothing I can't manage."

"Well, keep them all frightened. It's the best way. I'll get started with the rollback. Should only take a few minutes."

"Go for it," Dore Peretz said.

12:15 A.M.

Vance felt the cold steel rails, glistening lightly in the thin moonlight, and wondered how long it would take to set the charge.

He also wondered if his impromptu bomb would work as planned. It should. In the shop Cally had led him directly to a cache of British-made gelignite, left over from the days of excavation. He had shaped a so-called "diamond" charge which, when wrapped around a rail and detonated with a fuse, would produce shock waves that would meet at the center, then be deflected at right angles, shattering the metal. It was a little-known bomber's trick—one he learned from Willem Voorst—that usually produced total deformation and fracture.

He had insisted that she let him handle this one alone, claiming there was no need to endanger two people, and finally she had agreed. Dr. Calypso Andros: she had already proven she could take control of a situation, like the one up the mountain, and handle it. That cool would come in handy later.

He also liked her New York street smarts. Yet beneath it all, he sensed something was wrong. She mentioned some guy named Alan, then clammed up. Funny. Reminding a woman of some old boyfriend could be a mixed blessing. Sometimes you got to take credit for the other guy's failings. . . .

Well, that cuts both ways. Admit it, he finally lectured himself. Calypso Andros reminds you of Eva Borodin.

She was the temperamental Slavic beauty who had been the love—on and off—of his life. That was the bottom line. He still wore her wedding ring. He had loved her more than anything, and after she left he had tried everything he could think of to help forget her. None of it had worked. Even now, here, the thought of her kept coming back. . . .

But enough. Concentrate on the job at hand and get going.

Quickly he began securing the soft explosive. Although his instinct still was just to blow the whole gantry and have done with it, he agreed with Cally that that was a no-no. The idea was sabotage, not demolition. The difference might not be all that subtle, but there was a difference.

The gantry, a huge derrick on wheels, was illuminated by intensely focused floodlights from a battery across from the vehicles. The tracks were about sixty meters long, which suggested the distance it had to be away from *VX-1* before the vehicle could lift off. So if he could destroy the tracks close enough, the gantry would be stuck in place, making a launch impossible.

The gelignite should do it, he told himself. The charge was going to wrap almost perfectly around the rails. This ought to be a snap. . . .

At that moment, he felt a tremor in the rails and looked up to see the lights on the gantry flicker as its motors revved to life. Then it started rolling; like a monolith, slow and assured, it began inching away from the vehicle and toward him.

12:18 A.M.

"Okay, it's moving back," Helling said. "I guess this thing—"

Suddenly, as abruptly as it had begun, the gantry halted, its steel wheels screeching to a stop along the tracks.

"What happened?" Ramirez's eyes narrowed as he gazed out through the viewing window. A red indicator had come up on the console, flashing. The gantry, bathed in floodlights, was just standing there, stubbornly still.

"The control went into a safety mode." The German was staring at the console. "According to the lights here, the track sensors shut it down. Maybe the rails are obstructed."

12:19 A.M.

Good safety system, Vance thought. He could feel them now, beneath the explosive—electronic sensors on the tracks, a thin line of parallel wires held by insulators, had detected his tampering and halted the gantry.

Wait a minute, he suddenly thought, maybe I don't have to blow the track after all. Why not just short-circuit these wires and let the thing's own safety system shut it down? They may not figure out for hours what the problem is.

With a grin he began going along the track, feeling his way through the dark as he twisted the parallel safety trip-wires together every few feet, making certain they shorted.

12:20 A.M.

"Well, we don't have time to tinker with it now," Ramirez declared, feeling his pique growing. "There's only a problem if it's a malfunction of the motors, and they don't report a problem." He pointed down to the console. "So just switch it over to manual."

Helling stirred uneasily. "I'm not sure it's such a good idea to override the safety system. We don't know—"

"When I'm in need of your views, I'll ask for them." Ramirez cut him off. "Now go to manual and get on with it."

Wolf Helling was a risk-taker, but only when he knew the downside. If the gantry motors shut down, he figured there probably was a reason.

On the other hand, the first device already had been loaded onto VX-1, all systems checked, the preflight punch lists taken care of. Maybe it was better to go ahead and keep Ramirez's mind at ease rather than worry too much about the technicalities. After all, unanimity was as important as perfection.

"If you say so," he declared finally. "But it's risky. I take no responsibility for this."

He flipped the gantry control motors to override and shoved the operating lever forward. . . .

Outside the glass partition the huge gantry again began to inch along its steel tracks, moving away from the vehicle.

"See," Ramirez said coldly and with satisfaction. "It was probably a malfunction of the indicator lights. We don't have time to troubleshoot every little glitch that crops up. Now increase the speed and let's get on with it."

Wolf Helling, his precise Prussian mind clicking, was liking Ramirez's recklessness less and less. On the other hand, he knew better than to contradict the temperamental South American he'd hired on with.

"Let's keep the speed the way it is. And I think I ought to go out and check the track, just to be sure."

"If you want to, but don't take too long."

12:21 A.M.

Uh-oh. Vance felt the tracks suddenly shiver. Then with what sounded like a painful grind of metal on metal, the gantry started moving again. They'd decided to override the safety shutoff.

Okay, he thought, back to the original plan. He turned and retraced his steps to the place where he had left the gelignite, feeling along the track until his fingers touched it.

It was still in place, but there was no time now to set up a fuse.

Which meant there was only one other way to blow it.

Quickly he secured the diamond-shaped patch more tightly around the steel, then looked up to check the gantry. It was now about five meters away, its wheels inching along the rails with a ponderous inevitability as its electric motors hummed.

He pulled out his sailor's tin of matches and withdrew one. Relieved it was still dry, he scraped the match across the bottom of the can and it flamed in the dark. Next he quickly pressed the wooden end into the soft gelignite, making a target he could see from a distance.

After checking it one last time, he rose and dashed for the safety of the nearest shed, pulling the Uzi from his belt and chambering a round.

He leaned against a darkened wall and took careful aim, on semiauto. The gantry was only a meter away from the charge when he finally squeezed off a round. It kicked up a spray of gravel next to the rails, the small stones glistening in the floodlights like small shining stars as they erupted slightly to the left of where he had placed the charge.

Damn. He knew the match could be seen, as well as the flare of the Uzi, but maybe nobody was watching. In any case, he adjusted his aim and quickly fired again. But this time he had moved the sight too far to the right. Again the gravel splayed, another sparkle under the lights, but once more nothing happened.

Now the gantry's wheels were about to pass directly over the explosive. If the thing was going to be immobilized, he had one shot left. He took careful aim and squeezed the trigger . . .

To the sound of a dull click. His last round had misfired.

12:22 A.M.

"Something's going on out there," Ramirez yelled, grabbing Helling's arm. "I saw flashes of light. Somebody's shooting. See it? Over there." He was pointing.

"That's exactly why I wanted to check it out." At last, Helling thought. Maybe now he'll listen to reason. "Look, I'm going to shut this damned thing down right now. Till we know what's going on."

He hit the control and applied the brakes.

12:23 A.M.

He had just squandered his last rounds *and* his chance to cripple the gantry. He sighed involuntarily. *C'est la vie.*

At that instant, however, whoever was manning the controls locked the wheels and there was the loud screech of metal on metal. He watched the wheels slide across the patch of gelignite, creating instantaneous frictional heat.

Immediately a blinding white flare erupted from the tracks, followed by the loud crack of an explosion. He watched as the first steel wheel was sheared away and the gantry lurched awkwardly forward. Next the axle ground into the gravel next to the track as the motion of the giant tower tilted it askew. It had not toppled over, but it was leaning dangerously. Whatever might be required to repair it, the gantry was no longer functional. SatCom was shut down for the foreseeable.

He was less than happy with his handiwork. Cally's going to kill me—that was his first thought—after her long diatribe about not doing any big damage.

Then he watched as it got worse. The gantry jerked again as the axle cracked from the stress and began slowly to heel. Like the slow crash of a tumbling redwood—he almost wanted to shout "timberrrr"—it toppled forward, landing with an enormous crash that shook the very ground around him. Angle-iron and lights splintered into the granite-strewn soil that separated the launch pad from the rest of the facility. Now the gantry lay like a fallen giant. . . .

As he watched, he slowly recognized he had achieved nothing but malicious damage. By collapsing, the gantry was now out of the way, below the sight lines between the Cyclops system on the mountain and the vehicle. They still could launch.

VX-1 must already be armed, he realized; the bomb is aboard and set to fly.

12:24 A.M.

"Goddammit I warned you it was a mistake," Helling exploded, still stunned by the view out the window. The gantry had just heeled over and collapsed onto the track.

"At least it fell out of the way," Ramirez declared calmly. "No problem." He cursed himself for not taking Helling's advice. For once the German had been right. "Nothing's changed. We launch on schedule. But right now we have some unfinished business."

"What—?"

"That bastard from up on the mountain. He had to be the one responsible. I know it was him. I can smell it." He drew out his 9mm Beretta and clicked off the safety, then angrily motioned for Helling and headed out the door. "Come on, let's get the son of a bitch. I'm going to kill him personally."

12:25 A.M.

Now what?

Vance rose and started walking toward an opening he saw that led into the underground launch facility. Maybe, he was thinking, he could slip into Launch Control and somehow sabotage the vehicle itself. A dark tunnel branched off on his right—the lights were off—so he probably could go directly in.

Okay, he thought, assume one of the bombs must already be installed on the first vehicle and ready for launch. But given all the krytron detonators the Pakistani had, there could well be more. Maybe you should try and find them, see what you can learn. Could there be a way to disable the weapon now poised up there without having to reach it? Maybe disarm it electronically?

He tried to guess what the firing mechanism could be. Clearly if you were planning to deliver a nuke, you were going to need some way to control the detonation. So how did it work? Maybe a pressure apparatus that could blow it on the way down, during the reentry phase? Why not? As the vehicle encountered denser and denser atmosphere, pressure could activate a switch that sensed the altitude and instigated detonation at a preprogrammed height.

Or . . . another possibility was a radio-controlled device connected to the guidance system in the computer. That would be trickier, but it might ultimately be more reliable.

It also might be easier to abort. In fact, the whole thing might be doable from here on the ground. . . .

But what if he got caught? His Uzi was empty; Cally had his Walther; and nothing now stood between him and the terrorists except his own . . . bad luck.

As he edged into the darkened tunnel, he felt the coolness envelop him. The whole operation now felt as though it were in a shroud. . . .

He was almost at the end when he heard the steel door behind him slam shut. He whirled to look, but nothing betrayed any sign of life. Instead there was only stony silence, punctuated by the mechanical hum of the facility's underground environmental control system. But as he turned back, two figures stood in the doorway ahead.

Oh, shit!

He hit the floor just as it started, a ricochet of bullets slapping around him. Then, as abruptly as the fusillade had begun, it stopped. He was so astonished to still be alive he barely heard the voice from the smoky doorway cut through the sudden silence. Then it registered, accent and all.

"Is that you, my friend?" A pause. "You are like the cat with nine lives, and until a second ago you had used only eight. I assume your ninth got you through my colleagues' burst of impetuosity just now. But I want to see you before I kill you."

"Your counting system needs work," Vance said, still in shock. He gingerly pulled himself up off the floor, fully expecting to be shot then and there. The thought made him giddy, feeling like a Zen master living as though already dead. "I've got eight and a half left."

"So it *is* you." The accent was unmistakable. "Don't make me sorry I didn't let Wolf here finish you just now. However, this matter is personal. I want the satisfaction of doing it myself."

Vance stepped into the light. "Sabri Ramirez. I can't really say it's a pleasure to meet you." The giddy feeling was growing. "I feel like I'm going to need a shower, just being in the same space."

Ramirez stared at him, startled. "How do you know who I am?"

"I'll bet half the bozos who came with you don't know, do they?" Vance looked him over, feeling his life come back. Stand up and take it like a man. "Back from the dead. It's a miracle."

"Yes, I am back. But you soon will be entering that condition, and I doubt very much you will be returning."

Vance's mind flashed a picture of Ramirez strafing the Navy frigate, shooting the SatCom technician. Not to mention, he was planning to detonate a nuclear device somewhere in the world. Not a man given to idle threats.

He was also known to love torture, part of his personal touch.

"Incidentally," Ramirez went on, "perhaps you should pass me that Uzi. I assume the clip is empty, but it's liable to make my friend Wolf here nervous."

"Wouldn't want that, would we." Vance handed it over, metal stock first.

"Thank you." Ramirez took it and tossed it to the emaciated, balding man standing next to him. "By the way, you know my name but I still do not know yours."

"Vance. Mike Vance." Why not tell him? he thought. It hardly matters now.

"Vance . . . that name rings a bell . . . from somewhere . . ." The thoughtful look turned slowly to a smile. "Ah yes, as I recall you work free-lance for ARM." He paused, the smile vanishing as he mentioned the name. "So tell me, are they planning to try to meddle here? That would be a big mistake, Mr. Vance, I can assure you."

More bad news, Vance thought. Ramirez is no fool. He must have known we did the security for this place.

"I've got a feeling they're going to be interested in what happens to me, if that's what you mean."

Ramirez moved closer, looking squarely in his face. "You know, the eyes of a man always tell more about him than any words he can say. And your eyes give you away. You're lying, and you're scared." He stepped back and smiled.

"And I'll tell you something," Vance continued, meeting his stare. "When I look in your eyes, I don't see anything. But even a hyena can know fear. Your time will come." It was pointless bravado, but it felt good to say it.

"We'll see who can know fear." Ramirez scowled angrily at the use of the nickname he hated. "We will also learn something about your tolerance for pain, Mr. Vance. In very short order. You are not very popular with some of my men."

"They're not very popular with me." The defiance just kept coming; he wasn't sure from where. "And I've got some other news for you. You're about to find out that Andikythera is a very small, vulnerable objective."

"You persist in trying to antagonize me, Mr. Vance. I could easily have had you killed just now, and spared myself this pointless interview."

"Why didn't you?" The giddy feeling was coming back.

"I wanted to show you how stupid you really are."

He's right about that, Vance told himself. I think I've just proved it.

"But your nine lives have run out. I'm afraid I'm no

longer interested in this conversation." He turned away and motioned for Wolf Helling.

"Let me just shoot him and get it over with," the German said.

"Not just yet," Ramirez replied after a moment's thought. "No, I think Jean-Paul would enjoy softening him up first."

6:15 A.M.

"Mr. President," the voice said, "have you made your decision yet?"

John Hansen felt his anger growing. The voice on the other end of the phone exuded the self-assurance of a man who was holding something unspeakably horrible over your head. Either he could bluff with the best of them, or he knew exactly what he was doing. Which was it?

He looked over at Theodore Brock, who had been at his desk, just down from the Oval Office, early, arranging for the wire transfers of the funds to Geneva. The eight hundred million dollars had been placed in a numbered account in a branch of the Union Bank of Switzerland, just in case. The objective, however, was never to take the final step and transfer it into the accounts the terrorist had designated in Banco Ambrosiano. Brock now sat on the couch across, fiddling with his glasses. A cup of coffee sat next to him, untouched.

"We've accepted your proposal, in principle," Hansen replied, nervously drumming his fingertips on the desk. He scarcely could believe the words were emerging from his mouth. "We have some conditions of our own, concerning the hostages, but I think it's possible to come to terms, given time. Arrangements are being made concerning the money."

"According to the procedures I faxed you?" the voice asked.

"Not entirely," Hansen went on, beginning what was going to be his own gamble. "The funds will have to be handled through our embassy in Switzerland. It may take a few days."

There was a moment of silence on the other end, then,

"You don't have a few days, Mr. President. Time has run out. You have to make a decision. Either you honor our demands or you must be prepared to accept the consequences. And I assure you they are terrible. Which will it be?"

"It is going to be neither," Hansen replied coolly, sensing he still had leverage. "It is in both our interests to satisfy our objectives. Including the safety of the hostages on the island. If we have to work together to accomplish that, then we should. It's the logical, rational way to proceed."

"Mr. President, this world is neither logical nor rational," came back the voice, now noticeably harder. "The timetable does not allow latitude for delays. You—"

"Let me put it like this," Hansen interjected, trying to catch him off balance. "You have the choice of doing it the way it can be done, or not doing it at all. Which do you want it to be?"

"I've given you an ultimatum," the voice replied tersely, its sense of control returning. "The only question left is whether or not you intend to honor it."

Hansen stole a glance at his wristwatch, thinking. He needed to stall for time, but clearly it wasn't going to be so easy. The Special Forces had reached Souda Bay, but they would not be in position to begin an assault for several more hours.

"I told you I'm working on it," he said finally. "These things take—"

"The funds can be wire-transferred in minutes to the Geneva accounts I listed for you." The voice was growing cocky. "There's no need for brown paper bags and unmarked bills."

Hansen suddenly felt his anger boil, his composure going. Sometimes it was better to go with your gut than with your head. Then the scenario could be played out on your own terms. The hell with this bastard. Why not just call his bluff? He wasn't going to use the weapon, or weapons, even if he had them. He would gain nothing by that. The *threat* of using a bomb was his only bargaining chip.

"You know," he said, "I'm thinking maybe I don't want to play your game at all."

"That is a serious error in judgment, Mr. President. I am not playing games."

"As far as I'm concerned, you are." Hansen looked up to see Alicia ushering Ed Briggs into the office. God, he thought, do I look as haggard as he does?

"I'm offering you a deal." His attention snapped back to the phone and he continued. "Give me another day to arrange for the money. Another twenty-four hours. That's the best you're going to get."

"We both know that is a lie," came back the voice. "If you expect me to accept that, you are an even bigger fool than I imagined. Since you don't appear to believe my seriousness, the time has come for a demonstration."

"I'm waiting. The chances of you delivering a nuke, which is what I assume you have, are about the same as Washington being hit by a meteorite. The odds are a lot better that you'll just blow yourself up. Criminals like you are long on tough talk and short on technology."

"This conversation is getting us nowhere. So just to make sure we understand each other, let me repeat the terms once again. The eight hundred million must be wired to the accounts I listed at the Geneva branch of Banco Ambrosiano within the next five hours. If it is not, the consequences will be more terrible than I hope you are capable of imagining. The loss of life and property will be staggering."

"Keep him talking," Briggs whispered across. "Keep a line open. Dialogue the fucker till—"

Hansen cleared his throat and nodded. "Look, if you'll just hold off a few more hours, maybe something can be done about the problems with the money. You have to try and understand it's not that easy . . ." His voice trailed into silence and he looked up. "The bastard cut the line, Ed. He's gone." He cradled the handpiece. "Shit."

Will the son of a bitch be ruthless enough to use one of those nukes? he was wondering. You can't really know, he answered himself. With a lunatic, you damned well never know.

12:40 A.M.

Bill Bates was still in his office, trying to do some heavy thinking and put his problems into sequential order. The first problem was that the bastards were killing his people, mostly just to make an example and instill terror. The next one he wasn't so sure about, but from what he had seen in his occasional glimpses of Control, Cally was missing. Apparently she had gone off with the fucker who called himself Number One and hadn't come back. Was she down at Launch? Doing what?

Well, Calypso Andros was a tough cookie. They might pressure her and threaten her, but she would stand up to them. These terrorists were just cowards with automatics; he could smell that much a mile away.

The next problem was SatCom itself. He hated to find himself thinking about it at a time like this, but the company was built on a pyramid of short-term debt—construction loans that could be rolled over and converted to long-term obligations only if the test launch proceeded as scheduled. It already had been postponed once, and the banks were getting nervous. If these thugs derailed the Cyclops for any length of time, the banks were going to move in and try to foreclose on all the computers and equipment. The litigation would stretch into the next century.

SatCom. On the brink. High-risk all the way, but what a dream. Almost there, and now this.

He found himself thinking about his wife, Dorothy. She had been supportive—she always was—from the very first. Maybe after eighteen years of struggle she had had misgivings about gambling everything on this one big turn of the roulette wheel, but she had kept her thoughts to herself. Which was only one more reason why he loved her so. She had been all their married life, always there with a real smile and a hug when the going got the roughest. It made all the difference.

But now, now that the whole enterprise was in danger of going down the tubes, he felt he had let her down. For the first time ever. Even his briar pipe tasted burned out, like ashes. He had taken every cent he could beg or borrow and had gambled it all on space. Only to have a group of monsters barge in and wreck everything. Now what? He honestly didn't know.

He had flown an A-6 Intruder in Vietnam, but hand-to-hand with terrorists was something else entirely. The bastards had shut down all the communications gear when they moved in. The phones were out, the radio, and even his personal computer terminals had been shunted out of the system. He could count and he knew what automatic weapons could do. No, this one was out of his control.

He glanced around his office, paneled in light woods and hung with photographs of Dorothy and the two boys—his favorite was during a regatta in Chesapeake Bay. There also were photos of the Cyclops system and the *VX-1* vehicle, the latter caught in the austere light of sunrise, the blue Aegean in the background.

He shook his head sadly, rose, and made his way out into the cavernous room that was Command. The fluorescent lights glared down on a depressing sight—the staff disheveled and living in stark fear—one armed hood at the computer, another lounging by the doorway. . . .

12:45 A.M.

Georges LeFarge looked up to see Bates coming out of his office and into the wide, vinyl-floored expanse that was Command. He assumed the CEO had been sitting moodily in his office, dwelling on the imminent foreclosure of SatCom's creditors. He must have been puffing up a storm on his pipe because a cloud of smoke poured out after him. And he looked weary—his eyes told it.

Nobody down at Launch Control knew they had been taken over by terrorists. Peretz had carefully made sure that all communications from Command were monitored and controlled. Number One had gone down there, but he apparently had managed to fool everybody into thinking he and all his hoods were SatCom consultants. One thing you had to say for them, they were masters of deceit. Number One could pass for a high-powered European executive, and he was playing the authority thing to the hilt.

"Are you bastards having fun?" Bates walked over and addressed Dore Peretz.

The Israeli looked up and grinned. "More than that, we're making history. Fasten your seat belt, 'cause your first test launch is going to be a real show-stopper. A one-of-a-kind."

"This facility doesn't need any more 'show-stoppers,' as you put it, pal." Bates looked him over with contempt. "We were doing just fine before you barged in."

"Live a little, baby." Peretz beamed back. "Lie back and enjoy it."

"Let me break some news to you, chum. This organization isn't going to just roll over and give you the store. Now I want to talk to that greaseball who calls himself Number One. It's time we got some consideration for my people here. They need food and they need to be rotated so they can get some rest. There's going to be hell to pay, and in short order. I can guarantee it."

"Hey, man, ease up." Peretz leaned back, then rotated away from the console. "Everybody's okay. Don't start getting heavy. We're just about ready to party."

"Right." Bates walked past, headed for the door. "I want to see what you fuckers have done to my people down at Launch. I'm going over there."

"You're not going anywhere, asshole," Peretz declared, "so just sit down and make yourself comfortable." He turned and signaled the Iranian lounging at the door, barking something to him in Farsi.

The man was carrying his Uzi by the strap, almost as though it were a toy, but in a second he clicked to attention, brought it up, and chambered a round. Bates glared at him, then turned away, knowing when he was licked. He might try and take the bastard, but it probably wasn't worth the risk. Not yet. The time would come.

CHAPTER FOURTEEN

1:45 A.M.

"Isaac, wake up." She shook him, trying to be as quiet as possible. Outside a new storm was building, but the large barracks room in Level Three of the Bates Motel was dark and deserted, with the staff all now mobilized for the upcoming launch. "Thank God I found you."

His eyelids fluttered, and then he slowly raised up and gazed at her, his look still somewhere between sleep and waking. He seemed to be in a drug-induced, or shock-induced, torpor. "What? . . . Cally, is that you?"

"Isaac, there's been a disaster. I don't know where Bill is, but the gantry's been destroyed. He blew it up. Jesus, when I told him to be careful and—"

"Cally." He finally managed to focus on her presence. Then he looked around. "What's going on? Where—?"

"Everybody's down at Launch," she interjected impatiently. "These hoods have taken over the Cyclops and they've started a countdown. I want to get you out of here, and then try to radio someone. Now."

"What . . . what are you talking about?" He was still staring at her groggily. "Radio who?"

"The people who set up the original security system. They—"

"ARM?"

"They're coming in. To get rid of these hoodlums."

"Well, good luck. But the man who saved me, what was his name? He mentioned something about it. Then he disappeared. I don't—"

"That's who blew up the gantry. His name is Vance." She quickly recounted the story. "I told him not to blow it up, but he didn't listen. All he accomplished was to make things worse." She was so outraged she could barely speak. The idiot! The fuck-up!

Mannheim's mind seemed to be clearing. "A countdown. But why would Georges—?"

"He isn't involved, at least I don't think so. He's been replaced by one of their people. They've taken over Big Benny, somebody who knows how to run SORT."

Mannheim exhaled. "Then, what are we supposed to do?"

"It gets worse. Not only is the gantry gone, but I'm afraid they've taken Mike prisoner."

"Mike?" He was still trying to get his bearings.

"Vance." She was suddenly embarrassed by the implied familiarity. Isaac, she noted, hadn't missed it, and he raised an eyebrow. "Look," she continued, "he may be dead by now, who knows. But I want to get you out of here, and then try to raise ARM on the radio. They were going to delay everything for a day, but now they've got to get in here and stop the launch." She paused, shaking from the strain. "Isaac, I'm not as strong as I thought I was." Her voice quavered. "I'm scared to death. For you, for Bill, for Georges, for Mike. For all of us. Even worse, I'm scared for the world."

"What do you mean?" He was finally coming alive. With a faint groan he rubbed his glassy eyes and brushed back his mane of white hair.

"I've got a sneaking suspicion that those bastards have put a nuclear weapon in the payload bay of *VX-1*."

"Good God. And now you say the gantry is gone? How will we get it down?"

"Look, let's not worry about that part just yet. We just have to stop them from going through with the countdown. We can disarm the bomb later."

"All right, then." He was on the side of his bed, searching for his shoes. "Get me out of here."

She led him out into the darkened hallway. The separate rooms were all locked, giving no clue who was still around. Where was the SatCom security staff? she suddenly wondered. Were they locked up in their own safe little enclave somewhere? Wherever they were, they wouldn't be any help now. They undoubtedly were unarmed and demoralized.

With a sigh she pushed open the door and they stepped out into the storm. Wind was tearing across the island, bringing with it the taste of the Aegean, pungent and raw. It felt cool, a refreshing purge after the stuffiness of the Bates Motel. The rain lashed their faces, cleansing away some of the feeling of the nightmare, and she knew that the few wild goats that had not been captured and removed would now be huddled in the lee behind a granite ledge they liked, bleating plaintively. There was a wildness, a freeness about Andikythera, as the winds tore across and through the granite outcroppings—and the sea churned against the timeless rocks of the shore—that made it feel like nowhere else on earth.

Get practical, she ordered herself, forget the romance. The storm would probably be over well before morning, but in the meantime it would just make things that much harder for ARM to reach the island. If they made it at all, it would be around dawn, just in time to watch the launch. Damn Vance.

2:05 A.M.

"Somebody's on the frequency," Hans declared abruptly. The ARM team had been settled in for just slightly over an hour, trying to keep plastic sheets over them to ward off the rain as they attempted to alternate taking naps. However, in spite of the weather he had kept open the single-sideband frequency Vance had been using, just in case. Up until now, it had been a continuous hiss of empty static.

"What the hell . . . ?" Armont pulled back the plastic, wiped the rain from his eyes, and lifted a questioning eyebrow. Around them the dark Aegean churned against their granite islet. "Vance's crazy to be on the radio now. He'd better have a blasted good reason."

"It's not him. It sounds like a woman." Hans had a puzzled look on his face as he handed Pierre the headset, shielding it haphazardly from the rain.

"He mentioned something about a woman when we talked yesterday," Spiros said, snapping out of his morose reverie. "Maybe it's the same one. She was with him then."

"Well, whatever's going on, I think we all should hear this." Armont unplugged the headphones from the radio, then turned up the volume, the better to overcome the rain and roar of surf.

"Sirene, do you read me?" the voice was saying. "Oh, God, please answer."

"I copy," Spiros said into the microphone. He was as puzzled, and troubled, by this development as by all the rest. "Who the hell is this?"

"Thank God," came back the voice. "You can't wait. You've got to come in now."

"I repeat," Spiros spoke again, "you must identify yourself. Otherwise I will shut down this frequency."

"They've started a countdown. They plan a launch in less than six hours. And Mike is gone. I don't even know if he's dead or alive."

Spiros glanced around at the others, wondering what to do. The frequency was being compromised, but probably it was worth the risk. His instincts were telling him she was for real.

"Miss, whoever you are, you must identify yourself." He paused a moment, thinking. Then he asked, "Where is Ulysses?"

"I told you, he's disappeared. He screwed up and destroyed the gantry, and then he vanished. But I think they've already loaded a bomb in the payload bay of *VX-1*."

Spiros clicked off the microphone. "She knows Vance's code name. But half the Aegean probably knows that by now." He clicked the mike back on. "I'm giving you one more opportunity to identify yourself, or this conversation will be terminated."

"I'm Cally Andros, project director for SatCom. I was with Michael Vance when he talked to somebody in Athens named Dimitri yesterday morning. And I was with him a couple of hours ago when he was talking to you. How do you think I knew this frequency? What in hell do I have to do to convince you people that the assault can't wait? They have a countdown in progress. I don't know what they plan to do, but there's a very good chance a bomb is going somewhere."

"I think she's legit," Spiros said, clicking off the microphone again. "It adds up. Sounds like Mike was trying to shut them down and must have managed to muck things up. I thought he was better than that. But this is very bad news."

By now everybody was rousing, intent on the radio conversation. A storm was coming down, and now the whole plan was about to get revised. Again. Worse still, the insert would have to be managed without a point man. Unless . . .

"Dr. Andros," Armont began, "please tell me precisely what happened to Michael Vance. I want to know if he is still alive, and if so, where he is."

She told him what she knew, in a way that was repetitive and rambling. It also was convincing.

"Do you think they can launch in this kind of weather?"

"The storm will probably let up by daybreak. That's how the weather usually works here. I don't think it's going to be a problem."

"All right," Armont interjected. "Looks like we'd better come in. I would ask you where you are now, but that might compromise your safety. I do have one more request, though. Could you stay by the radio and assist us after insertion, telling us—as best you know—how the hostiles are deployed? It could be very helpful. And possibly save a lot of lives."

"Yes, I'll do anything you want me to. But you can't wait

until tomorrow night. If you do, there may not be any point in coming at all."

"Then stay up on this frequency," Armont said, and nodded to the others. "You'll be hearing from us."

It was a gamble, taking the word of some anonymous voice on the radio, but sometimes you had to go with your instincts. As he looked around, they all agreed.

2:09 A.M.

"Did you get it?" Radioman First Class Howard Ansel asked. The radio room at Gournes had been particularly hectic the last few hours, but he was glad he had thought of scanning single-sideband. Ansel was twenty-eight and had eyes that reminded people of the German shepherds he raised back home in Nebraska.

"It's on the tape," Big Al replied, lifting off his headphones and scratching at his crew cut. "But I don't have the goddamnedest idea what it means."

"Doesn't matter. It was somewhere off Andikythera. Which means it's automatically classified Top Secret. Whatever the hell's going on, it sounds like some bad shit. What was that about a launch? Going in? Is this some kind of priority exercise?"

"Who the hell knows? But we've got orders."

He picked up the phone and punched in the number for his supervising officer.

2:12 A.M.

Armont felt the cold surf slam against his leg as they slipped the two black Zodiacs back into the swell, taking care to avoid the jagged rocks along the water's edge. The surf was washing over them, and everything felt cold and slippery. Reginald Hall was the first to pull himself aboard, after which he looked back, as though trying to account for everybody and everything. The weather was starting to clamp down now, faster than anybody could have expected.

"Pierre, *vite, vite,*" Hans was already in the second Zodiac, tossing a line across. Their "insertion platforms," both equipped with small outboard motors, were lashed together with a nylon line. "Hurry up." He turned and used an oar to hold the raft clear. "We need to get moving before this thing gets ripped to pieces." Neoprene was tough, but there were limits.

Willem Voorst tossed the last crate of equipment into the second craft, then grasped a line Hugo had thrown and pulled himself aboard. Dimitri Spiros went next, and then Armont. The wind and current were already tugging them toward the south, so the outboards would have some help in battling the choppy sea.

Reggie Hall was muttering to himself as he tried to start the engine. He bloody well didn't fancy anything about the way things were going. Everything about this op was starting to give him the willies. When this much went wrong this soon, you hated to think about what things would be like when the going really got tough.

As they motored into the dark, Willem Voorst kept an eye on the eastern horizon, watching for the first glimmer, and prayed the storm would keep down visibility. He also monitored the compass and hoped they could stay on course. Where had the weather come from? The woman who had said her name was Andros was probably right, though; this one would blow out by dawn, but in the meantime it was a hell of a ruckus. And the reception coming up on the island wasn't going to be brandy and a dry bed, either.

"You know," Reggie was yelling, "this bloody weather might even be a help with the insertion. If it keeps up, it could be the perfect cover."

"What we really have to hope," Armont shouted back, "is that a storm like this might force them to delay the launch. She said it wouldn't, but who knows. Still, we can't count on it. By the way, how're we doing?"

"I think we've already made a kilometer or maybe a klick and a half," Hans yelled. "If we can keep making this kind of headway, we should make landfall just before 0500 hours. In time to join everybody for morning coffee." He looked around. "This has got to be the stupidest thing we've ever tried to do. We're just motoring into a shitstorm." He shook his head, and the raindrops in his hair sprayed into the dark. "I can't fucking believe we're doing it. I really can't fucking believe it."

2:15 A.M.

"Damn," Major General Nichols said, covering the mouthpiece of the phone. He was on the *Kennedy*, in Mission Planning, talking on secured satellite phone to JSOC Control in the Pentagon. "Gournes picked up some radio traffic on sideband. Some assholes are talking about trying to go in. Whoever the hell they're working for, they could screw things up royally." He spoke again into the receiver. "Do you have a lead on where they are?" He nodded. "Right, my thinking exactly. Which means they probably blew up that plane as a diversion. And our F-14 jockey suckered for it." He paused again. "No, we're not scheduled to go in for another twenty-four hours. But that may have to be pushed up. I'd say we have two choices. Either we interdict these dingbats, or we just go ahead and get it over with, take out the launch vehicle and—" He paused again.

"What do you mean, we can't?"

His eyes narrowed.

"Don't give me that 'classified' bullshit. I've got Top Secret clearance and I damned well have a 'need to know.'"

A long pause ensued. "Jesus! Now you tell me. 'Nuclear material'? What the hell does that mean? You're planning to send in my boys to take down a nuke! This is the first I've heard . . . Thanks a lot for telling me. Good Christ!" He paused once more. "Okay, let me think. I'll get back to you."

He settled the phone back in its cradle and looked around Mission Planning, the gray walls covered with maps. "Shit, this whole thing is coming apart."

"What is it?" General Max Austin asked. He was two-star,

with steel-gray hair. As the base commander for Souda, he had been placed in charge of Operation Lightfoot, code name for the action to retake Andikythera. Even though they had known each other for fifteen years, Nichols was not necessarily pleased to have this REMF, rear-echelon motherfucker, running the show. Austin had been given the undemanding post on Crete for a year mainly as an excuse to bump up his rank in preparation for retirement.

"The whole op is rapidly going to hell in a handbag," Nichols said. "The Pentagon conveniently left one small fact out of my briefing papers. I'd kill somebody, if only I knew who." He looked up. "Max, we may have to send the Deltas in tonight. Just get this damned thing over with."

"That's not possible," Austin declared without hesitation. "This operation can't go off half-cocked. You of all people ought to know that."

"Well, sometimes circumstances don't wait around for the textbooks. The Gournes SIGINT team just intercepted some radio traffic. Somebody's out there talking, and they know more than we do. They're probably free-lance clowns, most likely mercenaries, but they're claiming the bad guys may be about to launch one of the vehicles, within the next few hours. So they're planning to hit the place tonight."

"Well, they won't stand a chance," Austin said.

"I agree, but what they can do is royally fuck up *our* insertion. They'll disrupt the hell out of everything and probably get a lot of the hostages killed."

"Okay," Austin mused, sipping at his coffee, "we've got two problems here. Maybe they should be handled separately. First we interdict these guys going in, and then we decide what to do next."

"The best way to solve them both at once, two birds with one stone, is with a preemptory strike on the island," Nichols insisted again. "Right now. Tonight. We just go in and take the place down."

"No way, Eric," Austin interjected. "That's going to skew the risk parameters in our ops analysis. We'd have to scrap our computer simulation and virtually start over. Hell, that alone could take us three hours."

All those fancy analyses are best employed wiping your bum, Nichols heard himself thinking, almost but not quite out loud. We've got nobody on the ground, so we're working with satellite intel, and SIGINT—which ain't giving us shit 'cause those bastards aren't talking on their radios.

"Let me make sure I heard it right a minute ago," Nichols went on. "We can't just take out the launch vehicles, a surgical strike, because there's a chance there could be nuclear material on board?"

"You've got it right. I'd hoped not to have to tell you. So consider this Classified. The whole op has been jacked up to a Vega One. We've never had anything that serious before."

That's nuclear, Nichols told himself. Well, he figured, why not. If the terrorists did have a bomb.

"This damned thing is hot," Austin continued. "They don't get any hotter. So there's no way in hell I'm going to go around procedures. If you and your boys don't do this clean, it's going to mean our next command, yours and mine, will be somewhere within sight of Tierra del Fuego. If there's a nuclear incident here, the Greek government would probably tear up our mutual-defense treaty and convert the base at Souda into a souvlaki stand. Am I making myself clear?"

"If I hear you right, what you're saying is, no way can we afford to fuck this one up."

"I've always admired your quick grasp of the salient points in a briefing. So, we're going to do this by the goddamn book; we're going to dot every goddamn 'i' and cross every goddamn 't' and get every goddamn detail of this op, right down to the color of our goddamn shoelaces, approved, signed off, and ass-kissed in triplicate. That Iranian hostage disaster did not exactly make a lot of careers. Again I ask you, Eric, am I getting the fuck through?"

"In skywriting. The only small problem I see, sir, is that while everybody is carefully protecting their pension, those assholes on the island may start slaughtering hostages, or put this 'nuclear material'—which I have just learned about in such a timely fashion—into goddamn orbit. And then my Deltas are going to be in the middle of a shitstorm they easily could have prevented if they'd been given the chance.

They're my boys, and I don't really take kindly to that happening. Sir." He reached in his breast pocket for a cigar, the chewing of which was his usual response to stress.

"So what exactly do you propose we do?" Austin asked.

"The most obvious first thing would be to interdict this bunch of mercenary jerkoffs and keep them from going in there and getting a lot of people killed. I say we should find them and stop them, using whatever force it takes. There are enough civilians in harm's way as it is." He leaned forward. "Look, if we have to dick around waiting on the Pentagon before we can go in, at least we can stop these mercenary assholes. It has to be done. And we don't need some computer study before we get off our ass. I want to take them down, and nobody has to even know about it. If it comes out in some debriefing someday, we'll worry about it then."

"All right, maybe I agree with you," Austin sighed. "They should be interdicted. What do you want? A Pave-Low?"

"Just give me an SH-60. To pick them up. I'm going to put the love of the Lord into these amateurs, then bring them in. Hell, they're probably well-intentioned, just doing what somebody paid them to do." And who could blame that somebody, he found himself thinking, if it takes the U.S. of A. this long to cut through its damned bureaucracy and mount an operation.

"All right, I'll give you a Seahawk," Austin said. "It can be prepped and ready to go by"—he glanced at his watch— "0300 hours. Will that be enough?"

"Guess it'll have to be." By that time, he was thinking ruefully, we could be taking the island. And with that thought he decided to hell with protocol and fired up his well-chewed cigar.

"Look, Eric, I know what you're thinking," Austin said after a pause. "That an old fart like me is cramping your guys' style. And, dammit, maybe there's a grain of truth in that— hell, more than a grain. But here's the downside. If your Deltas go in half-cocked and get cut up, we're going to get blamed. On the other hand, if they don't go in till Washington says so, then, yes, maybe it'll be too late, but it's going to be on somebody else's service record, not ours. I'm protecting your boys, whether you see it or not. If we only go in on orders, then the Deltas are not going to be the ones taking the heat if this thing falls apart."

"Just get me the damned chopper," Nichols said quietly.

3:15 A.M.

Mannheim looked at her. "Cally, we need to try and find him. This Vance fellow. If his friends are going to try and come in, then they'll need him to help them. He'll know what they require a lot better than you will."

She found herself nodding grimly, agreeing. Isaac Mannheim was no dummy.

"They must either have captured him or shot him," she said. "Or both. He would have come back by now unless there was a problem. But if he's still alive, then they probably have him down at Launch. And it's going to be very dangerous for us to go down there, Isaac."

"I'm an old man. Maybe I've outlived my usefulness." It was strange talk for Isaac Mannheim, but he was turning wistful, perhaps even defeated. "I do know one thing. He risked his life for me. I owe it to him to at least find out what happened. So let me go by myself."

She did not like the sound of that. "Look, maybe I—"

"No, not you. They've got to be looking for you. But they probably just think I'm an old fool"—he laughed—"and maybe they're right. At any rate, at least I can go down there and wander around a bit. Everybody knows I'm harmless. As long as it doesn't look like I'm going anywhere, I don't think they'll bother with me. At least not right now. If they're busy with the countdown, they're not going to trouble with a deranged old man. I'm small potatoes."

"Isaac, you're a very big potato." She wanted to hug him. "But you're also just about the most wonderful man I know. I love you to death. Just be careful, please?"

Now it was his turn to smile, the old face showing its wrinkles more than ever. "I'm not dead yet. And with any luck I won't be for a while." He looked at his watch. "By the way, when do you think those friends of his are likely to show up?"

"They didn't say, but I expect they might get here in a couple of hours."

"Well, Dr. Andros, we're not licked yet. With any luck there won't even be a launch. Maybe the weather. In the meantime, why don't I check the empty storage bays in Launch. Just a hunch." He rose and kissed her, then began to shuffle down the hill.

3:20 A.M.

"I'd guess he's at about a thousand meters now," Pierre was saying. Above them the SH-60F Seahawk was sweeping past, clearly on a recon. "Maybe he won't pick us up, not with the swell this high."

Armont didn't really believe his own words. The Seahawk carrier-based helo, the U.S. Navy's preeminent ASW platform, had come in hard from the south and it was searching. The question was, what for?

Whatever it was, the guy was all business. And given his APS-124 radar—not to mention his forward-looking IR capabilities—eluding detection was going to be tough.

"They must have figured out we scammed them," Reggie declared. "I was afraid it was going to catch up with us. What with the electronic assets the U.S. has got deployed in this region, you'd almost have to expect it. Probably the fucking radio. Which means we've got to keep silence from here on in. *Damn.*"

Armont squinted through the dark. "Let's wait and see what happens. As far as I know, those things don't carry any cannon, just a couple of ASW torpedoes. We're a pretty small fish. Let's hold firm for now."

They hunkered down and motored on, watching as the Navy chopper growled on toward the north. Maybe, everybody was thinking, the crew had missed them. Maybe they were after somebody else. Maybe . . .

No, it was coming back again, sweeping, on a determined mission to locate something.

"They're going to pick us up sooner or later," Willem Voorst predicted. "It's just a matter of time."

The wind and sea were growing ever more unruly. But that was not going to save them. They all knew it.

"I've got a terrible idea," Reggie said, almost yelling to be heard. "It's going to mean we go in with a bare-bones complement of equipment, but I'm beginning to think we don't have any choice."

"What are you suggesting?" Armont asked, his voice almost swept away by the storm.

"We cut loose one of the rafts, leave a radio transmitting a Mayday. By the time they realize they've been had, we'll be at the island."

"What about their IR assets?" Armont wondered back.

"Okay, good point. So we set a flare, and maybe attach a couple of life jackets with a saltwater beacon. That'll engage their IR."

"And what do *we* do? This motor will still have an IR signature."

Hall thought a moment. "We could cover everything with some of the plastic camouflage. That should cut down the heat signature enough."

"Reggie, I don't think that's such a hot idea," Spiros yelled, the rain in his face. "We're not going to be able to shake them that easily."

"Don't be so sure. There's a good chance a decoy would keep them off our scent for a while. Might just give us enough time, mates."

The Seahawk had swept past again, banked, and now was coming back. Clearly working a grid, maybe getting her electronics up to speed. Nothing about it boded particularly well —for some reason it was lit, a long white streak in the dark. Long and lean and ideal to drop ASW drogues, the carrier-based Sikorsky SH-60F incorporated 2,000 pounds of avionics and was even designed to carry nuclear depth bombs, though the choppers were never "wired" for the weapon. Its maximum cruising speed was 145 mph, with a one-hour loitering capability. Given time, it would find them.

"Willem, how much farther do you reckon we've got to go to make the island?" Armont shouted over the growing gale and the roar of the two outboards.

"My guess is we're looking at another eight or ten kilometers. But I vote with Reggie. We've got no choice but to try a decoy setup. Let's keep this raft—the engine is running better—and start moving over whatever gear we absolutely have to have."

He knew there might well be some dispute over that, with each man having a pet piece of equipment he deemed himself unable to live without. But the men of ARM were pragmatists above all, and they would bend over backward to reach a consensus.

They began sorting the gear, hastily, and the selections being made cut down their assault options. Balaclavas would be kept, along with rappelling harnesses and rope. The heavier ordnance had to be left, the grenade launchers and shotguns. They quickly pulled over a case of tear-gas grenades, but the others they left. Radios, of course, had to be saved, and the Heckler & Koch MP5s and the Mac-10s. No Uzis: those were for cowboys. Each man had his own handgun of choice, but the rounds of ammo were cut down to a bare minimum.

As they sorted the gear, they were making an unspoken strategic decision concerning how the insertion would be structured. Without the heavy firepower, they would be fighting a guerrilla war, focusing on taking out Ramirez, and hoping the firefight would be over in seconds. If it lasted more than fifteen minutes, they were finished.

The result might well be an assault more risky than it otherwise would have been. But, as Reggie was fond of saying, you can't have everything. Sometimes you can't even come bloody close.

3:33 A.M.

"Seahawk One, this is Bravo Command. Come up with anything yet?" It was the radio beside Delta Captain Philip Sexton, who was flying copilot in the Seahawk. Lieutenant Manny Jackson was pilot, while the airborne tactical officer was Lieutenant James Palmer II and the sensor operator was Lieutenant Andrew McLeod. "Any hint of unintelligent life down there?"

"Andy says the damned radar's picking up too much chop, Yankee Bravo. Don't think we're going to find these bastards. It's the proverbial needle in the you-know-what. This baby finds subs, not dinghies. Looks like all we're getting so far is fish scatter. Just noise."

"Then you might want to see if the IR will give you anything," came Nichols's voice. "The fuckers have clamped down, total radio silence, but they've got to be there somewhere."

"Roger, we copy. Don't know if we've got the sensitivity to pick up a thermal, though. Not with this weather and sea."

"Copy that. So try everything you've got, even sonar. Or the mag anomaly detector. Hell, try all your toys. These bastards are close to slipping through, and no way can that be allowed to happen."

"You've got a rog, sir," Sexton replied. "I'll have Andy give the IR a shot and see what we get."

3:39 A.M.

"They're staying right on us," Hugo Voorst observed, looking up. "They don't have us yet, but they've probably figured out we'd make a beeline for Andikythera, so all they have to do is just work the corridor for all it's worth."

"Then let's get on with it." Armont nodded through the rain. "Do we have everything you think we might need?"

"We've got everything we can bloody well keep afloat," Reggie yelled back. "We're leaving half of what we need." He knew that seven men in the single Zodiac, together with their gear, was going to be pushing it to the limit. The sea was still rising, which meant they would be bailing for their lives as soon as they cut loose.

"All right, then, Willem, set the timer on the flares." Armont shook his head sadly.

"If we keep having to abandon equipment," Hall could be heard grumbling, "this is going to be a damned expensive operation. Where in bloody hell is it going to end? When we're down to a bow and arrow each?"

"It's beginning to feel that way now," Willem Voorst groused. He had finished and was clambering into the single raft. With his weight aboard, it listed precariously, taking water as the waves washed over. He settled in, grabbed a plastic bucket, and started bailing.

Now the Seahawk was coming down the line again, making an even slower pass. Time had run out.

"All right, cut her loose," Armont ordered.

The radio they left had been set to broadcast a Mayday; the engine was locked at full throttle; and a couple of life jackets with saltwater-activated beacons had been tied to a line and tossed overboard. The flares had been set to a timer, giving them three minutes to put some blue water between them and the decoy.

With a sigh, Dimitri Spiros leaned out and severed the last connecting line.

3:47 A.M.

"I've just picked up a Mayday," Jackson yelled. "From somewhere in this quadrant. I think we've located our bogey, and he's in trouble." He banked the Seahawk, trying to get a fix. "Not surprising with these seas." He gave the instruments a quick check. "They can't be far away. Andy, anything happening on IR?"

"Nothing to write home about. There's—Jesus! It looks like . . ." He glanced out the cockpit window. "The hell with the IR. We've got a visual on this baby. He's right down there." He pointed. "See it? Let's take her in and see what we can see."

"You've got it." Jackson hit the collective and banked, heading down. Yep, he thought, no doubt about it. There was an emergency flare. Maybe the fuckers had capsized. Maybe there was a God.

3:51 A.M.

"I think they went for it," Armont declared, his voice almost lost in the storm. It's going to take them a while to figure out the raft is empty, and then some more time to make sure there's nobody in those life jackets. I think we've milked maybe half an hour out of this."

"Then we're home free," Dimitri said, staring toward the dark horizon. "We should make landfall just before first light."

"One thing, though," Reginald Hall reflected. "We can't risk any more radio contact. We're clearly being monitored. So whatever happened to Michael, he's on his own."

Armont said nothing in reply, merely scanned the turbulent skies. Maybe, he thought, the weather had worked to their advantage, had saved them from interdiction by the U.S. Navy. But would it be enough to delay the launch? He was beginning to think the storm might clear in time—given the way Aegean downpours tended to come and go—and not even put a dent in the schedule.

3:54 A.M.

Ramirez walked into Command, wondering. Peretz was at the main workstation, the one normally controlled by Georges LeFarge, and he was wearing a big grin, the stupid one he sported so often. So what was the problem? He had sent a computer message to Launch, saying they needed to talk. What was this about? He suspected he already knew.

The room was busy, resounding with the clatter of keyboards, the whir of tape drives, the buzz of fans, the hum of communication lines, the snapping of switches. Above them a digital clock showed the countdown, clicking off the hours, minutes, and seconds, while next to it were the three master video screens: the first giving the numerical status of the Cyclops power-up sequence, the second depicting the Fujitsu's latest orbital projection, being lines across a flat projection of the globe, and the third showing a live feed from the base of *VX-1*, where the antlike images of SatCom Launch Control staffers could be seen methodically readying the vehicle, not having any idea what was about to go up.

"Got a little item to go over with you," Peretz said, in Arabic, not looking up from his screen. "A minor business matter."

"What's on your mind?" Ramirez asked in English. "We're all busy."

Peretz glanced in the direction of Salim, who was standing by the door, keeping a watchful eye on the staffers. Salim, he knew, spoke Farsi as a first language and English as a second. Like many Iranians, he had not deigned to learn Arabic. Peretz, on the other hand, spoke it fluently. Furthermore, he had brushed up on it in his recent experiences with the Palestinians. Ramirez, of course, had spoken it for almost twenty years, finding it indispensable for his business dealings in the Islamic world.

"The time is overdue for us to have a business chat," Peretz continued in Arabic, revolving around in his chair. "I've been thinking over the money. It strikes me that the split ought to be 'to each according to his ability,' if you know what I mean. You're a card-carrying Marxist, right?"

"If you insist," Ramirez replied, immediately realizing he had been right about the direction the conversation was going to take. He also understood the reason for the Arabic. "You may have the quotation in reverse, but I assume you did not call me down here to discuss the finer points of collectivist ideology."

"Nobody ever called you dumb, friend," Peretz went on, now settling comfortably into the mellifluous music of the Arabic. He actually liked the language better than Hebrew, understood why it was the perfect vehicle for poetry. "So I expect you won't have any trouble understanding this." He was handing Ramirez a plain white business envelope, unsealed.

Sabri Ramirez suppressed an impulse to pull out his Beretta and just shoot the fucker between the eyes. The only thing that surprised him was why this extortion—for that surely was what it was—had been so long in coming. Peretz had been planning this move all along.

After a moment's pause, he took the envelope and held it in his hand, not bothering even to look down at it. Instead he let his gaze wander around the room, taking in the rows of video terminals, some with data, some with shots of the working areas, together with the lines of shell-shocked staffers. Then his gaze came back to Peretz, a novice at the trade.

This inevitable development, in fact, almost saddened him. He had, over the past couple of months, acquired almost a fondness for the Israeli. He even had come to tolerate his irreverent humor, if that's what it could be called. Thus he had begun to wonder, in a calculated way, if they might have a partnership that could continue beyond the current episode. A good tech man was hard to find. . . .

"Do I need to bother opening this?" he said finally. "Why don't I just guess. At this point you feel your services have become indispensable, so you want to restructure the distribution of the money. You want to cut out the others, and I suppose there's even a chance you want to cut me out as well."

"Cut you out?" Peretz grinned again. "Never crossed my mind. The way I see it, we're business partners, baby, colleagues. I'd never, ever try and screw a partner, surely you know that. What do you take me for? No, man, I just think there's no point in giving monetary encouragement to all these other assholes."

"And what if I don't choose to see it your way?" Ramirez kept his voice calm.

"Well, there could be a lot of problems with the countdown, if you know what I mean. There's only one guy around here who could fix it. So I think teamwork is essential. You do your part and I do mine. The old 'extra mile.' "

"Your 'extra mile,' I take it, is to finish the job you were hired for in the first place." Ramirez found keeping his voice even to be more and more difficult. But he had to bide his time. A quick glance at Salim told him that the Iranian did not have an inkling of what was going on.

"You might say that." Again the inane grin.

"And mine is to restructure the dispersals of the money afterwards." Ramirez's eyes had just gone opaque behind his gray shades. "Something like that."

"Not 'afterwards.' *Now.* It's all in the envelope."

"Tell you what," Ramirez said finally, his anger about to boil over. "I'm going back to Launch, and I'll take this with me. What's the point in opening it here, raising questions."

"You'd better take this problem seriously, believe me," Peretz interjected, vaguely unnerved by Ramirez's icy noncommittal. "I'm not kidding around."

"Oh, I take you quite seriously, Dr. Peretz." He was extracting a thin cigar from a gold case. "I always have. You will definitely get everything you deserve."

"I intend to."

3:55 A.M.

Isaac Mannheim stumbled through the torrential rain, wondering if the terrorists were stupid enough to try a launch in this kind of weather. Actually, he found himself thinking, it might just be possible. The guidance system would be tested to the limit, but if the weather eased up a little . . .

The aboveground structures for Launch were just ahead, including the two pads with the vehicles sprouting into the sky. From the looks of things, they were both unharmed, with VX-1 clearly prepped and ready for launch. Then he paused to examine the collapsed gantry and shook his head in dismay, heartsick at the sight. *That* was going to cost a fortune to repair.

He shrugged sadly and moved on.

He knew it was going to be a beehive of activity inside the tech areas now. The entire SatCom staff was on duty, which was standard for a "go" power-up situation. Which meant that they had to be holding Vance somewhere out of the way. The question was where. Where? He tried to think.

There were some spare-parts bays, locations where items that constantly needed replacing could be held ready to hand. But everything was clicking now, with those areas pretty much out of the loop. So . . . maybe that would be the place to start checking.

The main entry-points for the bays were, naturally enough, from the inside. But there also was a large loading dock on the south that allowed gear to be delivered directly from the warehouse. Maybe that would be the logical place to try and slip in. He was feeling better now, energized. Why not go in, have a look.

4:22 A.M.

Jean-Paul Moreau punched him again, then waited for a response. There wasn't one, but only because Michael Vance was near to passing out. They had taken him not to the Bates Motel but to an unused room at the periphery of Launch. Its original purpose wasn't clear, but whatever it was, it no longer appeared to be used for anything—the ideal location to beat somebody's brains half out.

"You have a remarkably low tolerance for this, you sleazy *bâtard.*"

Vance merely moaned. He had been trying mystical techniques for blocking out the pain. God, he hated pain. So he attempted to focus his mind on something else, on little things like working on his boat, on making love, on Caribbean sunsets. Instead what he got was the vision of a nuclear bomb going off somewhere, and the anger he had felt when Ramirez and his thugs blew up the U.S. frigate. Still, any emotion, any feeling he could muster, seemed to drive back the pain, make it more endurable. Now he was focusing as best he could on the long-haired, blond French goon who was pummeling him. Whack. Love. Whack. Hate. Whack. Anger. Boiling, seething anger. It was almost working. Almost.

He moaned again. Then for one last time he tried to smile. "Jesus, what sewer did Ramirez dredge to come up with you guys?"

"Good. Good. Keep talking," Moreau said. "Sounds mean you are still alive. It means you still can feel." And he hit him again, hard in the stomach, taking his breath away once more. The moans had become airless grunts.

Jean-Paul Moreau had readily accepted the job of softening up the fucker who had caused them so much trouble. It was intended to be a partial compensation for his having endured the radar treatment, and also it felt good to be able to work over the very son of a bitch who had done it. There was, indeed, justice in the world. Justice that you made for yourself. He was now making his own justice, and it felt terrific.

Vance knew he couldn't take much more of a pounding without passing out. Moreau was a professional who didn't specialize in breaking bones; instead he confined himself to internal trauma. That seemed to be his particular area of expertise. He also was careful to make sure his victim remained conscious.

Which meant, Vance knew, that this part of the program was drawing to a close. He couldn't handle much more pain, the fact of which he knew this French thug with the streaming blond hair was well aware. What, he wondered, was the point anyway? Sadism? Ramirez was still waiting in line to dish out his own particular brand of revenge. And Ramirez had forgotten more about dispensing pain than this creep would ever know. . . .

Thunk. Another blow to the stomach took his breath away once more. He felt his consciousness swim back and forth, scarcely there any more. When was this going to end? He would have signed away anything just to stop the punishment for a few seconds, and he was on the verge of throwing up. Surely it had to be over soon. He felt like a boxer who had just gone fifteen rounds with no referee. Time for the bell.

His battered mind tried to put together a guess about what was next. Maybe after this Eurotrash had had his fun,

Ramirez would show up for the coup de grace. It would almost be welcome. Or maybe nothing was going to happen. Maybe Ramirez would just leave him to be blown up with the rest of the facility.

Where was Pierre? If ARM wasn't coming in for another whole day, who knew where this disaster was headed. What was Cally doing? And Bill? Were they safe?

He cursed himself again for screwing up the golden opportunity to deactivate the gantry and bring the proceedings to a halt. Instead of doing what he had planned, he tried to take a shortcut. Now he realized that had been a major mistake. And now, with ARM not coming in for another whole day, the only chance left was to try and stall.

4:37 A.M.

The wind was howling and rain spattered on the loading dock—it should have been protected, but you can't do everything—as Mannheim briskly made his way up the metal steps. The large sliding door was locked, but he still had the magnetized card that clicked it open. A button on the wall started it moving along the rollers . . . just enough to slide through . . . there, he was in.

Inside was a long hallway cluttered with various crates—either just delivered or ready to be removed, he was not sure—and he had to feel his way along, not wanting to risk turning on the lights.

For an instant, as he stumbled among the sharp corners, he really felt his age. This was not something for a retired engineering professor to be muddling with. He should be back in Cambridge growing orchids in his greenhouse. What in blazes was he doing . . . ?

Then he noticed the light emerging from under one of the doors, and as he stepped closer, he heard two voices. One of them belonged to the man who had saved him, Michael Vance. The other . . . the other had to be one of the terrorists. Now what?

4:51 A.M.

"You know, I hate to spoil all the fun you're having." Vance tried to look at Moreau, but he could barely see through the swelling of his puffy eyelids. "But I've got some unsettling news. You and the rest of Ramirez's hoods are about to be in a deep situation here. The minute you try to send that bomb up, you can tip your hat and kiss your ass good-bye. Better enjoy this while you can."

"What do you mean?"

"That nuke you've got primed. It pains me to tell you, pardon the joke, but your gang isn't exactly the crew of rocket scientists you think you are. The second the Cyclops laser hits the first vehicle, there's going to be a lift-off, all right. Only it's likely to be this island that's headed for orbit. And you with it. Why in hell do you think I was trying to stop it?" Was it true? he wondered. Think. Try to make it sound convincing.

"What are you talking about?" Moreau's blue eyes bristled.

"Just thought you ought to know the bottom line. If you're planning to liberate the oppressed masses or whatever, this is a hell of a way to start. By nuking yourself. That should really impress everybody with your dedication."

"You are going to die anyway, so what do you care?"

"Got a point there. Guess I'm just wasting my time. But there are a few people here on the island that I like—you, incidentally, are not among them—and I would kind of hate to see them get blown away because of your fucking incompetence." He paused, trying to breathe. "As it happens, I had a chat with the project director. She told me how that system works. The nuts and bolts are a little complicated, but it boils down to what happens inside the rocket when the Cyclops laser starts up. Surely you know the energy in the Cyclops creates plasma in the vehicle—that's loose atoms—which becomes the propellant." Vance looked at him. "You *do* know that, don't you?"

Moreau nodded, almost but not quite understanding what he was talking about.

"Good, because the interesting part comes next. You don't create this atomic soup called plasma without generating a lot of electromagnetic noise—in other words, radio garbage." You know, he thought to himself, it's getting to sound better and better all the time.

"These technical things do not concern me," Moreau declared with a shrug.

"They may not concern *you,* pal, but they might concern the bomb. What if one of the radio signals produced just happens to be the one that triggers its detonator? And believe me, with the smorgasbord of radio noise that plasma produces, the chances are easily fifty-fifty. I hope you feel lucky, asshole."

"I don't believe you." He sat down, in a spare chair, beginning to appear a little uncertain.

"You hotshots are a little over your head here. Maybe you ought to pass that information to the chief." Anything to get him out of here, Vance was thinking. Anything to give me a little time to recover. "I suggest you think about it." He struggled to rise, but then realized he was tied into the chair. "Congratulations. I think you just about beat me to a pulp."

"It was my pleasure." Moreau looked him over, his expression now definitely troubled. "Now I should beat you again for lying."

"If it's all the same, I think you might be smart to keep me conscious for a while longer. Maybe I can tell you how to solve your problem."

"If you are so wise, then tell me now." Moreau said.

"With all due respect, I don't talk to messenger boys." He tried to shift his weight, but his body hurt no matter what he did. "You wouldn't understand anyway. It's too technical. Why don't you let me have a chat with that genius you've got running the computer? He's the only one around here who could possibly understand what I'm talking about."

And he's the one, Vance told himself, who now holds the key to everything. Remove him and their whole house of cards crumbles.

"You mean the Israeli." He fairly spat out the words. "He's—"

"So, this operation is multinational."

"Peretz is handling the computer."

"Peretz. Is that his name?" Now we're getting somewhere, Vance thought. If I can get in the same room with the bastard, maybe I can rearrange his brain cells.

"He is supposed to be a computer specialist." Moreau's voice betrayed his contempt. "Maybe he is. But he thinks he knows everything. Whenever anybody tries to tell him anything, he just laughs and makes bad jokes. He won't listen to you."

"Well, why don't we give it a shot anyway?"

Moreau examined him closely, still skeptical but beginning to have second thoughts. "Why would you want to do this, anyway? Help us?"

"Like I told you, I figure you're going to end up detonating that bomb somewhere. Frankly I'd just as soon it wasn't fifty feet from where I'm standing, make that sitting. I do have a small sense of self-preservation left. So why don't you do everybody a favor and let me talk to this Peretz? He has to change the radio frequency that detonates the bomb to a digital mode. If that thing is controlled with plain old UHF, the Cyclops may just set it off before it ever leaves the pad."

Vance knew he was talking over this thug's head. He was talking over his *own* head. But who knew? His fabrication might even be true. The story, though, probably could use some work. "Look," he said finally, "why don't you raise him on that walkie-talkie and let me talk to him?"

Moreau frowned at the idea. "We've gone to radio silence, except for emergencies."

"I'd say this qualifies."

"That remains to be seen." He paused. "I'll go and tell him what you said. Then he can decide for himself what he wants to do."

"I don't want to belabor the obvious here, but time is running a little short."

"I'll be back. If he says you are lying, I may just kill you myself."

Whereupon he opened the door and walked straight into a befuddled Isaac Mannheim.

CHAPTER FIFTEEN

5:03 A.M.

They had used the same insertion procedure off Beirut three years earlier, so there was nothing about this that was new. Standard procedure. As had been planned all along, they donned scuba gear at five hundred meters out, packed their equipment in waterproof bags, and entered the churning water. After the raft was punctured, obliterating all evidence, the seven men of ARM set out, underwater, for the rugged shoreline of Andikythera.

Their scuba gear was invisible against the dark sea as, one by one, they emerged through the breakers and into the last remnants of rain from the storm. They faced a short ledge of surf-pounded rocks immediately abutted by a sheer granite cliff—exactly what they expected, indeed what they wanted.

They were greeted by silence from up above, which gave hope that the insertion had gone undetected. So far. They were in, with the only problem being they no longer had Vance to serve as point man. They would be proceeding blind.

But not too blind. Back in Athens they had studied the schematics of the facility carefully and had concluded the most vulnerable insertion point would be Launch Control. Added to that, Ramirez was last reported to be there, and the objective was to take him out as quickly and efficiently as possible. That also was the place where they believed they could shut down the operation quickest and get their hands on the weapons. Everything came together: hit Launch.

They had discussed renewing radio contact with the woman named Andros, in hopes she might be able to give them an update on the disposition of the hostiles and friendlies. But they decided to wait and see first if they could handle it alone. Radio security was nonexistent, as they had already discovered. For now, the downside of breaking radio silence outweighed the upside. Later, perhaps, when it no longer mattered.

After he had pulled off his scuba gear, Armont took out his IR scope and surveyed the top of the cliff and the coastline. Both looked clear.

"All right, it's going to be light soon," he whispered. "Let's get up there and get to work."

Dimitri Spiros nodded, then began donning an old SatCom uniform he had brought, left over from his days on the island, hoping to pass himself off as a company staffer if need be and get in position to act as point man—since Vance was not part of the picture now. Spiros would guide the unit in, using a secure radio to coordinate the overall operation with Pierre, and with Reggie, who would be standoff sniper.

By the time Dimitri was finished, they were ready. Marcel tossed a grapple up the side of the steep cliff and it lodged somewhere near the top. Next Spiros tested the line, then started making his way up, inserting silent spikes into the crevasses as he climbed. The granite was firm, with enough irregularities to hold onto. When he reached the top and signaled the all-clear, the others immediately followed, with Hans bringing up the rear after he had secured the gear with ropes, ready to hoist.

As the last black satchel topped the cliff, they went to work, breaking out the hardware they would need. The light of dawn had opened just enough for everybody to see what they were doing, yet remain little more than shadows in the early mist. Or was it fog? The dark made it hard to tell, but it was a magic moment that would not last long.

Since Reggie was the standoff sniper, he normally would have begun installing his IR scope, but now, with dawn so near, the need for IR capability was problematical. Not being seen was as great a concern as seeing.

Just ahead, barely visible, was the Rota-Barb fence. Since Spiros had installed it, he strode ahead and did the honors, cutting the razor wire quickly and efficiently. With daylight approaching, there was no time for niceties such as scaling; they would just have to take the chance that the security system was no longer operative.

They carried the equipment through, then scouted the approach. Up the rocky hill they could see two silver spires, now illuminated with spotlights. After a few moments of thoughtful silence, Reggie Hall nodded and pointed toward an outcropping of rocks located near the north entrance to Launch Control, indicating with hand signs that they would provide the best location for overall surveillance. He would set up there, a look-down spot from where he could handle the standoff-sniper chores, ready at any time to neutralize any hostiles who might emerge from Launch. It also was a good spot from which to monitor hostile radio traffic.

Having done this many times before, they were ready. Armont and Hans, together with the brothers Voorst, would lead the assault, while Marcel would be at the rear of the entry element, serving as defense man, covering for them and providing security. As point man, Spiros would supply backup for Marcel if things got hot or if somebody tried to ambush the entry team during approach and entry, or during withdrawal. The Greek would also be in charge of directing any pyrotechnics.

In addition to acting as commander, Armont would assume his usual role as security man, providing covering fire for the entry element during the assault and more close cover during withdrawal. He also would be in charge of any other equipment they might need.

Since the assignments reflected ARM's standard configuration, with everybody in their usual slot, there was no need to squander time reviewing who would be where. . . .

In moments they were ready, silencers attached, poised to move through the dark, early morning haze. It was providing a small semblance of cover, but not for long. They hoped they could take Launch Control fast enough that there would be no time for the terrorists to use hostages as human shields. If that happened, there was sure to be bloodshed.

Just to be on the safe side, Armont did a quick run-through of the assault with hand signals. He was just finishing when Reggie Hall's radio came alive in a burst of static.

"Sirene, please come in." It was a woman's voice. "Do you read?"

"Blast," he whispered, his face rapidly turning florid in the dim mist. "Didn't we tell her radio silence was essential?" He quickly switched on the microphone. "Ulysses One, get off this channel. Sirene is here."

"Thank God. But you've got to try and find Mike. Isaac went to look for him, but he hasn't come back."

"You mean Mannheim?" Armont took the microphone. "Where did he go?"

"He said he was going to try the empty loading bays down at Launch," she said. "He hasn't come back, so maybe he found him. Could you try there?"

Reggie turned to Armont with a questioning look that needed no words. It was, simply, What do we do now?

On this one, Armont had no better idea than anyone else. They all knew where the loading bays were, since the blueprints had made that plain enough. The problem was the sequence. Should they go ahead with the assault as planned, to take the time to try to find him and pull him out? Her intel on his location was just a guess, but it was a start.

ARM's rules always had been that their own people came first. So if they knew where Vance might possibly be, nothing else mattered. According to the rules, they had to drop everything and try to pull him out. Even if it jeopardized the operation. Those were the rules. No exceptions.

For that matter, Armont suddenly thought, why not try

and bring her in out of the cold, too? Then they would have a personal guide to the whole layout. It seemed to make a lot of sense, particularly since radio security was already shot to hell.

He clicked on the microphone again. "Can you meet us there? Where you think he is?"

"Copy. Give me eight minutes." And the radio clicked off.

I hope we've got eight to spare, Armont thought, checking his Krieger watch. The minutes were ticking away.

"Okay, we'll change the plan," he whispered. "We'll make the insertion through the loading bays." He nodded to Hans and the Voorst brothers, and without so much as a word they tightened their black hoods and headed up through the mist.

5:19 A.M.

She heaved a sigh of relief as she put down the microphone and prepared to stumble down the hill. She realized she had violated protocol by breaking radio silence, but she was almost as worried about Michael Vance as she was about the facility. And it was a disturbing realization. Or maybe not so disturbing. True, he had screwed up, but then everybody did that from time to time. Even Alan . . . there it was again. But come on, the resemblance was almost scary. And she was also beginning to hate him for the same reasons she had hated Alan. It was the anger, and maybe the guilt. . . .

She had told them eight minutes. So get moving. It was going to be tight. First find Mike, and Isaac. If that was possible. And then go on to the real business of the morning. Whoever was on the Fujitsu had to be stopped, even if it meant more damage to the facility. The cost no longer mattered. SatCom could be rebuilt, everything. But if one of those Third World bombs were set off somewhere, it would be another Hiroshima. The horror of it would be unthinkable.

She prayed a short prayer, something she hadn't done in twenty-five years, and started down the hill.

5:20 A.M.

Out the wide windows of Launch Control the searchlight-illuminated spires of VX-1 and VX-2 gleamed through the early mist. Sabri Ramirez studied them, thinking about logistics. With all the scrambled radio traffic in the area, he had a sneaking suspicion—more than a suspicion—that a Special Forces assault was being set up. But that's what all the hostages were for.

Everything was on schedule, just as planned. According to Peretz, the last tests of the telemetry had been completed and the countdown was proceeding without a hold. Outside, in the vast bay that was Launch, technicians buzzed, a sea of white coats. Lines of workstations showed voltage and amperage values for the power buildup in the coil. Calculations of wind shear were being made, and preliminary tests were being run on the guidance system. The "orbops" team, orbital operations, was busy running up orbital and attitude numbers, readying their input commands. The irony was, they still didn't have a clue they were about to send up a nuclear device. American ingenuity turned on itself, in a fearsome symmetry. . . .

"Take a look at what I found."

Ramirez whirled, hearing the voice, and was startled to see Jean-Paul Moreau coming in through the doorway of Launch Control leading the old Jew professor, Isaac Mannheim. Where did *he* come from? The old man was supposed to be sedated and sequestered away for safekeeping in the living quarters. Guess it hadn't worked. Here he was, bumbling about.

On the other hand, maybe this was a stroke of timing. He was about to be needed again, and this saved the trouble of having to go and get him.

"Where was he?"

"Wandering around the loading docks," Jean-Paul said, still shoving Mannheim ahead of him. "I think there's a technical question we need to run by him."

"What?"

"That bastard Vance just claimed that the Cyclops laser

may set off the device when it starts up. I didn't get it exactly. He wants to talk to Peretz. Something about plasma and stray radio frequencies."

"Sounds like an invention to me," Ramirez said, looking Mannheim over. The old man, his baseball cap askew, was clearly as mad as a loon. What would he know about anything? On the other hand, he *was* a scientist, so it wouldn't hurt to ask.

"Well, what about it, Herr Doctor Professor?" He walked over and straightened the old man's cap. "Is your laser going to produce random radio signals?"

"Of course not," Mannheim declared. "That's what is so ideal about this system. There's nothing to interfere with the telemetry. No static. No—"

"I thought so," Moreau muttered, cutting him off. With a flourish of his blond hair, he turned to go back to the loading bay. "I'm leaving him here. Vance was lying. Just as I thought. He's going to regret—"

The walkie-talkie on Ramirez's belt crackled and he grabbed it instantly. "What do you want? I ordered radio silence."

"Firebird One, this is Hacker," came the voice of Peretz. "I turned on the security system for a look-see, and lo and behold I think there's a possible penetration in progress. Down on the south shore. In sector fifty-six of the fence. Could be a malfunction, but maybe somebody ought to check it out."

Ramirez groaned silently. Was this the assault he had been half expecting? If so, it was coming quicker than he had planned. Which meant that having Mannheim here was definitely a stroke of luck.

"Wait." He motioned for Moreau, who had turned and was headed through the doorway. "I want you here till we find out what this is. Could be a false alarm, but then maybe not."

Okay, he thought quickly, where is everybody? Time to batten down. Peretz, of course, was in Command, along with Salim. Wolf Helling was here in Launch, coordinating telemetry between Peretz and the Pakistanis. Stelios was keeping tabs on the prisoners now in the living quarters, the Bates Motel. Jamal was on patrol around the perimeter—why hadn't he noticed anything?—together with the two Stasi. And Jean-Paul was here.

The first thing to do would be to raise Jamal on the radio and have him check out the situation there in the south. And if it really was a penetration, then the two most expendable members of the team right now were the Stasi. They were the cannon fodder. Let them earn their share.

"All right," he said to Peretz, "we'll check it out. Ten-four."

While Jean-Paul watched, he quickly raised Jamal on the walkie-talkie and repeated what Peretz had said. "It could be a malfunction of the sensors, but who the hell knows. If this is the real thing, then we'll have to take steps. But once we escalate, everything is going to get more complicated."

"I'll have Schindler check it out and get back to you in three minutes," Jamal barked back. "We'll keep the line open till I know for sure what's going on."

"All right, but you'd better get ready for trouble. My hunch is that this may be the beginning. If it is, then we've got our work cut out. You know what I mean." He clicked it off, then turned to Jean-Paul. "Okay, forget about Vance for now. I want you to go over to Command and help Salim get the security into shape. I'm not sure he knows what the hell he's doing."

"Check," Jean-Paul Moreau said. "I'll take care of everything."

He walked out the door and into Launch, then headed for the tunnel leading to Command. Ramirez, he knew, had a contingency that was supposed to stop an assault in its tracks. He only hoped it would work as planned.

5:23 A.M.

As she moved down the hill, dawn was beginning to show dimly through the fog to the east, promising an early morning clearing of the skies. The prospect made her fearful. The dark had been better, a shroud to cover mistakes. Now, without the fog, she would be almost as exposed as the barren rocks that pockmarked the hillside. The birds this morning were strangely silent, as though they knew ill doings were afoot. Even the pale, fog-shrouded glimpse of VX-1 and VX-2 down at the other end of the island had never seemed more plaintive. She had worked for almost three years to put those vehicles into space, and now she had to try and stop the very thing she had been aiming for all that time.

She had told the ARM team she could be there in eight minutes, but now she realized that was optimistic. Though she was moving as fast as she could manage, hugging the line of the security fence, the island seemed to be getting bigger all the time. And smaller.

The fence, which had seemed so reassuring when it was installed, wove among the trees and rocks as it went down the hill, almost a meandering presence. But it was not hard to follow, even in the reduced visibility of the half-dark and fog. The trick, she realized, was going to be finding the ARM team. Or maybe they would find her. Finding things was what they were supposed to be good at. . . .

Thank God. There was somebody up ahead, barely visible through the dim light. Only one, however, which immediately made her wonder.

She paused, drew a deep lungful of the fresh morning air, and waited to see what he would do. For one thing, he was moving along as though he was searching, yet with an air of owning the terrain.

Shit, it was one of Ramirez's men, out on patrol. She recognized him. It was one of the European hoods who had barged into Command the fateful evening now half a lifetime away.

Quickly she tried to melt into the shadow of a tall bush, but she was too late. His head jerked around and he saw her. Up came an automatic.

He was dressed in black, and as he approached her, he flashed a crooked smile, then produced a German accent. "So, it's you. We've been missing you."

"Which one of them are you?" She didn't know what else to say.

"I am Max Schindler," he replied, in heavily accented English. He was at least thirty pounds overweight, the hard-earned rewards of a lifetime of potatoes and strudel. He looked like a puffing, black balloon. "Number One vill be pleased to have you return to us. He thought you were an assault." He laughed as he gestured her forward with the weapon. "Come on. This morning, I think, is going to go quickly. Just another couple of hours and the real excitement will begin."

"I can hardly wait."

"Good"—it sounded more like *goot*—"you are going to have a circle-side seat." He seemed extremely pleased with himself, both with his own humor and with the fact that he had been the one who would be bringing her back.

"You mean ringside. Great." The time was already flashing by, she thought—the eight minutes she had given ARM were undoubtedly up—which meant they probably would be changing plans again, working their way. Would they just forget about her and move on? "Tell me, how did a smart guy like you end up working for a maniac like Ramirez?"

"Who?"

"The guy you call Number One. I hear he's really Sabri Ramirez. Didn't you know?"

The German's startled look betrayed his disbelief. His small, piglike eyes narrowed. "Who told you such a thing?"

"Just a little birdie."

Schindler shrugged, unconvinced, then pushed her on. "That's impossible. Everybody knows Sabri Ramirez has been dead for two, maybe three years."

Well, she thought, with any luck he soon will be.

"Whatever you say," she continued.

"It's absurd. Ramirez was South American. Number One is from Beirut. Now come on, hurry. Just keep your hands where I can see them." Schindler was almost shoving her around a rocky outcrop. "We have to get up to Launch before he gets impatient and sends somebody else out looking."

"Well, if you're in such a big rush, there's a quicker way

to get into Launch than the way we're going. We can just enter through the loading bays"—she pointed—"up there. We don't have to go all the way around."

"Are they unlocked?" He looked up and squinted through the mist. The bays were distinguishable by tall metal doors that were sized to accommodate some of the large vehicle components that had been delivered over the past couple of years. They could just be seen now, dark silhouettes against the horizon.

"The big doors are probably locked, but there's a side entrance that's always open." She paused. "Do what you want. But I guarantee you it's quicker than going around."

"All right"—he nodded, a quick bob of his beefy neck—"you lead the way."

What she really was thinking about was the rocks and trees covering that back route. This German blimp escorting her would be no match if she simply took matters into her own hands and made a dash.

Why not? It was a desperate move, but this was a desperate moment.

"Wait . . ." She bent over, as though to tie a shoelace, and when she came up, she was swinging. Schindler was tired, and perhaps because of that he was caught completely off guard, staggering backward. It was the moment of disorientation she needed. She grabbed at the Uzi, hoping to wrench it from his grasp. He may have been surprised, and overweight, but he had lost none of his dogged Stasi tenacity. His one-handed grip tightened on the weapon as his other hand flew up to defend his face.

Now she had one hand on the breech of the automatic, and with the other she reached out and seized the muzzle. It was the leverage she needed to swing the butt of the metal stock up against his jaw. The blow caught him with his mouth open, smashing his lower lip against his teeth and slicing his tongue.

He emitted a moan and yanked the Uzi away with both hands.

But now Calypso Andros was already stumbling through the brush, up the hill and into the fog.

Schindler felt his bleeding lip as he recovered his balance, and he fleetingly considered just taking her out with a
quick burst, nice and simple. Though Number One had insisted she be returned alive, he told himself he was mad
enough he didn't care. He wanted to kill the bitch.

But the second he took to make that calculation proved to
be crucial. She had gotten into the heavy brush that ringed
the hill farther up.

Scheisse.

He plunged after her, puffing and seething. It was one
thing not to have found her; it was another to have had her
within his grasp and then let her escape. He would be a
laughingstock, again. Wolf Helling, who had given him this
job, would be humiliated once more. It was unacceptable,
unthinkable.

The rocks along the fenceline were jagged, cutting into
his boots as he half ran, half stumbled through the dim light.
She was up there, somewhere. She had said something about
the loading bay, so she probably was headed there. In any
case, there weren't that many places to hide. It was just a
matter of time. Just a matter of time. . . .

5:24 A.M.

Ramirez was talking to Peretz again on his walkie-talkie.
"I've been monitoring the scrambled radio traffic, and I've
begun to have a sixth sense about the situation. I think we're
about to have some uninvited guests from the U.S. Special
Forces; ten to one it's Delta. Are you ready?"

"Jean-Paul just came in, and he says we're totally secure,
baby. SatCom thoughtfully lined this place with steel. Ain't
nobody gonna waltz into this little enclave of ours without a
press pass. Rest easy, man. Keep cool."

"Well, I'm thinking I should send you some more backup,
just in case." *What I really should do is shoot you and just
use the backup.* "By the way, how does the schedule look?"

"The countdown's now being handled entirely by the

computer. So far there are no holds. Lift-off is coming up exactly as scheduled."

"Good," Ramirez spoke back, "keep me updated on a ten-minute framework." He paused, thinking. "Incidentally, is there any way we possibly could speed it up?"

"Things are pretty tight as they stand. There might be some shortcuts, but I'm not sure I know this system well enough to start fooling around. If it ain't broke, don't fix it, know what I mean?"

"An original sentiment," Ramirez responded dryly. "But don't be surprised at anything that may happen here in the next ninety minutes. There may be a setup for an assault, but I'll take care of it."

"It's a tough game coming down here. But ain't nobody gonna fuck with us, 'cause we got all the big cards."

"They may try it, though. So make sure that place is tight, and have Jean-Paul and Salim double-check all the entries. The chances are good we're going to take a hit, and soon."

"No problem from down here. I told you we're covering it."

What do you know, you smart-ass? Ramirez asked himself grimly. "All right, but as soon as Jamal checks in, I'm sending him over there, too. And one of the Stasi. Stelios can handle the living quarters by himself. Just keep the countdown going, no matter what else happens."

"Okay, but the only way this thing is gonna fly is if you made those bank arrangements the way I wanted. One hand washes the other, as the saying goes. Otherwise, I'm just going to shut the whole thing down. I mean it, man."

"It has been taken care of," Ramirez said. "I faxed Geneva. They'd just opened that desk, but I should have a confirmation back in a few minutes."

With that announcement he clicked off the mike.

And smiled. Peretz's memo had explained he wasn't demanding blackmail; what he wanted was more like a equitable readjustment of the take. And why not? the memo had reasoned. Without his computer skills, nothing could have been possible. He wanted written proof that when the ransom money came in, it would automatically be split, with half going to a new account he specified.

What an amateur. It was almost depressing.

5:27 A.M.

She stumbled through the brush wondering where they were. They must have come in from the south, which meant they were already near the entrance to the loading bay. Go for that, she told herself, pushing on. The bramble was scraping her face and hands, tearing her clothes. She was going to look like she'd been run through a shredder, she thought. A bloody mess.

Then she heard something whiz by, the first shot, and knew the German was closing in, his weapon on semiauto. With a rush of desperation, she threw herself on the ground and tried to merge with the damp leaves and underbrush. And she felt terrible. Mike had screwed things up, but she hadn't done much better.

Then, out of the mist just up the hill, a figure appeared. Two figures. Three. Moving with quick, catlike motions. She wanted to yell, to warn them, but maybe all she would be doing was alerting the damned German hood trying to kill her. No, they were supposed to be professionals, so let them handle it their own way. . . .

Then she heard another whiz of a round singing by and saw a fleck of dirt fly up only inches from where she lay. Again the hard crack of the German's automatic followed.

All right, ARM. You're supposed to be such hotshots. Do something and do it now!

The three dark figures answered the shots as though they were in a ballet, all dropping to a crouch virtually in unison.

They were using silencers, so the rounds came as a series of dull thunks, but each figure fired only once, or at most, twice. And when she turned to look back, her pursuer was nowhere to be seen. . . . No, he was slumped over a bush, motionless.

As one of the hooded figures came up to her and began

lifting her to her feet, two of the others advanced cautiously on the German. Their caution, however, was unnecessary. He was as lifeless as the granite rocks around them.

Well, she thought, these guys sure know how to treat a lady.

5:28 A.M.

Jamal cursed the morning fog that had settled in, understanding it was probably moisture left over from the storm. Then he checked his watch and realized that Schindler was overdue. Which was typical. He was beginning to wonder how the German nation had acquired its famous reputation for punctuality. And efficiency. Both were, in his opinion, grossly undeserved. Helling's recommendation that those three screwups be brought along did not reflect well on his judgment.

He clicked on his walkie-talkie. "Firebird Six, do you copy? Is everything CQ where you are? It's check-in time."

There was no answer. The jerk had gone down by the south security fence, where something was amiss. Was he in trouble? Everybody was tied up now, getting ready for the launch. He wondered if they were going to find themselves shorthanded, not having as much firepower as they needed.

"Firebird Six, come in. Cut the games."

Again silence.

Which gave him a very bad feeling. There was no reason for the radio to conk out suddenly. The rule was they always kept their channels open.

This was trouble. Time to alert Ramirez. Either Schindler had fucked up, or they had been penetrated.

5:30 A.M.

Major General Eric Nichols was so relieved he scarcely knew whether to laugh or cry, and he rarely had been seen to do either. Actually, his feeling was more one of surprise. For once something was going right. After diddling and dabbling for almost ten hours, the Pentagon—Fort Fuck-up—had actually made a decision. It was so unprecedented it might even merit a place in the annals of military history. Such rare moments were to be savored.

Maybe they had gotten tired of running computer "risk analyses." Or maybe their damned computer had broken down. Whatever the reason, however, the exalted pay grades upstairs had decided to get off dead center and just let him assault the damned island. The op was a go.

The civilian assholes had been headed off at the pass, which meant one less thing to worry about. Now all that remained was to figure how to get the boys in safely and take down the place. And at last he knew there were nukes. Great communication system the Army had, making sure everybody had been briefed and was totally up to speed. Christ!

He sat still a moment after setting down the phone, breathing a short prayer. Although appearances would not suggest it, he was in fact a religious man at the core. He had been close enough to death enough times to conclude that there were indeed no atheists in foxholes, and he figured what was good enough for foxholes was good enough for the rest of the time. Besides, what harm did it do?

"All right." He turned and glanced at Max Austin. "I guess the computer has got everything planned. Looks like we can go in after all. How's that for efficiency? Just as it gets bright enough for my guys to be risking their asses, we get the green light. I'd say that's just about perfect timing."

Austin nodded slowly, then rose to check the teletype machine to see if the orders had really come through. This op was going to be by the book or not at all. If it turned into a nuclear incident, there were going to be inquiries up the wazoo.

"Looks like it's really going down," Austin said, yanking off a sheet. "So I'll cut the orders and get us mobilized here. How long before you can get your boys in the air?"

"Well, since this is going to have to be a daylight op, we might as well use the Apaches and not fuck around. We'll just hit the bastards with enough firepower to take out the command-control radars up on the hill. That ought to shut down any chance they could get anything launched. Then we've just got a hostage situation to deal with, and if we have to, we can just starve them out. It'll only be a matter of time. Maybe, God willing, we can keep the friendly casualties to a minimum."

Austin did not like the image of the headlines Nichols's assault plan suddenly conjured up. Any heavy property damage and there was going to be hell to pay.

"I don't like it, Eric," he said. "The word I get is that we're not to damage the infrastructure any more than is absolutely essential. Which means no first strikes on command-and-control. This isn't Iraq, for godsake; this is American property."

"You're saying my main orders are to save the infrastructure?" Nichols's tone was deliberately wry.

"You've got it. I want you to get in there fast, take down the hostiles, and get this situation the hell over with. That's the best way to put this problem behind us and fast. The last thing this man's army needs is a month's worth of gory headlines. Some quick casualties can look unavoidable and be over with in a day. A long-drawn-out situation can make us all look like jerks."

"I can't believe I'm hearing this."

"You didn't hear a damned thing, at least not from me. But if you know what's good for the Army, and for the country, you'll get in there and take down the place in a morning, neutralize the hostiles with extreme prejudice, and let the Army write the headlines with a press release."

Nichols knew what he was hearing: the groundwork for "deniability." And he despised it. This kind of "cover your ass" bullshit was one of the things that gave him such contempt for desk jockeys.

"All right," he said smoothly, covering his disgust, "if you want to play it that way, then we can sure as hell do it. I don't suppose my opinion in the matter is of a hell of a lot of interest to the Pentagon."

"Truthfully, no."

"Okay." He leaned back. "Doing it the Pentagon's way,

there would be two points we need to assault. There's the computer control center, and then there's the launch facility. There're probably terrorists at both, so we've got to take down both locations simultaneously. And both, unfortunately, are underground, which also means we've got to figure out how to get in, get down there, and do it fast."

"What would be your insertion strategy, given what we've just discussed?"

"Well, I've already got the alternatives rehearsed. Right now I think we should stage a diversionary landing on the coast by a SEAL team, then use the confusion to let the main assault team insert from choppers. My main worry is not the hostages, but getting my own boys shot up going in. It's going to be a cluster-fuck if some of those bastards can get a bead on the task force that's arriving by chopper. Could mean a lot of casualties. Let something go wrong and I don't even want to think about how many of my men could get chewed up. But we've been rehearsing that assault option and I think we can get twenty men on the ground in about ninety seconds."

The difference, he was thinking, was that he had been planning to do it under cover of darkness. To suddenly have to revise the entire strategy and try and take down the place in broad daylight was calling every assumption into question. But there was no time to try and devise yet another assault. Shit. All because Washington kept changing its signals, and when it did get them straight, somebody came up with this bullshit about minimizing property damage. It was a goddamn outrage. But that's what you had to expect when REMFs got mixed up in planning an op. Shit.

"Well, twenty men should do it," Austin said. "And there'll always be backup from the SEAL team that's providing the coastal diversion. They'll be there, in-theater so to speak."

"Right." You don't know fuck-all about how an op like this goes down, Nichols was thinking, and you have the balls to sit there and tell me how to deploy my resources.

On the other hand, it sounds easy. Too easy. That's what's wrong with it. The place would appear to be a crackerbox. But these bastards are pros, so they must already have thought through everything we have. Time to plan ahead of them.

"All right," Nichols concluded, rising. "I'll have everybody airborne in fifteen minutes."

5:38 A.M.

Vance twisted around and tried to see his watch. He couldn't make out the hands, but they both seemed to be pointing in the general direction of down. Whatever that meant exactly, the time had to be getting on toward dawn. The six hours that Cally had talked about, the six hours left before the liftoff: how much of that time was left? It had to be half gone.

What now? Maybe his cock-and-bull story had impressed the French hood enough to get him out of the room for a while, but it wasn't going to cut any ice with anybody who knew anything about lasers. Sooner or later, he was going to come back. Not something to let the mind dwell on.

One thing was sure: he felt like he had been run over by a truck. The blood from the beating was slowly starting to coagulate, crusting on his face. It had begun to itch, and something where his liver used to be was emitting stabbing bursts of pain. It would come, then subside, then come again. He tried to focus his eyes on the room, the piles of empty crates, wondering if maybe a sharp object was protruding somewhere, maybe something he could use to cut away at the cord that held his hands.

Nothing, and it was a stupid idea anyway, left over from too many B movies. But now his mind was beginning to attempt to function with a little more rationality, and along with that came the glimmerings of an idea. The bomb was aboard one of the vehicles and a countdown was under way, now being handled by Bill's supercomputer. There was no obvious way to stop it. Maybe, however, there was a not-so-obvious way. A last-minute reprieve. Assuming he ever got the chance.

He groaned and leaned back, wondering . . .

What happened next came so fast he couldn't really comprehend it at the time. Only later could he roughly reconstruct the dizzying confluence of events. But that was as it should have been. The door was suddenly slammed wide, and two smoke grenades plummeted into the room, followed by a flash grenade. Next, through the smoke and confusion three men dressed in black pullovers plunged through the opening and dropped to their knees, MP5s at the ready.

Jesus! He gasped for breath, blinded by the flash grenade but still trying to see through the billowing CS that was engulfing everything. In what seemed like less than a second, one of the men appeared by his side, and he saw a knife blade flash. A hand was slapped over his mouth as another rough set of hands yanked him from the chair. His legs were numb from the bindings, but they came alive as his weight went back onto them. Terra firma had never felt better.

The men's faces were all covered in balaclavas, but one of them gave two sharp clicks and, on that signal, they began to drag him out the door.

He knew better than to say a word. The whole operation had been carried out with clockwork precision and in perfect silence—except for the destruction of the door. Had there been any terrorists in the room, they would have been dead, scarcely knowing what had happened.

As they entered the hallway, one of the men pulled back his antismoke hood. "You look like hell," Willem Voorst said. "Can you walk?"

"In a manner of speaking." He felt pain shooting up through his wobbly legs. "I suppose I should ask what took you so long, only it hurts to talk. You weren't scheduled in for another day. What happened?"

"We moved up the timetable, though you'd be amazed how many people didn't want us to show up," Marcel remarked, his Belgian calm returning. "The entire U.S. Navy, to be exact. We were made to feel very unwanted."

"That's going to seem like a Welcome Wagon compared to what's coming up." He paused and tried to inhale the comparatively smokeless air of the hallway. "What's the plan? Do you want to try and take out Launch Control, or do you want to move on Command? . . ." That was when he saw Cally. "How did you get down here?"

"Somebody had to lead these guys in," she said matter-of-factly. Her face was scratched and her shirt torn. "No thanks to you. All we have to thank you for is blowing up the gantry."

He just groaned. "Things got complicated."

"But you waited until it moved over the explosive before you blew it. I saw the whole thing. How could you be so *crazy!*" Her anger was boiling. "That wasn't what we agreed to."

"Like I said, things—"

"*Please,* give me a break. If you worked for me, I'd fire you on the spot." It was clear she meant every word. "So after you screwed that up, what was I supposed to do? I had no choice but to get on the radio. Now look at the mess we're in. What *happened?*"

"To tell you the truth," Vance answered, "I'm not even quite sure myself."

"Great. Just great."

"It's a jungle out there."

"No kidding."

"Later. I'll tell all," he said lamely, wanting desperately to change the subject. "Right now, though, there's the matter of Ramirez. And by the way, it is him. We had a one-on-one."

"What did he tell you?" Armont asked, his interest suddenly alive. "Did he say what he wanted out of all this? Ransom or what?"

"We didn't make it that far. A personality conflict got in the way."

"No hint? Nothing?"

"Just that he knows exactly what he's doing. They're going to launch an atomic bomb. Kill a lot of people somewhere. And I don't think the payment of ransom is going to make them call it off. They're going to take the money, then go ahead and do it anyway." He rubbed a hand across his face, trying to feel a cut, then drew it away and examined the blood in the half-light, not quite sure what he was seeing. "But I still think that if we take him out, the rest of them will fold." He looked at Cally, trying to meet the outraged glare she was bestowing on him. "Any idea where he is now?"

"The last I knew, he was in Launch," she said, still visibly fuming.

"Then I guess that's the first objective."

"Jesus, do you want to go in shooting?" She looked around at the motley men of ARM. "Those are my people in there, you know, my friends. It could be a bloodbath."

"Doesn't have to be." Spiros had pulled back his balaclava and was shaking Vance's hand with an air of genuine contrition. Maybe trying to cheer him up after Cally Andros's blast. "Michael, I'm damned sorry about all this. The whole thing is my fault, really."

"Spilt milk," Vance replied. "Now we have to look ahead."

"Well, it's my spilt milk, as you say," Spiros declared, "and I want to clean it up myself. If all we need to do is take down Ramirez, I think I can get in there and maybe do it without too much in the way of pyrotechnics."

"What do you mean?" Armont asked.

"Let me go in by myself, alone. I've got a uniform, so I'll just be another Greek mechanic. At least we should try that first. See what I can do."

"Dimitri, that's a heroic offer," Armont said, "but—"

"No, it's not heroic, it's realistic. It's a chance, but one I think we should take."

"We don't stay in business by taking chances," Armont declared, vetoing him on the spot. "We go in as a team."

"All or nobody," Hans said. "It may not always be best, but those are the rules."

"Exactly." Armont closed out the subject. "All or nothing. So let's get out the blueprints and start assigning the entry-points."

CHAPTER SIXTEEN

11:16 P.M.

"It's him," Alicia's voice came back over the intercom in the Oval Office. By now it looked as disheveled as the Situation Room in the basement.

"What?" Hansen said. "The son of a bitch is on the phone again? At this hour?"

"What do you want me to do?" she asked.

"Just a minute." He clicked off the intercom and returned to his other call. "Caroline, I don't know. Just play it by ear and do the best you can. Press Secretaries get paid for giving non-answers. Tell the goddamn *Post* we have no comment. Try and make a deal. Say you'll give their team an exclusive, deep background, just for them, if they'll hold off another few hours to give us time to sort this out. Tell him we promise not to give the *Times* anything fit to print until after their deadline tomorrow. The late edition." He paused. "You're probably right, but give it a shot anyway. Look, I've got to go."

He reached over and pushed a second button on the console.

"Yes."

"Mr. President," came the voice, its accent more pronounced now, "I know you think you can recover this facility with an assault, but I want to assure you that any such action would be a very costly mistake."

"The only mistake that's been made so far was made by you. Going there in the first place." Hansen glanced at the listing of his commitments for the next day. Ted would have to cancel all of them. This wasn't how the presidency was supposed to be. Nobody told him he would be spending days on end negotiating with a criminal threatening mass murder.

"Let me put it like this," the voice went on. "If there is an assault, all I have to do is retire to the lower level of the facility and then detonate one of the nuclear devices I now have armed. It's radio-controlled."

"If you want to commit suicide, then go ahead," Hansen said. What kind of bluff was that? he wondered.

"Let me put your mind at ease," came the voice, as measured and secure as it was foreboding. "My revolutionary colleagues and I will be at the main power coil, which is buried at least three hundred feet below the bedrock here. It is a ready-made bomb shelter. Any invading force, however, would be vaporized, along with all the civilians."

"You'd never escape," Hansen shot back. "What's the point?"

"That remains to be seen. But what you have to ask yourself is whether you are prepared to have a nuclear disaster in the Aegean."

On that point, Hansen admitted to himself, the son of a bitch had a point. The political costs, not to mention the economic costs, would be staggering.

"Look," he said, "you're proposing a scenario neither of us wants. It would be irresponsible and immoral. Though I suppose those points don't disturb you very much."

"Let me help your thought processes. You have twenty minutes, starting now. If at the end of that time you can't assure me that the assault has been called off—please don't bother to deny that one is imminent—then what will happen will be on your hands." He paused. "Incidentally, I also will bring Professor Mannheim to the phone then, and you can explain to him why he is about to die. I am putting this line on hold. You now have nineteen minutes and forty seconds." The phone went silent.

Hansen stared at Ed Briggs, sitting bleary-eyed across on the couch, then returned his gaze to the desk, noting the time on the digital clock.

6:25 A.M.

"Alpha Leader, this is SEAL One," crackled the radio. "Bearing two-zero-niner. Range five hundred meters. No hostile fire."

"Roger," Nichols replied. "Continue inbound." He clicked off his walkie-talkie, then turned around and yelled to the men in the back of the Huey.

"Okay, heads up. The assault is now in progress. We go in at 0630 hours."

The Deltas nodded as they checked their watches and spare ammo clips. The twenty-three men were all wearing black pullover hoods, each with a thin plastic microphone that looked like a phone operator's. Over these they had Kevlar helmets with protective goggles and light balaclavas, while their bulletproof assault vests included pockets filled with grenades and extra ammo for their H&K MP5 assault submachine guns.

Nichols was using a squad of ten Navy SEALs to stage a diversionary assault on the shoreline, the same kind of diversion that had been employed so successfully by the SEALs in the war to liberate Kuwait. After leaving the carrier, they would approach the island at forty mph in a pair of Fountain-33 speedboats, powered by 1,000-hp MerCruiser engines. About one kilometer offshore, they were scheduled to disembark into two motorized Zodiac rubber raiding craft that they had lashed to the bow. If all went according to plan, they would hit the coastline in full view and provide diversionary fire, giving the real assault team an opening to take the two main objectives.

That's when the serious action would begin. Nichols and his men would then come in using Army choppers—two HH-1K Huey gunships and two AH-64A Apaches. The Hueys would hover and drop off the insertion teams, while the Apaches would provide backup firepower that—with their 30mm chain guns, Hellfire missiles, and 70mm folding-fin rocket pods—could easily be mistaken for the end of the world.

The assault was timed down to the second. Three minutes after the diversionary SEAL action began, the two Hueys would set down in the middle of the island and pour out the real assault teams, one team to storm Command and the other to hit Launch Control, massively. He figured if they took both at once, there would be no place for the terrorists to hide. That was the best way they knew to accomplish their first objective, which was to neutralize any nuclear devices safely.

The outstanding unknown, of course, was the location of those devices, and their state of readiness.

You had to assume terrorists weren't suicidal, Nichols told himself . . . but yet, what about Beirut and the Marine barracks, demolished by a suicide mission? Such things were never outside the realm of possibility. So if these crazy fuckers decided to go out in a blaze of glory, it wouldn't exactly be a first. . . .

"Alpha Leader." The radio came alive again. "SEAL One objective secure. No sign of any hostiles down here."

"Copy, SEAL One." Shit, Nichols thought. The bastards didn't go for it. They're battening down, planning to make a stand. And why not? They've got hostages. They think we're not going to hit the place.

They've got another thing coming. It's just going to be bloodier than we had hoped. If they start using the hostages for human shields . . .

"Request permission to advance toward Launch Control," came the radio again. "If we're going to provide that diversion, we're going to have to go in."

Why not? Nichols thought. We're already improvising, but maybe the bastards can still be drawn out. It's worth a try.

"Roger, SEAL One," he said, checking his watch. "Watch yourself. It could be a setup." He knew the SEALs were lightly armed, with only a German Heckler & Koch submachine gun each, plus a couple of M16s specially equipped with M203 grenade launchers, the so-called "bloop tube." Still, those boys could raise some hell.

"Confirmed."

"Copy. We'll slip in here for five. Kick hell out of anything that's not nailed down."

"Roger, Alpha Leader. If they show their heads, they're gonna know we're in town."

6:26 A.M.

"All right," Armont declared, "we make the insert here." He tapped his finger on the blueprint. "We hit the nerve center of Launch with flash-bangs and tear gas, and take it down. If we're lucky, Ramirez will still be there, and that should be the end of it. He always controls an operation totally. Nobody else will have any authority. That's his style. If we handle it surgically, there shouldn't be any major casualties among the friendlies."

The area around Launch Control was still foggy, illuminated mainly by the lingering spotlights on two vehicles. No technicians were in evidence, since the final stages of the countdown were under way and nothing remained to be done to the exterior of VX-1. The dry ice "propellant" had been installed and now the action was underground, where the subterranean energy-storage system, the superconducting coil, was being primed. At this point, most of the staffers were monitoring the last-minute computer checks of the in-flight systems.

"Sounds good," Reggie said, pointing to a spot on the blueprint. "I'll position myself right there, where I'll have a clear shot at the main points of ingress and egress. Now let's move it before somebody checks in with the security system and picks up our penetration."

Everybody else agreed, signifying it by a last-minute review of weapons and gear. Everybody, that is, except Michael Vance, who had been thinking, and worrying, about the irreversible step that a frontal assault would represent. What if Ramirez had left Launch and gone back to Command? The man had a habit of keeping on the move. It was an innate part of his inner nature.

"You know . . ." He rubbed at his swollen face and winced at the pain. "I'd like to suggest a different tack. A sort of 'look before you leap' approach."

"What do you mean?" Armont asked distractedly, anxious to get the assault under way while there was still a lingering cover of fog and semidark.

"Pierre, before the team shows its hand, why don't you let me test the waters a bit. See if I can't be a decoy long enough to make them show *their* hand."

"Care to explain exactly what you have in mind?" Armont asked, always willing to listen, if skeptically.

"They know I'm here. They don't know about the team, at least not yet. And, more to the point, we don't know if Ramirez is really in there or not. But assuming he is, instead of storming the place, why not let me first see if I can't draw him out, at least give us a preview of his resources."

"How would anybody go about doing that?" Reggie was double-checking the sight on his Enfield L85A1 assault rifle, still anxious to get moving.

"Well," Vance went on, "he wants me. So maybe this is not the worst time to use our heads instead of hardware. Why not use me as bait?"

"Michael," Armont interjected, "whatever you have in mind, you've done enough already. This isn't your fight, and I can't in good conscience ask you to do anything more. You just take care of those bruises and let us handle it from here on out. Tell you the truth, you look like hell."

Vance paused, trying to get a grip on his own feelings. "All right, maybe it's just a vendetta on my part, unprofessional, but the real truth is I'd like the chance to take him down myself." He realized he had truly come to hate Ramirez, a killer without a conscience who deserved anything he got. "Besides, there's another reason. I think he's got an old professor in there somewhere, and I confess a certain fondness for the man, in spite of all his bungling. If you rush the place, God only knows what he's liable to do. Probably get himself killed."

"I can understand you might feel you have a personal stake in this," Reggie Hall said finally, "but what exactly do you think you can do? Remember the old saying, Shakespeare or somebody, a hero is the bloke who died a-Wednesday."

"I don't plan to try and get killed. But why not let me take some flash grenades and a gun? Go up there by the gantry and generate a little excitement. If he's still there, maybe I can draw him out. He won't realize I've got backup. You take it from there."

"I'm not sure I like it," Armont grumbled, slamming a clip into his automatic. "If you ask me, there's been too damned much impromptu strategy on this op already."

"On the other hand, Michael has a point," Hans interjected with Germanic logic. "If we can separate Ramirez from the hostages, it could prevent a lot of danger to the friendlies. My only worry is that if it doesn't work, then we've blown the element of surprise. All of a sudden we've got a firefight on our hands."

"We've got a firefight anyway," Marcel observed, "no matter what happens. So why not?"

"I agree it's a gamble," Vance paused. "But the alternative could be a genuine disaster." He took an MP5 from the bag of hardware they had brought and checked the clip. "Does anybody strenuously object?"

"I do," Cally finally spoke up, her anger at him seeming to soften. "We'll probably have to come and pick up the pieces. But you're right about Isaac. Knowing him, he's liable to just walk into a line of fire, out of sheer absentmindedness."

"All right." Vance looked around. "While the fog is still in, I want to go up." He was pointing. Why wait for a vote? Nobody seemed to be strongly against it. "I'll come in from up there"—he pointed—"by the base of what's left of the gantry, and try to draw him out. If nothing else, it'll be diversion. If it doesn't work, you can still go in."

"All right, you win," Armont said. His eyes betrayed his lingering misgivings. "But you're making yourself a target, so don't try any heroics. If Ramirez does show his face, let us take it from there. This isn't your game."

Willem Voorst nodded and pulled out an extra vest, already festooned with grenades. He handed it to Vance, who slipped it on and secured it, wincing silently from the pain in his rib cage.

"Just be bloody careful," Reggie Hall said. That and nothing more. British understatement.

Calypso Andros had no such reserve. Her hair plastered across her face, she reached up and impulsively kissed him on a swollen cheek. Then she whispered good luck.

6:31 A.M.

"Alpha Leader, this is SEAL One. I think we've spotted some hostiles."

With a smile, Nichols clicked his radio to transmit. He was in the lead Huey, now hovering slightly more than a kilometer away from the shoreline of Andikythera.

"I copy, SEAL One. What's your status?"

"We're ready to get acquainted. Are you synchronized?"

"Roger," Nichols's terse voice replied back. "I want all hell to break loose. And any bad guys you can pin down or neutralize will be much appreciated. We insert in ninety seconds."

"We roger that, Alpha Leader. SEAL One team on full auto."

Nichols turned to his pilot, Manny Jackson. "Okay, it's a go. I want us on the ground in nine-zero seconds."

6:32 A.M.

Vance moved quickly up the hill, toward the toppled gantry. Already he had a view of the wide sloping window that was the center of Launch Control, and he could see figures there, though not clearly enough to know if Ramirez was one of them. Maybe they were SatCom staffers or . . .

No. There was Ramirez, talking on the phone. And standing beside him was the man Vance had come to love . . . Isaac Mannheim. The old professor looked haggard, a perfectionist man who had despaired. He clearly had lost touch with time and place. Then Ramirez handed him the phone and barked something at him. Dejectedly he took it and started speaking.

Damn. Any half-competent sniper could take out Ramirez here and now. He thought he was safe, and he had never been more exposed. But this was not a job for an amateur, not with Mannheim so close.

Okay, he thought, guess this is going to have to happen the hard way.

He extracted a flash grenade from the vest Willem had given him and got ready to pull the pin.

6:33 A.M.

"Johan, he'll do it," Isaac Mannheim was saying into the handset that Ramirez had thrust into his face. "They have two devices. One is on *VX-1*, ready for launch, and the other one is here. They say they've rigged a radio-controlled detonator on it. He's going to use it if you don't do whatever it is he wants."

"Let me talk to the son of a bitch again," Hansen said.

"All right, Johan. Please talk to him." Mannheim handed back the receiver. His hand was shaking.

"Have you made a decision, Mr. President?" Ramirez inquired.

"Yes, goddammit. I've got an open line to Gournes. You

can listen while I issue the order to hold off the assault for six hours. Does that satisfy you?"

"It will do for a start," Ramirez said. "Then we can talk about the money."

And he listened as Hansen spoke tersely through the secure communications link to Mission Control on the *Kennedy*.

What he did not hear in Hansen's conversation was the incredulity on the other end of the line. But the assault is already under way, General Max Austin was declaring, stunned. They were in communication with Nichols, and the SEALs were about to open fire on the hostiles.

"Just scrub the operation," Hansen barked. "That's an order."

"That was a wise decision," Ramirez said, listening. "Now about the money."

"Check with the bank in fifteen minutes," Hansen said, a note of resignation in his voice. "It will be deposited. Now, I want you out of there, all hostages safe, and those weapons disarmed and left."

"You have nothing to worry about," Ramirez declared, scarcely able to contain his sense of triumph. "You have made a decision for humanity."

"Just get the hell gone. And don't try my patience." This time it was Hansen's turn to abruptly break the connection.

Ramirez was cradling the receiver, savoring his triumph, when a blinding flash erupted from the direction of the fallen gantry. And there, in the momentary glare, stood Michael Vance.

6:34 A.M.

The leader of the SEALs, Lieutenant Devon Robbins, spoke into his thin microphone. "Can you see them? We could use an IR scope." The SEALs had split into two teams, as was their practice, and he was leading the first.

"Hard to make out much in this fog," came back his point man, Lieutenant Philip Pease, who was leading the second team. Pease was exactly twenty meters away, all but invisible because of his dark commando gear. He was studying the men up the hill with a pair of 8×30mm Steiner stereo-optic binoculars. Though they were designed for low light, he still could not see clearly. "But they're dressed in black, and they look like they're armed."

"What else can you ID?"

"They're not together, exactly. It's almost as though they're deploying for something."

"What the hell are they doing outside in the first place? Does it mean the fuckers haven't gotten around to taking over the launch facility yet? Maybe they're getting set up for their next move."

"Can't confirm anything, SEAL One. Just too much damned fog. . . . Wait, yeah, they've got assault rifles of some kind. Looks like some big-time shit. That's a definite confirm."

"Do they look like they're setting up?"

"All I can tell for sure is they're moving, spreading out. Something's about to go down. Got to be baddies. Who else could they be?"

"All right, SEAL Two, our mission is to create a diversion, shake them up, and let Nichols's chopper teams handle the heavy lifting. Those Apaches can make a man give his heart to Jesus."

"You've got a rog on that, SEAL One. But if we're here to make an impression, I say let's give them a big Navy welcome. Time for a close encounter."

"We came to play. Get—"

A flare blossomed from somewhere up in the vicinity of the vehicles, illuminating the fog into a huge white cloud, vast and mysterious.

"What in hell!" yelled Pease's voice on the radio. "That was farther up. Maybe it's a two-point assault."

"Looked like it was over to the left. Can you tell what happened?"

"Must have been a flash-bang. These assholes brought their own boombox."

"Okay, SEAL Two, we've got a mission. First things first.

For now we just neutralize those bastards in black. Looks like half our hostiles are outside and in the clear. On the count of three."

The SEALS all clicked off the safeties on their MP5s and took aim, wishing they could see something more than dark, vague outlines in the fog.

6:35 A.M.

How the hell, Ramirez wondered, did Vance get on the loose again? Moreau was supposed to have taken care of him. Had *he* screwed up, too?

I should have just let Wolf kill him in the first place and had done with it. This time, I'll just handle it myself.

He checked his pockets, making sure he had extra clips for his Beretta 9mm and then he headed through the door leading into the open bay of Launch. The SatCom systems engineers and ground-control specialists, not privy to the wide windows of Launch Control, had no idea what had just happened outside. They were too busy worrying about the fog, making the final checks of the electronics, monitoring the countdown clicking off. And all of them had laid side bets on whether the launch, now scheduled for less than an hour and a half away, would be able to proceed. The wagering leaned toward the fog clearing in time.

Ramirez strode past the bustling gray SatCom uniforms with a single-mindedness that characterized his every move. How the hell, he was wondering, did Michael Vance get on the island in the first place? He was one of the back-office support types for ARM, a financial guy. Nobody had ever ID'd him in an assault. It made no sense that he was here, when none of the rest of the ARM operatives were around. Why Vance, who was a nobody?

All the same, he had specialized in screwing up things ever since the initial penetration. He had managed to wreck the Hind, destroy the gantry, make a general nuisance of himself. The time had come to put a stop to the annoyance and then get moving. If the money had been delivered, as

Hansen had claimed, then it was time to move on to the next phase. Just take care of a few banking transactions, then put the egress plan into motion.

He hit the lock control on the door, which had long since been defaulted to manual, and strode out, his Beretta ready. The problem now was finding that bastard Vance in the fog, but the reflected light off the spots illuminating the vehicles was going to provide visibility. Besides, the bastard was a cowboy, took chances right and left. He also didn't seem to be a particularly competent marksman. . . .

6:36 A.M.

"There he is," Pierre Armont said, peering through the fog with his Tasco Infocus Zoom binoculars. They did not require focusing, and with a touch of a lever he jacked up the power from six to twelve. "I want the sucker myself. We missed him in Beirut, but this time . . ."

Up above, Sabri Ramirez was gliding along the side of the fallen gantry, an automatic in his hand. Ramirez, Armont knew, was famous for his Beretta 9mm, used to such deadly effect over the years. It was his trademark, always employed for assassinations.

But now, finally, after all the years. There was the Hyena, exposed and clear. One shot. One shot would do it.

"He's mine." Armont leveled his MP5, captured Ramirez in the sight, and clicked it to full auto. Vance was a genius. He had lured the Hyena from his lair. Take him out, and the whole op would be over in time for morning coffee.

6:37 A.M.

Ramirez was edging down the side of the gantry, the cold angle-iron against his back, when there was an eruption of gunfire down the hill. It was controlled, professional fire that seemed to be coming from two locations. An assault.

Well, fuck Hansen. The President had lied, claiming he

had called it off. Had he lied about the money, too? The
fleeting thought made him seethe. But one problem at a time.

He quickly ducked behind the fallen gantry, disappearing
into the shadows. One more phone call, then a check with
Geneva. If the money hadn't been transferred, Souda Bay
and the American Sixth Fleet were both going to disappear in
a nuclear cloud. In fact, they were anyway. What better way
to cover an egress?

6:38 A.M.

"What in—" Armont emitted a curse as all hell broke
loose behind them. A fusillade of automatic-weapons fire
rained around, from somewhere in the direction of the shoreline. It was almost like covering fire, not well directed, and
since everybody on the ARM team had long made a practice
of minimizing exposure at all times, he didn't expect immediate casualties. But what in hell! Had Ramirez's terrorist team
encircled them, drawn them in? He felt like an idiot.

"Hostile fire!" He gave the signal to get down and take
cover, swinging his hand from above his head to shoulder
level, but that was nothing more than redundant instinct. The
ARM team was already on the ground, ready to return fire if
so ordered.

Nobody, however, was wasting ammo on the darkness.
The team had little enough to spare, and besides—why give
away your position and create a target? The third consideration was that ARM never fired on an unknown. They were,
after all, civilians and answerable. An army could wreak whatever havoc it pleased and later blame everything on the heat
of battle. ARM had to be damned sure who it was taking
down.

By the time Armont's yell died away, everybody on the
team had already found cover behind the random outcroppings of rocks. Everybody, that is, except Hugo Voorst, who
spun around and stumbled backward, moaned, then collapsed.

6:39 A.M.

"Hold your fire! Goddammit, hold your fire." The SEAL leader, Lieutenant Devon Robbins, was pressing in his earpiece, incredulous at what he was hearing. Around him the team was on the ground, in firing position, keeping the terrorists up the hill pinned down. Next would come the assault. "Roger, Alpha Leader, I copy. Does anybody know what's going on with this whole fucked-up op? . . . I copy."

He looked around. "We just got aborted."

"What the *fuck* do you mean," the SEAL next to him, John McCleary, said. He was slamming another clip into his MP5.

"The team is extracted. Now." Robbins could scarcely believe his own words.

"You have got to be fucking kidding," came the radio voice of Lieutenant Philip Pease. "We've got the assholes. A couple of grenades from the blooper and then we take them. They're history."

"Hey, I just report the orders, I don't give them," Robbins replied. "Immediate egress. That's the word. Who the fuck knows?"

"But what about the choppers? Nichols is coming in with the Apaches."

"Gournes says they're scrubbed, too. Everybody's on hold. Nichols just about ate the fucking radio. He's going apeshit."

"Well, the hell with Gournes," came a third voice, through a black pullover. "Maybe we had a 'radio failure.' The fuckers are pinned down. Let's just go ahead and take them down. The whole op is blown. Now they're going to know we're coming in."

"They probably figured on it anyway," Robbins said, clicking on the safety of his MP5. "But who the hell cares. We're out of here. Flint, you've got the rear. Use it. I'm on point. Let's hit the beach. In five. Pass it on." He switched on his radio. "Listen up. Anybody not in a Zodiac in five mikes swims."

6:40 A.M.

Georges LeFarge had been studying Peretz, trying to figure out what was going on. One thing was sure: the countdown was about to switch into auto mode—which meant the
priming of the superconducting coil would begin. When that
happened, the Cyclops would be entering a very delicate,
and dangerous, phase. Shutting it down after auto mode com-
menced required the kind of familiarity with the system he
was sure Peretz did not have. Mess up then and you could
literally burn out the huge power storage ring buried deep in
the island's core—which was why the Fujitsu was deliberately programmed to thwart any straightforward command to
abort. Ironically, the fail-safe mechanism was designed not to
shut down the Cyclops, but rather to carry through. At this
stage, the only way to abort the launch sequence safely was to
bleed off the power using the Cyclops's main radar, the way
they had done early last night. To simply flip a switch and
turn everything off would be to risk melting the multimillion-
dollar cryogenic storage coil down under. The whole thing
was as bizarre as it was real. By continuing the countdown
until everything went into auto mode, Peretz was creating a
monster of inevitability.

He was currently trying to explain this to the Israeli, hoping the guy could conceive the gravity of what he was about
to do. "You don't understand," he was pleading, his voice
plaintive above the clicks of switches and buzz of communications gear in Command, "you're going to risk—"

"Hey, kid, chill out." Peretz did not bother to look up
from his terminal. A strip-chart recorder next to him was
humming away as voltage and amperage checks proceeded.

"But look." Georges pointed to the screen of an adjacent
workstation. "You've got less than three minutes left to abort
the power-up. After the auto-test sequence it's doing now is
finished, the superconducting coil starts final power-up.
That's when everything switches to auto mode. It's all automatic from then on. For a very good reason."

"Hey, that's why we're here, kid." Peretz was grinning his
crazy grin. "This is not some fucking dry run. This is the big

one. I've got no intention of shutting it down. We're gonna launch, dude."

Dore Peretz knew exactly what the critical go/no-go points in the countdown were; he had researched the Cyclops system extensively. He also knew that after auto mode, there would be no altering the orbital abort and the timing of the detonation. Once auto mode began, he was home free. He could split.

The trajectory he had programmed with SORT was not for Souda Bay but for low orbit. One orbit. The abort had been preset. The bomb was going to be delivered right back here on Andikythera. It was brilliant. Get the money in place, get out, and then wipe out the island, all evidence of the operation.

Including Sabri Ramirez.

The world would then think that all the terrorists were dead. And they would be—all, that is, except Dr. Dore Peretz.

In truth, he was thinking, this was almost the most fun he'd had in years. The actual most fun had been the memo he had presented to Sabri Ramirez concerning the new split of the money. All along he had thought the phrase fifty-fifty had a nice solid ring. What point was there in spreading the ransom all over the place? Giving it to a bunch of assholes?

Which was why Dore Peretz had, two weeks earlier, established an account in the same Geneva bank where Ramirez was having the money delivered. The memo had instructed Ramirez to advise the bank to move half the money into that account as soon as it arrived. And when funds were deposited into that account, the bank was instructed to move them yet again—well beyond the reach of anybody.

All he needed now was proof that Ramirez had faxed the bank with the new instructions. So had he? The time had come to check in with the bastard and find out. Then it was over. All he would have to do after that was commandeer the chopper and get the hell out.

The only missing link was somebody to fly the Sikorsky,

and the perfect choice for that little task was in the next room, a certain Vietnam fighter-pilot turned CEO. . . .

He motioned for Georges LeFarge. "Okay, everything's set. Auto mode. We've got exactly sixty-eight minutes to lift-off. Is that enough excitement for you?"

LeFarge did feel something of a thrill, in spite of his better judgment. He didn't know why Peretz would want to abort the flight—which he knew was what SORT had been programmed to do—but at least *VX-1* was going up. And when you worked on a project like this, there was only one real payoff—when the vehicle left the pad. All the months, years, of preparations led up to that final moment. . . .

"I want Bates," Peretz declared, pointing toward the closed office door. "So, go and get him. That's an order. It's time he got in on the fun. After all, this is his baby.

Georges turned away from his useless workstation, still shaken by the sight of auto mode clicking in, and walked back toward the door. Bates had been locked in there, mainly to keep him quiet. But now things were starting to happen. Several members of the terrorist group had come in, started readying weapons, and were acting nervous.

Well, Georges thought, maybe they're worried the U.S. might just get off its ass and come in, do something about this outrage. The terrorists had plenty of heavy weapons, and now they were checking them out and slapping in clips of ammunition. Bill Bates was not going to like what he saw. . . .

He opened the door and motioned for Bates to come out. He slowly rose from his chair, looking beat and haggard, and came. Georges's first impression was that he was missing a large slice of his old zip. He looked like a man near defeat—exhausted, even disoriented.

"How are you feeling?" Peretz asked.

"How do you think?" Bates growled, looking around at all the assembled terrorists now readying their weapons. The place was turning into an armed camp.

"Just a friendly inquiry," Peretz went on, flashing his empty grin. "We're about to start the fireworks up at Launch, and I didn't want you to miss out on any of it." He paused to check the countdown scrolling on the terminal in front of him. "So . . ." he continued, turning back, "I think it's time we three—you, me, and Georges here—took a small stroll and checked out how things are going."

"Mind telling me what in blazes you're up to?" Bates demanded. His voice was still strong even though he had lost much of the spring in his step. "If you fuckers have killed any more of my people, I'm going to see to it personally that—"

"Take it easy, man," Peretz interjected. "As long as nobody causes any trouble, then nobody gets hurt." He turned and motioned for Jean-Paul Moreau. "Keep an eye on this place. He swept his arm over the sea of technicians and systems analysts. "Everything's right on target with the countdown." It was an impromptu private joke, a spur-of-the-moment thing, that he found delightful.

Jean-Paul Moreau, his reflexes now slowing slightly from lack of sleep, did not get the joke, and he did not like the feeling he *was* getting. Dore Peretz was a canny little fucker, and he suddenly seemed in a great hurry to get out of Command. Was the *bâtard* up to something? It was puzzling, and troubling.

He adjusted his blond ponytail and gazed around the room, now a cacophony of preflight activity. Keeping everybody in line was the least of his problems. These white-shirted engineers were so scared that if you said jump, they'd all stand up and ask how high. No, what bothered him was not knowing what the damned Israeli had up his sleeve. Peretz was planning something, probably intending to leave somebody to hold the bag.

And it wasn't hard to figure out who that somebody was. . . .

"You know," he said to Peretz, "everybody has orders to stay at their posts and keep security, in case there's an assault. You pulling out of here is not part of the plan."

"Hey, I've been handling this thing so far, and the launch is set. Now I need to check on the telemetry and data hookups at Launch—if that's okay with you. I've taken care of my end, so now all you've got to do is keep any of these assholes from getting on the computer and trying to screw things up. Nobody so much as touches a keyboard, got it?"

"Got it." Moreau nodded, hating the little son of a bitch even more.

"Good," he said, turning back to Bates. "Okay, baby, we're gone."

CHAPTER SEVENTEEN

6:58 A.M.

Hugo Voorst was lying propped against a rock, his shoulder bandaged with white strips of gauze from the first-aid kit. Now that the flow of blood had been staunched, Marcel was injecting him with a shot of morphine to quell the looming pain. Happily the hit was clean, just a flesh wound and nothing serious, but he would be of no further use on the mission. Worse still, he actually had become a liability. The only thing to do was to leave him where he was, with an H&K machine pistol for protection, and proceed. You didn't like to abandon anybody, but . . .

Voorst, for his own part, mainly felt sheepish. Giddy though he was, the result of mild shock, his Dutch stoicism was still holding up. "I'll be all right," he was saying, a slow grin covering his face as the narcotic kicked in. "Sorry to be a party pooper."

"You got lucky," Hans soothed, checking the bandage one last time. "You get to take a little time off. But you may still have a chance to give us some backup if things get hot."

Armont had not said anything, leaving the kidding around to the younger men. They needed it to keep up their macho. The hard truth was, the whole operation was rapidly turning into a disaster of the first magnitude. Everything possible had gone wrong. And now he had no idea where Vance was. The situation had gone red, the odds deteriorating rapidly.

Ramirez had been lured out, but he had been saved by the deus ex machina of an unexpected but short-lived attack from their rear. What had that been all about?

Then he noticed a glint in the sky, through the early dawn, and realized it was a helo, far in the distance, banking as its pilot began turning back. He looked more carefully and counted four. All egressing.

"Take a look." He pointed toward the cluster of tiny dots slowly diminishing in the dim sky. "Looks like somebody showed up just long enough to screw us, then aborted. And now Mike is back in the Belly of the Beast." He turned and peered at the fog-swathed floodlights, now growing pale as dawn began arriving in earnest. Around them the dull outlines of trees and rocks were lightening into greens and granite-grays. "With the damned rocket still sitting up there ready to blast off.

"All right," he continued after a thoughtful pause, "we know where Ramirez is, but after all the shooting around here, the idea of a nice clean insertion will have to go by the boards." He returned his gaze to Launch Control. "No way in hell could we take Launch by surprise now. Ramirez has got to know something is brewing. Which means we're going to have to do things the old-fashioned way. Bad news for the hostages if they don't know how to get out of the way, but we've got to deal with the bomb, no matter what."

There was muttering and grumbling. ARM men did not fancy excessive gunfire. They had all long passed that age of youthful denial when men thought they were invulnerable. They had seen too much.

"By the way," Armont abruptly interrupted everybody's chain of thought, "what happened to the woman who was here, Dr. Andros? Was she hit?"

Nobody had noticed, up until that point, that she was

absent. They quickly checked the rocks around the area, but she was nowhere to be found.

"Forget about her," he finally decreed. "If she doesn't want to stay with us, then she's not our problem." He thought a minute. "Maybe we should break radio silence and see if we can raise Vance. He took a unit with him."

"I'm against it," Willem Voorst declared. "As a matter of fact, I'm against doing anything. If the U.S. is planning to come in here and take down this place, then why should we risk our own ass. Let's just get in a secure position and let them do our work for us. We've never had that kind of help before. It might be refreshing. I think Michael can take care of himself. Why—"

"No, we can't wait for them, whoever it was." Armont cut him off. "I don't know what the hell they were really up to. And besides, if that little demonstration we just had was any indication, their mode is going to be to shoot first and ask questions later. So we have to finish our job, just get it over with. And I'll tell you what I think. Since Launch is a muck-up now, our best bet is to keep Ramirez off guard for a while and go ahead and take down Command. Immediately, before they realize what's going on. With any luck, maybe they won't be expecting it." He looked around. "Make a three-point entry, flash-bangs and tear gas. Just blow out the place." He paused to let the words sink. "Well," he continued finally, "does anybody disagree?"

There were nervous frowns, but nobody did. Instead, they began silently collecting their gear.

11:59 P.M.

Hansen had returned to the basement Situation Room, where maps and operation plans cluttered the teakwood table and littered meal trays, grease encrusting on the white china, were piled up in the corner. No stewards were allowed in the room, and nobody else was going to clean up. He had not slept for a day and a half, and he was now showing a ragged shadow of beard. Ted Brock had heard some of his aides upstairs commenting to each other *sotto voce* that he had never seemed older.

"All right," he said. "I've called off the assault and given the bastard six hours to clear out. I've also released the money, had it wired to the account he wanted. So maybe now he'll leave quietly. Our deal is that he frees the hostages unharmed, disarms the bombs, and gets the hell out of there. But I'll tell you something else: he's not going to live to spend a dime. The minute he's airborne, his ass is ours. I want him shot out of the sky, and the hell with the consequences."

"He'll probably take some civilians along with him," Briggs said. "Hostages. We could be looking at some dicey press."

"All right, then, so we won't shoot him down; we'll just force him down, the way we handled that Libyan passenger jet with terrorists aboard. There was official flack for a week or so from the usual quarters, but off the record everybody was applauding. When you do the right thing, the world makes allowances for how you manage it."

Briggs remained skeptical, but he kept his thoughts to himself. He wanted to have as little to do with the operation as possible. Sooner or later there would be loss of life, he was sure of it, and the chances were the losses would be massive. He had no interest in making the history books as the author of a civilian massacre, terrorists or no terrorists.

"All right, Mr. President, I'll tell the Deltas to keep their powder dry until we play this one out." He had already heard from General Max Austin, who said Nichols was fit to be tied, eating his cigars instead of smoking them. Who could blame him? To have a Commander-in-Chief micromanaging an anti-terrorist op violated every known canon of military strategy. There might be a more surefire recipe for disaster, but it was hard to conjure one offhand.

Hansen, for his own part, recognized the pitfalls of giving the terrorists more time. However, he hoped it would end up being the rope—make that false confidence—that would hang them.

He had wired the "ransom" money to the numbered account at Banco Ambrosiano, as requested. There, his intelligence on the ground was reporting, the eight hundred million had been split and transferred to several other accounts. Then portions of it had been immediately wired out —to a destination not yet known, though it damned well would be. What, he wondered, was that all about? Were the terrorists in the process of screwing each other? It was a possibility. Everything was a possibility. But it also was smart, because it made recovering the funds that much more difficult. They were, in effect, laundering it even before they had made their getaway. These characters, whoever they were, were taking no chances.

7:03 A.M.

"Load it on now," Ramirez was saying. "We're taking it with us." He flashed a smile from behind his aviator shades. "You never know when you'll need a nuke."

Abdoullah couldn't believe his luck. He had been sure that Number One intended to try and kill him. But now it turned out to be the others, the ones he'd sent over to Command, that he planned to leave in the lurch.

Dawn was breaking, but there still was enough early fog to mask their movements partially. It was definitely time to get the show on the road. One of the bombs had been installed on the VX-1 vehicle and a countdown was under way. When that bomb devastated Souda Bay, nobody was going to be worrying about a lone chopper somewhere over the Med. And with the other weapon still in their hands, the whole operation was going like clockwork. The money was in place —he was now rich—and they were packing to leave.

The bomb they were now loading actually made him think. Maybe, he mused fleetingly, he could just kill Number One and return it. It would be the final revenge for what the bastard did to Rais.

No, that was stupid. Better to just take the money and run. Lose the heroics. In fact, given how things had gone so far, the whole thing was almost too good to be true. In fact, that bothered him a little. More than a little. He had seen too much double-dealing already to believe anything Number One said or did.

He trusted Dore Peretz even less. The Israeli, he was sure, had a private agenda of his own. He always seemed to. Maybe he was planning to divert the bomb and take out Tel Aviv. He was crazy enough.

But who cared? They were getting out. Better still, Number One had indicated he intended to take the old professor, the Jew, with them. With him on board, Number One had declared, there was no danger that the U.S. President would order the chopper shot down. The old guy made a perfect passport.

But with Souda Bay being incinerated as they made their egress, it hardly seemed to matter. . . .

He grasped the lever on the forklift and, aided by Shujat, hoisted the bomb through the cargo hatch, guiding the edges of the crate. It weighed almost as much as they did together, but by now they were used to managing it. Interestingly, it still was wired to its radio-controlled detonator, with the explosive charges intact. He had the momentary thought that it should be disconnected, but now there was no time. That was something that should be done with extreme care. Maybe he would take care of it after takeoff, when they were airborne.

"Be careful," Ramirez went on. "But don't waste time. The vehicle is going up, and then we're going to be out of here. In less than an hour."

7:08 A.M.

"Team Two CQ," came Hans's voice on the walkie-talkie. He and Marcel were in the overhead ventilation duct above Command, which had been depicted in great detail in the blueprints. Hugo Voorst had been left to fend for himself, while Willem had split off with Dimitri Spiros, forming Team Three.

"Team Three CQ," Willem reported next. "Ingress looks like a go." He and Dimitri were at the rear exit, which passed through Bill Bates's office. They had entered through the tunnel that connected Bates's office and the living quarters. The door had been set with C-4 and was ready to blow.

"Copy. Team One CQ," Armont whispered into his own radio. He and Reginald Hall were now in the outer lobby, and just ahead of them stood the doors that led into Command. Together the teams formed a three-pronged attack that would seal off all egress. "Take down anybody with anything in their hands. And watch out for Michael. I don't think he's in there, but you never can tell."

"If he is," Willem Voorst's voice said, "he'll know what to do."

As they waited, Reggie gazed around Reception in disgust. The deserted guard desk looked as though it had been strafed by an automatic, almost as if the terrorists intentionally were wreaking as much destruction as possible.

"Cheeky bastards," he muttered under his breath. "Why do these terrorist blokes always think they've got to trash a place?"

"Reggie," Armont whispered back, "these gentlemen did not attend Eton. You have to learn to make allowances. And right now they appear to be trying to deliver an atomic bomb into somebody's backyard, which would tend to suggest they're not model citizens. One has to expect a disheartening want of tidiness in such an element." He checked his watch. "All right, get ready."

Ahead of them the doors to Command were closed— who knew if they were locked or even booby-trapped? But it didn't matter. The C-4 had already been attached around the frame. Exploding it and the other door opposite would serve as a diversion, drawing the first fire and giving Hans and Marcel the moment they needed to make their own ingress, rappelling in under cover of flash grenades and mopping up.

That was the plan, at any rate. A three-point entry, with flash grenades and tear gas. It usually worked.

Armont clicked on his walkie-talkie again and checked his watch. "All teams alert. Assault begins in three-zero seconds. Starting *now*."

7:09 A.M.

Peering down into the room through the overhead grating, Hans felt his palms grow sweaty. This was the moment he always hated. Even after all his years with the assault squads, *Spezialen-satztrupp*, in GSG-9, he had never gotten over this moment of soul-searching panic.

Twenty seconds.

He glanced up from his watch, then tested the rope he and Marcel would use to rappel down into the room. Finally he adjusted the hood of his balaclava one last time in an attempt to quell his nerves. It never worked, of course, and it wasn't working now. Still, he always did it. More helpful was checking the clip on his MP5. He had a spare taped to the one now loaded, making it possible to just flip them over. A third was taped to his wrist. It should be enough. Ten seconds.

That was the moment—it always happened—when he felt his mouth go dry. Bone dry.

7:10 A.M.

Reggie, who normally served as standoff sniper, almost always used an old AK-47 he had had for fifteen years and kept honed to perfection. Nothing fancy, just deadly accuracy. Today, however, he was keeping it in reserve, since this was close quarters. At the moment he was going with his sentimental British favorite, an Enfield L85A1 assault rifle that was the last product of the old Enfield Arsenal. Its special sling meant it could be carried behind his back, and it was short, virtually recoilless, and a marvel to behold on full-automatic.

For his own part, Armont had a Steyr-Mannlicher AUG assault rifle, augmented with a Beta hundred-round .C-Mag supposedly only available to government organizations. He didn't like to bother changing clips, which annoyed him as a waste of precious time, and the circular, hundred-round dual magazine gave him—so he claimed—all the firepower he needed. Besides, he liked to say, if a hundred rounds weren't enough to take down an objective, then you hadn't planned it right and deserved to be in the shit.

He gave five clicks into his walkie-talkie, which meant five seconds, then stood back as Reggie got ready to blow the C-4.

7:10 A.M.

"Looks like you got it right," Peretz said with a crooked smile. He was examining a fax whose letterhead read Banco Ambrosiano, Geneva. Ramirez had just passed it over, and the correct account number was there, together with the amount in dollars. His piece of the money, his *bigger* piece, had been transferred to the separate account he had specified. By now, according to the instruction he had left, it was already on its way out. Home free.

He counted the zeroes again, not quite believing it. The villa he had set his heart on was his. He had just acquired four hundred million dollars. Some *countries* weren't worth that much, for godsake.

"Your generosity is touching." He folded the paper and slipped it into his shirt pocket. He had left ironclad instructions at the bank. The minute the funds were transferred, they would be wired to a bank in Nassau, Bahamas, a bank known only to him. That way, Ramirez would have no chance to fiddle the money back.

Ramirez said nothing, merely smiled. The fact was, this little Israeli creep was an amateur. Five minutes after he had wired the instructions, he had sent a second fax, countermanding them. That was the last thing to worry about. More important was that Peretz had left his post at Command and come down here to gloat. So it was a good thing he had sent Jean-Paul and Jamal over there to keep an eye on things. They also had taken the last Stasi, Peter Maier, with them. Schindler had disappeared, presumably lost when the U.S. began its aborted attack. They had proved to be useless, a fact he was going to point out to Wolf Helling just before he shot him between the eyes.

This crude attempt at blackmail by Peretz was perfectly in character, had in fact been telegraphed from the start. Which was why all the contingency plans had been necessary.

Given Peretz's particularly obnoxious demand, he was tempted to move the plan ahead and just shoot the son of a bitch now. Unfortunately, though, he might still be needed. So the best course for the moment was just to let him think he had gotten away with it. Besides, it was a trifle early to finish thinning the ranks. All in due time. . . .

7:11 A.M.

It could have been the sound of a single explosion, even though it had taken place at the two opposite entries to Command. Then, as one, Team One and Team Three were inside, just behind the harmless explosions of flash grenades and charges of CS they had blasted into the room.

Willem Voorst of Team Three was in first position as he virtually pounced through the door just blown away with C-4, which now was a curtain of smoke. While he sprayed the ceiling with rounds, sweeping left to right, Dimitri Spiros was in second position, automatically sweeping right to left.

"Get down," Voorst yelled in English, hoping the civilians would be quick. Staffers dove for the gray linoleum, many yelling in pure terror. In Voorst's experience, a couple of curious morons always wanted to stand up and watch the action, frequently a lethal form of entertainment. This time, however, everybody fortuitously hit the floor.

On the far right, Salim Khan yelled and brought up his Uzi, mesmerized by the balaclava-covered face of Voorst, but the Dutchman was already far ahead of the game, and a single burst from his MP5 dropped him, taking away the left side of his face. The bearded Iranian pilot never realized what had happened, pitching forward without so much as a final prayer.

One away, Voorst thought. But that was an easy one. An amateur.

On the opposite side of the room, Armont was in first position and Hall was in second—both poised to take down anybody who showed hostile intent. Together with Team Three at the back, their two-point entry was like a Wagnerian crescendo that began a piece of music instead of ending it. The melody was still to come.

Armont squinted through the hood of his balaclava into the billowing CS that was enveloping the room. The confusion that obscured the difference between friend and foe dismayed him. ARM had had no photos of the terrorists to work with, no intelligence—other than the ID of Ramirez—concerning their physical appearance.

The back of his mind, however, was telling him that they all were dressed in black, just as the members of the ARM team were. So everybody with a gun looked alike; the difference boiled down to who was shooting at whom.

Reggie, in number-two position, had the best eyes of any of them, and he had moved in behind Armont, those eyes sweeping the room. Try not to waste the bloody place, he was lecturing himself. Show some class.

With the surprise still fresh, it now was time for Team Two to appear, completing the three-point assault. Through the smoke two black figures appeared out of nowhere, rappelling down into the very middle of the chaos. First came Hans, followed by Marcel, both holding the rope in one hand, an MP5 in the other.

While Willem Voorst and Dimitri Spiros were still firing, hoping to draw the attention of the hostiles away from Team Two, Hans rotated on his rope, and took measure of the room. He had less than a second to get his bearings and to analyze the immediate threat from hostiles, the peril to friendlies, and the one-time opportunities a quick window of surprise offered. The main thing was to try to cut down the most senior, experienced hostile in the room.

In the millisecond before his feet touched the floor, he saw what he had hoped for: a man dressed in black, with long blond hair tied back in a pony tail, carrying an Uzi. Better yet, he recognized him. Jesus! It was Jean-Paul Moreau.

Interpol wants that bastard, he told himself, but they want him alive. And there's a private bank-consortium bounty on his head of five hundred thousand francs. He's found money. Alive.

7:11 A.M.

"What the hell!" Ramirez glanced at the TV monitor that was next to the array of instruments and video screens looking out onto the launch pad.

Peretz whirled to look, as did Bill Bates. The scene was Command and the image had grown fuzzy, as though the room were filled with smoke. But there was no mistaking the chaos. SatCom staffers were on the floor, while flashes of light darted across the screen as the camera automatically panned back and forth.

Jesus! Bates thought. It looks like Nam. It's an assault. Who could it be? Had the U.S. decided to get off its butt and start protecting its citizens? They damned well had taken their time about it. . . .

Now he could see who was doing the shooting, and most of it seemed to be coming from pairs of men dressed in black. There were—

Abruptly the screen went blank, switching to video noise. The panning camera had been drilled by somebody's stray round.

7:12 A.M.

Through the chaos of the flash grenades and the tear gas Moreau had missed seeing Hans and Marcel rappelling down. Instead he paused for half a second, then hit the floor and rolled, ponytail flying, intending to get as many of the hostages as possible between him and the two members of the assault team at the front. He figured the firepower would come from there. The rear entry, with the two guys firing at the ceiling, was the diversion, intended to throw everybody off.

He knew better. You never looked where the other side wanted you to. That was playing into their hands. He got off a burst from his Uzi, leaving a line of craters in the cinderblock walls next to the front door. Wide and high. Bad placement. But the game wasn't over; it was just beginning.

Now he had repositioned himself so that a terrified cluster of SatCom staffers were between him and the front, and a line of terminals protected him from the rear. Good. In the momentary pause, he slammed a new clip into the Uzi.

These assholes aren't going to shoot up the hostages, he told himself. That wasn't how professionals worked. And these guys, wearing balaclavas, were professionals. They were fast, moving quickly, and not providing a real target. *Merde.* But now you've got the advantage. Just concentrate and take them out, one by one. You've been in tougher spots before.

Dimitri Spiros, approaching from the rear, also had seen him, the blond-haired terrorist who rolled behind a line of workstations. But Spiros had not recognized him; to the Greek he was merely another hostile to be taken down. He switched his MP5 to semiauto and carefully took aim between the terminals, waiting for the creep to show himself.

Hans was not planning to wait. As his boots touched the floor, he took aim and got off a single round, carefully wounding Moreau in the right bicep. The French terrorist spun around, startled, but he sensed no pain. Instead he felt satisfaction at knowing, now, where the third entry-point had been. Life had just been simplified. A three-point entry: standard, no problem. All you had to do was keep your wits.

He whirled and got off a burst toward Hans and Marcel, sending them diving to the floor, then returned his attention to the pair at the front. But now those two *bâtards* had taken cover. Where was Jamal? Salim was dead, the stupid Iranian. Good riddance. But where was his brother? Why wasn't he helping?

As it happened, during the first few seconds of the assault,

Jamal Khan had been making his own calculations. He had been figuring an assault was overdue, and he had been prepared for it for several hours now. He had long since donned a bulletproof vest, and he had made sure he had two Uzis at hand, both loaded, together with five spare clips.

The moment the first flash grenades went off, he rolled beneath a row of workstations and shoved a handkerchief over his face, ready for the tear gas he was sure would come next. Now he was surrounded by a frightened cluster of SatCom staffers. The perfect shield.

Marcel had also surveyed the room as he rappelled in, and—by previous arrangement—he had focused on the right half, whereas Hans took the left. He had seen Jamal's roll and started to cut him down with a blast, but then he thought better of it: there were too many friendlies to take a chance on ricocheting lead. Just get into position and do it right.

Pierre Armont also had seen Jamal duck out of sight, and he felt his heart sink. The element of surprise had been used with all the effect it could, and the result had been one terrorist killed and one wounded. Now they were entrenching. Bad, very bad. . . .

Then a man on the other side of the room shouted something in German, choking from the CS, stood up, and brought around an Uzi. That one was stupid; he had identified himself and he was wide open.

Armont dropped him with a single burst, before he could even get off a round. Clearly an amateur terrorist, he was standing in the clear, and Armont's well-placed rounds sent him into a macabre dance of death.

Hans watched with satisfaction. Okay, he thought, that's two. Now what about Moreau. It would be nice to take him alive, help salvage something from this damned expensive disaster.

Moreau, however, had no intention of being taken alive; in fact, he had no intention of being taken at all. He had rolled into the shelter of a computer workstation and begun to spray the entrance indiscriminately. Fortunately the shots were wild, posing no threat to the ARM team or anybody else unless by ricochet.

By now Hans had taken cover behind the terminals situated in the center of the room. This wasn't the movies, with the assault team standing tall and shooting from the hip, particularly with all the friendlies milling in the haze of tear gas. Besides, there were plenty of hostiles, including the young Arab who had provided himself a secure redoubt behind a row of workstations, surrounded by hostages. He knew that stray bullets could not be tolerated. What to do? If Moreau kept this up, he would have to be taken down, lethally, and damn the money. A shame, really. The scene was rapidly turning into a standoff. The worst thing that could happen.

But first things first. Determined to bag Moreau alive, he lobbed another canister of CS across the room and into the clump of people and hostages where the Frenchman was. A half-second later it exploded, spraying its noxious powder across a full quarter of the room, and as that was happening, he threw another flash grenade. The friendlies would be blinded and overcome, he knew, but the effects would only last for a few minutes and by that time everybody could be dragged into the open air. It was better than being mowed down in a hail of fire.

The two grenades had the desired effect insofar as they momentarily disoriented Moreau. And they gave Hans the opening he needed to get in behind the row of terminals against the wall where the French terrorist crouched. It was the last, best chance he would have to take the bastard alive.

Moreau was on the floor now, gasping from the CS as he tried to get an angle on what was happening. He knew he was going to be rushed, but he wasn't sure from which direction. And as Hans moved in, that hesitation proved to be a profound, primal mistake. Before he could plan his next move, the German was on him, an MP5 against his neck. He tried to bring up his own Uzi, but by the time he had it halfway around, Hans had kicked it aside and intercepted the move.

With a yelp of pain Moreau twisted away, trying to recover, and managed to slam his left leg against Hans, knocking him off balance. Both were now cursing loudly, mingling their epithets with threats. The battle would have been even, had it not been for the fact that Hans was wearing an encumbering balaclava.

Hans's flash grenade had illuminated the entire room with its blinding explosion, and now Dimitri Spiros was making an end run along the far wall, just below the huge projection TV screens, trying to encircle Jamal before he had a chance to recover completely from the glare. Across the room, Reggie saw what was happening and opened fire into the ceiling, hoping to keep the Iranian pinned down, or at the very least draw his fire. Confusion reigned.

Willem Voorst, who was in the center, analyzed the situation with a clearer eye. The damned little Arab was not going to be taken down easily. Spiros was heading into danger. Not thinking.

"Dimitri, *no!*"

"The little fucker," Spiros yelled. He was already moving, impossible to stop. His Greek passion had superseded his better judgment, for he was not wearing his bulletproof vest —a container of those had been left inadvertently when the seaplane went down—and he was in no position to put himself in harm's way.

Jamal was coughing and choking from the CS, but he had not yet been totally immobilized. He saw Dimitri, a hooded figure in the smoke, and responded by instinct, bringing around his Uzi and getting off a burst. Although Spiros had seen it coming and tried to duck and roll, he was not quick enough. Two rounds caught him in the chest, but not before he had gotten off a well-practiced three-round burst from his MP5. One of the slugs entered the center of Jamal's neck, above his bulletproof vest, and literally ripped his throat open.

The Muslim radical who had helped kill two hundred and eighteen defenseless Marines in Beirut collapsed in a pool of blood, having exacted one last price. Dimitri Spiros was down, gravely wounded.

Willem Voorst was at his side in an instant. He took one look, then rose and sent another blast of automatic fire into the Iranian Jamal, whose life blood was already ebbing rapidly. It was an impulsive act of anger definitely out of character for ARM, but the vengeance of the moment seemed to call for something.

Jesus, Hans thought as he watched the tragedy unfold, still grappling with Moreau, this is turning into a disaster. How did we manage such a screwup. And how many more of the bastards are there? They're like vermin who keep showing up, just when you think you've got them all.

The area around him had become a cacophony of gasping, coughing SatCom staffers, many moaning in fear, all near shock. But it works both ways, Hans thought. If there are any more terrorists hiding among the terminals, they're probably in the same condition.

Now, though, there was no motion anywhere in the room. It looked to be over.

"Clear," Marcel said, the first, his voice garbled by the balaclava.

Hans crunched a knee against Jean-Paul Moreau's face and heard him moan. "You little fucker," he yelled in French, and slugged him as hard as he could. It had the desired effect. Moreau's body went limp, but Hans, wanting to take no chances, immediately yanked his arms around behind his back and handcuffed him.

"Clear," he yelled, still breathless.

"Clear," called Reggie, but not before looking around one last time, squinting through the smoke. He thought, hoped, it was true. A bloody great mess, that's what the assault had been, and Ramirez was still on the loose.

"Objective CQ," Armont announced finally, even as he surveyed the scene with bitterness and horror. Dimitri had screwed up twice, unforgivable, and now he was on the critical list, hemorrhaging from the two holes in his chest, barely conscious, with blood seeping out of the corner of his mouth.

While Willem Voorst was already bent over him, trying to begin stabilizing the crisis, Armont moved quickly to his side. "Hang on, *chéri*. Can you hear me?"

Spiros nodded, though whether it was in answer to the question no one could tell.

"Don't move. The blueprints show there's an emergency

medical facility here. They probably have a supply of plasma. We'll pull you through."

This time Spiros tried to smile and raised his hand slighty, but Armont gently took it and laid it back on the floor.

"Save your strength. We may need you again before this is over."

Then he rose up and looked around the room. "Start clearing everybody out of here. And make sure there aren't any more of these fuckers hiding among the friendlies."

Was it a clean job? he wondered. Did we hit any civilians? There was enough gunfire to create a real possibility that somebody got nicked, or worse.

He watched as Hans began shouting orders for the evacuation. The air in the room was starting to be slightly breathable again, and everybody seemed able to move. Three terrorists lay dead, and a fourth wounded and handcuffed. All wore black pullovers. Maybe, he thought, just maybe we had a little bit of luck on our side after all. It was about time.

But who could talk about luck with Dimitri lying there on the floor, gravely critical. God damn the whole operation. It was Spiros's fault, but this was no time to recriminate. He looked like his lung was punctured. In fact, that was an optimistic prognosis. It could be much worse. . . .

Well, Armont thought with relief, the SatCom people seem okay. Chalk up one for marksmanship. Guess that's why we get paid so well.

He looked up at the large computer screen being projected on the wall at the end of the room, which showed a countdown in progress. Ramirez's scheme was still on track, though there was still almost half an hour's time left. What now?

"All right," he declared, "let's make up a stretcher and get Dimitri down to their medical room."

Hans pulled a syringe from the medical kit he always had with him and gave the Greek a heavy shot of morphine in his inner thigh. In moments it had surged through his system, causing his eyes to glaze and the moaning to stop. Willem checked the wound again, then took some more gauze pads and continued working. He figured if Spiros could be gotten on intravenous plasma within the next fifteen minutes he might survive.

Willem Voorst was finishing the construction of a makeshift stretcher from chairs and cushions, while Hans was checking over the civilians as he ushered them out into the hallway, making sure none were injured . . . and too deeply in shock to realize it.

He also was running an interrogation. "Who here knows how to stop the countdown? Just shut the damned thing off?"

Nobody offered up his or her services, possibly because nobody wanted to be held responsible for causing a meltdown in the multimillion-dollar storage coil. There also was a more practical reason.

"Georges LeFarge was in charge of the countdown," a coughing, nervously shaking young man finally volunteered. "He's not here now. The Israeli guy took him over to Launch." He paused. "But the Fujitsu is in auto mode now. We can't just flip a switch, at least not without doing horrific damage to the coil. It has to be discharged through the Cyclops."

"Then can you do that?" Hans asked.

"Not without Cally or Georges here," he replied decisively. "You screw it up and you're talking millions of dollars." He shrugged. "No way would I attempt it without somebody's say-so." His voice trailed off.

Hans pondered this, then shrugged. "Okay, you're saying everybody here is scared to tinker with the Cyclops. So we'll still have to take down Launch and get to the vehicle." He glanced back toward the smoky room, thinking aloud. "But we were going to have to anyway, to get Ramirez. Once we're there, maybe we can find a way to disable the vehicle some other way."

The staffer looked dubious. "I don't know how. There's only one real way to do it, by bleeding off the Cyclops. Anything else would be too dangerous. Maybe—"

"Hans," Armont was shouting, interrupting them. "Come and help Willem carry Dimitri through the tunnel. Do you remember where the medical room was from the blueprints?"

"I memorized everything," he shouted back. "What do you think I get paid for?"

"Then get on with it. Maybe there'll be somebody there who can help out. Otherwise, you two just became doctors."

"I'll save him," Willem declared, trying to sound as confident as he could. He knew, as they all did, that it would be a long shot. "But what are you going to do now? We still have to get Ramirez."

"I'm aware of that," Armont snapped back. "But first we've got to get these people out of here and somewhere safe." Then he had a thought. "Maybe you should take them with you. Over to the Bates Motel. We could make that our collection point for friendlies."

"All right," Hans agreed, partially, "but this is no time to split up. You'd better come with us. If we run across any more of these assholes, we'll need backup."

Armont nodded, realizing it made some sense. "Okay, then get the people."

Hans looked down and checked over Jean-Paul Moreau. The Frenchman was bleeding, too, but nothing about his wound appeared to be serious. A tourniquet should hold him. "Some of them can carry out our friend here." For a moment he considered telling Armont who their captive was, but then he decided to do it later. Moreau might be more useful if he didn't realize he had been recognized.

Then, with Armont on point and leading the way, they headed through the tunnel that connected Bill Bates's office to the living quarters. Minutes later Command sat as empty as a tomb, impotent and useless as the countdown continued to scroll, the Fujitsu working the will of Dore Peretz.

CHAPTER EIGHTEEN

7:12 A.M.

"Hansen lied," Ramirez was saying as he took one last glance at the snowy TV monitor, which moments earlier had shown the chaos in Command. "The son of a bitch lied. He didn't call off the assault after all. It was just a stalling tactic." He turned to Peretz, anger deep in his eyes. "We've been double-crossed."

"What do you care what happens to those assholes?" Peretz remarked calmly, flashing his pale grin. "Good riddance. Let's just take the old guy, like we planned, and get the hell out of here. We've got the money, so who gives a shit."

"You have an inelegant but concise way of putting things," Ramirez concurred. "But there's a final phone call I need to make. I want Hansen to know what will happen if he tries to interdict us."

"Well, while you're doing that, I'll check out the chopper," Peretz went on. "When we split, I don't want any problems."

"Is that why you brought him?" Ramirez pointed at Bates.

"Might as well have someone with some aviation experience look it over." Peretz smiled again. "Besides, I think we may have just lost Salim in all that excitement over in Command. So we're going to need a pilot, right? What better than a war hero."

William Bates had been monitoring this exchange, not quite understanding the underlying dynamics. He did perceive, however, that Peretz was playing the scene as though he were in a game, and it looked like a contest with only a single winner. Number One, however, was not the kind of guy who struck you as a loser. But then Peretz didn't seem like the losing type either. The Israeli was one wily son of a bitch, and he had something up his sleeve. Was he intending to screw Number One somehow and get away with all the marbles? Just how he intended to do that was not yet clear, but there was no mistaking his faked attempt at calm. If Number One didn't catch it, he was dumber than he looked. And he didn't look dumb.

What, he wondered, had happened to Mike? Did the message LeFarge had passed along, "Ulysses has landed," mean he was on the island somewhere? And if he was here, had he called in ARM? Were they the ones who had just stormed Command, not the U.S.? Whoever did it, they hit the wrong place. The murdering bastard who called himself Number One was *here*, and he was about to get away scot-free.

7:12 A.M.

Vance wanted to kick himself. He'd screwed up again, managing to blind himself with his own flash grenade. And having done that, he'd thought it the better part of discretion to take cover and hope Pierre and the team could take out Ramirez with a clear shot. Instead, Ramirez got away.

Why didn't they get him? Instead they got into some kind of firefight. Heck, he thought, if I'd known they were going to blow it, I could have tried to take him out myself, half blind or no.

Now, though, Ramirez was back in Launch, in the control room. Worse still, he told himself, I've really screwed things up. I blew the element of surprise. Now what?

He sat down, feeling like a prisoner of the fog, and began to engage in extensive self-recrimination. He was afraid to use the radio, and he didn't know where the ARM team was. Everything had to be rethought. . . .

"Michael, is that you? Are you all right?" Cally was a pale apparition in the half-light, now working her way around the remains of the gantry.

"I'm terrific."

"Thank goodness. I almost gave up on finding you."

"What happened down there?" He was relieved to see her, but otherwise he still felt miserable. Also, he wondered if she was still angry.

"We got ambushed by somebody. From the direction of the shoreline. I didn't know there were so many of them." She looked back down the hill, puzzled. "It was strange. There was a lot of firing, and then it just stopped. But one of your guys got hit."

"Who?" Our first casualty, he thought. The disaster grows.

"I don't know his name. I think he was Dutch."

"Willem or Hugo?" Vance loved them both and felt his heart turn.

"I don't know, but it looked like he's going to be all right. I decided not to stick around."

"So you don't know where they went? Pierre and the team."

"Haven't a clue."

Vance sighed. "Okay, the way I see it, we've only got one chance left. But I have to get Bill to help."

"That's going to be next to impossible. They're still holding him in Command."

"Not any more. I think I saw him through the window there a couple of minutes ago." He pointed. "There in Launch."

"That's not a good sign." She sighed. "It could mean they

may be getting ready to leave. And they're probably going to take him with them."

"Then we've got to break protocol. Get on the radio and try to locate Pierre."

12:15 A.M.

"Look, you bastard," the President was saying into the phone. "I've done everything you asked. I've deposited the money and pulled back all American forces for six hours. Now you're going to live up to your end of the agreement. You're going to disarm those weapons and get the hell out of there. No hostages. I personally guarantee you safe passage." If he'll believe that, Hansen was thinking, he's still writing letters to Santa.

"Who do you think you're talking to?" Ramirez asked. "There's a force on the island right now, that's got my people under fire. I no longer can take responsibility for anything that happens."

"I don't know what you're talking about," Hansen replied, genuinely puzzled. Had the Deltas countermanded his orders? Carried out a rogue operation? If so, there was going to be hell to pay. "If there's somebody there, they're not part of the American armed forces. That's your problem, not mine."

"It is your problem. I want you to put a stop to it."

"How the hell am I supposed to do that, exactly?" What can he be talking about? Hansen was still wondering. "If you can't handle your situation, then maybe you'd better go back to terrorist school. I've kept up my end."

Ramirez proceeded to tell the President two things. First, when the Sikorsky took off from the landing pad, Isaac Mannheim was going to be on board, a hostage. He was their insurance. That much was true. The second was a lie.

"The other thing you should know is that we have armed a nuclear device and secured it on the island. The detonation sequence is radio-controlled. If there is any interference with our egress, no matter at what point, we will not hesitate to detonate it."

"You do that," Hansen said, "and you'll be tracked to the ends of the earth. That's something I can guarantee you for absolute certain." He had visions of his presidency going down in ruins. And if the story of the money ever came out, the headlines . . .

"Then you also have the power to guarantee that it doesn't happen. Think about it." With which cryptic farewell, the connection was severed, for the last time. The fact that a fifteen-kiloton nuclear bomb was about to obliterate Souda Bay, Crete, and the Sixth Fleet in a matter of minutes was not mentioned.

7:18 A.M.

"Ulysses to Sirene. Do you read me?"

When his radio crackled, Armont was in the medical facility of the Bates Motel, watching as a plasma IV was attached to Dimitri's arm. He immediately grabbed for it.

"I copy, Mike, but make this quick. Are you all right?"

"Never better. Where are you guys? Sorry to break radio silence, but I think Ramirez may be getting ready to pull out. Could be now or never."

"We took down Command," Armont said into his walkie-talkie. "Neutralized four of the bastards and cleared it. Looks to be a clean job as far as the friendlies are concerned. A minor miracle, considering. And when we got here to the Motel, there was a Greek, one of them, but we took care of him."

"Nice work."

"That's the good news. They're all here with us now, and they seem okay." He leaned out and took a peek down the hall. The SatCom systems engineers were all collapsed on the floor, drinking Cokes from the machine at the end. "There's bad news, too. In the first place, nobody there would shut off the countdown. They're just afraid to do it. Has to do with melting some kind of coil. The bird is still going up."

"What's the second place? The other bad news?"

"Dimitri got shot up. He's in pretty bad shape. We're in

the emergency room now, just keeping him alive. We've got to evacuate him out of here and soon."

"I hear you," Vance replied back. "But the only way I know of right now is with one of the helos, either the Agusta or their Sikorsky. How long can he hold on? We still need to take out Ramirez. I haven't given up."

"Michael, the airspace is closed around the island. Totally shut down. I guarantee it. There's no way he could get a chopper out. He's trapped, going nowhere. We're staying with Dimitri till we're sure he's stabilized, and then we'll come down there and handle that son of a bitch. All in time."

"All right," Vance said. "Take care of Dimitri. In the meantime, let me see what I can do at this end. And while you're there, you might want to sweep that place for explosives. I think they were planning to get everybody inside and blow it. I found some C-4 on a timer down on the second level. By the elevator. There may also be some more of them hanging around there, so be careful."

"Only way we know."

7:20 A.M.

Major General Eric Nichols was in the *Kennedy*'s Mission Control room, fit to be tied. Now he was beginning to understand how the attempted rescue of the American embassy hostages in Tehran could have turned into such a disaster.

He lit a cigar and tried to relax. The op would be back on track in—he checked his watch—another five and a half hours. Unless, of course, the orders got changed *again*.

Then the blue phone on his desk rang. . . .

"Well, I'll be damned," he said, hanging up a few moments later. "I knew this was going to be a cluster-fuck, but I think we've just expanded the term." He looked over the Deltas waiting with him. "Would you believe it's back on? Something happened, who knows what. But the sons of bitches are pulling out, and they've threatened to nuke the place if anybody tries to stop them. We're ordered to get in there before anybody can get off the ground, keep them from

having the chance. I don't know if we're going to make it."
He grinned. "But I'll tell you one thing. This time we're
going to just take the place down once and for all. And the
hell with micromanaging from Fort Fuck-up or anywhere."

"Fuckin' A, sir," Lieutenant Manny Jackson declared,
reaching for his flight jacket. "I say we just do a standoff with
Hellfire missiles. Take out their damned space vehicles and
any choppers they've got. Then they can just stick their nukes
up their ass."

"Sorry, Jackson, but that's still our last resort. If we hit the
vehicles, there's the risk of nuclear material getting loose. No,
what we're going to do is take down their radar power source,
the so-called Cyclops, and any choppers they have, which
ought to put them out of business. And if that doesn't cause
the bastards to throw in the towel, then we'll call in a Tomcat
and lay a couple of laser-guided missiles right into those underground bunkers."

Nichols had studied the satellite photo intelligence they
had, as well as site plans and blueprints obtained from
SatCom's executive offices in Arlington, and he knew exactly
where a missile would have the best chance of penetrating
Command and Launch Control. There might be some civilian
casualties, but they sure as hell wouldn't have the nukes in
there. A quick, decisive operation.

"All right," he added in conclusion, "let's rock and roll.
And this time there's going to be no recall, I don't care who
tries."

7:21 A.M.

"How does it look?" Peretz was asking. He and Bill Bates
had just climbed aboard the Sikorsky, cold and gray in the
light fog.

Bates had already checked it over from the outside. It was
military, and it appeared to be on loan from the Pakistani Air
Force, with the markings clumsily painted over. But it appeared to be in pristine shape. Good maintenance.

"Let me see." He walked to the cockpit and looked over

the rows of instruments. Nothing obvious seemed amiss. "If there's fuel, it should be able to fly. After all, it got in here from somewhere."

Peretz nodded with satisfaction, then clicked on his walkie-talkie. "Firebird One, Bates says there may be some problems with the nav gear. He wants to start it up and give it an instrument check. Probably just feeding me some kind of bullshit, so why don't you send out Helling for a minute? He should be in on this."

"What?" Bates mumbled. "I didn't—"

"I copy you," came back Ramirez's voice. "What seems to be the problem?"

"Probably no big deal. Claims it's the in-flight computer. Something to do with flight control."

"All right," Ramirez replied. "I'll send Wolf out if you think you need him." The walkie-talkie clicked off, to the accompaniment of static.

"What are you talking about?" Bates looked up, feeling a chill. "I don't see anything here that looks like a problem. Who the hell knows if the in-flight computer is—"

"Just shut up," Peretz barked. "Now, start the engines."

"But—"

"Just do what I tell you." He was now grasping a Walther 9mm with what appeared to be boundless self-assurance.

"You're the boss." Bates nodded, settling into the cockpit. He suddenly realized that something not on the schedule was about to go down. All along he'd had a feeling Peretz was up to something. Now it was more than a feeling.

With a tremble of apprehension he hit the ignition button, then started spooling up the power on the main rotor. Everything seemed to be working normally, just as it should. This old crate, he figured, had a lot of hours on the engines, but there was nothing to suggest any kind of problem.

Coming toward them now, across the tarmac, was the famous German terrorist, Wolf Helling. Bates glanced through the windscreen and looked him over, thinking he looked annoyed. He had the hard face and eyes of a killer, the kind of face you could only earn the hard way.

Suddenly the whole scenario clicked into place. This Israeli character was about to try and pull a fast one on everybody. He had set the vehicle to launch and now he was getting out. But what about the German? Was he in on the scam?

Probably not, from the disgruntled look he had. Besides, this guy Peretz was the quintessential loner. He had his marbles and the hell with everybody else.

"What's the problem?" Helling asked as he stepped lightly up the metal steps of the Sikorsky. "Is something—?"

He never had a chance to finish the sentence, as a dull *thunk* punctuated the placement of a 9mm round directly between his eyes. The half-bald leader of Germany's notorious Revolutionare Zellen pitched into the chopper, dead before he reached the floor pallet.

"Fucking Nazi," Peretz said to no one in particular. "I've been waiting a long time." Then he stepped over the body and headed for the cockpit. "Okay, it's about to be post time, baby."

"You're going to bug out, aren't you?" Bates had turned around and was staring at him. "You son of a bitch, you've got VX-1 set to launch and now you're leaving while the leaving's good."

"It's not going to be that simple," he responded calmly. "But we are about to make an unscheduled departure. You will be flying."

"And get shot down?" Bates said, rising and walking back from the cockpit. "Come on, this place has got to be surrounded." He had hoped, now feared, it was so. Surely the word on these terrorists was all over the world by now. "You have got to be kidding. No way am I taking this bird up. You're on your own, pal. I refuse."

"That would be a serious mistake, health-wise." Peretz smiled back. "Because if you give me the slightest hint of trouble, you're going to enjoy the same fate as this Nazi klutz, starting with your kneecaps. I would advise you to be cooperative." He smiled again.

"Do what you want," Bates said, not quite feeling his own bravado. "But you'll be flying it yourself."

"Don't press me, asshole," Peretz said. "Besides, there's a

nuclear weapon in that crate there." He pointed. "Nobody's going to lay a finger on us."

7:22 A.M.

"Do you know how to handle this?" Vance handed Cally the MP5 he was carrying. He had brought it up the hill to try to take out Ramirez, but after the fiasco with the flash grenades, he hadn't fired a shot.

"I've got a pretty good idea," she replied, some of the old pique coming back. "Somebody'd better use it. Besides, it doesn't exactly require postgraduate research."

"Sometimes it takes some thought to keep from getting killed." He sighed, then proceeded to show her how the safety worked. "Okay, what I need is for you to give me some cover when I make the move. Call it our last-ditch effort."

"What are you going to do?"

"What else? It's time I had a talk with Ramirez. If you can't lick them, join them."

"You're kidding." She laid down the automatic and glared. "You're going to just give up?"

"No, I'm going to offer him a deal. Maybe it'll work, and maybe not. But I don't know what else to do."

She stared at him incredulously. "What kind of deal?"

"I don't know yet. I'm making this up as I go along. But maybe if I can get in close to him, I can try to slow him down." What would happen, he was wondering, if Ramirez saw him again? Just shoot him on sight? It was possible, but then again maybe not. It was worth a try. "But you've got to help. Create a diversion that'll give me an opening."

"All right, then." She shrugged. "Just tell me what you want me to do."

Now he was fiddling with his Walther, checking how many rounds were left in the clip. There were two. He cocked it, then slipped it into the back of his belt, pulling down the shirt over it.

"See that window there?" He was pointing toward the glassed-in viewing station of Launch Control that overlooked the pad and the vehicles. "I want to get him there, where you can see us both. Then when I give a signal, a thumbs-up, I want you to open fire."

"On you both?" She looked incredulous.

"How about trying very hard not to hit either one of us. Just start firing and distract them. Then I'll try to take care of Ramirez. Somehow."

"You know, I don't know why you're doing this, but it seems awfully dangerous."

"Maybe I'm trying to make amends for being such a screwup." He was half serious.

"That's very noble, but frankly I think we'd better wait for your friends from ARM." She picked up the automatic and examined it again, then looked him over. "To be brutally honest, they've got a slightly better track record."

"Good point. Except now they've got a casualty to worry about, and we're running out of time. So this has to be solo." He kissed her, this time on the lips. "Wish me luck."

"You're really going to do it, aren't you?"

"I'm going to try." He finished tucking in his shirt.

"You're crazy. You won't listen to anybody."

"Sometimes that's a help." He kissed her again, more lightly than he wanted to. Was she still mad? It was hard to tell, but she was definitely distant. "Okay, get ready. And for God's sake, don't hit *me*. Fire wide."

"Wide?" She grinned.

"Extremely wide."

7:24 A.M.

"Thought you might be getting lonesome." Vance had walked into Launch Control, directly through the entrance next to where the fallen gantry had been. Ramirez had met him, with his Beretta 9mm trained on him from the instant he came in the doorway.

"Always the joker, Mr. Vance." Ramirez did not appear to think he was very humorous. "I see you're roaming around again, like a cat."

"Nine lives, remember."

"Yes, I should have put an end to them earlier." He gestured Vance forward with the automatic. They now were in Launch Control, the wide windows looking out over the vehicles. "But then I wanted you to myself."

"Here I am." He felt a chill. Was Ramirez just going to shoot him before he had a chance to do anything?

The terrorist, however, seemed to have other things on his mind. "You know, you've been missing out on a lot of the fun. There was something of a ruckus in Command just now. As it happens, it was on that TV there." He pointed to a monitor, its screen now filled with snow. "A decidedly second-rate entertainment, but I watched awhile anyway."

"Sounds exciting. Want to tell me what happened?"

"The broadcast encountered technical difficulties before the end. For all I know, the show may still be going on. But perhaps I should break some news to you. That assault force, whoever they were, merely saved me the trouble of tidying up myself."

"You were planning just to murder all your helpers anyway, right?" He settled into a sculptured chair next to a console, as casually as he could manage. "Neatness. Guess I should have thought of that."

"You should have thought of a lot of things, Mr. Vance."

"And how about you? Did the ransom money come through? I assume this operation had a price tag attached."

He laughed. "Of course the money came through. All eight hundred million. What do you take me for?"

"Respectable chunk of change. So why in hell are you going to still launch an A-bomb?" Even Vance was impressed by his perfidy. "That's not very sporting."

"I'm not a sporting person."

"That's hardly a news flash." He felt his outrage spilling over. "Mind telling me the target?"

"Not at all. I'm going to incinerate the U.S. air and naval base at Souda Bay. The Americans don't care anything about civilians, as they have shown any number of times, but they are very attached to their Sixth Fleet."

"Jesus, you're totally mad." It was worse than he had

imagined. "You're going to kill hundreds, thousands. How in hell can you do that?"

"Easily. As a matter of fact, it's as good as done. In a few minutes." He checked his watch, then glanced up and examined Vance a moment. "It looks like Jean-Paul did a fairly good job. I should have told him to just finish it."

"He got close enough, believe me."

"Looking at you, I'd have to agree." He smiled, eyes behind his gray shades. "All right, Mr. Vance, I assume you came back in here for a reason. What is it?"

"The truth is, I'm dropping by to see if we couldn't talk over a deal."

"I don't really think so."

"You may be able to set off a bomb, but the way things stand, no way are you going to get out of here in one piece." He was trying out the speech he had been rehearsing. "In case you didn't realize it, the U.S. Navy has the airspace around the island totally closed down. The skies over the eastern Med are currently an F-14 parking lot. But if you'll put a stop to all this insanity, release the hostages, then—"

"Don't try to bluff me, Mr. Vance." He gestured him forward. "Come, take a look at my collateral."

He led the way across to a second row of workstations, these on the side and closer to the window. "When I leave, which is imminent, I will have company. A certain professor. I think you've met him."

And sure enough, there in the corner sat Isaac Mannheim, looking as though the world had already ended. The old man appeared to be in a dark space of his very own, his face pitifully sunk in his hands.

"It can't be stopped," he was mumbling, almost incoherently. "Damn them. There should be a special rung in hell for them."

"Don't worry," Vance assured him. "There is." He turned back to Ramirez. "It isn't going to work. The U.S. is not going to be bluffed."

He hoped it was true. Somehow, though, he didn't feel all that confident. Ramirez was smart, very smart, and the U.S. had a history of screwing these things up. Just outside the window *VX-1* awaited, primed and about to lift off. Unlike the space shuttle, it had no clouds of white condensate spewing out; instead, it stood serene and austere, its payload prepared to wreak havoc on thousands of unsuspecting U.S. citizens. The loss of life would be staggering.

"He got Johan to call off the assault," Mannheim continued, interrupting his thoughts. "It was because of me. He wanted to save me. He did, but he only made things worse. He should have just let them kill me and have done with it."

Vance examined him and stifled a sigh. Now he had Mannheim to worry about. He didn't want Cally to start shooting up the place with him in the room, so he couldn't go to the window and signal her the way he had planned. What to do?

"Look," he said finally, turning to Ramirez, "if you need insurance, why not just take me and let Mannheim go? You and I have some unfinished business. He's not part of it."

"He will go, all right. With me on the helicopter. You, on the other hand, are . . ." Ramirez glanced out the wide window and fell silent as he studied the Sikorsky. The main rotor was starting to power up, and something about that seemed not to sit well with him. Suddenly he seemed galvanized. He glanced at his watch, then checked the safety on his Beretta.

Vance watched this, wondering what to do. Was this the golden moment to try and take him? There were only the Pakis outside to worry about. . . .

But Ramirez was already moving, grabbing Mannheim by the arm. Abruptly he stopped, turned, and took aim at Vance, somewhere precisely between his eyes.

Vance blanched. Jesus! Go for the Walther and get it over with.

But before he could move, Ramirez laughed and slipped the hand holding the Beretta into his pocket, then gave a nod of his head, beckoning. "Mr. Vance, I think I would like to have you join us after all. You're right. We still have a few matters to settle." He stepped aside and motioned. "But the time has come to bid farewell to Andikythera."

Ramirez was still dragging Mannheim along as they passed through Launch, pausing only to nod lightly toward

the two Pakistanis, who immediately snapped to attention and
followed. Amidst all the excitement of the pending launch,
nobody seemed to notice. They passed through the outer
door and onto the tarmac as an ensemble, Ramirez holding
Mannheim by the arm and guiding him.

7:31 A.M.

Bill Bates looked through the Sikorsky's wide windscreen
and saw them coming. The time had arrived, he realized immediately, to make a move. Now or never. The Israeli's attempt to pull out early had just been cut off at the pass, so
why not see what would happen if the scenario got shut down
entirely?

He reduced the power, listening to the engines wind
down, and rose.

"Guess my part of this is over," he announced. "You've
got a go system, so have a nice day. I'll be seeing you
around."

Peretz's eyes momentarily flashed confusion, but he was
wily enough to recover immediately.

"Your help has been much appreciated," he smiled
quickly. "Thank you for checking everything out."

Should I tip off Number One, Bates asked himself. No,
that fucker is nobody's fool; he's already way ahead of this
little twerp. And the second he sets foot in here and sees that
dead German hood, there's going to be a lot of heavy-duty
explaining to do.

Now Peretz was moving jauntily down the Sikorsky's folding steps, carrying his Walther with an air that proclaimed
nothing amiss.

Time to get out of here, Bates told himself. There's going
to be hell to pay.

He rose and headed down the stairs after Peretz as rapidly as he could. "Mike, where've you been?" He waved at
Vance. "We can't go on meeting like this. What do you say we
just pack it all in and go sailing?"

"Fine with me," Vance yelled back. "No time like the present. . . ."

At that moment, a shot rang out from somewhere in the direction of the fallen gantry, whereupon Peretz whirled, leveled his Walther into the mist, and got off a burst on full auto. Emptying the clip.

The scene froze, like a tableau. Vance's first thought was that Peretz had overreacted. Nervous. And probably with good reason. But at least Cally was trying to do her share. The problem was, the quarters were too close.

The two Pakistanis were still standing on the tarmac, not quite understanding what was happening, but Ramirez sized up the situation in an instant. He shoved Mannheim up the steps ahead of him, ducked into the protection of the Sikorsky's open door, and then turned back. Peretz was slower, caught standing on the foggy tarmac next to the bottom step. When he realized his Walther's clip was empty, he fished another out of his pocket and quickly began trying to insert it.

"That won't be necessary, Dr. Peretz." Ramirez's voice was like steel. "Let me take care of it." Whereupon he leveled his Beretta 9mm and shot a startled Abdoullah squarely between the eyes. Before Shujat realized it, he shot him, too, point blank in the left temple.

"What in hell are you doing?" Peretz yelled, watching them fall. He was still trying to shove a new clip into his automatic, but now he was losing his touch and it jammed. "That's not how we—"

"I suppose you thought me some kind of fool," Ramirez replied, shifting his aim. "It's time I laid that fond illusion of yours to rest once and for all."

"I don't appreciate your tone of voice." Peretz was still struggling frantically with his Walther.

"And I don't appreciate you trying to make off with this helicopter. We have just lost a crucial element of our relationship, the element of trust."

"I never knew our 'relationship' had all that much trust in it." Peretz looked up defiantly. "We had a business arrangement. I've kept up my end to the letter."

Vance watched the exchange with mixed emotions. He

realized that Peretz, being no idiot, knew the situation had just gone critical. He had begun stalling for time. It wasn't going to work.

But after Ramirez finishes with this computer clown, he told himself, Bill and I are next. And with that thought, he reached around under his shirt and circled his fingers around the Walther.

He had been right.

"It's over, you little son of a bitch." Ramirez fired point blank into Peretz's chest. The Israeli jerked backward, stumbled, and crashed, slamming his head against the hard asphalt. He didn't move.

Uh-oh, Vance thought. Now it's our turn.

He was standing next to Bates, while around them were three bodies of terrorists. Ramirez, however, was safely inside the open doorway, out of range for Cally.

Does she realize what's about to happen?

She must have, because just as Ramirez leveled his black Beretta to finish off what he had started, there was another burst of fire from the direction of the gantry. It was the diversion Vance needed. He dove for the tarmac, rolled, and extracted the Walther he had shoved into his belt.

Come on, baby, keep giving me cover.

"Mike," Bates yelled, seeing the pistol as he, too, dove for the tarmac, "shoot the bastard. *Now.*"

Vance aimed for the doorway, but it was already closing, the steps coming up. Sabri Ramirez was not a man to engage in gunplay for the fun of it. He was about to be gone. A second later the main rotor, which had been idling, immediately began to whine into acceleration.

"We blew it," Bates boomed, his voice now almost drowned by the huge GE turboshafts.

"The Hyena," Vance muttered, pulling himself up off the asphalt. "Headed back to his lair. And there's not a damned thing anybody can do about it."

"Not with Isaac on board," Bates concurred. "Sorry I yelled. You really didn't have a chance." He was shielding himself from the downdraft as he tried to stand up. "The fucker is getting away without a scratch. Looks like he pulled it off."

"Right," Vance said, watching the giant Sikorsky begin to lift. "But maybe there's one thing left we can do. How about trying to remove that bomb"—he pointed up at *VX-1*—"before that thing goes up?"

"What in hell are you talking about?" Bates turned to squint at the silver spire. "There's no way."

"Well, I don't know, what about using the Agusta? It's probably still flyable." He had turned back to watch the Sikorsky bank into the thinning fog. Ramirez was just barely visible through the windscreen, smiling as he disappeared into the mist.

"There's no time. Peretz told me that *VX-1* is set to lift off at seven forty-eight. The bastard had it timed exactly." Bates glanced at his watch. "That's just a few minutes."

"No balls," Vance snorted. "Bill, for godsake, let's give it a shot. Maybe we can at least disable it, turn it into a dud."

Bates was still dubious as he gazed upward. "Buddy, I don't want to be hovering over that thing when the Cyclops kicks in. Do you realize—"

"Come on, where's your backbone." He waved to Cally, who was now coming around the corner of the gantry. "Thanks for not shooting me."

"When I saw Ramirez start killing everybody, I assumed you two were next. It was then or never." She looked exhausted.

"You assumed right. We were on the hit list. Thanks." He kissed her on the forehead, where her hair was still plastered. "Now will you help me talk some sense into this guy? I say we could at least try to mess up the bomb before the Cyclops launches it. They've got it programmed for Souda Bay."

"You're kidding." Bates was transfixed.

"That's what he claimed. Come on, let's . . . hang on a second." He turned and trotted over to the doorway of Launch, where he seized a coil of electrical wire. "This may come in handy." Coming back, he punched Bates's arm. "Let's give it a try. No guts, no glory."

"Souda Bay. Christ!" Bates glanced again at his watch. "Mike, we've got less than nine minutes."

7:38 A.M.

"I copy," Nichols said into his mike. "When did the chopper lift off?"

"The AWACS picked it up at . . . just after 0730 hours," came the voice from the *Kennedy*. It was General Max Austin. "The bastards are bugging out."

"So what do we do now? Try and intercept them?"

"We're taking care of that from here. Fixed-wing. First, though, we've got to figure out if there really are hostages aboard, like they claim. But don't worry about it. There's nowhere they can hide. Your mission is still the same. Secure the facility. There could still be some of them left, so just interdict anything that tries to egress."

"That's a confirm. If it moves, it fucking dies."

CHAPTER NINETEEN

7:42 A.M.

Dawn had arrived, though the mantle of light fog was still adding a hazy texture to the air. The sun-up had a freshness that reminded Vance of the previous morning, the first glimmerings of daybreak. Now, though, visibility was hampered by the residual moisture in the air, just enough to give the world a pristine sheen. What would the morning look like, Vance wondered, if a nuclear device exploded at Souda Bay on nearby Crete? It was a possibility difficult to imagine, but the results were not.

Bates began spooling up the power, and slowly the blue-and-white striped Agusta Mark II started lifting off the pad. Fortunately it had been prepped the previous day and was ready to fly.

"This is going to be dicey, Mike," Bates yelled back from the cockpit, his voice just audible above the roar of the engines. "I don't know how exactly you expect to manage this."

"I don't know either," Vance yelled in reply. "Try and see if you can hover just above the payload bay. Very gently."

Cally was helping him circle the insulated wire about his waist, then his crotch, making a kind of seat. Finally he handed her the free end and shouted, "Here, can you secure this around something?"

"Around what?" she yelled back.

"Anything that looks sturdy. And then hang onto it."

"Ever done this before?" She had found a steel strut by the door. "I haven't."

"Are you kidding! That makes us equally experienced."

"Well, remember one thing—the downdraft from the main rotor is going to buffet you like crazy. Be prepared."

"Right." He was already trying mental games to avoid vertigo. The closest thing he could think of was looking out the windows of a tall building, and even that scared him. He liked working close to the ground. Very close.

As Bates guided the Agusta quickly down toward the launch pad and the vehicles, visibility was no more than a quarter of a mile. And since he had not bothered switching on the radar, he was totally unaware of the two Apache AH-64s now approaching from the south at 180 mph. It was a mistake.

7:44 A.M.

"Sir, we've just picked up some new action on the island," Manny Jackson, in the first Apache, said into his radio. He could scarcely wait to get in and take down the island. These camel-jockey terrorists needed to be taught a lesson once and for all. He had lost a cousin, nineteen years old, in the Beirut bombing, and this was the closest he was ever going to get to a payback. "Guess there were more of the bastards. Ten to one they're taking up another chopper."

"No way are we going to allow that to happen," Nichols declared. He was in the lead Huey, two kilometers back. "The first batch may have got away, but not these. From now on, nobody down there moves a hair. We're about to teach them a thing or two about air supremacy."

"They don't seem to be going anywhere. Just moving

down the island. What do you think it means?" He was wondering what a lot of it meant. Why was Souda Bay being evacuated? They weren't calling it that, but an evacuation was exactly what was under way. A big hurry-up to get the fleet into blue water, all nonessentials ordered to take a day off with pay, a sudden token of "thanks" from Uncle Sammy for jobs well done. Bullshit. . . .

"Probably picking up hostages," came back Nichols's voice. "Who the hell knows? But our mission is to make sure they don't leave the ground."

"You've got it, sir." He reached down to the weapons station and flipped the red switch that armed the Hughes 30mm chain gun. Its twelve hundred rounds, he figured, should be enough to handle the problem.

7:46 A.M.

"What in blazes is he doing?" Pierre Armont wondered aloud. He was standing with Reginald Hall at the southern entrance of the SatCom living quarters, the Bates Motel, gazing out over the launch pad and trying to make sense of what he was seeing. Five minutes earlier they had watched in dismay as the Sikorsky lifted off. Now this.

"Looks to be some damn-fool trapeze stunt," Reggie Hall muttered, shaking his head. "He's going to get himself killed. What in bloody hell?"

He caught his breath as he watched Vance begin rappelling down some kind of thin line dangling out the open door of the chopper, spiraling from the downdraft of the main rotor. It *was* something of a circus aerial act—definitely not recommended for civilians. He clearly didn't have the slightest idea how to use his arms to stabilize the spin. A rank amateur. . . .

What was that sound? His senses quickened and he turned to squint at the southern horizon. Through the light fog he could hear the faint beginnings of a dull, familiar roar, and he realized immediately it was choppers coming in. He quickly pulled out his Tasco binoculars and studied the morning sky—two helos, both looking like ungainly spiders. Yes, they had to be Apaches. What else.

Great, he thought, once more the U.S. has got its timing dead on. The first time they showed up and managed to keep us from getting Ramirez, and this time they decide to drop in just after his Sikorsky took off, probably taking him and the last of his goons out, undoubtedly with a few hostages for good measure. From all appearances, he had gotten away. Again. It was sickening.

Now the gunships were dropping altitude and moving in, boldly, with the authority their firepower commanded. He wondered if the teams on board might actually be unaware that Ramirez had escaped.

"We ought to go out and signal them in," Armont said. "Let them know how useless—"

Warning flares erupted from the Hughes 30mm in the nose of the first Apache, missing the Agusta by no more than fifty meters.

"Christ! They don't know who the friendlies are." He immediately canceled his impromptu plan to head out and wave. The U.S. Army was in no mood to dialogue.

"Do they think Mike's a terrorist?" Reggie asked, incredulous. But even as he said it, he realized that must be exactly what they thought. They were going to try to force down the Agusta. Or shoot it down.

"Reggie, draw their fire!" Armont yelled. Almost by instinct, he raised his Steyr-Mannlicher assault rifle and opened up on the lead helicopter, going for the well-protected GE turboshaft on the left. "Don't try to kill anybody, for godsake. Just distract them."

"This is insane," declared Willem Voorst, who had come out to see what all the excitement was about. "What are you doing? I don't want to go to war with the United States of America."

Then he noticed the blue-and-white Agusta hovering over VX-1, Vance dangling, and put it all together. Without a further word he aimed his MP5 and got off a burst, watching as it glinted harmlessly off the second Apache's left wing.

Miraculously it worked. The Army's favorite helicopters

were huge, with a main rotor almost fifty feet in diameter, but they could turn on a dime and these did. They came about and opened fire with their chain guns on the cinderblock portico where Armont and Hall and Voorst were ensconced.

The 30mm rounds tore around them, sending chunks of concrete flying, but the structure was temporarily solid enough to provide protection. Armont ducked out and got off another burst, keeping on the heat, then back in again.

Now the Agusta was hovering just above the nose of the VX-1 vehicle, and Vance had disappeared on the other side. What, Armont wondered again, could he possibly be doing with the vehicle . . . ? Then the answer hit him, as transparent as day.

Merde! He's going to try and retrieve the bomb.

Good Christ, he thought, the man has gone mad. He may know how to trace hot money halfway around the globe, but he doesn't know zip about a nuclear device. He'll probably set the thing off by accident and blow the entire island to—

A spray of cannon fire kicked up a line of asphalt next to where he was standing, and he retreated for cover deeper behind the cinderblock portico. They're not going to fool around long with that chain gun, he told himself. We're going to be looking at rockets soon, and then it's game up.

"We've done what we can for Michael," he yelled, getting off one last burst. "We've got to get back inside before they get tired of playing around and just fry this place."

"I hear you," Willem Voorst agreed, already headed deeper inside. "Mike's on his own."

7:47 A.M.

Vance had never been more scared in his life. This made a day at a stormy helm seem like a Sunday stroll. The downdraft was spinning him violently now, a lesson that rappelling was not for the faint of heart. Then he remembered some basic physics and held out his arms, helplessly flapping like a wounded bird. But it was enough, as his spin immediately slowed.

He was dizzy now, but when he came around, he got an overview of the launch facility, and the glimpse made him realize that something had gone terribly wrong. What were those? Two Apache helicopters were hovering and they were firing on . . . on the Bates Motel. Just beyond the fallen gantry.

Why! Ramirez and all his goons were gone or dead.

Bill Bates, who also had seen it all, had a better understanding of what was under way. It was a massive failure of communications. Thinking as quickly as he could, he started negotiating the Agusta around, situating VX-1 between him and the Apaches. The fucking Delta Force had come in like gangbusters and was shooting at the wrong target. There was no time to try to raise them on the radio, and besides, he only had two hands.

Down below, Vance slammed against the hard metal of the nose, and then rotated, one-handed, to try to take measure of what to do next. It wasn't going to be easy, that much was sure. The payload bay was sealed with a Teflon ring, which was itself secured with a series of streamlined clamps that were bolted from inside, designed for automated control. But . . . there also was lettering next to a thumb-operated hatch that read EMERGENCY RELEASE.

He flipped it open and, bracing himself against the side of the silver cone to try to overcome the destabilizing downdraft, looked in. A red button, held down for safety by another thumb latch, stared back.

What the heck, he thought, you've got nothing to lose. He flipped the thumb safety, and then—bracing himself to try to slow his erratic spin—slammed a heel into the button. Nothing happened for a second, but then the Teflon clamps on the cargo bay began to click open one by one.

Up above him, Cally was yelling something, but he couldn't make out her voice above the roar of the engines. Anyway, whatever it was, it would have to wait. There was only one thing left to do, and he had to press on. The clamps were now released, but the cargo bay was still closed. . . .

At that moment, he began experiencing yet another failure of nerve. There could only be a minute left, two at most, and he didn't have the slightest idea what to do next.

Then he noticed the heavy release levers, positioned beneath the Teflon clamps and circling the three sides of the streamlined door. Once more bracing himself against the slippery side of the nose, he began clicking them open, starting on the left and working his way around.

Time is surely running out, he told himself. This could end up being the stupidest stunt ever attempted. The roar of the Agusta above was so deafening he could barely think. He felt all of his forty-nine years, a weight crushing down on him with the finality of eternity. . . .

Then the last clamp snapped free, and he watched as the door opened by itself, slowly swinging upward. It was heavy, shaped like the pressure door on an airplane fuselage, and designed to withstand the frictional heat of space flight. But the spring mountings on the recessed hinges were intended to open and close automatically.

And there sat a metallic sphere outfitted with a jumble of connectors and switches. So that's what a bomb looks like, he marveled. It was somehow nothing like he had imagined, if he had had time to imagine.

Now Bates had lowered the helo just enough to allow him to slide inside and take the weight off the line. Finally he could breathe, but again the matter of passing seconds had all his attention. If the vehicle really was going up at 7:48, then there probably was less than a minute left now to get the device unhooked and out.

He looked it over, puzzling, and decided on one giant gamble, one all-or-nothing turn of the wheel. It was a terrifying feeling.

Quickly he untied the wire from around his waist, and began looping it around the metal sphere: once, twice, three times. There was no time, and no way, to disconnect the telemetry, so the device would simply have to be ripped out. One thing was sure: if it blew, he would never be the wiser.

When he had the wire secure, or as secure as he could make it, he looked out the door and gave Cally a thumbs-up sign, hoping she would understand. She did. She turned and yelled something to Bates, and a moment later the Agusta began to power out as the pitch of the blades slowly changed. The line grew taut, then strained against the sides of the bomb, tightening his knots.

Will the wire hold? he wondered, and does this little toy helo have enough lift to yank this thing out of here? It's like pulling a giant tooth.

Then there was a ripping sound as the connectors attached to the sphere began tearing loose. So far so good, he thought. At least the telemetry is now history. If the vehicle goes up now, it'll be orbiting a dud. Mission partly accomplished.

Then the bomb pulled away from its last moorings and slammed against the side of the door, leaving him pinned against the frame, unable to breathe. But he instinctively grabbed the line and wrapped his legs around the sphere, just as it rotated and broke free. As it bumped against the doorframe of the payload bay, he barely missed hitting the closing door, but he ducked and swung free, into the open air, riding the device as though it were a giant wrecking ball.

7:48 A.M.

"Those bastards firing on us have gone inside," Philip Sexton yelled. "Let them wait. Let's stop the damned chopper from egressing." He was pointing through the windscreen of the Apache. "Orders are to keep everybody on the ground."

Manny Jackson hit the pedals. Nothing to it. There, almost in his sights, was the striped Agusta chopper, with a terrorist hanging beneath it. Probably fell out. He was hanging on to something, though what it was you really couldn't tell through the thin mist.

It didn't matter. The guy was open and in the clear. This was the beginning of what was going to be a marvelous operation, taking these bastards down. With a feeling of immense satisfaction, he reached for the weapons station.

And then his world went blue.

7:49 A.M.

Cally stared out the open door of the Agusta and felt her heart skip a beat. A beam of energy, so strong it ionized the air and turned it deep mauve, seemed to be engulfing Michael. Staring down, she was almost blinded by its intensity. He was there, she was sure, but where she could not tell.

Then it shut off for a second, and she realized it had been directed toward the base of VX-1. Next came an enormous clap of thunder as the splintered air collapsed on itself, sending out shock waves. Just like lightning, she thought. The Cyclops is sending energy as though it were lightning. . . .

Then the blue flashed again, and this time it began microsecond pulses, like a massive strobe light. All the action was now highlighted in jerky snippets of vision, as unreal as a disco dance floor. The air around the beam was being turned to plasma, ionized pure atoms . . . but the next burst of energy came from the propulsion unit of VX-1, which slowly began discharging a concentrated plume out of its nozzles, a primal green instead of the usual reds and oranges of a conventional rocket.

The Cyclops had just gone critical, right on the money, ionizing the dry-ice propellant in VX-1. Would the impulse be enough to lift it off? she wondered. Was Isaac's grand scheme going to work? Years had been spent planning for this moment. She felt her heart stop as she waited for the answer, totally forgetting the man who was dangling just below the chopper, bathed in the hard, pulsing strobes.

7:50 A.M.

As Manny Jackson grappled for the collective, blinded by the intense monochromatic light engulfing him, a clap of thunder sounded about his ears, deafening him to the roar of the Apache's turboshafts.

What in hell! Had one of the nuclear devices been detonated? No, his instincts lectured, he was still alive. If it had been a nuke, he would be atoms by now, sprayed into space. This had to be something else.

Now his vision was returning, the blue receding into quick flashes, and the chopper seemed to be stabilizing. Maybe, he thought, I'm not going to be permanently blind. But I've got to get this bird on the ground. We'll just have to take our chances. Then the realization of what had happened finally sank in. The damned Cyclops laser had switched on. They had arrived too late. . . .

He was thrown against the windscreen as the Apache slammed into the asphalt and collapsed the starboard leg of the retractable gear.

"Jesus!" He turned back to the cabin, forehead bleeding, and yelled, "Everybody okay?"

The assault team was still strapped in, and nobody seemed the worse for the bumpy landing. The Apache was a tough bird, hero of tank battles in Iraq.

"No problem," came back a chorus of yells. They were already unfastening their straps and readying their weapons.

"All right," he bellowed, killing the power. "Everybody out. Let's take cover and kick ass."

7:50 A.M.

Vance heard the thunder and felt the shock wave almost simultaneously. He gripped the wire, trying to hold on, and felt it cut deep into his palms. The pain seemed to work in opposition to the numbing effects of the shock wave that had buffeted him, assaulting his eardrums and his consciousness. For a moment he forgot where he was, shut out all thought, and just hung onto the wire with his last remaining energy.

In the Agusta up above, Bates was struggling with the controls, trying to keep stabilized as the pressure pulse from the Cyclops swept down the island. The dangling bomb, and Vance, were serving as a counterweight, holding the small commercial helo aright. It was all that kept it from flipping as the sudden turbulence assaulted the main rotor.

The energy that filled the air now had yet another release.

As his eardrums recovered, Vance heard a new roar, deeper and throatier than the sound of the Agusta, welling up around him. Down below, wave after wave of pressure pulses were drumming the air, and he watched spellbound as *VX-1* shuddered, then began to inch upward into the morning sky. It was a gorgeous sight, the lift-off of the world's first laser-driven space vehicle.

Was Cally watching this moment of triumph? he wondered. She should be ecstatic, even in spite of all the rest.

But would the vehicle make it to orbit? he suddenly asked himself. With the payload gone, wouldn't the weight parameters be all out of whack. But then maybe it didn't matter. The mere fact that it was going up should be enough to cover Bates's contractual obligations with his investors.

That was down the road. He was so mesmerized by the sight of the lift-off that he had totally forgotten he was wrapped around a nuke, hanging on for all he had as the asphalt loomed fifty feet below, like Slim Pickens riding the bomb down in that famous closing scene from Kubrick's *Dr. Strangelove*.

Then the pain in his hands refocused his attention. The bomb down below, he figured, was now permanently inoperable. But Ramirez still had Mannheim as a hostage, and he had made good his escape. Which meant he was still in the terrorists' catbird seat. Using innocents for a shield rather than slugging it out fair and square.

As the Cyclops continued to pulse, and *VX-1* edged upward into the morning mist, Bates steered the Agusta toward the old landing pad where it had originally been parked. In moments he had eased down the bomb, just as though settling in a crate of eggs, no more than twenty feet from where they had taken off five minutes earlier. It was a marvel of professionalism.

As the weapon bumped onto the asphalt, Vance had a sudden thought. The damned thing was useless now, and harmless. But what about the other one, the one Ramirez had taken with him in the Sikorsky.

"Michael, are you all right?" Cally had leapt from the open door of the Agusta, looking as disoriented as he had ever seen her. "You were only a few feet away when the Cyclops turned on. For a minute there, I couldn't even see you. What was it like?"

"Try the end of the world. Like a thousand bolts of lightning, all aimed at one place."

"A perfect description." She smiled and reached to help him stand up. "I'd never realized there'd be a thunderclap when it switched on at full power. God, what a sight." She was beaming at the thought, exhilarated that all SatCom's work had been vindicated.

"You know," he said, "speaking of the end of the world, we came pretty close. I hate to think what would happen if a bomb actually went off on Crete."

"I've got a sinking feeling the end of the road wasn't going to be Crete at all," Bates declared, stepping down from the Agusta. "I've been thinking. Something that little Israeli prick let drop as we were coming out to start up the Sikorsky finally sank in. He was rambling on about retargeting the vehicle. You know, I think it was going to come back _here_. He had the trajectory set to begin and end right here on Andikythera. After he bugged out, of course."

"Nice," Vance said. "I actually kind of admire his balls. He was going to nuke Ramirez."

"_And_ us."

"That part's a little harder to like, I grant you." He turned and gazed down toward the two Apaches that had landed. "By the way, what were those all about? The Delta Force saving us?"

"Who knows?" He seemed to have a sudden thought. "Let me get on the radio and try to call them off. Before they actually end up killing somebody."

"While you're doing that, I'd like to try and raise Pierre. Find out what's happening at his end."

"There's a walkie-talkie in the cockpit," Bates said. "Use it."

7:55 A.M.

"Michael, thank God it's you," Armont said into the mike. "Guess what, we almost went to war against the U.S. Special Forces. We have just surrendered. Incidentally, nice work up there. Or maybe you just got lucky." He laughed. "Seeing you rappelling leads me to suggest that you probably ought to stick to other lines of work."

"I hear you," Vance said. "By the way, the bad news is Ramirez got away."

"So he was in the Sikorsky?" Armont sighed with resignation. "Blast, I was afraid of that."

"Well, this may not be over yet. The vehicle got up, but we're not quite sure where it's headed, bomb or no bomb. I want to try to get into Command, or what's left of it, and try to find out. Before some Delta cowboy fires a Hellfire missile in there."

"Good idea," Armont agreed. "It would also be nice to keep a handle on Ramirez's getaway chopper. But I assume somebody will interdict him. The almighty U.S. Navy owns this airspace, as we found out the hard way."

"Don't count on anything. He took along Mannheim as a hostage. Insurance. This guy is no slouch. I'd be willing to bet he's got something up his sleeve. One thing he's got is at least one more bomb. Bill saw it on the chopper. And he might be just crazy enough to use it, God knows where."

"Then I don't know what the U.S. can do if he's got a hostage, *and* a bomb. They're sure as hell not going to shoot him down. Where do you think he's headed?"

"That's question number two, but if we can get into Command, maybe we can figure out a way to track him from there. Somehow."

"Good luck," Armont said quietly, and with feeling. "And stay in touch."

8:01 A.M.

Dore Peretz's chest still felt like it was on fire, a burning sensation that seemed to spread across the entire front of his torso; in fact, he felt like shit. And he had almost been blinded by the intense blue laser strobes that had purged the island when the Cyclops kicked on. However, in all the confusion surrounding the lift-off of VX-1, nobody had bothered to wonder where he was. That part suited him fine.

Donning the bulletproof vest around midnight had been the best idea of his life. . . . No, that wasn't true. The best of all was coming up.

Sometimes, he thought, life could have a moment so delicious it made up for all your past disappointments. And you could either seize that moment, or you could forever let it pass, wondering what it would have been like. Not this one, baby.

As he passed through the lobby, he noticed the security door leading into Command had been blown away with some kind of military explosive. Probably C-4. Curious, he paused and assessed the damage. Hey, the television down in Launch hadn't really done the assault justice. Must have been one hell of a show.

Then he stepped inside and checked out the scene.

Jesus! The place was a mess, showed all the signs of a bloody assault. Luckily, however, the emergency lights were working, their harsh beams perfect for what he wanted to do now. There was definitely plenty of evidence of gunfire, flecked plaster from the walls, and over there . . . Christ! It was Jamal, or what was left of Jamal. Little fucker's neck looked like he'd had a close encounter with a chain saw. Not far away was Salim, shot in the face. Then, on the other side of the room, was the body of the last German Stasi, Peter Maier. His demise had come neatly, right between the eyes.

Smooth piece of work, you had to admit. The only asshole unaccounted for was Jean-Paul Moreau. So what happened to that arrogant French prick? Did he escape, get captured? . . . Who gave a shit?

Meditations on fate, the absolute. The truth was, it was

more than a little chilling to see the bodies of three dudes you'd come in with only a day before. . . .

Well, fuck it. These other guys had known the risks. If they didn't, then they were jerks. Down to business.

He knew what he was looking for, and he had left it next to the main terminal. And there it was.

While he was working, he would block out the ache in his chest by thinking about the money. Hundreds of millions. Tax-free. Even if you spent ten million a year, you could never spend it all. What a dream.

Then he had an even more comforting reflection. Everybody had seen him shot. They wouldn't find the body, but they would naturally assume he was dead, too. He would have the money, *and* he would be officially deceased.

He almost laughed, but then he sobered, recalling he had only a scant few minutes to wrap things up.

He slipped the component into its slot, then rummaged around for the connectors. He had left them dangling when he removed the black box, and they were conveniently at hand. They were color-coded, and besides, he had a perfect photographic memory and knew exactly what went where. Seconds later the diodes gleamed. On line.

Okay, baby, let's crank.

The real radio gear, he knew, was in Bates's office, which stood at the far end of the room, its door blown away. Bates had plenty of transmission and receiving equipment in there, so that would be the perfect place to take care of business.

He picked up the device, now ready, and carried it with him, heading over. The main power switch that controlled Bates's radios had been shut off, but it was just outside the door and easy to access. He pushed up the red handle, and walked on through, watching with satisfaction as the gear came alive. Over by the desk was Bates's main radio, a big Magellan, already warming up. Life was sweet.

He clicked on the receiver stationed next to the transmitter and began scanning. Ramirez, he figured, would probably be on the military frequencies now, spewing out a barrage of threats about blowing up Andikythera. That had been the agreed-upon egress strategy, assuming the confusion created when the bomb took out Souda Bay wasn't enough.

And sure enough, there he was, on 121.50 megahertz, just as planned. Peretz decided to listen for a minute or so before breaking in.

"I won't bother giving you our coordinates," came his voice, "since we show a radar lock already. I warn you again that any attempt to interfere with our egress will mean the death of our hostage and a nuclear explosion on the island."

How about that, Peretz thought. The getaway scenario is still intact, right down to the last detail. Gives you a warm feeling about the continuity of human designs.

He and Sabri Ramirez had planned it carefully. The Sikorsky would be taken to fifteen thousand feet, its service ceiling, whereupon anybody left would be shot. The controls would then be locked, and they would don oxygen masks and jump, using MT-1X parachutes, the rectangular mattress-appearing chutes that actually are a nonrigid airfoil. MT-1Xs had a forward speed of twenty-five miles per hour and could stay up long enough to put at least that many miles between the jump point and the landing. They were, in effect, makeshift gliders, and they presented absolutely no radar signature. While the Sikorsky continued on its merry way, on autopilot, they would rendezvous with the boat that was waiting, then be off to Sicily, with nobody the wiser. The chopper would eventually crash into the ocean halfway to Cyprus, leaving no trace.

The only part about that plan that bothered Dore Peretz from the first was whether Sabri Ramirez was intending to kill him along with the rest of the exit team. Nothing would prevent it. There was supposed to be some honor among thieves, but . . .

Enough nostalgia. The moment had come to have a little fun. He flicked on the mike. "Yo, my man, this is your technical associate. Do you copy?"

There was a pause in the transmission, then Ramirez's voice came on, loud and clear. "Get off this channel, whoever you are."

"Hey, dude, is that any way to talk? We have a little business to finish. By the way, how's the weather up there? Chutes still look okay?"

"What in hell," came back the voice, now abruptly flustered as the recognition came through. "Where are you?"

"Dead, I guess. But hey, I'm lonesome. Maybe it slipped your mind I was supposed to be part of the evacuation team."

"What do you want?"

"Want? Well, let's see. How about starting with a little respect."

"Fuck you, Peretz."

"Now, is that any way to talk? If that's how you feel, then I just thought of another small request. I also want you to transfer your part of the money into my account at Banco Ambrosiano. As a small gesture of respect. I want you to get on the radio and see about having it arranged. Or I might just blow the scenario for you." He had to laugh.

There was radio silence as Ramirez appeared to be contemplating this alternative. It clearly was unpalatable.

"You've got a problem there, my friend. One of time. I'm sure we're being monitored, so let me just say there's been a change of plans. You would have been part of it, but unfortunately . . ."

"Hey, asshole, there's no change of plans. You figured it for this way all along. But now there *is* going to be a change. I hate to tell you what the new scenario is . . . yo, hang on a sec."

He had looked up to see Bill Bates and Michael Vance entering the office. "Come on in and join the fun, guys." He waved his Walther and grinned. "We're about to have a blast."

Vance walked through the door, bloody and exhausted. "And I thought Ramirez was the only one who could manage to return from the dead." He tried to smile, but his face hurt too much. "Either he was using blanks, or you were wearing a bulletproof vest. Somehow I doubt it was the former. So what happened? Have a business disagreement with your partner in crime?"

Peretz was grinning. "That's how it is in life sometimes, man. Friendship is fleeting." He gestured them forward.

Bates had moved in warily, still stunned by the carnage among the workstations in Command. "I suppose I have you and Ramirez to thank for tearing up the place out there." He walked over to the desk. "Nice to see that my radio gear is back on and working."

"It's working fine," Peretz replied, then waved his Walther toward the couch opposite the desk. "Now sit the fuck down. Both of you."

"You're staring at *beaucoup* hard time, pal." Vance did not move. "I can think of several countries who're going to be fighting over the chance to put you away. This might be a propitious moment to consider going quietly."

"Quietly?" There was a mad gleam in his eye. "I never did anything quietly in my life. You're in luck, asshole. You're about to have a front-row seat at history in the making."

He turned back to the radio and switched to transmit. "Yo, my man, looks like we have nothing more to say to each other. Which means it's time for a fond farewell."

What's he about to do? Vance wondered. He's about to screw Sabri Ramirez, but how?

Then it dawned. There was one bomb left, and Bill had said it was on the Sikorsky. Probably radio-controlled, and Peretz had a radio, right there. God help us!

"Hey," he almost yelled, "get serious. What you're about to do is insane. You don't use a nuke to take out a single thug. Even a thug like Sabri Ramirez. You've gone crazy."

In fact, Vance told himself, Peretz was looking a little, more than a little, mad. He had a distant fix in his visage that was absolutely chilling. The world had been waiting decades now for a nutcake to get his hands on a nuclear trigger. Maybe the wait was over.

"Look, peckerhead, I'm sorry if you find this unsettling." Peretz was still holding the Walther. "However, don't get any funny ideas." He laughed. "You know, it's almost poetic. For years now Israel has been the world's biggest secret nuclear power, but nobody ever had the balls to show our stuff. I'm about to become my nation's most daring ex-citizen."

He turned back to the radio. "You still there, asshole?"

There was no reply. The radio voice of Sabri Ramirez didn't come back.

"He's jumped." Peretz looked up and grinned a demented grin. "He's in the air. Perfect. Now he'll get to watch."

He plugged in the device he had been carrying, a UHF transmitter. Then he flicked it to transmit, checked the liquid crystals that told its frequency, and reached for a red switch.

"*No!*" Vance lunged, trying to seize the Walther as he shoved Peretz against the instruments. The crazy son of a bitch was actually going to do it.

Peretz was strong, with the hidden strength of the terminally mad, and after only a second, Vance realized he didn't have a chance; he was too beat up and exhausted. Bill Bates, too, was suffering from absolute fatigue, but he also leapt forward, grappling with Peretz and trying to seize his automatic.

With Vance as a distraction, Bates managed to turn the pistol upward. Peretz was still gripping it like a vise, however, and at that moment it discharged, on automatic, sending a spray of rounds across the ceiling. Vance tried to duck away, and as he did, Peretz kneed him, shoving him to the floor. Bates, however, still had a grip on his right wrist, holding the pistol out of range. Again it erupted, another hail of automatic fire, but as it did, Bates managed to shove Peretz against the desk, grabbing his right elbow and twisting.

The Walther came around, locked on full automatic, and caught Dore Peretz in the side of his face. As blood splattered across the room, Bates staggered back, while Peretz collapsed onto the desk with a scream, then twisted directly across the transmitter.

He was dead instantly. And as he crumpled to the floor, almost by magic, the background noise from the radio on the Sikorsky stopped, replaced by a sterile hiss.

"Thank God," Bates whispered, breathless, and reached to help Vance up. "Are you okay, Mike?"

"I think so," he mumbled, rising to one trembling knee. "At least we—"

The room shook as a blistering shock wave rolled over the island. Outside, the distant sky above the eastern Mediterranean turned bright as the midday sun. Fifteen thousand feet above the Aegean, a blinding whiteness appeared unlike anything a living Greek had ever seen.

CHAPTER TWENTY

12:10 A.M.

"My God," the President muttered, settling the red phone into its cradle. "They did it. The bastards detonated one of them. NSA says their SIGINT capabilities in the Med just went blank. An electromagnetic pulse."

"I don't believe it," Morton Davies declared. Sitting on the edge of his hard chair, the chief of staff looked as incredulous as he felt. "We're tracking their helicopter with one of the AWACS we brought up from Rijad. The minute they set down, we're going to pick them up, rescue Mannheim and any other hostages, and nail the bastards. They know they can't get away, so why . . . ?"

"He'd threatened to nuke the island," Hansen went on, "but I assumed that had to be a bluff. Why in *hell* would he want to go ahead and do it? It didn't buy him anything at this stage."

Edward Briggs was on a blue phone at the other end of the Situation Room, receiving an intelligence update from Operations in the Pentagon. As he cradled the receiver, he looked down, not sure how to tell Johan Hansen what he had just learned. Mannheim.

"What's the matter, Ed? I don't like that look. What did—?"

"Mr. President." He seemed barely able to form the words. "Our people just got a better handle on . . . It wasn't Andikythera."

"What?" Hansen jerked his head around, puzzlement in his deep eyes. "What do you mean? Good Christ, not Souda Bay! Surely they didn't—"

"The detonation. Our AWACS flying out of southern Turkey monitored it at around fifteen thousand feet. As best they can tell. They still—"

"What!"

"They say it looked to be about seventy miles out over the eastern Med, in the direction of Cypress. Which is exactly where they were tracking—"

"You mean . . ." His voice trailed off.

"That's right," Briggs said finally. "They think it was the helicopter. The one they were flying out. An old Sikorsky S-61 series, we believe. It—"

"What are you saying?" Hansen found himself refusing to believe it. "That those idiots nuked *themselves*?" What the hell was the Pentagon talking about? . . . My God. Isaac was—

"Doesn't exactly figure, does it?" Briggs nodded lamely. "The electromagnetic pulse knocked out all our nonhardened surveillance electronics in the region, but Souda's intel section was hard-wired into our backup SAT–NET and they claim they triangulated it. Everything's sketchy, but that seems to be what happened."

"I can't believe it," Hansen said, running his hands over his face. They were trembling. "The whole situation must have gotten away from him. That's . . . the only way. It must have been a macabre accident. Christ!"

"A damned ghastly one," Briggs agreed. "But I think you're right."

"It's the only explanation that makes any sense," Hansen went on. "He probably decided to take one of the bombs with

him, hoping to try this again, and something went haywire."
He suddenly tried a sad smile. "You know, I warned that son
of a bitch he didn't know what he was doing, that he'd probably end up blowing himself up. Truthfully, I didn't really
think it would actually happen, though." He turned back to
Briggs. "The Pakistanis said the weapons they had were
about ten or fifteen kilotons. How big is that, Ed, in English?"

"Okay," Briggs said, pausing for effect, "that would be
like a medium-sized tactical, I guess." Truthfully he wasn't
exactly sure.

"Well," Hansen mused, "I'm still convinced they intended it for Souda Bay. And if they'd succeeded . . . but as
it stands, I guess it was more like a small upper-atmosphere
nuclear test. A tactical nuke, you say? The very term is an
obscenity. But, you know, NATO had those all over Germany
not so long ago, on the sick assumption that the German
people couldn't wait to nuke their own cities." After a long
moment, during which a thoughtful silence held the room,
Hansen continued. "Tell me, Ed. What kind of impact would
a weapon like that actually have at that altitude?"

"My guess is the effects will be reasonably contained."
He was doing some quick mental calculus. "Okay, if you were
directly under it, you'd have been about three miles away, so
you'd have taken a shock wave that would have knocked out
windows. And maybe produced some flash burns. But we had
the region cleared of civilian traffic, so maybe we're okay on
that score."

"What about fallout?" Hansen asked.

"Well, at that altitude the radioactive contamination
should be mostly trapped in the upper atmosphere and take
several days to start settling. By that time, it'll probably be
diluted to the point it'll be reasonably minimal. Nothing like
Chernobyl. Hell, I don't know the numbers, Mr. President,
but then again he was over some fairly open waters. Besides,
like I said, we had a quarantine on all civilian air and sea
traffic—guess we see now what a good idea that was—so
maybe we can be optimistic."

"The bloody fools just committed hara-kiri, and took Isaac

with them." He found himself thinking about the warning his aged father had given him that the job of President would age him half a lifetime in four years. He now felt it had happened in two days.

"There's more," Morton Davies said, clicking off a third phone and glancing at the computerized map now being projected on the giant screen at the end of the room. "SatCom's laser-powered rocket did go up. That's all they know for certain, but they think it's going into orbit. Whatever the hell that means."

"What about the Deltas?" Hansen asked finally, remembering all the planning. "And the assault? Did they—?"

"Right. Good question." He beamed. "JSOC Command reports that the Deltas are on the island now and have it secured. They even retrieved the bomb that those bastards were planning to put on SatCom's rocket. They managed to get it removed before the launch."

"How?"

"I haven't heard yet, but at least we can take pride in the fact that this country's antiterrorist capabilities got a full-dress rehearsal. And they were up to the job."

The President nodded gravely, not quite sure what, exactly, had been proved. That America could go in with too little, too late? If so, it was sobering insight.

"All right, Morton, get Caroline in here first thing in the morning. I want her to schedule a television speech for tomorrow night. Prime-time. I don't know what I'll say, other than our Special Forces minimized the loss of life. It's going to sound pretty lame."

"And what about the money? Is that going to get mentioned?"

Hansen laughed. "Not in a million years. That money's going to be traced and retrieved today, or else. The Swiss know when to play ball. And by the way, nobody here knows anything. About any of this. No leaks, or off-the-record briefings. And I mean that. The less said, the better."

"That might apply to the whole episode, if you want my opinion," Davies observed.

"You know, Morton, yes and no." He turned thoughtful.

"Maybe some good can come of this disaster after all. It might just be the demonstration we all needed to start the process of putting this nuclear madness to rest, once and for all. The genie managed to slip out of the bottle for a couple of days, and now we see how it can happen. I think it's time we got serious about total disarmament and on-site inspection."

Edward Briggs always knew Hansen was a dreamer, but this time he was going too far. He did not like the idea of America scrapping its nuclear arsenal, even if everybody else did the same. "That's going to mean a lot of wheeling and dealing, Mr. President. It's going to be a hard sell in some quarters."

Right, Hansen thought. And the hardest sell of all was going to be the Pentagon. "Well, dammit, nothing in this world is easy. But this is one move toward sanity that may have just gotten easier, thanks to that idiot on the island. I'm going to rework that speech I've got scheduled for the General Assembly. We lined up the Security Council, including the Permanent Members, for the right reasons once before. I'm going to see if we can't do it again. This time I think we've got an even better reason."

8:23 A.M.

"All right, we can evacuate them on a Huey," Eric Nichols was saying. "They'll take care of them on the *Kennedy*, courtesy of the U.S. government. But just who the hell are you?"

He was in the upper level of the SatCom living quarters, talking to a man in a black pullover who was packing a pile of Greek balaclavas into a crate. What in blazes had gone on? He had arrived in the lead Huey, to find one of the Apaches crash-landed, only one SatCom space vehicle left, and the Deltas on the ground, futilely searching for terrorists. But instead of terrorists, they had only come across this group of men in black pullovers, who had surrendered en masse. Turned out they were friendlies. And now this guy had just asked for a Huey to take out a couple of their ranks who had been shot up, one pretty badly.

"My name is Pierre Armont," replied the man. He seemed to be the one in charge, and he had a French accent.

"I mean, who the hell *are* you? And all these guys? CIA?" Nichols couldn't figure any of it. Two minutes after he landed, a shock wave pounded the island. Then when he tried to radio the *Kennedy*, to find out what in good Christ had happened, he couldn't get through. There was no radio traffic, anywhere. He had a sinking feeling he knew what that meant. And now, these clowns. They didn't look like regular military, but there was something about the way they moved. . . .

"We're civilians," Armont said cryptically. "And we're not here. You don't see us."

"The hell I don't. What in blazes do you mean?" Nichols didn't like wiseacres who played games. The problem was, these guys clearly weren't desk jockeys, the one type he really despised. No, they seemed more like a private antiterrorist unit, and he didn't have a ready-made emotion for that.

"As far as you and the U.S. government are concerned, we don't exist," Armont continued. "It's better if we keep things that way."

Nichols looked around and examined their gear, trying to figure it. The stuff was from all over the place—German, British, French, Greek, even U.S. And not only was it from all over the globe, it was all top notch, much of it supposedly not available to civilians. Where . . . and then it hit. *"You're the jokers we were trying to keep from coming in."*

"You did a pretty good job of slowing us down." Armont nodded.

"Not good enough, it would seem." He laughed, a mirthless grunt. "You're a crafty bunch of fuckers. I'll grant you one thing, though. At least you knew enough not to put up with micromanaging from the other side of the globe. You ended up doing exactly what we would have if anybody had let us. Vietnam all over again." He was reaching into his pocket for a Montecristo. He pulled out two. "Care to join me? Castro may not be able to run a country for shit, but he can still make a half-decent cigar."

"Thank you," Armont said, taking it. He hated cigars.

"By the way, I'm Eric Nichols."

"I know," Armont said. "JSOC." He had followed Nichols's career for years, always with an idea in the back of his mind. "I also know you've got one more year till retirement, but you don't seem like the retiring type."

Nichols stared over the lighted match he was holding out and smiled. "Tell me about it." Then he looked around at the men of ARM, the pile of balaclavas and MP5s, vests of grenades. And discipline, plenty of discipline. It was a sight that did his heart good. "Your boys look like they've been around."

"In a manner of speaking." Whereupon Pierre Armont proceeded to give Major General Eric Nichols an overview of the private club known as the Association of Retired Mercenaries. Including the financial dimension.

Nichols nodded slowly, taking deep, thoughtful puffs on his Montecristo. He was already way ahead of the conversation. "I think we might need to have a talk when all this is over. A look into the future."

"It would be my pleasure," Armont said. "Dinner in Paris, perhaps. I know the perfect restaurant." He did. Les Ambassadeurs, in the Hotel Crillon. French, though not *too* French. Rough-hewn Americans like Nichols always got slightly uneasy when there was more than one fork on the table and the salad came last.

"Sounds good to me," Nichols said. "Just as long as I won't be getting any asshole phone calls from the Pentagon while we talk."

"I can virtually guarantee it," Armont replied. "But in the meantime, we do need a favor or two from you. For starters, we would much prefer to just be numbered among the civilians here." He smiled. "That is, after all, what we are. Civilians with toys."

"And some pretty state-of-the-art ones at that," Nichols said, looking around again. "But I sometimes have problems with my vision, can't always be sure what I'm seeing. Like right now, for instance. I can't seem to see a damned thing."

"Oh, and one other favor," Armont continued, nodding in

silent appreciation. "We took one of the terrorists alive, a certain Jean-Paul Moreau, who is wanted in a string of bank robberies all over France. It's Action Directe's idea of fund-raising. We'd like to remove him back to Paris. There're some . . . parties there who will pony up enough bounty to cover the costs of this operation and make us whole. How about it? For purposes of your mission debriefing, can you just say the precise number of hostiles remains to be fully established? When we get back to Paris, he's going to fall out of a bus on the rue de Rivoli and be captured." He paused, hoping. The Americans might not go for this one. "We would be particularly grateful. And so would several financial institutions I could name."

Nichols drew again on his Cuban cigar, starting to like this Frog a lot. "Why the hell not? If you're not here, then I can't very well know who you take out, can I? Never heard of the guy."

"Thank you very much," Armont said, and he meant it. This was indeed a man he could work with. "I'm glad we see the situation eye to eye."

"Somebody at least ought to come out of this cluster-fuck whole," Nichols reflected wistfully. "Jesus, what a disaster."

Armont had turned to watch as the Deltas began easing Dimitri onto a metal stretcher. He seemed alert, and he even tried to lift a hand and wave. Armont waved back and shouted for him to take it easy. "By the way, that Greek civilian over there is named Spiros. He runs a security business out of Athens and never leaves town, which is why he wasn't here."

"Got it." Nichols nodded. "Guess a lot of things didn't happen today." He looked around. "But I've still got one question. We've already counted about half a dozen dead hostiles. So if nobody was here, then who exactly took down all these terrorist motherfuckers?"

"Well," Armont explained, "we both know Delta Force doesn't exist either. So maybe this Greek sunshine gave them terminal heatstroke and they all just shot themselves."

"Yeah," Nichols concurred with a smile, "damnedest thing."

9:31 A.M.

"Georges, what do you think?" Cally asked. "Can it be saved?"

"Well, first the good news. The Fujitsu is okay." He wheeled around from the workstation. Command was a shambles, but he had managed to find one auxiliary terminal that would still function. That workstation, and the lights, were on, but not much else. "It was buried deep enough in the bedrock that it escaped the EMP, the electromagnetic pulse, from the blast. If we'd lost our sweetheart, we'd be dead in the water."

"Any telemetry?"

"Yep." He smiled. "The tapes were on. We had Doppler, almost from liftoff. The Cyclops computed our acceleration from it, and the results look to be right on the money. The not-so-good news is that the last telemetry we recorded, just before the bomb went off and the Cyclops crashed, showed that *VX-1* was about three minutes away from capturing orbit. I think we probably made it, but I still can't say. However, since Big Benny was already reducing power, getting ready to shut it off anyway, maybe, just maybe we got lucky."

She sighed. "When will you know for sure?"

"Right now I'm trying to get Arlington on-line and tied into here. I'm hoping we can patch into their satellite receiving station. Anyway, I should know in a few minutes, assuming the vehicle is still sending back telemetry."

"Care to venture a guess?" She collapsed into a chair next to him. This was the first time she had been in Command for several hours and it seemed almost strange. Whereas the staff over at Launch Control had opened the champagne immediately after lift-off, still not fully aware of all the behind-the-scenes drama, the Command technicians were too shell-shocked to think, and they were only now slowly drifting back in. Not the people in Launch, though. All they knew for sure was that they had done *their* job, even if the gantry had collapsed for some mysterious reason. *VX-1* left the pad without a hitch. They had a success.

"Well, if I had to lay odds," Georges went on, "I'd guess

we captured orbit, but it's going to be erratic. However, if we can get the Cyclops up and running again, maybe we can do a midcourse correction." He tapped something on the keyboard. "Yet another first for the never-say-die SatCom team."

She had to laugh. "You look pretty cool, Soho, for somebody who just lived through World War Three."

He tried unsuccessfully to smile. "Hey, don't go by appearances. I tried to open a Pepsi just now and my hands were shaking so badly I finally just gave up and went to the water fountain. Cally, I'm a wreck. I'm still quivering. God." He pulled at his beard, then absently added, "I'm going to shave this off. What do you think? It isn't me."

"It never was." She had refrained from telling him that earlier, but now he seemed to want to talk about trivia, maybe just to take his mind off all the heaviness around. And there were two new things she did not want to tell him. The first was that millions of dollars were riding on his every keystroke. The second was that she was thinking a lot right now about somebody else.

9:43 A.M.

"Mike, I can't believe it," Bates said, hanging up the phone. The one in his office was among the few still working, and it had been ringing off the wall. "Know who that was?"

Vance had not been paying heavy-duty attention. He had been thinking about the woman out there now talking to the computer hacker with the scraggly beard.

"What? Sorry, Bill, I wasn't listening."

"Hey," he laughed. "Your mental condition isn't what it might be. Tell you the truth, you look like a guy who just mixed it with a twenty-horsepower fan, and lost. You really ought to go over to medical and get your face looked after."

"The Deltas are probably still over there. If I showed up, I might just get arrested. Don't think I could handle an interrogation right now. Better to hide out for a while longer." The fact was, he still felt too disoriented to think about how he must look. He hurt all over, and he almost didn't care.

"Whatever you say." Bates shrugged. "Anyway, that guy on the phone just now was a Jap by the name of Matsugami. He just happens to run NASDA."

"What's that?" Vance asked, trying to clear his mind enough to remember the initials. The information was back there somewhere, but he just couldn't reach it.

"You really are out of it, buddy. You of all people ought to know perfectly well it's their National Space Development Agency. He says they're disgusted with all the failures they've been having with the American and European commercial rockets. He wants to talk about a contract for SatCom to put up their next three broadcast satellites. That means we get to haggle for six months while they try to trim my foreskin, but I think we'll get the job. Laser propulsion is suddenly the hottest thing since Day-Glo condoms. That bastard who took us over just gave us a billion dollars of publicity." He laughed. "I'd almost like to kiss what's left of his ass, except it's probably somewhere in the ozone about now."

"Well, congratulations."

"Wait till Cally hears about this. She just may go into orbit herself."

"You've been on the phone for an hour." After Peretz was carried out, he had collapsed onto the couch in Bates's office and tried to go to sleep, but the goings-on had made it impossible. Bates had been talking nonstop. "What else is happening out there in the world Ramirez was planning to nuke?"

"He did nuke it. He just didn't manage to nuke it the place he intended." Bates leaned back in his chair. "Well, it turns out good news travels fast. Since VX-1 is up, our two prime banks in Geneva are suddenly engaged in intimate contact between their lips and my nether parts. 'Roll over your obligations? Mais oui, Monsieur Bates. Certainement. Avec plaisir. Will you need any additional capitalization? We could discuss an equity position.' The cocksuckers. It was almost a shame to piss away that weapon on empty space. I could have thought of a much better use."

"Hallelujah." He felt his spirits momentarily rise, though not his energy. "Maybe this means all that stock you paid me for the boat will end up being worth the paper it's printed on. Truthfully, I was beginning to worry."

"Told you it'd all work out," he grinned. "No faith. Come on, amigo, I've got to break the news to the troops." He strode to the door, or the opening that was left after the C-4 had removed the door, and surveyed the remains of Command. The technicians and systems analysts were filing back in, but mostly it was a scene of purposeful lethargy. The horror of the last day and a half had taken a terrible toll. Eyes were vacant, hair unkempt, motions slow and aimless. Several of those who had previously quit smoking were bumming cigarettes.

He whistled with two fingers, and the desultory turmoil froze in place. "Okay, everybody," he said, his voice not quite a shout. "It's official. We're back in business. You've all still got a job."

The glassy-eyed stares he received back suggested nobody's thoughts had extended that far yet. Nobody was in a particular mood to let themselves think about the future.

"That's the good part," Bates went on, oblivious. "The other news is there won't be bonuses or stock dividends this year. We'll be lucky just to service our debt. But anybody who hangs in there for twelve months gets half a year's pay extra, as a bonus. I'll do it out of my own pocket if I have to. And if you play your cards right, we could be talking stock options, too."

There were a few smiles and thumbs-up signs, more to hearten Bates, whom they revered, than to celebrate. Nobody had the capacity left to feel particularly festive. At the same time, nobody was about to abandon ship. Not now, now that they were needed more than ever.

Vance was leaning on the wall behind him, watching it all and thinking. Okay, so Bill was about to be rich, and SatCom had gotten enough free publicity to last into the next century. But the real notoriety should be going to the question that had haunted the world for four decades: what would happen if terrorists got their hands on a nuclear device? This time the consequences—although intended to be devastating—had in fact been peripheral, an inconsequential detonation somewhere halfway into space. But the question that still hung over the world was, what would happen the next time? It was a question Bill Bates had too much on his mind today to think about. Maybe he never would.

9:51 A.M.

J.J. shook his head in disgust as he looked over the shambles that was the gantry. Dr. Andros had just phoned from Command, asked him to undertake a preliminary assessment of the condition of the facility, just to ballpark the extent of damage. The assignment was already depressing him. Still, from what he could see so far, things could have been worse. There was no obvious physical injury to VX-2 or to the transmission antennas up on the hill, though the testing and corrections could take weeks. The gantry was a total loss, no doubt about that, but otherwise the major physical structures on the island appeared unscathed. The main reason, naturally, was that almost everything important—including the superconducting coil and the Fujitsu—was well underground.

The main scene now was all the bodacious helicopters, Hueys, on the landing pad and all the Army commandos milling around. Jesus! How did everybody in Launch Control miss what was really going on? Looking back, the whole thing was fishy from the word go.

Now the Army types were collecting the bodies of the terrorists and acting like they had cleaned up the place all by themselves. Guess that was going to be the official story. . . .

Mr. Bates had already come down to Launch, shook everybody's hand, and thanked the crews for hanging in there. He looked a little shook up, but he wasn't talking like it. Totally upbeat. You had to love the guy. He also delivered the news that as soon as things settled down, SatCom was going to kick some ass in the space business.

Jordan Jaegar looked up at the brilliant Greek sunshine and grinned in spite of himself. Shit, he couldn't wait.

10:22 A.M.

"It's all been handled," Armont was saying. Vance had finally decided to venture out of Bates's office and see how things were going. The Bates Motel had taken some heavy gunfire around the entrance, but it was still usable, with the ARM team milling around and readying to depart. Down below, the sea had never looked bluer. "Nobody knows anything. Our favorite state of affairs."

Vance was still trying to take it all in. "How's Spiros doing?"

"They took him out on one of the Hueys," Armont said. "Hugo went, too.

"Are they going to be all right?"

"Hugo's okay. He even knocked back a couple of Guinnesses before he left, saying they would help ease the 'stabbing pain.' Can you believe? As for Dimitri, the Deltas had a medic along, and he gave him a better than fifty-fifty shot. Said nothing vital seemed beyond repair."

"Thank goodness for that at least."

"Poor guy, he felt personally responsible for the whole mess. I think that was why he sort of lost his better judgment there for a second when we rushed Command and got careless."

"It can happen," Vance said. Looking back, he decided he had lost sight of better judgment several times over the past few hours.

The rest of the ARM team was checking out the gear and tying crates, all the while working on their second case of beer. Departure was imminent.

"Well," Vance added finally, "it was a nightmare, start to finish. What more can you say."

"Well, not entirely," Armont observed, a hint of satisfaction creeping into his voice. "Bates is going to let us use the Agusta to fly back to Paris. And when we get there, one of the terrorists who got blown up is going to suddenly reappear. Jean-Paul Moreau."

"Know him well," Vance said, remembering the beating and his sense of hopelessness at the time. "Better not let me see the bastard. He might not make it back to Paris in one piece."

"Well, Michael, that would be very ill-advised. He's worth a small fortune. If the Greeks were to get hold of him, he could piss on the court system here and keep it mucked up for years, so we're taking him straight back to Paris." He paused to glance around. "Nichols is giving us an Apache escort as far as international airspace will permit. But you don't know anything about any of this. Keep your nose clean."

"Nichols?" The name didn't mean anything, but then his mind was still mostly in neutral.

"Major General Eric Nichols. No reason you should know him. Runs the Deltas. Good man, by the way. First rate. I've had my eye on him for a number of years. Could be he'll end up being our first Yank. Well, our second besides you."

"So this was really a recruiting drive." Vance laughed. Suddenly he was feeling almost giddy again, this time from the release of all the stress.

"You take them where you can get them." Armont nodded, then looked around and whistled. "Okay, everybody, bring down the Agusta and start loading the gear. We're gone." He turned back to Vance. "How about you? Coming?"

"No," he said, almost not even catching the question. "Think maybe I'll stick around. Make sure Bill is okay. You know, unfinished business."

"Right." Armont laughed. "I think I saw your 'unfinished business,' Michael. Don't you think she might be a little young for you. You're starting to get like me now, middle-aged."

"Well, working for ARM doesn't help, but then you do have a gift for pointing out the obvious." The way he felt, starting over looked tougher all the time.

"On the other hand, why not. As a romantic Frenchman, I can only wish you *bonne chance.*" He patted him on the back. "What more can I say."

"Thanks." Vance had to smile. Armont was gallant to the end, and a man who prided himself on knowing what things mattered in life. "At my age, you need all the luck you can get."

"*Merde.* In this life you make your own luck." With which pronouncement he shook hands, then yelled for Hans to bring over the list of gear for one last inventory.

7:47 P.M.

It was the end of the day and he could genuinely have used a tequila, double, with a big Mexican lime on the side. Instead, however, he had something else on the agenda. After an early dinner with Bill Bates, he had talked Calypso Andros into a stroll down to the harbor, there to meditate on the events of the past two days. They had agreed in advance not to talk about Isaac Mannheim's death; Cally declared he would have wanted it that way. His life was his legacy.

"I wonder if this island will ever be the same again," she was saying as she leaned back against a rock. "You know, it was peaceful once, before SatCom took over— there actually were sheep, a whole herd—but even then it had a kind of purposefulness that was just the opposite of chaos. *We're* the ones who disrupted it. SatCom. We remade it in our image, and we tempted fate." She sighed. "God, this whole disaster almost seems like a bad dream now. I wonder if the island will ever know real peace again. There'll always be the memory to haunt everybody."

"You know, when Ulysses came back to *his* island, he discovered it had been taken over by a bunch of thugs. So he took away their weapons, locked the doors, and straightened things out. It set a good precedent."

"Well, it didn't exactly happen that cleanly this time, but we did get them all. Every last one. And about half of them, you took care of yourself. One way or another."

"Please," he stopped her. "Let's don't keep score. It's too depressing."

"I'm not depressed. At least not about them. They came in here and murdered people right and left. They deserved whatever they got. Good riddance. The human race is better off."

"That's pretty tough," Vance said. "On the other hand,

whereas they claimed to be terrorists, they really were just extortionists. At least Ramirez and Peretz were. For them this was all about money. Kidnapping and ransom. So maybe you're right. The penalty for kidnapping is death. They were looking at the max, no matter what court ended up trying them."

"I'd say ARM just spared Greece or somebody a lot of trouble and expense. Performed a public service."

"I suppose that's one way to look at it." He smiled. "But somehow I don't think Pierre's going to get so much as a thank-you note. It never happens. Things always get confused like this at the end, but as long as he and the boys come out whole, they don't care."

His voice trailed off as he studied the sea. Along the coast on either side, the pale early moon glinted off the breakers that crashed in with a relentless rhythm. Yes, a bomb had exploded somewhere up there in space, but the Aegean, even the jagged rocks around the island, still retained their timeless serenity. The Greek islands. He never wanted to leave. Right now, though, he was trying to work up his nerve to talk seriously with Dr. Cally Andros—and the words weren't coming. How to start . . . ?

"Are you still here?" She finally broke his reverie. "Or are you just gazing off."

"Sorry about that." He clicked back. "I was thinking. Wondering if you'd still be interested in . . . in what we talked about yesterday."

"What?" She looked puzzled, then, "Oh, you mean—"

"Taking a sail with an old, slightly beat-up yacht-charter operator."

"You're beat up, there's no denying it." She laughed. "I hope you keep your boats in better shape." She looked him over and thought again how much he reminded her of Alan. The mistake that affair represented was not one to be repeated blindly. Then again . . . "But I don't consider you old. Experienced, maybe, but still functioning."

"Is that supposed to mean yes?"

"It's more like a maybe." She touched his hand. "What were you thinking about, exactly?"

"What else? The Odyssey thing." He looked out at the horizon, then back. "Seems to me it deserves another try.

> *Oh, the pearl seas are yonder,*
> *The amber-sanded shore;*

If you'll pardon my attempt to wax poetic."

She smiled. "Plagiarist. I know that one. And I also know there's another line in it that goes,

> *Troy was a steepled city,*
> *But Troy was far away.*

Far away. Get it? Or maybe it doesn't even really exist at all."

"Oh, it exists all right. You just have to want to find it." He picked up a pebble and tossed it toward the surf, now rapidly disappearing in the dusk. "So what are you trying to say?"

"I'm saying that maybe Troy was a real place and maybe not. But that's almost beside the point. What it really is is a symbol for that something or somebody we're all looking for. Whatever special it is we each want. Like when I came here to work for SatCom. Space was my Troy. It was what I wanted. And when you tried to re-create the voyage of Ulysses, you were thinking you could make something that was a myth into something that was real. Big impossibility."

"You're saying the search for Troy is actually just an inner voyage, and I got caught up in trying to make it literal. The boat and all."

"Well, that's what myth is really about, isn't it? We make up a story using real, concrete things to symbolize our inner journey."

"You're saying Ulysses could have sailed up a creek, for all it mattered?"

"That's exactly what I'm saying." She leaned back. "Shit, I want a pizza so bad right now I think I'm going crazy."

Vance was still pondering her put-down of his Odyssey rerun, wondering if maybe she wasn't onto something. Maybe he had learned more about himself in two days on the island than he would have learned in two years plying the Aegean.

"All right," she said finally. "I'm sorry. I've busted your chops enough. You asked if I'd like to take a sail, and I said maybe. The truth is, I would, but I've also got a journey of my own in mind."

"What do you mean?"

"Well, before I tell you, maybe I'd better make sure you meant it. For one thing, what are you going to sail *in?*"

"Good question." Up until that moment he had not given much thought to personal finance. The truth was, he was broke. "I don't know if I can scrape up enough money to build an *Odyssey III*. It's a problem."

"Well, I'll tell you what I think. I think Bill owes you at least a boat for all you did."

He shrugged, not quite agreeing with her on that point. You don't pitch in to help out an old friend, then turn around and send him an invoice. "Maybe, maybe not. But in any case, it would be minus the ten grand I owe him for the bet I lost."

"Come on"—she frowned—"that's not fair."

"Maybe not, but a deal's a deal. Poseidon was the god of the sea, and the god of anger. This is Greece, so maybe the old gods are still around. Maybe I tempted Poseidon and pissed him off. Anyway, the sea got angry, and that's how it goes. The way of the gods. Ten big ones."

"Well," Calypso Andros said, "speaking of gods, Aphrodite was the goddess of love and beauty. The Greeks were smart enough to give you a selection. So you ought to think about burning some incense to her next time. Or something. Maybe fall in love. I hear she likes that, too."

"Good suggestion." He glanced over.

"Michael, I feel so rootless," she said finally, leaning against him, strands of hair across his shoulder. "Not close to anybody, really. Now that SatCom doesn't need my mothering any more, I want to try and start a few things over . . . and the *place* I want to start is Naxos. My Odyssey."

He just nodded, understanding.

"I want to go back to my old home," she went on, almost a

sad confession. "I haven't been there for over twenty years. We had such a beautiful little whitewashed house. Looked out on a bay. It was tiny, but I still sneak back there in my dreams. I want to make sure it survived."

"Don't think you have to worry. The shock wave was probably well dissipated by the time it hit Paros and Naxos. Fact is, I doubt it did any real damage to any of the islands."

"Then why don't we go there together? Your Odyssey and mine."

"It's a done deal."

"Good." She straightened, suddenly becoming business-like. "Just as soon as we find out about VX-1. If it made orbit and if anything is salvageable. Georges should know by to-morrow morning. Then I want to split for a while."

"It would do us both good. Have to. And you know, since we're definitely going to need some transportation, I think I'm getting an idea." He nodded down toward the twenty-eight-foot Morgan, pristine white, bobbing at anchor in the harbor. "Looks pretty seaworthy to me. Think Bill would mind?"

"With all the SatCom stock I've got now?" She reached out and touched his face. "I'll just fire him if he says a word."

Biography

Thomas Hoover

After writing two non-fiction books on Japan and China, THOMAS HOOVER published an internationally best-selling novel of India, *The Moghul.* This was followed by *Caribbee,* another historical novel that found a wide audience in the U.S. and Europe. He then turned to contemporary fiction with the successful Wall Street thriller, *The Samurai Strategy,* which was followed by the high-tech thriller duo *Project Daedalus* and *Project Cyclops.* Formerly an executive with an international consulting firm, he lives in New York and is currently at work on a new novel set in Central America.